D0897888

The Giant Book of
Erotica

The Giant Book of Erotica

Edited by Maxim Jakubowski

Magpie Books, London

MAXIM JAKUBOWSKI was born in England but educated in France. Following a career in publishing, he opened London's now famous MURDER ONE bookshop. He has published over 60 books, won the Anthony and Karel Awards, and is a connoisseur of genre fiction in all its forms. His recent books include six volumes in the *Mammoth Book of Erotica* series, as well as the *Mammoth Book of Pulp Fiction*. Other well-received anthologies include: *London Noir*, three volumes of *Fresh Blood*, *Past Poisons*, *Chronicles of Crime* and *Murder Through the Ages*. A regular broadcaster, he is the crime columnist for the *Guardian*. His fiction includes *Life in the World of Women*, *It's You that I want to Kiss*, *Because She Thought She Loved Me*, *The State of Montana* and *On Tenderness Express*. He lives in London.

Constable & Robinson Ltd
3 The Lanchesters
162 Fulham Palace Road
London W6 9ER
www.constablerobinson.com

First published in the UK as
The Mammoth Book of Best New Erotica by Robinson,
an imprint of Constable & Robinson Ltd 2001

This edition published by Magpie Books,
an imprint of Constable & Robinson Ltd 2005

A copy of the British Library Cataloguing in
Publication Data is available from the British Library

ISBN 1-84529-201-4

Printed and bound in the EU

1 3 5 7 9 10 8 6 4 2

Contents

CONTENTS

CONTENTS

Acknowledgments

MOVEMENTS by Michael Hemmingson, © 2000 by Michael Hemmingson. First appeared in AQUA EROTICA, edited by Mary Anne Mohanraj. Reproduced by permission of the author.

AFTER LOSS by Tabitha Flyte, © 2000 by Tabitha Flyte. First appeared in BEST WOMEN'S EROTICA 2001, edited by Marcy Sheiner. Reproduced by permission of the author.

A WALK IN THE RAIN ON THE WILD SIDE by O'Neil De Noux, © 2000 by O'Neil De Noux. First appeared in NOIROTICA 3, edited by Thomas S. Roche. Reproduced by permission of the author.

WEIGH STATION by Debra Hyde, © 2000 by Debra Hyde. First appeared in DESIRES, edited by Adrienne Benedicks & Shivaji Sengupta. Reproduced by permission of the author.

A JOHN'S STORY by Samuel R. Delany, © 2000 by Samuel R. Delany. First appeared in 1984. Reproduced by permission of the author and Voyant Publishing.

THE ROOM, AFTER SHE LEFT by Adam Barnett-Foster, © 2000 by Adam Barnett-Foster. First appeared in GARGOYLE 42. Reproduced by permission of the author.

ACKNOWLEDGMENTS

THE EDITOR VS. THE AUTHOR by Anya Ross, © 2001 by Anya Ross. Reproduced by permission of the author.

MONKEY SEE by Matthew Branton, © 2000 by Matthew Branton. First appeared in ALL HAIL THE NEW PURITANS, edited by Nicholas Blincoe & Matt Thorne. Reproduced by permission of the author and his agents, Gillon Aitken Associates.

BAHN by Zoe Constantin, © 2000 by Zoe Constantin. First appeared in CLEAN SHEETS MAGAZINE, May 2000. Reproduced by permission of the author.

BOTTOMLESS ON BOURBON by Maxim Jakubowski, © 2000 by Maxim Jakubowski. First appeared in DESIRES, edited by Adrienne Benedicks & Shivaji Sengupta. Reproduced by permission of the author.

THE HEART IN MY GARDEN by Carol Queen, © 2000 by Carol Queen. First appeared in LIBIDO MAGAZINE, Fall 2000. Reproduced by permission of the author.

LES JARDINS DE KENSINGTON by Justine Dubois, © 2000 by Justine Dubois. First appeared in THE EROTIC REVIEW, September 2000. Reproduced by permission of the author.

SODOMY AND SORCERY by Mark Ramsden, © 2001 by Mark Ramsden. Reproduced by permission of the author.

DO WHAT YOU LOVE by Susannah Indigo, © 2000 by Susannah Indigo. First appeared in CLEAN SHEETS MAGAZINE, April 2000. Reproduced by permission of the author.

HOW TO WRITE AN EROTIC STORY by Bill Noble, © 2000 by Bill Noble. First appeared in SCARLET LETTERS MAGAZINE. Reproduced by permission of the author.

ACKNOWLEDGMENTS

PULL ME IN THE PULLMAN CARRIAGE by Helen Lederer, © 2000 by Helen Lederer. First appeared in GIRL'S NIGHT OUT, edited by Chris Manby & Fiona Walker. Reproduced by permission of the author and her agent, Curtis Brown Ltd.

LITTLE DEATHS by Heather Corina, © 1998, 2000 by Heather Corina. First appeared in SEXILICIOUS. Reproduced by permission of the author.

DEMETER'S GARDEN by Catherine Sellars, © 2001 by Catherine Sellars. Reproduced by permission of the author.

JACK by Cara Bruce, © 2000 by Cara Bruce. First appeared in BEST WOMEN'S EROTICA 2000 edited by Marcy Sheiner. Reproduced by permission of the author.

IN THE PINK by Isabelle Carruthers, © 2000 by Isabelle Carruthers. First appeared in SUSPECT THOUGHTS MAGAZINE, 2000. Reproduced by permission of the author.

USHERETTE by Jacqueline Lucas, © 2000 by Jacqueline Lucas. First appeared in THE DEVIL, issue N. Reproduced by permission of the author.

DEATHROCKER, SEX BOY, AND FUCK by Thomas S. Roche, © 2000 by Thomas S. Roche. First appeared in CLEAN SHEETS MAGAZINE, August 2000. Reproduced by permission of the author.

DA DA by Toby Litt, © 2000 by Toby Litt. First appeared in THE EROTIC REVIEW, March 2000. Reproduced by permission of the author and his agent Mic Cheetham.

DOWNTOWN by Hanne Blank, © 2000 by Hanne Blank. First appeared in SCARLET LETTERS MAGAZINE, 2000. Reproduced by permission of the author.

ACKNOWLEDGMENTS

ONE IN THE HAND, TWO IN THE BUSH by Lauren Sanders, © 2000 by Lauren Sanders. First appeared in KAMIKAZE LUST. Reproduced by permission of Akashic Books.

NEW YORK, NY BY WAY OF TAOS, NM by M. Christian, © 2000 by M. Christian. First appeared in ALL YOUR MIND. Reproduced by permission of the author.

ONLY CONNECT by Lauren Henderson, © 2000 by Lauren Henderson. First appeared in THE NEW ENGLISH LIBRARY BOOK OF INTERNET STORIES, edited by Maxim Jakubowski. Reproduced by permission of the author.

QUIET by Lucy Moore, © 2000 by Lucy Moore. First appeared in CLEAN SHEETS MAGAZINE, January 2000. Reproduced by permission of the author.

THE LITTLE MERMAID by Cecilia Tan, © 2000 by Cecilia Tan. First appeared in AQUA EROTICA, edited by Mary Ann Mohanraj. Reproduced by permission of the author.

FRIED BLONDE TOMATOES by Robert Schaffer, © 2000 by Robert Schaffer. First published in DESIRES, edited by Adrienne Benedicks & Shivaji Sengupta. Reproduced by permission of the author.

CHAMELEON by Francisco Ibañez-Carrasco, © 2000 by Francisco Ibañez-Carrasco. First appeared in SUSPECT THOUGHTS MAGAZINE, 2000. Reproduced by permission of the author.

BUTT HUT by Matt Thorne, © 2000 by Matt Thorne. First appeared in THE NEW ENGLISH LIBRARY BOOK OF INTERNET STORIES edited by Maxim Jakubowski. Reproduced by permission of the author.

ACKNOWLEDGMENTS

PASSENGER by Sidney Durham, © 2000 by Sidney Durham, First appeared in LOVESEAT STORIES (Renaissance E Books). Reproduced by permission of the author.

THE SURVEY by Mary Anne Mohanraj, © 2000 by Mary Anne Mohanraj. First appeared in BEST WOMEN'S EROTICA 2000, edited by Marcy Sheiner. Reproduced by permission of the author.

MURIEL THE MAGNIFICENT by Marilyn Jaye Lewis, © 2000 by Marilyn Jaye Lewis. First appeared in THE NEW ENGLISH LIBRARY BOOK OF INTERNET STORIES, edited by Maxim Jakubowski. Reproduced by permission of the author.

WASABI PUNANI by Christine Pountney, © 2000 by Christine Pountney. First appeared in THE EROTIC REVIEW, July/August 2000. Reproduced by permission of the author.

BELOW THE BELTWAY by Simon Sheppard, © 2000 by Simon Sheppard. First appeared in STRANGE BEDFELLOWS, edited by Dominic Santi & Debra Hyde. Reproduced by permission of the author.

SUBCULTURE by Sarah Veitch, © 2000 by Sarah Veitch. First appeared in SUBCULTURE. Reproduced by permission of the author.

THREESOME by Daniel James Cabrillo, © 2000 by Daniel James Cabrillo. First appeared as 'Two Obsessions, Pique & Melissa . . . & Doc and One Night' in CLEAN SHEETS MAGAZINE, 2000. Reproduced by permission of the author.

Movements

Michael Hemmingson

I. Suite for an End to a Marriage

The first time I saw my wife fucking another man, she was by our Jacuzzi the night of The Party. I was fairly convinced it would be the last party we'd throw as husband and wife.

Actually, she was with two men. One was a fellow I didn't know and he was fucking her from behind – his large, hairy hands tightly grasping her hips in an attempt to control the backward thrust of her pelvis as if she were a wild animal. The other one (my best friend) had his dick in her mouth. She was taking this dick down her throat pretty deep, and he was no bigger than myself. She never did that for me. Maybe she never liked my dick; and this is something I could believe, given the recent sour circumstances of our marriage.

"I don't think I'm in love with you anymore," she told me three months before. I was trying to have sex with her. Her pussy was dry like a dry cunt. Finally she pushed my hand away and said she didn't want to. We hadn't made love in quite a while.

"What do you mean?"

"Is it hard to understand?" she said. "How can I illustrate it any better? *I don't think I'm in love with you anymore.*"

"I see," I said.

"No," she said, "you don't."

We tried the marriage counselor routine, and that only

proved to drive us further apart, snickering at all the flowery, New Age suggestions the counselor was trying to sell us.

"What a fucking waste of money," my wife said.

Her name is Beryl, by the way.

I stood there, looking out the kitchen window, and watched Beryl fuck. The one who was my best friend, his name is Art.

I wasn't surprised. The night seemed to be heading for this. Beryl was on the warpath to have sex with someone – other than me.

"I'm feeling frisky tonight," she said when she pulled me aside during The Party.

She was drunk. I told her so.

"So I'm *drunk*," she said, "and I'm feeling *good*."

I wasn't feeling good. "Thanks for the information."

"I just want you to know," she said, "that I might do something *wild*, I might do something *sexy*, and I don't want you to get in the *way*."

"I won't," I said.

"I don't want you to get in the way of my being *happy*."

"I won't," I said.

It started, I suppose, with her dance – or striptease. She put on some electronic music, the kind that gives me a headache. I don't know where she got this music. She began to dance, and had an audience of men cheering as she lifted her skirt and flashed her panties; when she opened her blouse and exposed her tits. She had small, pointed, brown breasts. She was a tall, slender woman with long legs and tanned skin and straight blond hair, a very appealing woman to many men.

"That's some wife of yours!" someone said to me, slapping me on the back.

"Yeah," I said.

Beryl had stripped down to her thong. Drunken hands groped for her. One pair of hands belonged to Art. Beryl giggled and ran out back and jumped into the Jacuzzi.

Watching her fuck, I knew it was the hottest sight I'd ever viewed. It was better than watching a porno: this was real.

I wasn't the only person watching, either. Several men, some I knew, some I didn't, moved toward the threesome. I moved with them. We were all like mesmerized cattle.

Two months ago I was sitting in a bar with Art. We were on our fourth or fifth drinks.

"I think Beryl and I are getting a divorce," I said.

"You think?" Art said.

"Probably," I said. "She doesn't love me anymore."

"*No*."

"Yes."

"*No*."

"She said this."

"Do you still love her?" he asked.

"I'm not sure," I said. "I think I do."

"What went wrong? You two used to be the happy fun couple."

"I'm not sure," I said. "I think she might be having an affair."

"You *think?*"

"I wouldn't put it past her."

When Beryl was done with Art and the man I didn't know, she started having sex with two other men. The Party was becoming something else. Other people departed – old friends giving me strange looks. Someone said, "You didn't say this was going to turn into an *orgy*." It was past one in the morning anyway, the time for most parties to start winding down.

Art, with his clothes back on, passed me.

I grabbed his arm.

"Hey," he said softly.

I just looked at him.

"We should talk," he said.

"Yeah," I said.

The Party was over, people were gone. Four a.m. I lay in bed, listening to my wife taking a bath. The door was unlocked. I went in. She stared at me. She was sitting in the tub, water and soap all around her. She started to say something, I held up a finger to stop her. I unzipped my pants and showed her my hard prick.

"Do you plan to do something with that?" she said.

"I have some ideas," I said.

"You look all worked up."

"I am that," I said.

"I haven't seen your dick that bulging and red since . . . since we first met."

I approached her, my body shaking. "Did you like fucking those men tonight?"

Softly, "You know I did."

"I could tell. I haven't seen you fuck like that since . . . since we first met."

She said, "Did you like me fucking those men?"

I grabbed Beryl's head. I was fast and she was surprised. I pushed her face into my crotch. I bunched up her slick wet hair in my fists, like I was angry. I was more horny than angry, or on a fine line that crosses both conditions. She took my cock in her mouth. I wondered how many loads of come she'd swallowed this evening. Mine would be just another. Beryl pulled my pants down and grabbed at the flesh of my ass, yanking me forward, so that I was partially in the water with her, getting wet . . .

In bed, I asked her how long she'd been fucking Art. I knew that tonight wasn't the first time – the way they were with each other: that familiarity of the body. Beryl said, "For a while now."

II. Sonata for a New Phase in Marriage

The three of us were in the Jacuzzi. This was inevitable, this had to happen; I knew it, Beryl knew it, Art knew it.

We'd had dinner. It was a quiet dinner. I savored every bite of the mushroom sautéed chicken Beryl had prepared, the scalloped potatoes that reminded me of being a child and eating Mother's well-cooked meals. It was a warm night. Beryl suggested we relax in the Jacuzzi, drink wine. Art wanted beer. Beryl drank wine. We got naked, acting like excited, modest teenagers doing something daring and naughty, and went into the water.

It was a clear night out, a lot of stars.

I was also drinking wine.

"That's Mars up there." Beryl pointed at the sky, to a bright star with a red tint.

"Think there's life up there?" Art said.

"Mars? Or elsewhere?"

"Mars."

"Sure," she said.

"What do you think?" Art asked me.

"As long as they don't invade us," I said, "I don't care."

"I'm glad you're not mad," he said.

"I'm not mad," I said. "I keep telling myself I should be. But I'm not."

"It's good that you're not," Beryl said. "It means you're growing. It means you're moving in the direction I am, and that makes me happy."

Art waded through the water in her direction. She giggled. He backed her against the Jacuzzi wall. They kissed. I sipped my glass of wine and watched him kiss her. I watched him lift her body up, sit her on the edge of the Jacuzzi, spread her legs, and go down on her. Beryl liked this. She ran her fingers through his wet hair and made familiar sounds of pleasure. I knew those sounds like a distant cousin one has fond memories of. She leaned back, propping herself on her elbows, and let Art work his tongue between her legs, his hairy hands rubbing her stomach and breasts. She looked at me and said, "Come here and stick that dick in my mouth."

I got out of the water. The hair on my body was matted, I was dripping. I liked walking about like this, my cock pointing the way. I crouched before Beryl so she could take me in her mouth as Art continued to eat her pussy, grunting sounds coming from his throat.

We then moved away from the Jacuzzi to a lounge chair, where she sucked on us both: Art and I standing close, almost touching, Beryl going from one cock to another. I could smell Art's body. I could smell the musk from his crotch, and I wondered if I was emitting any odors he could sense. Needless to say, the smell of sex permeated the immediate air around us.

We took turns fucking my wife. Art went first. I wanted to watch them; watching them made me want her all the more.

"Whore," I whispered in her ear when it was my turn.

"Yeah," she said, "talk dirty to me."

When we went to the bed, Beryl wanted us both inside her at the same time. "One in my kitty," she said with a seductive voice, touching herself, "and one in my booty."

"I have hope for us," she said later.

We were lying in bed alone. The sex had been good. I remembered a night, not a month ago, when we were in bed together and she had said, "We should just have wild sex right now, that'd solve all our problems," but neither of us could do it.

"That's good," I said.

"I really do." She kissed me.

I kissed her back.

"I feel so sexual, so alive again. I want to fuck more men. I want to fuck *a lot* of men. I love you. Will you help me do this?"

She could have done it by herself, or with Art, but she wanted me involved, and I wanted to be involved. And Art, of course, wished to be there too.

It started with the gang bang. Art made the arrangements for this, being the resourceful fellow that he is, getting the guys Beryl had fucked at The Party together for another go at it. There were nine of them in all, more than I had originally imagined. Had my wife really fucked nine men that night? I suppose so. Ten, including Art. Eleven, including me.

If I should ever think that what happened was just a wild fantasy, or a dream, I have the evidence on videotape. It was, yes, Art's idea to capture this night for posterity. When he suggested it to Beryl, she got this wild look in her eyes and said, "Yes." I was beginning to know that look better and better. I wanted her to say no. I wanted her to say no because I liked the idea myself.

(A number of times, alone, feeling lonely, thinking of the life I once had, I will put that tape into the VCR and watch. I will watch my wife fuck all those men in a single session, fucking in every combination possible.

Others have watched her. Hundreds, thousands, all over the world. This is really what this story is about.)

It was Art's idea – again – to create a Web site and place stills from the gang-bang video on it. He created the Web page and allowed people to access it for free. In a matter of days, the site was getting thousands of hits. Art said this was a combination of posting stills to various news groups with sexual themes, and the help of a number of search engines.

After a month, he – or we – announced that the whole video-tape could be purchased for $34.95.

In a matter of weeks, two thousand orders came in.

First we were just some people doing kinky things, and now we were in business.

We were, I guess you can say, pornographers.

III. Solo in the Jacuzzi, with Memory

I was alone in the Jacuzzi. It was another clear night. That red star was indeed Mars. I stared at it. I wanted to go there. I wondered what sex life was like on Mars.

In the bedroom, in the house, Art and Beryl were fucking. He had been fucking her in the ass when I had left, and came out here, turned on the jet streams, and sat in the warm bubbling water. I closed my eyes while looking up.

In the water, I thought about the two of them. I pictured his cock going in and out of her butt, the muscles of her sphincter contracting with each thrust. As I thought of this, I started to become aroused. The image in my head was far more enticing than returning to the bedroom and seeing and smelling it. In my mind, I was the director, I was in control, and I made my own movie of the act.

I also pictured scenes from the night of The Party.

I touched myself. I had my cock in my hand under the water, and I began to jack off.

I watched my semen clump in the water and float to the top, getting caught in a whirlwind of bubbles, spinning around, blending in with water and chlorine.

Intermission

How We Met

I met Beryl at the recital of an experimental cellist; he was on tour for his new CD. In the first half of his performance, he presented classical pieces by Debussy and Mozart. I had difficulty listening – I kept glancing at the blond woman who was sitting alone, across from me in the small concert hall. She was wearing black slacks and a white cotton blouse. She kept looking at me as well. We talked during the intermission. Small talk: *what do you think of the cellist? Oh, he's good.* We sat together for the second half, and the cellist presented his own iconoclastic work, hooking his instrument to microphones, adding special effects, or playing along with a tape full of strange sounds. Toward the end, he did a manic solo and broke two strings. After, I asked the blond woman – Beryl – if she'd like to go get some coffee. "No," she said, "but how about a beer?" Two months later, we were living together. Six months later, we were married.

IV. Quartet

"We've been approached with a business deal," Art said on the phone. Beryl and I were on separate phones in different rooms, listening together.

"Go on," she said.

He said, "There's this couple – here in the city – who have a successful on-line business. They do the same as us: sell videos and pix of them fucking, or the wife fucking some guys. Then they started to make and distribute vids of other couples. Acting as distributors, growing their business. You know. They came across our Web site, and they want Beryl. I mean, they can sell five times the amount of videos we do. Or so they say."

"What does this mean?" I said.

"More money," Art said.

"More money," Beryl said, "sounds good to me."

This couple – Fred and Donna – invited the three of us for dinner to talk about the possibility of a business venture. Art drove in his own car and was late. Beryl and I were both nervous and we didn't know why.

They had a nice, modestly furnished suburban house, not the kind of place you'd think a big Internet porn outfit would be located. Fred and Donna were also the kind of couple you might see at a PTA meeting – almost conservatively dressed, quiet, and friendly. They were in their late thirties, attractive and unassuming.

Over dinner, we talked about our lives, not sex.

I wondered why I was here. I was expecting drugs, hard booze, triple-X love acts.

Fred suggested we go to the water.

They also had a Jacuzzi, but this one could fit ten people. It was very nice and spacious. Fred and Donna disrobed before us and got in. Donna was a bit on the chubby side, but had a magnificent tan and silicone-enhanced breasts. Fred, I was quick to notice, didn't have a hair on his well-muscled body, and his dick had to be ten inches long.

Art stripped and jumped in. Beryl and I took our clothes off slowly, still uncertain, and joined the party.

We were all drinking champagne, by the way. It always begins with some kind of party.

"You have a great body," Donna said to Beryl.

"Thank you," Beryl said.

"I'd love to fuck you," Donna said.

"I'm not bi," Beryl said.

"Too bad," Donna said. "But maybe Fred can fuck you. I like to watch him fuck other women."

"Sounds good to me." Beryl laughed.

"You got a look-see at his tool?" Donna said.

"Oh, yes," Beryl said. "I wonder if I could take it."

"It takes some getting used to," Donna said. "His cock is very nice."

"Yeah," Beryl said.

Art and I looked at each other.

"Let's talk business," Fred said.

"Let's," Art said.

"This past year," Fred said, "we've cleared three million in sales."

I almost choked on my champagne. Beryl did.

"You're shitting me," Art said.

"No," Fred said.

Donna smiled. "We'll make more each year."

"Porn is the backbone of e-commerce," Fred said, "and the amateur market is in a boom. A huge boom. There are dozens, hundreds of people like us making a living off pleasure. We have something many people out there want."

"Intimacy," Donna said, "and love."

"This business saved our marriage," Fred said. He drew Donna close to him. They held each other. They kissed. "We wouldn't be together now," he went on. "It added . . . excitement. It delivered us from an absolutely dull life, the same thing day after day. You know what I mean."

"I was ready to leave him," Donna said. "I wanted something more."

"We both did," Fred said.

"And we found it," Donna said.

Beryl and I looked at each other. I moved to kiss her. She kissed me. Art looked away.

"We like what you have," Donna said.

"We can get rich together," Fred said.

"I like the sound of that," Beryl said.

"Me too," I said.

Fred said, "So let's fuck and seal the deal."

We all laughed.

"Hey, buddy," Fred said to Art, "there's a camera in the house, and a light. Why don't you get it."

Art nodded and got out of the water. He looked lonely, walking away wet and naked. I can't say that I felt sorry for him.

Donna moved to me, and Beryl moved to Fred. I took Donna's large breasts in my hands and rubbed them. Her pink nipples were pointing at me. Beryl was stroking Fred's big dick and she said something like, "Oh, my." He sat on the edge of the spa, and Beryl did her best to take him in her mouth.

"You want me to suck your dick too?" Donna whispered. "What do you want me to do? I'll do anything, anything."

Art set up the camera.

Donna and I got out of the water to fuck. I had her on her back, her thick legs on my shoulders. She smelled strongly of perfume. She reached up and bit my nipple as I fucked her. Beryl was still sucking on Fred.

"Hey," Fred said, turning to me with a smile. "I think I'm about to come in your wife's mouth."

Art didn't join us. As he operated the video camera, he jerked off. He was now an observer. I could see it on his face: something was missing. He looked lonely and I didn't care.

V. Epilogue

Our hair was still wet when we got in the car. We were electrified. The sex had been good, the idea of success even better.

I touched my wife's face.

"We don't need Art," she said.

"I was thinking the same thing."

"Our marriage will work, won't it?"

"I hope so."

"We can be as happy and wealthy as Donna and Fred."

I wanted to say that we *were* Donna and Fred. We'd just made love to our mirror images, and it was caught on tape.

I started the car.

"Turn on the heater," Beryl said. "I don't want to catch cold."

I did, and as we drove, the warmth started at our feet and moved up our bodies and to our faces. We were holding hands the whole way.

Home, our hair dry, we went into our own Jacuzzi and fucked in the water and under the stars, and there was only us, and it was very nice again, for a while.

After Loss

Tabitha Flyte

After the tears had been shed, the damp tissues were buried in wastepaper baskets, and we had all given up asking *why, why, why*, Robert said that he should go back home. My sister Sarah said no: she felt she should stay overnight to keep an eye on Mum, even though my brother was still living at home back then. (He moved out a few months later. He said it wasn't the same without Dad).

I couldn't bear to stay in the family house so I asked Robert if he wouldn't mind dropping me at my flat, even though it was way across town. My eyes were blurry from crying, and I hate night driving even at the best of times. Robert said it was no problem.

Saying goodbye wrung more tears out of all of us. My sister and I hugged each other unusually tightly and I promised to call early the next morning. As I left the house I had a sick feeling in my gut: *what if they died too?*

Robert drove so effortlessly it was almost as if he weren't driving at all. I watched his big hand as he glided through the gears. He was a cool customer but I knew he was upset too. He and Sarah had been dating for eight years; as Mum said, he was almost family. In fact, he probably got on with each of us *better* than family. I don't think he and Dad had ever conversed deeply, but they'd laughed about a broad range of things, as men do, and together they'd teased Sarah and me, the crazy sisters.

"I feel terrible," I said desolately when we arrived at my place.

"I'll come in for coffee," he said, and I knew that he meant a talk. Robert had been trying to talk us around for the last few days. He was full of correct homilies, lines from books on bereavement counseling.

In the bathroom, my face in the mirror looked unfamiliar. My eyes were over-bright and my expression seemed new, but not fresh-new. Surely I didn't have more lines, more gray hairs than last week? I pinched my cheeks, trying to bring some color onto the pale palette. I changed out of my formal black clothes into a dressing gown.

In the living room Robert was sitting on the floor, cupping his mug of cocoa. When he saw me a sympathetic look crept across his serious face. It was too gentle. Annoyingly, it started me off.

"Robert," I dribbled, "I need a cuddle." The words just spilled out like a leak.

"It's all right," he said. I swear I would have killed him if he'd said, "Let it out" or "Have a good cry."

I sat down beside him, and he put his arms around me. It had been so long since anyone, any man, had touched me that for a split second I almost didn't know what to do. I tensed. It was a shock, just to be there, to be held. Eventually I relaxed. I felt the stress leave my body, and my muscles all seemed to flop. With my family I had tried to be so strong; now, with Robert, I defrosted.

Robert didn't let go. He held me in his warmth. He was a big cuddly bear. "It's all right, 's all right."

Men and women hug so differently. When I am hugged by a woman I feel that the arms around me say, "Yes you can do it, you can." When I am held by a man I feel that I am being told, "No, you don't have to do it, you don't."

A sob, a groan – I didn't realize immediately that it was he who was sobbing, not me. He was crying into my shoulder. I remembered Sarah saying, almost contemptuously, that he couldn't even watch a romantic film without welling up.

"It's OK," I whispered. It was my turn to comfort. I patted him awkwardly. This was my grief, not his, yet I was proud; if *he* was this bereft, think what sorrow *I* was entitled to. His face had that comical look men sometimes get when they cry; he was trying to cheer up, but grief literally pulled the corners of his lips southward.

I felt the carpet beneath my dressing gown burning against my thighs, but I hung onto him, squeezing him alive. How good it was to comfort someone rather than have him walk on eggshells around me.

"'S OK," I whispered. He looked at me for a second and then his face was comfortably looming over mine. His mouth moved onto mine, tender, searching.

"It's OK," I repeated firmly.

We kissed, and our lips parted and our tongues peeped out, cautious at first, tentative. Then, as his lips warmed mine, I couldn't stop my tongue from prying into his mouth. His tongue felt so good, like an extension of our comfort, a sharing of our pain. His wet tongue inside my mouth was like transference, like a mother giving her baby food. It was sweet, soft nourishment somehow – well, that's how it felt at first. I cupped his face, his beautiful face, and I felt moisture between my legs, but it didn't feel wrong or anything, just friendly. We held each other tight. He was massaging my back, making big circular strokes, and our mouths were widening and our tongues becoming more adventurous. I made a little whimpering noise and he pulled me closer.

OK, we weren't being so friendly then, but the opposite of friends is enemies, and we were still friends – we'd just slid along the sliding scale. It didn't feel like a big change, or an abrupt turn. It felt warm playing with tongues. Arousal dampened my knickers. Rising heat. Maybe we shouldn't have, but it was nice, so nice, not to be alone. We were like kids too young to know any better, playing doctors and nurses. He kept pulling back and studying my face but I couldn't stand having him look at me. I wanted his tongue inside me, his mouth wrapped around me. I didn't want him to see me; I felt like my face was just fragile skin stretched over skull. People say faces are beautiful, but they are just mineral, just shells. I wanted him to squiggle in my hole, to blot away my anger. I was becoming exuberant, feeling good, physical, for the first time in weeks. I felt that strange twist in my sex, the reminder that I was not dead.

How can you be dead when you feel like this?

Somehow, I don't know how it happened, but my dressing gown was gaping and he was down lower, sucking at my tits. I remember looking at his face, his tufts of dark hair, pressed into my collarbone. I felt womanly, maternal. I knew I couldn't stop this. There was no reason to stop. This was the best way to comfort someone. If I could do this for everyone, every man, then surely the world would be a better place. Imagine on the subway, healing the soulless faces, touching their hands grimy from newspaper print, letting everyone who needed it suck me there, hold me tight. I would spread sustenance, warmth, fulfill some fantasies.

My nipples were hard and he was rolling them around in his mouth, sucking them like candy, pulling at them. I still felt tender toward him, tender toward everything – but I felt crazy too. Go lower, I wanted to urge, go south. I wanted him to suck my clit before I exploded.

He was kissing me again, little angel kisses on my lips and my chin. He was pulling me onto him, and I let him because he was so upset, and if I was making him feel just a little better, it would make me feel a hundred percent better. To see my nipples harden and pinken was something I just wouldn't have expected at a time like this.

At a time like this.

I was leaning over him so that my breasts kind of plopped into his mouth. I was thinking how lovely it was. Nothing else. I know that you are supposed to be wondering tortured thoughts – *Where will this go? How will this end?* – but I didn't wonder about any of that. In fact, I thought he, we, wouldn't go further. I thought this was it, a complete story. But then he yanked my dressing gown up at the back and his hand landed on the cusp of my ass. Fuck!

Jesus, it felt nice. The hole between my legs turned liquid from his hands toying with my butt. I was making little noises of approval. These fired him up: the next instant he was sucking my breast furiously, fiercely, harder than before. I thought, *What about the other one? What's wrong with that one?* Then he moved over and nursed my other nipple and I was controlling his head, urging him on. Even to myself I sounded like one of those women in the dirty movies, telling him to suck me, telling him how horny he made me.

I felt like he was taking possession of my body. He was really moving in, and I didn't know how I felt about that. At the same time I was thanking God that someone was taking control of me. It was glorious to let someone else be responsible for a change. I was sitting lightly on his hands, and he was massaging my naked buttocks. Biting my titties. Did he know how creamy my cunt had become? Did he realize that I would fuck him like a shot, bereavement or no? He looked me in the eyes again before another round of bruising kisses.

"Robert," I murmured, "what are we doing?"

I suppose my intervention came too weak, too late.

It did not take much for the poor man to slide one finger, just one culpable finger, between my legs. And it took just one exploring finger to change the way of the world and to make all of our decisions. His finger found my cunt, wandered up my creamy slit. I was wetter than the ocean. He groaned his surprise. Still, as soon as his fingers were slithering around in my moistness, I knew that this wasn't right.

Sarah will kill me.

I had never fancied Robert before, and I say that in all honesty. But I wanted him now. Oh, yes. I wanted him to fuck me like I wanted nothing else in the world.

His finger filled my sex. And he had such massive fingers, and his other hand, the hand on my buttocks, was clenching me tight. Exploring where it shouldn't, gliding up and down the gap between my cheeks. Oh, God, Robert, do it to me more.

Sarah will never find out.

More fingers were involved. One was on my clitoris, flicking gently, Oh, God, Robert, you are going to make me come. I was burning up. I was re-entering the earth's atmosphere, or maybe I was halfway to heaven.

Sarah taught you well.

I felt that he wanted me on top of him, but I wouldn't. I didn't want to straddle him but to be annihilated by him. *Fill me up.* Wasn't I the "victim" here? He pressed down on me – not questioning, not fainthearted, but assertive. *This is my right, my primitive right.* His cock grew huge against my thigh. *Yes, bigger, you bastard, as big as it will go.*

My wetness coaxed him to be brave. In the tremors of our bodies, our grief was forgotten. He started kissing me again. Long deep dark kisses, knowing kisses, victorious kisses.

Sarah aged twelve asking Dad what erogenous zones were. "Places that are hot," he'd said, winking at me.

My dressing gown was parted and Robert was sucking powerfully on my nipples, yearning at them, serenading them with his pointed tongue.

I wanted to feel alive again.

Remind me that I am not dead. Show me that I am flesh and blood, and squealing cunt, and horny thighs, and breasts, and curly pubic hair. He went there, between my legs, with his lovely, clever tongue. He licked me there, my wet pussy, sucking out my loneliness the way people suck out the poison of snakebites. He pushed me down so I was lying with my dressing gown askew, legs open, bent at the knees, not caring what he did to me. My shutters were thrown open. He was fielding my pussy, soaking his face and rubbing it against me.

"You're so good."

I wondered how we compared sister to sister. Did we taste the same? Would we come the same? He licked and licked and I moved, rocking against him, making his face so wet that he had to pull away and wipe himself. And then he was back, determined, vibrating my clit, tongue and fingers, fingers and tongue, and I was cunt-up, eaten up, losing it, losing him. I thrust against his licking face, mad for it. The orgasm stole through me, big shudders following little ones. Embarrassed laughs of disbelief followed my roars of approval.

And then he was up; up and ready to insert his big cock inside me to blot out our pain. He fiddled between my legs and found my welcoming space. After the hors d'oeuvres, my cunt was hungry for the main course. He moved to enter me.

"Do you have a condom?" I hissed.

No.

Then we couldn't fuck, we can't fuck because tonight is definitely not the night the first grandchild will be conceived, not by him and me. I didn't trust him not to come the moment he entered me. I would, why wouldn't he?

Oh shit, the interruption, the aching, I needed fucking like I never had before. This emptiness had to be filled. *Let me escape just for a minute again into the oblivion of orgasm.* My body was still shaking from the tremors of the last one, the aftershock. *Do it again before it wears off and we wake up from this dream. Fill me up, fuck me up.* It had to be all of it, his hands on my tits, his mouth on my mouth, and his throbbing dick thrusting up my hole.

"Up my ass," I whispered. I knew Sarah wouldn't. I knew he wanted to, and I knew she wouldn't agree to it. "It's dirty," she'd insisted during one of our private sex chats. Well, I was dirty, a fucking whore. *So fuck me, hurt me, harder, deeper, go where you shouldn't go, come when you shouldn't be thinking about fucking, do it to me when you should be crying, or praying, or drinking sweet tea and eating plain biscuits.*

I got up on my hands and knees, doggy-style. I must have looked a sight with my ass up in the air, waving it about, jiggling it, at a time like this. I liked looking like this. He caught hold of my cheeks and pulled them apart, exposing me, wasting me.

His breath caught. "It's so tiny," he said cautiously. It was the first time for both of us, I think.

"Yes," I said, though I didn't know, how could I know? Dwarfed next to his rigid rod. His fingers sneaked their way around to my underbelly. He put his face forward and nuzzled me again. I clamored for more. I was bewitched.

I wanted it up there.

Things were not normal. Things were unnatural. Him here, me here, making out like teenagers on the carpet, fingering each other in places we didn't know. But I didn't want to be alone; I didn't want time to think. He was a bandage for my wounds, and, I suppose, I was for his.

He held me open and probed my hollow softly with his index finger. It wouldn't budge so he sucked his forbidden brother-in-law finger and put it damp in my forbidden sister-in-law hole. I was anxious, impatient, and terrified. The puckered valley was temporarily sated by the explorer. He entered me. I loved him entering me. I wanted to buck and shout and shudder. He was stroking my buttocks with his bigness, showing me what he was made of. Kneading me with his shaft of neediness.

"Are you sure?"

Sure? What was there to be sure about in this world; nothing would ever be sure again. I could only gulp my fucking willingness. My willingness to be fucked all over. I saw us in the mirror, his mesmerized expression, concentration and the work ethic etched on his lips. He was going to screw me like I needed to be screwed.

He pushed forward. I felt my insides tear and howled, "No, no, no!" We all make mistakes. To think I could do this with him was a big mistake. But he held steady, thank goodness, he stayed still and waited for my expansion. I could accommodate him, yes, I could. More than that. I wanted to hold him inside me, up me. I scrambled back against him, mashing and grinding. He wrapped his arm around me, perching his hand over my pussy. His hand looked like a diver poised to launch into the deep blue sea. He dove. I felt the trigger, the chase, the splash. All holes filled, all bases covered.

I slammed back again and again to feel his cock work up and down that new place, that uneven road. His hand worked magic on my clitoris and I slammed back, again and again, sighing and coming, and breathing hard, and promising I loved him, and I knew I was alive, I was really alive.

He sped up, and was groaning hot cunts and fucks in my ear, and we jerked against each other, together but not together, alone in our excitement, our exalted incredible comings. I couldn't stop myself from wailing as his cock sliced through me.

Afterwards he disappeared into the bathroom, where he probably examined his prick and tried to wash the guilt off him. *What the fuck have I done?* I knew he must have been feeling that, because I was. He dressed hurriedly, like a man who has overslept on the day of the big company presentation.

"Well, if there's anything you need . . ." he said, backing away toward the sanity of the street. The car sat loyally against the curb like a puppy faithful to its owner.

"You've already said that."

I watched him walk away. I watched him intently almost to convince myself that he *had* been there, inside my house, his head between my legs, his cock up my ass. As soon as the car drove off he seemed to erase, or vanish. But not completely. My skin felt different, touched, and the hole, the passage, felt used and unfamiliar. Later, no matter how I tried to contort and distort my memory, I could never drive out the events of the day. I realized I had simply exchanged one kind of grief for another.

A Walk in the Rain
on the Wild Side

O'Neil De Noux

Judy was plenty scared. Two seedy-looking men leered at her legs as they sat across the aisle of the narrow streetcar. She looked up at the only other person on the car, the driver, and tugged nervously at the hem of her tight silver minidress. The driver was too busy driving through a tropical New Orleans rainstorm to notice anything else on the streetcar at one in the morning.

Judy told herself to calm down. This was what she'd planned when she climbed into the shortest dress she owned earlier that evening. Checking herself in her full-length mirror, as she built up confidence to leave her house dressed like that, she felt excited. The slightest bend at the waist gave a clear view of her thin white panties. Her dress was so short, she had to pull her black thigh-high stockings all the way up to her ass, to keep the top of the hose from being seen when she walked.

Finishing her make-up, Judy had rolled dark red lipstick over her lips and took a look again in the full-length mirror. She'd run her hands down her hips to straighten her dress and turned. Not bad, she thought. At thirty-two, she still had a good figure and damn nice legs. She just wished she could tan, so her skin wouldn't look so – white. She ran a final brush through her long brown hair and slipped her Smith and Wesson .38 snub-nosed revolver into her purse. After a third glass of wine, she decided to go braless.

Judy squirmed in her seat and realized it wasn't fear that made it difficult for her to breathe now – it was her dress. Her dress was *shrinking*. She should have known better. Everyone knows, never wear crêpe in the rain. It shrinks.

It hadn't been raining when she walked over to Carrollton Avenue to catch the streetcar. She'd immediately flashed a well-dressed man with green eyes when she sat across from him. She felt a blush cross her face as she crossed and uncrossed her legs, watching him stare at her legs every time she uncrossed them. She told herself this was all part of the plan. She felt him looking up her dress, and liked it. The wine helped.

Getting out on Canal Street to wait for the return trip, she didn't notice the clouds overhead. The rain caught her just before the streetcar arrived. It was a typical, late summer rainstorm that came down in torrents. It ruined her hair and drenched her dress. Stunned, Judy climbed aboard the streetcar.

Sitting on one of the bench seats that faced the aisle, near the rear of the streetcar, she wiped the water from her face and arms. It was then she felt someone staring at her. She watched two young men move directly across the aisle from her. The black one was tall and wore a wild African shirt. The other, a ruddy-looking man with a reddish face, looked like a Portuguese pirate. They stared directly at her legs. She crossed her legs immediately. The way she'd been sitting had given them more than a good view up her short dress. She felt a flush on her face again. These were the type of men she was looking for, but hadn't expected them so suddenly, nor the way they were looking at her – as if she was dinner. She stole glances at them as she wiped the rain from her arms. Pulling her purse close, she was soothed by the weight of her .38.

Younger than Judy, the black man looked to be in pretty good shape, with bulging biceps. His companion, also in great shape, was about Judy's age and wore a grey T-shirt and torn jeans. His complexion looked as if he'd spent years under the hot Louisiana sun or on the deck of a tramp steamer. Judy felt nervous as they ogled her legs, and fought to calm herself.

The streetcar slowed as the rain increased, slamming against the side windows in sheets. Judy struggled with her dress; it was getting tighter around her waist by the second. Tugging at the dress did little good. She looked down; it looked as if it had been painted on. The tops of her stockings were completely exposed. The dress pressed so tightly around her breasts, it hid nothing.

Judy looked up at her two spectators and saw that they had noticed her dress was shrinking. Judy had to uncross her legs to pull her dress down as much as she could; but even holding it down failed to cover her panties now. Looking at the two men, seeing them staring at her crotch gave her another flush. Excited and frightened at the same time, it was a rush, sexy and dangerous. She felt her heart beating. She looked out at the rain, feeling the cool damp air through the cracked window while the men stared between her legs, her dress shrinking by the second.

Then the streetcar stopped. The driver called back to them. "There's some cars blocking the tracks 'cause of the flooding. I'll be right back." He bolted out the door before Judy could say anything.

The rain slammed against the streetcar. Outside, St. Charles Avenue was flooded.

The dress was so tight around her chest, it was cutting off her breath now. It must have been on her face, because the black man said, "Say, lady, that dress is shrinking you to death."

"It's crêpe," she answered nervously, then deepened her voice immediately. "It shrinks when it gets wet."

He leered at her crotch. Judy looked down and saw that her dress was halfway up the front of her panties.

"How do you wash it?" The man asked.

"Huh? Oh, I have to send it to the cleaners."

"Oh."

Both men grinned.

It was then the black man said, "My cousin lives right over there." He pointed to a two-storey wooden house down Euterpe Street. Euterpe? That was the very street she'd planned to get off at and walk down in her daring dress, to find someone, anyone that would talk along the block between St. Charles and Prytania.

The wind howled loudly and shook the streetcar.

"Look, y'all," he said, "I ain't staying on this streetcar. Y'all better come with me to my cousin's. I think there's a tornado out there."

At that moment, a gust of wind slammed against the streetcar, rocking it so hard Judy almost fell out of her seat. The man reached over and grabbed her arm. Then he pulled his hand away quickly and said, "I'm sorry. I didn't mean to touch you."

Judy watched him move to the open front door and step out. Standing now, Judy realized her dress had crawled halfway up her ass. The thought of being left alone on the streetcar was scary enough – but she wasn't alone. The pirate was still there. She looked back and saw his dark eyes staring at her rear end. Composing herself, she moved forward and looked out at the darkness of Euterpe Street. The man stood out in the rain, in knee-high water, his hands in the pockets of his jeans as he looked back at Judy.

She gulped and told herself this was where she was supposed to get off. If he had a cousin who lived on Euterpe, then she was half finished with her mission.

Overhead a lightning bolt flashed, followed by a roll of thunder so loud Judy jumped and followed her movement right out of the streetcar, right for the black man. With her heart pounding, she followed him down Euterpe Street. She lost both high heels and was completely drenched by the time they made it to the back porch of a three-storey wooden tenement. Pausing to wipe themselves off, the man told her his name was Donnie. Judy told him her name was Marsha. From below, she heard a voice call out.

"I'm Sam!" It was the pirate. He'd followed. Shielding his face with his hands, he said in a heavy accent, "Can I come up on the porch too?"

Donnie told him to get up before he drowned. Then Donnie quickly excused himself and went up a flight of stairs. Judy heard him moving on the wooden stairs above, then heard him coming down.

"Damn, he ain't home."

Judy couldn't breathe any more. She wanted to just ask him the question, but felt herself going lightheaded. She had to unzip her dress. Tucking her purse under her left arm, she reached back and tried unzipping the dress with her right hand. Her purse fell. She bent over and grabbed it. Standing, she felt faint.

She struggled with her zipper again and managed to get it down a couple inches but then it stuck, so she asked Donnie to help. He moved around and tried, but only managed to get it down another inch. Judy wiggled and looked up at the bright porch light they stood under. The men would get a good view in about a minute. She had to get out of that dress, braless or not.

"Let me," Sam said.

Donnie stepped out of the way and Judy felt Sam's strong hands on her zipper. After a few seconds of struggling, he said, "I'm trying not to rip this, but—"

"Rip it," she told him. "I can't wear it again."

She felt Sam's knuckles now, digging against her back as he ripped the dress completely off. Instinctively Judy put her arms over her breasts. Donnie, who was standing in front of her, got a good look before she covered them. He looked up at Judy's face and smiled.

"What do I do with it?" Sam said, holding up the ruined silver dress.

Judy grabbed it and threw it off the porch into the rain.

Donnie removed his shirt and threw it out in the rain too. So did Sam. Before long, they were all standing in their drawers. Judy pulled her hair out of her eyes and watched the men stare at her breasts. Her nipples were erect as she stood there, half-naked with the two strangers.

Turning to Donnie, Judy said, "I could have used your shirt."

"Want I should go get it?"

It was lying in mud, so she told him no. The rain seemed to increase. Aided by the wind, it blew in on them in waves. They edged to the wall of the building. Donnie, always the leader, had another idea. He told them to wait a second and then went back up the stairs. He scrambled down a moment later.

"Come on," Donnie said, "we can get out of the rain."

He led them upstairs and around the side of the building and pointed to a high window. "It's vacant. I just climbed up there." He held his hands together to give Sam a boost. Judy was next and a moment later, found herself tumbling into Sam's eager arms. His hands conveniently ran across her breasts and caressed her ass momentarily.

Judy tucked her purse against her breasts and pulled away. Donnie climbed in a second later. She looked around the room and saw that they were in a empty apartment, illuminated only by the bright street lights streaming through the windows.

"I thought your cousin lived here," she said.

"He lives in the next apartment. This one's vacant." Moving next to her Donnie added, "You're bleeding."

Looking down at her panties, Judy saw a dark stain of black grease along the rear of her panties. Away from the light, it looked like blood. It looked gross.

"Take it off," Sam said, as he pulled his drawers off and threw them across the empty room. Donnie followed suit.

Looking into Donnie's eyes, Judy heard herself say, "Just don't hurt me."

Donnie's large brown eyes widened as he spread his arms and said, "Lady. Nobody wants to *hurt* you. That's for sure."

Turning her back to them, Judy pulled off both stockings and used them to try to wipe the grease from her panties and rear end. She only succeeded in spreading it. So she sucked in a deep breath and slipped out of her panties and used them to wipe the remainder of the grease from her ass. Then she threw the panties and stockings across the room, too, and stood there stark naked with two strange men, in the middle of a storm, in the middle of an empty room, in the middle of a night that was anything but empty.

Craning her neck around slowly, she saw them standing in the window light, their bodies glistening from the rain. She saw the erection between Sam's legs as he stared at her naked ass. Donnie, wiping the rain from his arms, was completely erect. He had a long, thin dick that stood straight up.

Judy felt a weakness in her legs as she stood there. Her stomach bottomed out. Looking down at the floor, she saw that it was fairly clean, at least by the window. So she moved to the wall, put her purse down and sat, pressing her purse against the wall. She pulled her legs up against her chest and waited, her chest rising with each breath. After a moment, Judy leaned her head to one side and began to wring the water from her long hair.

Without a word, Donnie moved up, took her hair and wrung it out, gently. Sam moved on the other side of Judy and sat cross-legged, his dick sitting up stiff between his legs. When Donnie finished with her hair he sat next to Judy, also cross-legged. In the ensuing silence, Judy looked at Donnie and then at Sam and watched the two men examine her. Slowly, Judy let her knees down and leaned back against the wall, her arms falling to her side. She crossed her legs and closed her eyes and felt their gaze tracing their way up and down her body. Slowly she moved until she sat cross-legged between them.

Opening her eyes, Judy saw Donnie on his knees, leaning close and staring at her face. Hesitating, he leaned closer and moved his large lips toward hers. She felt her heart thundering in her ears. He parted his lips slightly and leaned even closer. Judy felt her head turn one side and they kissed. Donnie kissed her ever so softly at first. She felt his tongue probing hers as the kiss became more intense. Judy frenched him back long and hard and felt his fingers on her breasts.

Donnie pulled her away from the window, lying her down, just beneath the window. Kissing his way down her neck, he kissed each of her breasts as his fingers found their way between her legs. Then she felt Sam's hands on her ankles as he gently moved them apart, wide, wider, until she was completely open. Donnie's fingers slipped inside the folds of her pussy.

It was unbelievable. Judy felt so many emotions as Donnie climbed on her and pressed the tip of his long dick into her. She sighed at the penetration and curled her back and almost came immediately as this lean young man began to fuck her.

"Oh!" She reached down and grabbed his ass.

Donnie pressed his tongue hard into Judy's mouth as his dick plunged into her, his balls slapping against her ass. Judy came in a rush and came again just before she felt him explode inside, felt the gush of his climax as he pounded her. He pumped a full, hot load into her and cried himself as he came. Kissing her softly again on the mouth, Donnie moved off. Judy kissed him back and felt Sam move between her legs and press his wide cock into her.

Sam fucked her long and hard and came in spurts. Moving off, he curled up next to Judy and said, "Man, you are a beautiful."

She smelled their semen mixed in with her pussy-juice, smelled their sweat on her chest as they lay there catching their breaths.

When Donnie was ready again, he asked her to stand up and put her hands on the window sill. Spreading her feet wide, he moved behind Judy and sank his dick into her doggie-style. His hands on her hips, he rocked against her and rode her, moaning and grunting as he jammed her. Judy could hear the sloshing sound of his dick moving in and out as he fucked her again.

Rubbing his hands over her ass, he gasped, "White girl, you got one great pussy."

Sam moved beneath Judy and began sucking her nipples as Donnie fucked her. She didn't think her legs would hold out until Donnie came again. But she held up and he came once more.

Then Sam pulled her down and mounted her and screwed her again. He rode her a long time, kissing her neck and mouth and breasts, working his large dick in her until she came again. When he came, he cried out something in Spanish.

Judy watched both men lying on their backs after, their dicks flaccid and spent. She watched their breathing decrease. But – she was still hot. Moving over Donnie, she pulled her hair back with her left hand and took his dick in her right hand and kissed it and licked it and sucked it until it was up again. Then she climbed on it and rode him to another spurting climax. Then she did the same with Sam.

Curling between the men, she felt Sam when he rose and climbed out of the window and left. Much later, with the rain subsiding, Donnie told her he lived a couple buildings down. Judy picked up her purse and asked the question as casually as possible.

"I know a guy who lives on Euterpe. Jimmy Walker."

"Yeah? He used to live in my building, just downstairs." Donnie's brow was furrowed now. "Jimmy's bad news. How you know him?"

Judy pressed herself against Donnie and french-kissed him again.

"That's my secret," she said

"Well, he stays on Prytania now. Atop that food store painted green and yellow. But he's bad news, lady."

Donnie took Judy's hand and led her, naked, into the night to his apartment. Judy felt so naughty and sexy walking naked in the light rain, right on the sidewalk of Euterpe

Street. Just before turning to Donnie's tenement, two men sitting on a porch across the street whistled and Donnie waved to them.

After a hot shower, they went to sleep in Donnie's bed.

The next morning, Judy awoke with Donnie's big dick pressed against her stomach. Donnie was awake and looking at her. He rolled Judy on her back, climbed on her again and gave her another good long fuck.

Later, he gave her a pair of shorts and a T-shirt after and led her down to his beat-up T-bird. Passing around the corner, on streets still wet, Donnie pointed to a wooden building painted green and yellow and said, "That's where Jimmy stays now. But he's bad news, lady."

She made note of the address. She had him let her out on Carrollton. As she started to climb out, Donnie reached over and fondled her breasts once again. She walked home after he pulled away. Going straight for the telephone, Judy called Homicide and waited on the line for the lieutenant.

"Lou, this is Judy Wilson. Third District Patrol. I have Jimmy Walker's address."

"You do?"

She gave the lieutenant Jimmy's address.

"Good work. I'll let you know if we get him."

Judy took another long shower and climbed naked on her bed. She lay there with closed eyes and remembered the excitement, the feeling of getting gang-banged by two strangers.

She must have fallen asleep; the phone woke her. It was Homicide.

"We got him," the lieutenant said. "I don't know how you found him, but that was good work, officer."

"Thanks," Judy said, hanging up and feeling so good that they'd finally caught that no-good, rotten cop-killer Jimmy Walker. Closing her eyes again, she thought about that, about how she had found Walker when no one else could.

Then she thought about what she'd done and her breath-

ing increased as she lay on her back on her bed. Her eyes
snapped open. She felt hot again, very hot. She replayed her
walk on the wild side, replayed every scintillating moment.
And it felt delicious.

Weigh Station

Debra Hyde

At first glance, we knew we'd changed since college. I had some wrinkles; he was greying. My hair was a shorter, sassier red; his black, brooding beard was a distant memory. I was in the throes of a mid-life crisis; he was already a widower. Life had made me tough as nails; tragedy had shown his vulnerability. As we embraced, our bodies provided further confirmation: we'd grown fleshy with age.

But we hadn't changed enough to break our intentions. We kissed, deeply.

His tongue slipped into my mouth, meeting mine, playing a capricious, darting game of tag. I was stunned to find his kiss still felt the same and, as we Frenched to the old familiarity, I discovered we were still capable of the heat of mutual attraction. We were heading for a mutual meltdown, proof that old lusts die harder than old loves.

He reached for my breast, cupped it, caressed it. It was a softer, fleshier thing, no longer pert and perky, time having done its duty well. I hoped that when I took my top off, he wouldn't think National Geographics.

I caressed his back, shoulders and moved to his chest. He had had a crevice where pecs met breastbone and I wondered if that lovely spot still existed. It did, but it had lost some definition. Good. That evened things up. I buried myself in dedicated kissing, losing myself in arousal, trying to forget the weight of aging.

He pinched my nipple lightly between two fingers. "You

still like to go bra-less," he noticed, pulling away from my kiss.

"Even at work, if I can get away with it."

"You use to drive the guys nuts, you know, with the way your nipples use to show through."

I giggled. "Womanly badges."

He started nibbling on my ear. "And still arresting."

I hoped with age came wisdom, once our clothes came off.

A jolt between my legs told me to stop worrying and start enjoying. A jolt like that had started it all, years ago in younger days. I was wedged between him and his roomie in the front seat of roomie's car, cruising, and, as we turned a corner, I leaned into him. He put his hand on my knee, as if to balance me. An electric touch, it had forced me to make up my mind about him, lose the boyfriend, and make myself available to him.

His touch was still electric enough to make me available.

We peeled our tops off and our torsos pressed the flesh. His warmth and the feel of his now plentiful, now salt-and-peppered chest hair were familiarity, renewed. We rubbed our bodies together – petting body slams – and his hands strayed back to my breasts. Fingers tugged at nipples while his mouth travelled downwards for its follow-up. He remembered, rightly so, that his mouth upon my nipples would flare the fuel between my legs.

I went for the belt buckle, then the zipper, to free him. His cock, firm and ready, and my hand, grasping and eager, raced to meet each other. I remembered the spire that he was, the girth that had satisfied, but as I caressed his length, I realized I'd forgotten the actual feel of him – soft, with a stiff inner core. He moaned, still sucking. I swayed backwards onto the bed, wanting him to explore more of me, wanting him to reclaim what he'd once known well.

Letting go of each other, he helped me shimmy from my skirt, surprised to find me pantiless and shaved.

"No bush," he smiled. He lingered, looking at me, slowly

bringing his fingers to my pussy, touching my hairless cunt, examining the mound and crevices as if he'd never seen them before.

"You remember that time I shaved, don't you?"

"Yeah," he said. "But I thought you were being weird and I was embarrassed. Of course, years later, I realized that I was the weird one."

"No, no you weren't. I was the weird one. Still am."

"So you claim." Ah, his old habit of discounting me. The stiff inner core in another form.

Unaware of his subtle attitude, he smiled gently and focused on my pussy, examining me. He placed a finger on my clit, pressed down, making me groan.

"I understand how to work this better," he told me, gazing into my eyes briefly, then returning to my cunt. His finger began to circle it, rubbing, pressing on occasion, working my arousal. But he was also intent on exploring the nuances of my folds and he spread me with his other hand. There, he found a little surprise.

"Whoa!"

"Labia rings."

"I see."

"Go ahead, touch them. You can even tug on them."

He was tentative in his approach, in that initial touch, so, like a new lover showing him the ropes of my pleasure, I demonstrated, tugging, rotating the rings, then directed his hand back into place.

"I love having small weights hanging off of them and being taken from behind," I confided.

He gulped, shocked, much the same as he had years ago when he saw me shaved. I laughed softly but sensitively. "Don't worry. You don't have to do that stuff. Make love to me the old way and I'll be more than satisfied."

He relaxed into a slight smile and, without further ado, went down on me. His tongue knew more now than then, so much so that it forced me to stop comparing past and present. He concentrated on my clit, swirling, pressing, lips gently nipping now and then for added effect. Fingers wandered to my slit and played there with the rings, then found their way into me. Wet, my cunt accepted them.

I remembered how he would sometimes eat me to such arousal that I'd beg him to bury his fingers in me, all of them, deeply. He'd cater to my craving, sinking as much of his hand into me as he could to appease me, four fingers to the knuckles, enough to make me come and, when he pulled out, to feel empty, voided. Then, we had been too inexperienced to know we were toying with fisting.

Now, imagining the possibility of completing that play – my greedy cunt engulfing his hand, his every little twitch threatening me with orgasm; the very thought of grabbing him, squeezing him and squeezing one off in the process – imagining all that, while his tongue and his fingers played with me, I came.

And a new eagerness exploded with that orgasm. "Let me suck you," I begged.

He pulled away from me, shed his pants completely, and climbed on top of me. "No," he said in my ear as he hovered over me.

"Please."

"No."

He sank his length into me. "I want pussy," he said by way of explanation. He started fucking me and observed, dispassionately, "You're wetter than I remember."

"Things change," I managed to say before caving to the feeling of his full cock.

"Good, you feel incredible. Just right."

My cunt throbbed back its own acknowledgments.

He took a nipple in hand, pinching it to go with the motions.

"And you taste delicious, you know that?"

He kissed me to prove it.

He knew how to mix me just so: deep strokes, long and succulent; drawing the head of his cock to the edge of my kissing labia, teasing me; shallow, swift ones to test me, wear me down. I neared, he knew it. He plunged into me.

"Grab my ass," I begged him. "Please."

He did and I cried out, bucking at the feel of his fingers grabbing my cheeks, nails digging into my flesh. He reached down, took my nipple in his mouth, sucked, then bit.

I exploded around him, aware only of his cock in my spasming clutches, his bite, and my own lightheadedness as the bed rocked and creaked its complaints. I collapsed beneath him and he freed me from his grip. He watched me as I rested and returned to lucidness, slowly fucking me the whole time, as if it were some minor habit.

"Roll over," he said, withdrawing.

I did and he uttered, "Good God."

Now he saw why I jumped when he grabbed my ass. I sported bruises, compliments of a recent paddling.

"You really did become a masochist."

"I warned you I had."

"Yes, you did."

He touched my bruises gingerly and, though I flinched fully and suddenly, I also moaned with the same passion I had expressed with other touches. He knew it but still waxed serious, the past catching up to him.

"I did this to you," he said, remorseful. "I made you a masochist."

"Love made me a masochist," I declared firmly, sparing him the details. "Come on, forget it. Fuck me."

I backed my still wet cunt up to his cock and pressed him into business. He aimed himself at me and entered. It felt reluctant.

"You can't hurt me," I counselled him. "Just do me."

He took me by the hips and slowly worked me, testing me. I made noise about how big he was, how good he felt, how much I wanted it. Stroke by stroke, he convinced himself that, indeed, he would not hurt me. He relented, finally, and indulged himself by plundering me. I upped the dialogue, begging him to fuck me harder, to tear me up. Ruin me, I said.

In times past, that would've sent him and he would've

come. But that was then. Or maybe it was my poor choice of words. *Ruin me*, I guess, only works on a sadist.

"Roll me over," I offered.

I did. He climbed aboard again and I wrapped my legs around his waist. While he resumed his fucking, I played with his nipples, pinching and pulling. An old trick, my fail-safe.

He started shaking, head to toe. He was nearing, just like old times.

"Oh, God," he muttered. The signal was the same, time-less.

He slammed into me repeatedly, relentlessly, shivering, groaning, finally holding his cock still so he could better feel each ejaculation. Wet warmth flooded me, making me shiver.

Just like old times.

Downtime followed. Lying there, we resumed looking at each other's bodies, memorizing them. Our skins were softer, our bodies bulging a bit in spots, yet his cock, my cunt looked essentially the same. And they spoke to each other in the same hurried sentences of long ago.

But we weren't just cock and cunt. Our entireties had changed, bodily in countless little ways, soulfully in ways profound.

He looked at me now, wanting to revel in the body before him but too perplexed by what he saw. There, in that look, I had my answer: happiness couldn't be had here; the gulf between the unattached bohemian and the widowed married was too large for anything but solace and respite.

You can't go home, I wanted to tell him but words failed me, so I drew his head to my chest, held him, caressed his hair.

Solace, then, I decided silently.

He sighed and started, "I wish . . ."

"Shhh," I consoled. "I know. Sometimes I wish too."

Long ago, though, I learned that wishes don't sustain; dreams do. And, laying there, with him in my arms, I realized that the sudden harshness of widowhood had dashed his dreams, dreams he had yet to replace, dreams that, when they came, wouldn't include me because I was incapable of embracing them. Because years ago, after him, I had abandoned my own chance at sustenance and gypsied my way through life, forever too skittish to trust in dreams, forever eluding them.

Now, I could be a weigh station at best, a momentary rest as he moved through life. And, despite my own longing to have him and have him often, I could live with those limitations. Love had, indeed, made me a masochist and a good one at that. The only problem was, from what I could tell, he didn't like to make me flinch.

A John's Story

Samuel R. Delany

Lately I haven't spent that much time down on that strange fold in the city that seems to collect so many crumbs and so much lint: 42nd Street itself? Well, there's pretty much the same collection of Puerto Rican loose-joint dealers and pill hawkers, in their tank tops or with their shirts off for the July afternoon, with their homemade tattoos and their endless deals and arguments, laughing in little bunches, now one running out after this score or that one, or half a dozen of them standing around, squinting in the sun, while the white or black policemen amble by, with pretty much the same dazed look as the dealers. Now and then, in jeans and a too-tight top, or in some theatrically short skirt high over heavy, greyish thighs, one of the white or Puerto Rican prostitutes strolls through with a friend or stops to laugh or argue with this or that dealer.

Like a streaming veil, across it all rush the hot, sweating, ordinary people, the guys in shorts, the guys in gym suits, the office women in loose, dark dresses and the waitresses in tight, light ones, the black couples on their way to the movies, the five eleven-year-old Puerto Rican boys feeling grown-up and expansive because they're disobeying parental orders ("Don't you go down to that place, today! Hear me?"), the younger cousins from some Hispanic family with a kiddie stroller and a blue canvas bag for the baby bottle, the fried chicken, and the pasteles, him in a white T-shirt and grey-brimmed hat, her in a red-striped top and orange pants, them and the four kids going to *Conan the Destroyer* at Brandt's Lyric, or the three fourteen-year-old white girls, coming out of the subway by the newsstand, vigorously chewing their gum and wandering through it all, wide-eyed, in from Brooklyn, on their way to one of the (slightly) better movie-houses up on Broadway.

Around the corner, the Puerto Ricans still give way to the black grifters. About half the time, the middle-aged black shoe-shine guy is there by the phone booths, in his baseball cap and glasses, with his portable stand, still with his gaffes and goofs on all the passing women, white, brown, yellow, and black: "Oh, darling, you are *so* beautiful I don't think I can *stand* it!" Immediately, he tips his cap to her boyfriend, who's looked back, surprised: "Take care of that lady, sir. She's a truly good woman . . .! Want a shine?" The Beer & Burger on the corner right now is in the process of being changed into a fried-chicken joint; its glass windows are covered with plywood; the construction involves some digging in the sidewalk on the Eighth Avenue side; for the last two months, the plywood partition – on that busiest corner of the city – has taken up half the sidewalk, so that the pedestrians must veer out, around the wire trash baskets, over the clotted gutter, breaking at the phone booths, some squeezing in front, some striding behind and into the street, before swinging back onto the sidewalk to continue up by the gay burlesque house ("Hot! Gay! Kinky! Bizarre!"), the peepshow, the green front of the Irish hot-plate bar and toward the blue awning of the Barking Fish, the Greek pizza and souvlaki joints, and the corner liquor store and tobacco shops with their glassed-in inner walls, the little overpriced delis.

At 46th, beyond the porno movies, out in front of the blue wall and wrap-around glass window of McHales [I still think of it as Your Spot], it's a lot calmer than it used to be. Further up the Avenue, the Haymarket has been closed for getting on a year now, if not two; that's what used to bring in the serious hustlers, with the Fiesta, on 46th, and O'Neal's, on 48th, taking up the overflow spilling in either direction. But since then, O'Neal's has become the bar for the hard-core working men – myself, I never did like the atmosphere; and if, in the last year, I've walked in and out of there three times, just to see what's going on, I'm surprised. And the Fiesta, which used to be able to offer at least three or four 20-year-old junkies for the johns to choose from on a good day, doesn't even attract that much trade any more. The men who want a couple of beers' worth of relief from the high pressure of O'Neal's just come to sit and relax, with or without a trick. I've only had half a dozen beers there in twice that many months.

Still, it's the strip in the city where, for years, it's always seemed to be happening – and yet, if we're honest, it never happens *enough* at any particular hour, day, or season . . .

I'd gone into that Eighth Avenue porn theatre, the Cameo. In the lobby, in his blue uniform, cap and a brown sweater, the bored security guard sat on his stool, his billyclub over his lap, and didn't look up, even when I went over beside him to look at the poster in the glass case above his shoulder: Seka and Mai-Lyn were sharing some new Oriental sex-opera. Coiling over the four-color poster, a scaly dragon spread huge wings from one side of the glass case to the other, flicking a forked tongue above the two stylized bare-breasted skin stars.

"Hello, honey . . . want a blow job?"

The security man still didn't look up. I did, though: Wearing a gray, sequinned blouse with the shoulder torn, and torn-off jeans, a very tall, very black queen – at least a head-and-a-half taller than I am – nodded at me from the door to the orchestra.

"No," I said.

He flashed me a wicked look. "Don't know what you're missing, honey." His lips were maroon. His eyes were touched with gold glitter about the lids. "I give a truly beautiful blow job. Five dollars. Complete with Kleenex, wipe-up service, and a cigarette afterwards – if you smoke menthol . . .?" He held up a pack of something I sure wouldn't smoke.

Whenever one of these characters comes on to me, I'm always torn between saying, "Take a walk," and laughing.

He said: "You ain't gonna do too much better than that in here. We're under new management, you know."

"I don't have any money." And I laughed.

He raised his chin as if to say, "*Ahhh . . .!*", put away the pack, and moved to the steps that lead up to the Cameo's balcony, where the serious hustling goes on, anyway. As he walked up beside the pay telephone, grinding his buttocks at me dismissively in his frayed cut-offs, I shook my head – for the benefit of the security guard. Who still didn't look. So I went into the door to the orchestra.

In darkness I walked to the side aisle and gazed down over the scattered and flickering heads of the all-male audience.

The dozen committed jack-off artists were seated widely down towards the front. Most, however, were divided between the bored and the business-like, each of whom ignored the other, and none of whom would make use of what he'd watched till back in the privacy of his own bedroom or bathroom.

On screen, blonde Seka closed her china blue eyes and caught her breath as Mai-Lyn dropped her face into the bulge of a shaved cunt, black hair falling forwards over high cheekbones touched with Revlon blush, so that you could just see her tongue, through the dark strands, trolling like a red mouse between the folds of plump pussy-flesh as Seka moved her thighs.

An occasional young black queen or aging white faggot drifted listlessly in the aisles, while, big as Thanksgiving Day balloons, the two women's hands, their thin fingers and long red nails brushing, joining, entwining, suggested something between lust, friendship, and a film editor's whim. Then, from another angle, Mai-Lyn pushed her other hand down between her legs, as, from behind, the camera caught the melons of her buttocks. She spread her cunt-lips, and – once – quivered as though she'd hit something inside her moist envelope, igniting a pleasure momentarily beyond that called for by her $300 per day contract.

Out of the light I found a seat towards the side of the theatre, put my hand between my legs, moved my knees up against the back of the wooden seat ahead of me, and looked at the screen . . .

The thin kid who slipped in to sit two seats away wore grey sweatpants and a grey sweatshirt with the hood up – which the Cameo's air conditioning, always on minimal, just doesn't warrant in mid-July. I glanced over and thought: Now here's some seventeen-year-old Chinese queen, going to try and hustle me.

I was wondering how long I was going to go on being polite to the guys who kept bothering me.

In return for my very uninterested glance, I got a dazzling friendly smile. Well, I thought, at least he's not wearing makeup.

The kid immediately moved over, with a movement that was mostly hips, into the seat next to mine, shoulder against my shoulder, legs (with knees together) leaning against my legs; he touched my thigh with a hand as feminine as any I've ever seen, the nails long and neat under clear polish. "Do you want to have some fun?" he said in a surprisingly girl-like voice, with just the faintest accent – not foreign so much as simply from some other part of the country, or even of the city. Then, almost as if the question was a joke, he leaned towards my ear to hide his dark, Oriental eyes from me and laughed in a way that, I'm not kidding, made me think of small bells.

"Look, sweetheart," I said, "you're working. I'm just here to pull on my own prick a little, all by myself. Why don't you go find somebody else to hit on?" I like to be polite to any working man or woman, but I also know that, sometimes, with the desperate, you have to be firm. "I don't bring any money with me when I come into these places," I said. "So even if I fall asleep after I come and you or one of your friends slips back and slits my pockets, all you'll find is my subway token home. Believe me."

I felt his lips brush my ear: "Not for money!" came the intense whisper, still on the edge of laughing. "Just to have a good time! You know . . . you and me!"

The Oriental kid sat back now and took a finger and drew it diagonally across the sweatshirt's chest – "Cross my heart" – and then diagonally the other way – "and hope to die! I just want to have a little . . ." He shrugged. ". . . fun!"

As the grey cloth gave under that slender hand, I realized there was something under that sweatshirt. The breasts there were about as large as tea-cups stood upside down. And the first thing I thought was: on a guy as slender as that, they're just too big for even the most intensive hormone treatments. While, at the same time, I also figured any transsexual who'd actually saved the $6,000 I'd heard the operation costs these days would have *certainly* gotten them bigger.

I frowned. "*Are* you a girl . . ." I asked, disbelieving, looking closely at the young, Oriental face with the straight black bangs inside the grey hood.

For answer, the lower lip pulled in between the teeth in an effort of concentration and decision. Quick glances left and right; then the delicate hands hooked into the waist of the sweat pants while he (or she; at this point I was really befuddled) lifted hips a little from the theatre chair and slid the elastic waist down the substantially full hips (no panties) until the black bush of pubic hair pushed over the rim. "Touch me there! Go on! I like it! Touch me . . .!"

I touched . . . well, yes, *her*. In the hot closure between her legs, soft with dark hair, my fingers bunched up in the crevice, opened up when she moved her legs apart some, and my middle finger found the warm lips and slipped through them to find that always surprising inner heat.

Now I *know* what a pussy put in by a plumber feels like. (The working girls call it a "roll and tuck job." And *that's* $20,000 or up.) I've had my hands *and* my dick in more than one. Scar tissue is scar tissue; and it feels like a scar. Also, neither KY nor Vaseline – there since leaving the house that morning – has the same texture as a lady's natural moisture.

Her hands came together to press mine further in, and the elastic of her sweat-pants pulled over my wrist.

"Hey, look . . ." I whispered. "If you got some pimp waiting in the back of the theatre to beat the shit out of me when I don't come up with any bread . . . I mean, I'm not kidding you: I'm broke! You can go score with somebody else–"

She moved her thighs on both sides of my hand. "I know. But I don't *want* any money! I already crossed my heart, didn't I?"

"Well, look . . ." I took a breath; and, yeah, moved a finger.

"Please," she whispered. She put her mouth up against my ear again. "I gotta get somebody to eat my pussy for me!" Her thighs kept moving around my hand, and the lips of her cunt rubbed, with them, on the sides of my two middle fingers, which, without even trying, I was working deeper into the tight, the narrow, the wet, the hot. "I really want it . . . I'm so hot! You like to eat pussy?" she asked me, breathlessly – with, between "to" and "eat," a catch in her voice as if one or another of my knuckles had brushed the same spot that, minutes before, had made Mai-Lyn twitch.

I took a deep breath myself. "Fine wines," I said. "French food . . .? There's nothing I like better! Hey, who are you? What's your name?"

Her voice caught again, only this time there weren't any words around it. She pressed my hand still harder, and whispered, her lips still tickling my earlobe: "My sister just bought this theatre. You want to meet her?"

"Huh?" I said, turning to look at her. (Really, I've always been kind of curious who owned some of these scum-bag houses, but I've just assumed it was organized crime; certainly not the sister of some seventeen-year-old Oriental nymphomaniac.) "Your sister? What do you –?"

What she did to stop my question was, with her diagonally-lidded eyes wide, stick her tongue in my mouth. Then her eyes closed. And maybe, for a moment, I closed mine too. Cool lips moved on mine. Her hot tongue moved over and under my own, while moments of air came between our mouths, which we both kept pushing closer, in order to drive the cool spots from between them. I got my other arm around her. Moments later, when our mouths dragged apart and my face was in her neck (the hood of her sweatshirt had fallen back, and I could hear her breathing in time to the work I was doing between her legs with my hand), I growled into her collar: "Oh, honey, I'm gonna eat your pussy till you shiver like the San Francisco earthquake! I'm gonna tongue your clit till you're crazy enough to run all the kooks out of Bellevue! I'm gonna eat your cunt till you can't even fucking *walk!* I'm gonna suck your goddamned pussy till –" but didn't finish, because suddenly we were both going after each other's tonsils again.

When one or the other of us stopped to breathe, she whispered: "All right. You come meet my sister, then . . ." and pulled back, both her small hands flat against my chest. Her straight hair was long, I saw, now that her hood had fallen; it was held on one side by the kind of long, white barrette little girls wear. On the other side, it hung down by her face before it went back in her collar.

On screen, panting Mai-Lyn pulled at her cunt-lips, while Seka's paler, pinker tongue caressed and caressed the wet snatch Mai-Lyn held further and further open.

"Come on," she said. "Let's go. Now. Please . . .!" She glanced around again. "We can't do it here!"

Which was kind of a surprise, because God knows enough of these crazy queens do a lot worse. But then, this was a real girl.

I looked around too, for the first time since she'd sat there.

Two black guys in the row behind us, a Puerto Rican in the row in front wearing just his undershirt, and a red-headed white guy, narrow-shouldered, about nineteen, and with glasses, who'd slid into our row two seats away, all had their scrawny little peckers out, beating off for all they were worth, getting off on me making out with this crazy Oriental chick. (Actually, one of the black flashers wasn't so little, either. But never mind.) "Ah, shit!" I said, loudly. "Yeah, come on. Let's go!"

While the red-headed kid tried not to catch the head of his dick in his zipper, I pushed in front of him, holding her by her arm.

As soon as we hit the aisle, she was a step, three steps, five steps ahead. Hurrying behind her, I watched her hips working as she half walked, half ran towards the back of the theatre: her sweatshirt was no longer tucked into her pants, and bare flesh showed across the top of her buttocks, so that, even in the dim light, I could see two inches of the crack in her ass. Her black hair had come out of her collar and swung against her shoulders. I wondered how I could have thought she was a boy or even a transsexual. Though, Lord knows, enough of both work that place!

At the back of the Cameo, the men's room is left of the entrance: The door is always open, and the pale yellow light falls out from the steps leading down to the very busy, very smelly urinals.

Right of the entrance is the soft-drink machine; next to that stands the water-cooler, and beside that is a door that's almost always locked. It says:

Ladies

In most porno theatres, ladies' rooms are pretty superfluous; though, if a couple does come in and the woman really wants to use it, she can sometimes get the key from the cashier or the manager – unless they decide she's a pro.

About a year ago I was in the theatre when the men's room broke down and got locked up for the day; so, with a hand-written sign on a paper towel scotch-taped to the door jamb, they opened up the ladies' room for male use: a set of steps down a narrow, paint-peeling stairwell to a cubicle one-quarter the size of the men's, with a sink and single stall at the bottom.

The pipes over the ceiling had dripped a lot. And it stank.

The girl went right to that locked door and from the front pocket of her sweat-shirt got out a key. As she was fooling around with it in the old lock, I went up behind her, slid my hands under the back of her pants to hold both of her buttocks and, while I kneaded them, began licking her neck. She laughed and turned the door-knob.

The door opened, and the first thing I saw was that the light inside was very red. She moved into it, and practically pulled me, stumbling, in behind her – till my hands came loose from the elastic.

She reached past me and yanked the door closed sharply, while I blinked, surprised, looking up and down. Somebody had done a hell of a lot of work on this place since the men's room broke.

We were at the top of a stair, yes. But it was three times as wide as I remembered. The walls were covered with that red-flocked wallpaper like they have in Tad's Steak Houses, only the design was more complicated and, as I looked around, I was pretty sure it was also a lot more expensive. Brass banister rails were fixed to the walls. And the only smell in the place was as if somebody two or three days ago might have burned a little incense there. The stairs themselves ran down beyond a kind of beaded curtain made with lots of transparent glass globes on gold chains, so you could just see beyond it. The scarlet carpet here on the upper landing, which ran off under those hanging baubles to cascade down the steps, had a nap long enough to attack with a weed-whacker.

"What the *fuck* . . .?" Not very original. Still, it's what I said.

She stepped away from the door, looked around, turned to me, smiling, and began to push her sweatpants down over her hips, wiggling them, with her beautiful Oriental pussy coming into view over the waistband that slanted left, slanted right, till at last the pants fell around her ankles. She stepped free, first with one bare foot (leaving her sandals somewhere in folded material), then with the other. Arms crossed over her stomach, she pulled up the sweatshirt from beautiful tits that were bigger than I'd thought, under that loose grey.

Smiling, she shook out her dark hair and slipped, naked, between the beaded curtain, starting down.

I didn't slip. "Hey –!" I crashed through clattering globes.

Five steps below, she'd stopped, turned back, and, with one hand on the polished banister, watched me. She moved a finger from her tit up towards her neck and back, breathing hard.

There was some kind of light right beside her – more brass, with all sorts of crystal hanging around it; but, though she was clearly lit, I couldn't see much beyond her.

As I started down, she leaned forwards, reaching out with both hands and just . . . well, caught my crotch. So I stopped. "I want to suck you . . ." she whispered. "I wanna suck your beautiful penis . . .!" (Only girls say "penis" with that uncertain excess enthusiasm compensating for a conditioned embarrassment, which, for the duration of the word, leaves them a-quiver someplace where they cannot know the judgment upon them.) She got my belt open, pulled apart the top button on my jeans, and slid my zipper down. "I want to suck you and make you feel so good . . .!"

"Eh . . . sure," I said, wondering if I should help with the undressing; but she slid my pants down my hips and pulled my underpants down. The next thing, she was on my cock like a covey of hot, frenzied oysters. I let her suck; and she sucked *very* well. I caressed her black hair, rubbed her neck, then reached down to play with her tits. A breast in each hand, I rolled her nipples between the sides of my fingers. Now some women, when you play with their tits, it doesn't do shit. Others, well – she was one of the others.

Kneeling on the steps at my feet, her body began to quiver, then got real still (just her tongue going inside her mouth over my dick), then she'd quiver all over again, moving her head forwards and back. She sucked and shivered at the same time – while I kneaded her breasts I could feel her tongue vibrating at the base of my balls. I mean, while she sucked me her *shoulders* blushed!

I could've come any time. But after about a minute, I said: "Oh, baby, let me get my face in that pretty pussy." I pulled my cock from somewhere deep inside her head. (Really, that's what it felt like.) As I stood up, her breasts slipped out of my hands.

My pants down around my thighs, I kind of hobbled around her, running my hands over her sides, her tits, her ass; then kissing them, then licking them, while she stretched out along the banister, one arm above her head, one hand back to follow me around; she kept trying to touch my ear.

Behind her, I turned, sat on the carpeted stair, and wedged my head up between her legs. She lifted the outside one to the step above, and I ate pussy like crazy. There was the faint smell of soap, the faintest taste of salt, and a faint odor of some toilet water or perfume she must have dabbed earlier that day on some other part of her body. With my nose full of soft cunt-hair and her thigh hot against my left ear, she started to flex pussy-muscles around my tongue; I licked, now deep inside her, now lifting the little knob of flesh at the folded roof of her cunt, now trolling through the sparse forest of her pussy, and digging deeply, then lightly, then doing it all over again, while she breathed, then moaned, then grunted; the muscles of the one leg against my ear actually shook, as though some musician had plucked the nerve that ran the length of her thigh like a harp string, while she whispered: "My . . . sister! Oh, yes, my . . . sister! You come back here, a lot! Yes. We'll do this lots and lots. My sister, she'll *love* you . . ."

Now a funny thing happens to your cock when you take it out of a hot mouth: it feels a little cold. Now and then I kind of played with it, which felt good, but what I really wanted was to make her freak out, and mostly I held on to her legs and licked.

She was pretty nearly over her hump.

Me too.

But suddenly, something hot and soft was on my dick, and a hand was leaning against my leg. Someone from down below had crawled up the stairs to suck me!

Given we were in the hall to a porno theatre ladies' room, I thought some queen who'd been downstairs had come up to lend a mouth. Not that I mind who sucks on my crank as long as I'm getting mine, but I kind of wanted to know who it was and say, "Hey, motherfucker, I *see* you . . ."

I pulled my head out and looked down.

Another oriental face looked up, eyes smiling, with my dick a couple of inches in her face. This woman was about 35. Her lips around my cock were red as the skin of polished delicious apples. Her eyelids were blue with make-up, her cheeks coloured with rose blush, and I could see that she wore black stockings, and black, high, high heels. Her nylons were held on by a black garter belt. She kneeled on the step below me, the stiletto of one heel pointing back into shadow. Her heavy breasts were full and naked.

With red nails long as those of Seka or Mai-Lyn, she took my dick softly and lovingly in her hand and licked it, now and again gazing up at me with eyes lidded by that Oriental fold pulled down over her eyes' inner corners – or perhaps she gazed, I realized a moment later, at that other pussy still hanging inches over my head.

The first girl came down a step to stand beside me, her hand on my shoulder, her leg against my arm. "My sister!" she panted. "See! She likes you!" Then she said something in chink. And between licks, her sister said something in chink back. (I bet it was something like: *See, he likes you too*, with the answer: *Far fucking out!*) "I told you she would . . ." came down to me in English.

I thought about saying, "Eh . . . glad to meet you. Real nice porno theatre you got here," but it didn't seem appropriate. I said instead: "Suck on daddy's *dick*, mama!" and reached down for her fuller, swaying tits. "Suck on it and make it dribble!" At the same time I nuzzled over toward the crotch of the younger one, leading with my tongue.

The older one did (suck my dick, that is), and I got my face
back home into pussy-land, feeling the nails on the older
one's hand flex against my belly like a kitten's claws, while,
with those on the other, first she tickled the delicate place
behind the sack of my nuts, then must have reached back
between her own legs to do a Mai-Lyn.

Her mouth's engine seemed to roar around my cock. And
the pussy over my face worked my jaw till the base of my
tongue was sore.

The three of us kept getting closer, till they were embracing above me. I ducked my head, took a breath, slid down a
step, and stood up. Touching a shoulder of each with each of
my hands, I moved around to look at them from the side,
close enough to see the faint down on the younger one's cheek
and the grain in the rouge on the older one's; my breath
shifted gears in their ears' cartilages. Turning, brushing,
pressing, one pair scarlet, the other pink-white, their lips
moved centimetres apart. Their tongues travelled over and
around each other, more than crossing the distance between.

They pulled their mouths apart, leaned back in one another's arms, their flattened breasts rounding. Swaying,
those seventeen-year-old tits and 35-year-old jugs brushed
nipples. The stockinged legs of the older one bent, rubbing
my knee, as, panting, she lowered her face across her sister's
belly.

I sat down on the other side of the steps, leaned against the
brass banister, my cock in my hand, and watched. (Yes, I'd
come once; and I was pretty near it again.) In their very
different ways, they were very beautiful women. The older
licked out that cunt I'd been so happy in, her tongue
spreading, thinning, now going straight up into the red gorge
separating the black hair, now dipping forwards, now sliding
back, while, with her red claws, she massaged her own pink
clit at the vault of the raw declivity falling through the hair
between the black bands of her stocking tops. The younger
one's head was back against the wall. She smiled at me once,
then closed her eyes, her lips touching and parting, now

wetting under a sweep of her tongue, now drying with her loud breath, to stick and pull open as if she whispered dirty words in a language I didn't know and couldn't quite hear. Articulating them, her tongue made little twitches in her mouth.

When I came the third time, the older sister was standing against the wall, her hands high and wide on flocked crimson and her head down, while, squatting behind her, her little sister ate out her asshole with such avidity that, as I watched black hair shake down on those naked shoulders, as I heard the standing one cry out while the one on her knees grunted like some mad and famished gorilla, I was sure would leave one or the other of them sobbing on the steps in a minute, just from sheer excitement.

I say I'd come three times, now; and they'd each gone panting and quivering around the bend seven, ten, or more, in quivering, jaw-clenched (the younger one) or keening (the older) orgasmic cascades. And I *still* wanted another shot.

I thought about saying something like, "Hey, make room for me, ladies," but I just got up, stepped over, while they pulled apart a little, breathing heavily, both of them blinking at me with faint perspiration under their dark hairlines. Then the older one smiled as if I was the greatest thing since disposable chopsticks. Somehow we were all holding each other, and I felt their different-sized breasts against my naked chest; then all three of us spent a lot of time with our tongues in the other two mouths. Without stopping, we were all three going down the steps together in a way that could have been real clumsy, but, because nobody tripped, I hardly noticed.

For a while, I know, I sat on a step again, with two sets of thighs hot on each ear, while they rubbed cunts and kissed, and I ate double pussy that, I'm not kidding, made me shoot a forth wad off through my fist and into the dark. (We're talking an hour-and-a-half, two hours, here.) Then I was up, holding the older one around her shoulders, while she ran her nails over my back, and I kissed her, rubbing my cock (*still* hard!) from her pussy-hair up over the edge of her garter belt, while the younger one, crouched down where I had been, between our legs, rubbed my thighs with her small hands and flicked her tongue back and forth between the base of my dick and her sister's snatch. I began to quiver in a combination of heat and indecision on which hole, mouth or cunt, I should put it in first. I think it went in one, then the other, then back, then back again. But it all felt so good, I couldn't tell you which was which.

Down there, my balls kept dragging over her face. So she licked them too.

When I shoot a few times, close together like that (and, no, it doesn't happen *that* often), finally I lose the edge between coming and not-coming. My hard-on gets permanent, and my whole body becomes sensitive. Orgasm at that point is beyond what most of us think of as pleasure. It becomes more like a burning that spreads through the whole body, at many times the intensity of your ordinary, satisfying come. The fire runs from the back of my throat and deep in my ears down to the place below my kneecaps, to my insteps and the skin behind my ankles. Really, it's like my whole body becomes pure dick. (During one of those, sometimes juice comes out, and sometimes it doesn't – but there were already four wet spots on the carpeted steps around us.) And I was on my way to one of them, nearing it, falling away, and nearing it again; I kept on having the fantasy that the whole red stairwell was one raw, pulsing cunt while I was a man-sized cock, fucking it.

They were embracing, were kissing, and I was behind the younger one, with her hair damp in my face, and the underside of my prick running up and down her ass's scalding crevice, while over her shoulder, in much less light, I watched her and her sister's lips close and open around their tongues. (We were much further down the stairs now; it was much dimmer.) I tried to make my movements especially gentle, almost slow-motion, because I knew I was on some edge that, if I let myself go over, I'd be on them both like a

fucking animal – as slow as I moved, I was close to the kind of
frenzy where I could have bitten a tit or an ear or sunk my
teeth to the blood in a cunt-lip without even meaning to. As I
moved to their side, one of them held my dick and one of
them held my balls; and they still kissed and rubbed
snatches; I leaned to get my own face in between them –

When their mouths came apart, and I slid my tongue out
against theirs, the tongue of the elder seemed, for a moment,
terribly long; and, in that half-dark, I could have sworn its
end, six inches from her small, white teeth, was thin and
forked. The back of the younger one felt so smooth and
warm. But my hand, moving on the older one's shoulder, felt
cool and, as it moved, encountered something like cloth –
rough cloth; or even leather. I moved my hand down, away
from the roughness, while she took some great breath that
thickened her waist, and the garter belt that, fifty times now,
I'd run my tongue or my fingers or the head of my dick
under, front and back, suddenly went limp, raddling against
my palm.

The thing had snapped!

Again, I wondered whether I should say anything, but I
didn't even know if the older sister spoke English.

My hand went down to her buttocks; and something
seemed *very* wrong – as if one of her legs was bent much
too far back, or, as I ran my hand around it, as if she had a
third leg, or something, there. I moved my hand up again,
and the small of her back was not only cool, but cold; the
roughness I'd felt, here and there, before, actually changed
under my hand to a hardness like plastic, like metal.

I opened my eyes and pulled back.

Then I staggered back.

Because her face turned to me – and it was as long as an
iguana's; the eyes in it had reversed their slant till they were
almost vertical, big as the bottoms of beer bottles, and yellow
as urine. Her face was that of some beast and covered with
black scales; and the breath, which, between us, had been a
three-way thunder, was suddenly cut by her liquid *Hissss* . . .

Glimmering, her tongue snaked out a foot, flickered, and forked. What I'd felt at her haunches was not a leg, but a thick, saurian tail that swept the stairs first to pound my wall, then to crash the far one. Great wings rose behind her, their talons high as the ceiling, their tremendous folds fluttering hugely, looking for space to expand.

Her stockings ripped from her expanding thighs.

Beneath black hair, made little blades by the sweat, the younger turned her boyish smile to me. "You like my sister . . .? This is her place now!" No longer red except for the highlight from the lights further up, a claw moved black talons tenderly from the younger one's breast to her belly. I slipped down a step, grabbing for the banister behind me, started to run up. But one wing swung out to block the stairs – and the light. In sudden dark I could no longer see the younger one at all. So, turning, I barrelled down into black. Slipping on the carpet, I only kept from going head over heels because I was still holding the rail.

I ran down, kept running, and underfoot I could tell that there was no more rug.

Then I saw a light, like day, below. I ran for it, came down to the end of the stairs, and sprinted out into it, only stopping halfway across the theater lobby.

From his stool, the security guard looked up.

I took a breath and turned, almost falling, to stare back up past the pay phone to the balcony steps.

Then I looked at the guard again. Under the poster of Seka and Mai-Lyn, he frowned, dropping his hand from his billy-club. I tried to say something, but found myself looking back at the stairs I'd half-tumbled from because . . . something was coming down:

The black queen who'd tried to hit on me when I first came in stepped into the light. When he saw me, he frowned too; he adjusted the shoulder of his sequined blouse, letting his head fall to the side. "You look like you been busy, honey . . . You comin' up for air before getting yourself into another session? . . . Too bad it wasn't with me!"

I looked down at myself.

My shirt was open and hanging off one arm. My jeans were apart and pushed so far down my hips you could see public hair and the top of my dick.

Behind me, the guard finally said: "Look, fella! We let a *lot* of things go on in this place. Upstairs, you can take your pants off and get fucked in the aisle if you want. I'm just here to see nobody picks your pocket while you do. But you *still* gotta put your clothes on before you come out. Otherwise I ain't gonna let you in here no more. Comin' down here like that, I don't care *what* you're on, it just don't look right. And the new owners don't want you to go quite *that* far, know what I mean?"

I turned again, started to speak.

Then I pulled my pants up, trying to tug my shirt together with one hand, buckle my belt with the other, and shove my shirt-tails down inside at the same time, while I shouldered out the glass doors into the July evening. I went down Eighth Avenue, squinting to get the goddam buttons into their goddam red holes, while I passed half a dozen guys who weren't wearing any shirts at all in the muggy heat.

In his cap and glasses, the shoe-shine guy was pulling the dirty canvas cover down his stand.

My entire body tingling, I swung around the plywood partition, onto crowded 42nd, making for the subway.

The Room, After She Left

Adam Barnett-Foster

The camera pans across the room. A slow, steady but almost languorous movement. Noting every feature, every detail, methodically scrutinising all angles, colours and shapes as it glides along. Every single sign of absence.

This is a room where we made love.

Me and her. Me and she. She and I. I and her. The two of us.

She who has left. Whose name I must no longer mention.

Furniture, walls, standard issue prints (sailing ships, landscapes after Napoleonic battles, Audubon birds), bedspreads, windows, floral-patterned curtains, heavy wooden doors, a bed.

Does a bed have memories? Of the million fucks, of the endless embraces, the sighs, the despair, the words said and unsaid? Like an imprint in a pillow after heads have followed bodies and moved on. To the hotel corridor outside, to the lobby, the road outside, to the rest of their lives?

Hotel rooms don't belong to this world. They can be anywhere. A Trust House Forte shaped like the Pentagon building, close to Heathrow airport, frayed carpets. Adobe walls and Indian rugs draped across the floor in Scottsdale, Arizona, close to Phoenix and the John Ford desert of orange horizons and countless cactii. A modern tower overlooking Puget Sound in Seattle, rain crashing in gusts against the bay windows. Or a room in a small bed and breakfast chalet in the Italian Alps facing Mont Blanc, the nearby peaks crested with snow, the early morning sky bluer than blue and a healthy chill lingering in the air. Or again a hotel for students in Paris' *Quartier Latin*, where the bed can extend upwards, bunk-like, in times of necessity, last floor reached by a thin lift cage that can barely accommodate two bodies without an added single piece of luggage. Let's not even evoke New York hotel rooms: the Plaza, the Algonquin, the Chelsea, the Iroquois, the Gershwin. Take your pick.

Like Gene Hackman in *The Conversation* listening to the silent sound of lovers in a distant place. Eavesdropping on the memories abandoned by the wayside.

"Is this where it happens?' A woman's voice, hushed, shy. Hers.

"Yes." A man's voice. Darker. Mine.

"Kiss me, then."

The sound, electric, charged with emotion, of lips meeting.

An echo of lust imprinted through the memory layers of the room. A further memento of the lost past.

"Undress. I want to see your cock."

"And I want to see your body. Now. Badly. Every square inch of your skin. Watch my fingers map the territory, my fingers roam your intimacy."

"Yes."

The voices of several fucks, the awful sound of a togetherness which was too shocking too envisage just a few weeks before when we were strangers to each other, business acquaintances no more, respectively married to others by the virtue and authority of a magistrate or a priest.

The now empty room bears witness.

_ To the way she shifted across the bed as we lay there so lazily, in no hurry to rush the inevitable first penetration and lowered her lips towards my cock and took me inside her mouth. The heat. The moistness. One of my fingers lingering on the edge of her puckered sphincter, then moving forward, pressing against the closed ring of darker flesh and slowly inserting myself into her most private, aromatic warmth.

Sounds: breath held back, gentle moans, the velvet friction of white flesh against flesh.

And right now: utter silence as she walks down a south London street to greet another man, a husband, with a look of innocence on her face and guilt in her mind, her skin still tingling from my lips, her cunt still full of my juices. But infidelity cannot be read on the horizon of a face, or finger marks long faded away on the panorama of her nude body. Maybe only, the sole clue to the mystery of lust that might betray us, the smell of sex. In her breath, despite the Polo mints.

On my fingers, as in an empty hotel room I bring them closer to my nose and inhale the fragrance that still lingers there of her juices and nacreous innards. On my shrivelled cock which I haven't yet washed – the room is booked until late afternoon; I am in no hurry – where her strong fragrance still seeps deep into the flesh, bathing its roots, reminding me of how well we fitted together genitally, as if engineered for each other.

Outside, a jumbo jet takes off for parts unknown, a shadow against the insulated window which no outside noise penetrates.

So, this is it. We met, we flirted, we hesitated, we took a conscious decision to be selfish, we fucked.

Just a room.

A stain on a white sheet, some secretion or another, hers or mine; stray hairs on the cushion which looks more like a punch bag after the battle, lighter, curly pubic ones lower down the bed.

"You don't have to do it, you know . . . It's our first time, there's no rush . . ."

"But I want to,"

"Love you."

A look of amusement in her eyes as she interrupts the delicious activity in progress.

"Am I a bad girl because I suck a guy's cock on the first date?"

Mischief.

"Who said I was looking for a good girl?"

"So you were actively looking, were you? And I just came along at the right moment?"

"Well, I was the one who made the initial approach . . ."

"Your letter to my office?"

"Yes."

"I knew I wanted you since that day in Manchester."

"Did you really?"

"You bet."

"Come to think of it, you did give me a strange look while I was there reading my paper."

"That's what you think . . . I'm short-sighted, so you shouldn't attach too much importance to the look in my eyes . . ."

"Is this our first argument, already?"

"I'm not arguing."

"OK. Keep on sucking . . ."

Watching her head bob up and down in his lap. Her curls wild, uncountable. The almost invisible scar on her right ear lobe, highlighted by the sepia light peering through the orange regulation curtains. The whiteness of her skin, porcelain. Her large arse paler than pale close to his cheeks. A moan. A gasp.

The room records it all. Testimony for a further trial, record of evidence for the day of reckoning, filthy reasons for impeachment, actions that might one day bar them from the portals of paradise and plunge them into flames eternal. A mouth, thin-lipped, greedily gobbling a thick, heavily veined penis, a finger twisting inside her rear, manual sodomy, unhygienic, wonderful. The way their bodies relax into twisted postures that no other couple could imitate for fear of cramp or worse. But then, disappointingly, the room also knows that in just a few days, another visiting couple, older, darker-skinned, will succeed in even more extreme sexual gymnastics. The room knows.

Rooms always know. Like shadows.

And do not judge.

And keep their secrets.

Our secrets. In another room, before I knew her, long before I could even justify any morbid jealousy, she made love to another. Was it even her husband. Dublin? Scarborough? Paris, near the Gare du Nord? But I guess it was more vanilla, less pornographic. Surrounded by another four indifferent walls, antique furniture, sounds of a Chinese matron being fucked to high heaven on the other side of the thin partition, police sirens piercing the rhythm of orgasm, I melted Suchard white chocolate squares inside an Australian woman's cunt and later watched her lick the sticky residue and her own juices clean off me.

Ah, the strange etiquette of hotel room sex when the person you are doing it with is new! Allowing the water tap to run as noisily as possible as you sit on the toilet while your new partner waits for you in bed, just a few metres away, to stop her hearing the pee splash against the water, or the turd unroll out of you with extravagant farting noises. Waving arms in air to disperse the foul, personal smell. Listening to her pee and getting a hard on and wanting to ask her if you can watch . . .

Preliminary inventory.

A bedside table where she leaves her wedding ring and contact lens solution. The rumpled stockings at the foot of the bed, her lace-up resoled boots, her bunched-up knickers (when she moves to the bathroom and you get up and tidy the mess, you can't help but raise them to your nose, to smell the crease, slightly stained, soiled, through which you had earlier fingered her when you were both still partly dressed), her handbag (make-up kit, two separate shades of lipstick – before and after the fuck? – a pair of tweezers, a wallet with just twenty pounds in cash and her credit cards – her second name is Edwina, she'd never told you that, and orange, tissues). The carpet has cigarette holes. If you peer closer to examine the blanket all concertina'd up at the end of the bed, you can make out the hieroglyphic, faded patterns of previous come-stains from past generations of adulterers and lovers. The bedside lamp sheds a flickering light, distorting the colour of skin, the hidden darkness of sexual organs.

"Jeez . . . I'm so damn sensitive there. Every time you touch it, it's like a flash of electricity coursing through me in overdrive."

"Really?"

"Yes. My husband" (she carefully refrains from mentioning his name, naked as she is in the embrace of another man) "seldom touches me there, but somehow it doesn't have the same effect, you know."

"You're wonderful. Many other women wouldn't have dared admit that."

"Just the way I feel."

He kisses her. I kiss her. I kissed her.

Time loses all its meaning.

Never have we been so alone, in our forgotten island of lust.

"One day, would you . . ."

"Yes, I would like you to fuck me there. Very much . . ."

His mind races. Butter. Extra lubrication. Genuine fear of harming her. The madness of this intimacy they have so quickly reached.

His heart breaks. Straight through the middle, where it hurts the most.

She walks out into the corridor. Time for the train back to the conjugal bed. He follows her silhouette as her characteristic gait takes her down the endless hotel road, just like the one in the Coen Brothers' *Barton Fink*. He distractedly thinks this would be a perfect image, a fade away as end of a wonderful story, the camera raising itself on a crane as she moves away, long legs, tousled hair, from him. But in life, things don't end that simplistically.

He is no longer part of the room. He closes the door. Without her. Smells. The imprint of her tattooed deep into his flesh. Dresses. Leaves. Settles the bill with one of his credit cards. Makes his way to the car park, an empty black promotional tote bag swinging from his shoulder, no longer carrying the bottle of white wine he'd brought earlier. Car keys. Ignition. Motorway.

The room after she has left: empty, lonely too but still inhabited by her presence, a pervasive feeling of her.

The silence.

The cold.

Soon, the floor maid enters. Her electronic pass affords her entry to all rooms. In her closet, a red light had lit up, indicating 404 was now ready for cleaning. A day let only.

She pulls the cart behind her. Looks ahead at the relative untidiness, bed spread open, towels on the bathrobe marble floor, tap still dripping in the shower, a half empty bottle of wine by the bed. Clean ashtrays. Curtains still drawn.

The maid sniffs the air. A smell she is all too familiar with.

"Fuckers," she recognises.

The Editor vs. the Author

Anya Ross

Insomnia, an aching back and a fractured heart were passing acquaintances, but inner turmoil was a constant companion, the only one he could rely on never to leave him.

Long after he'd left, she wanted to remember while he wanted to forget. In a world of fragile hopes she had found the right man in the wrong circumstance. Yet she remained optimistic.

from the Novel by the Author

At times I had to pause and lay my pen aside as his words took my breath away. Still, I began to dread these editorial sessions; working with the author was like dancing on broken glass. There was a raw immediacy to his writing but the manuscript was littered with errors and inconsistencies and its pages were now covered in my red marks. At the publisher's suggestion we went through the corrections at my flat. My initial strategy had been "Flatter, suggest, discuss, persist, win". It had worked for about ten minutes: my calm and collected nature was being tested.

His novel was a challenge in both scope and length, leaving as many questions unanswered as asked: he wanted the reader to work. Our job was to cut and polish this rough diamond, but the conflict between my precision and his flawed genius exasperated us equally: he was unable to accept criticism graciously and could not concede a point without losing his temper, while I debated my corrections with more force than was justified. We were now way over our deadline due to our inability to compromise.

During our fifth meeting we fought over one paragraph endlessly. A man and a woman are sitting side by side at a desk discussing a complex architectural plan. He draws an amendment on the page, the woman leans over him to correct it, her breast brushing against his cheek. I explained that this was anatomically impossible. He disagreed vehemently. I shifted my chair closer to his and said, "Look, I'm reaching across you towards the desk. My shoulder is brushing against yours but my breast is nowhere near your cheek."

He said nothing, but I caught a brief look of surprise and defeat. As I repositioned my chair he wrote in the margin: "Point taken".

The following day I was working on the manuscript alone. The antagonist forces himself on a colleague, his brutality bordering on the dangerous. It wasn't believable, but as I read on, my pen remained motionless in my hand. I reached the end of the chapter and realised my heart was pounding. Damn, I was turned on. I had to go and lie down. My T-shirt pulled up and knickers discarded, the only hands I could imagine touching me were the author's. I tried to replace his presence but couldn't. I came quickly, annoyed at myself but still believing the scene was implausible.

He walked through the front door, avoiding eye contact and barely acknowledging my greeting. I steeled myself for the next few hours' work.

When we reached the sex scene he read my note in the margin. "What do you mean it's implausible?"

I took a deep breath. "It's too brutal and too fast. You have two people who don't even like each other. One minute they're arguing, the next he has his tongue in her throat, his hand down her skirt and he's yanking her knickers up her crotch – and she likes it. It just wouldn't happen."

Anger flashed in his eyes but I refused to give in. His hand slammed down on the desk and he said, "Right." He stood up, kicked back the chair and grabbed my shoulders, forcing me to stand. He kissed me hard as he thrust his hand down the back of my jeans. I tried to pull away but his hold was too strong. I felt the fabric of my knickers twisted in his fist and as his body pressed against me his hand jerked upwards. I wanted to cry out but his mouth stopped me.

His hand relaxed against the small of my back and I realized I was gripping his shoulders. In shock and breathing fast I was unable to let go of him. He looked at me with an expression I hadn't seen before: it was devoid of anger.

Finally he spoke: "Tell me, is it still implausible?"

I couldn't answer.

He stroked my hair. "Is she turned on, or is she not?"

I nodded and whispered, "Point taken."

Certainty is always dangerous because there is no room for debate. He knew, he always knew, and this alarmed her even more than her doubts.

Chapter One

He straightened the chair, sat down and returned to the page as if nothing had happened.

"He's mad," I thought as I discreetly adjusted my underwear. We had each scored a point via the physical rendering of a sexual episode, but if the writer's aim is to seduce the reader with his words he had taken that intention to a higher level. Shaken and confused, I pictured the tableaux to come.

The remainder of that chapter was an extension of the sex scene, and my comments in the margins were decidedly critical. Was this man not getting laid? Though I knew nothing about his personal life, whether he was married, divorced, celibate – and he certainly wasn't gay – I sensed these encounters were based on fantasy rather than reality. Moderation was an alien concept and every episode was set in the extreme: bondage, domination, abasement, discipline and a few for which I had no terms. He was obsessed with underwear, but not the sheer minimalist kind. The women wore big, plain white knickers – no doubt from Marks & Spencer – and tights. It was the latter I found most offensive.

"What's wrong with tights?" he asked.

"No one looks sexy in tights."

"But these are real women, not Penthouse Pets."

"I think you'll find that even real women like sexy underwear." I was baiting him, irritated by his sartorial assumptions of good girls versus bad. "I take it you don't like your women to dress up for you?"

I regretted the question instantly. It was hostile but also flirtatious and his response caught me off guard.

"What would you wear?"

I paused and for the sake of research answered honestly. "If I were wearing a skirt, say on a fifth or sixth date, I might wear stockings."

"I've never seen you in a skirt."

His observation surprised me, but I had the feeling he'd never seen a real woman in stockings either. "Trust me, it's bare legs or stockings."

I was about to win the argument, or so I thought. "Prove it," he said. "Put on your stockings . . . and that dress," he said, pointing to a photograph of me in a strapless black lace ball-gown.

What should have been an unwelcome request was now a clarion call heralding the memory of his hands on me.

Men are blind and women are deaf.

Chapter Three

As I walked into the living room, the lining of my dress rustling against my stockings, I questioned my motive and his; this could only lead in one direction. But this man was unpredictable, perhaps to him it was just research.

I stood a few feet in front of him and he leaned forward, looking only at my face. Holding his gaze I realized I'd mistaken the colour of his eyes: they were now as unfathomable as a nameless ocean. His thick black hair was shot through with grey and each line on his face held a story; I'd read some of them but the untold tales beckoned.

Eventually he scanned the length of my body, all the way down to my high-heeled shoes. He gestured to the hem of my dress. "Show me."

I gathered the lacy material in my fingers, gradually revealing my legs. I stopped at my knees.

"Go on."

I lifted it higher, exposing my thighs. I paused again, prolonging the moment, but his expression told me little.

"That's enough," he said and sat back in his chair.

The hem dropped to my ankles and my stomach sank in humiliation at the thought of his studying me for investigative purposes only. I felt utterly foolish, modelling a costume of seduction for a man whose idea of sexual etiquette included unflattering lingerie and American Tan hosiery. I was about to retreat to my bedroom, jeans and T-shirt ready for me on the floor.

"Take it off," he said.

Relief flooded through me as I unfastened the back of my dress. I let it fall to the floor and stood before him in a pool of black lace. When I looked into his eyes they were deep blue: an emotional refraction had caused a change and I needed to gauge its angle.

He drew me towards him, his knees pushing my legs apart. As he ran his hands down me from my bra to the tops of my stockings I shivered, wondering if this tenderness might switch at any moment, like the volatile dark figure that lurked throughout his novel.

He pulled me down onto his lap and when he stroked my face I flinched; it was the touch of the familiar and the threatening, its message ambiguous. In his book it was a gesture signalling both pure love and misplaced trust. When he reached my throat I gasped.

He looked almost wounded. "Did you think I was going to hurt you?"

I shook my head, wondering which of us had misunderstood. I was waiting for the switch, anticipating a sudden pressure. But it didn't happen.

Men need to feel stronger than the women they are with, but when it comes to real strength, women beat them hands down every time.

Chapter Five

His kiss was curiously hesitant as he led me back to safety. I laid my hands on his shoulders and sensed his strength: his build was powerful, but the muscles quivered at my touch.

He fumbled at my bra-strap with an awkward urgency, as though I might vanish at any second. My lips let him know I wasn't going anywhere. When his finger traced the outline of my left nipple he moaned with me. He was fully dressed while I was nearly naked, my vulnerability exposing a need in us both.

I leant back and guided him downwards, his breath warm against my skin. He kissed my nipple, a barely there whisper of intention, his restraint so unexpected, as if he were both unsure of his right to be there yet certain of my willingness to be guided. And I was. Despite the unsettling reaction to his exaggerated telling of my own fantasies, we shared identical lines of dialogue, some of which he had already spoken in that low reassuring voice. Even when he'd been angry with me his voice was always diverting.

As the pressure of his mouth on my nipple increased I stroked his hair, as soft as warm silk under my fingers. "Who is this man?" I thought. Softness and hard edges, tentative and assertive, tender but with the potential to change course

at any moment. I had made too many assumptions based on
fictional acquaintance. So far I had misread him completely.

"Do you love me?" he asked.
"Almost as much as you love me," she said, and he smiled
because he knew it was true.

Chapter Seven

He lifted me from his lap and led me into the bedroom. I lay
back and stretched, almost purring in anticipation as he
closed the curtains and turned on the bedside light. As he
held my hands above my head his voice poured over me:
"You're perfect, and I don't just mean your body."

Intrigued and flattered as I was by his declaration, I
assumed its meaning would soon be revealed. I smiled and
looked into his eyes: they were as distinctly green as they had
been deep blue a few minutes earlier.

"But –" he paused, all tenderness gone. When he spoke
again, his words were slow and deliberate: "You are a very
bad girl."

A hundred different thoughts raced through my mind,
none of them safe. The most important was that I hadn't
finished the novel: what if the heroine ends up in some
twisted sex game with the sadistic anti-hero? Or worse.

"You haven't read the last chapter, have you?"

I shook my head and turned away from him, remembering
that the anti-hero had green eyes.

"Are you frightened of me?"

I knew the line but couldn't remember how the heroine
had answered. I had to fake it: "No."

"Good girl."

"Stupid girl," I thought. I already knew his fantasies were
dangerous and now I had no way out. I was virtually naked
on my own bed with a man who was ten times stronger than
me. A few moments earlier his big masculine body had made
me feel small and protected. Now it alarmed me.

"You know I'd never hurt you."

I wanted to believe him but the contradictions were so extreme, the shift so rapid that I couldn't tell if he was the dark figure or a divine messenger. In a perfect world he would be both.

"You like the unpredictable, don't you?"

I couldn't answer. Yes might mean danger; no might mean another switch.

"Shh," he whispered, stroking my face.

I flinched again at the gesture I knew so well.

"Don't be scared. I thought you understood."

I didn't understand at all and shook my head.

"Chapter Eight. It's the one scenario we should all aspire to."

Chapter Eight . . . I struggled to find the running order. I knew it wasn't the forced encounter we'd already enacted, and I hoped it wasn't the sadomasochistic couple with a taste for rubber.

"Please tell me Chapter Eight is set in Devon," I said, remembering the one genuine love affair. In an ideal world this couple would have found life-long happiness.

"And it's only circumstance that keeps them apart."

My heart leaped in relief and delight; their sexual compatibility and adoration had left me breathless. "Thank God it's not Chapter Twelve," I said.

He laughed. "As if."

The man and woman in Chapter Eight are never named, but to the enlightened reader they will be familiar: lovers who *know* each other without having to say a word. I was looking into the eyes of the man in the story, experiencing what the woman felt or perhaps it was because it was already written, in both senses.

I suddenly realised he had never spoken my name. And now it seemed right; the anonymity was as implicit as the trust. Fiction or not, its creation was the very essence of him, and I felt I already knew him as intimately as a lover. Having spent hours and hours together focused on his words, I'd become as passionately committed as he was, despite the antagonism. I knew my emotional investment had earned his respect.

An illicit affair by necessity propels passion, and the couple's need for each other was almost painful. Their time together was limited, but accelerated love fires the most intense emotions since crisis might end it at any moment. They knew it was too good to be anything but short-lived. In his book their story is never resolved. I wanted to believe that they might find a way to be together, but I doubted it.

These thoughts flashed through my mind in a moment of deliverance and foresight: we were about to live what had previously been fantasy.

"I adore you": it was a safe euphemism.

Chapter Eight

"The woman in Chapter Eight, is she real?"

He smiled and said, "She is now."

It was the ultimate compliment: he had seen beneath the surface, whereas I had taken him at face value. Had I stopped to analyse the heightened emotions I might have recognised the attraction sooner. Owing to the editorial process our own relationship had accelerated, but I hoped we would improvise on a theme rather than follow the script to the letter. He had no need to disclose his sexual likes and dislikes, I already knew. As for mine, he was reading me flawlessly.

How confusing it is for men now that women no longer need rescuing.

Chapter Nine

He was still fully dressed but my near-nakedness no longer made me feel vulnerable; in his beautiful hands I was free from harm. Tracing the curve of my hips, he lingered over the straps of my suspender belt. "You might be right about the stockings."

I acknowledged his concession with a "told you so" grin. He slapped me playfully on the bottom, but hard enough to let me feel its impact.

"That's for being so smug."

I had been chastised for a minor misdemeanour, another subtle variation on his fictional inclinations.

There is no desire without restraint, but walking hand in hand with fear he almost let her slip away.

Chapter Eleven

Crouched at my feet, he looked up at me and said, "Do you remember their code?"

I did, but I wanted to hear him explain it.

He moved up the bed, his legs straddling me. "The code is a safety device," he said, releasing my stockings from their straps. He slipped them off me and ran his fingers down my bare legs. I responded by lifting my calf to his face and he rubbed his cheek against it like a cat making friends. "You need a safe word," he said, "so I know how far to go. I want you to resist me, but 'No' doesn't mean 'No', it means 'Go on', no matter how you phrase it, and 'Please stop' means anything but stop."

My breathing was shallow and fast as I imagined what he might do that would warrant a safe word.

"I don't need one," I said, not quite believing it.

"Oh, yes, you do. You have no idea what I have planned for you. I've been thinking about it for weeks."

I was stunned. The attraction must have been immediate.

"When we met, I watched you read over those first few pages and thought 'Who is this self-possessed, smiling woman?' "

I faltered: the false attribute left me exposed. There's a

price to pay for masking our secret fears and its coin is confusion. He had recognised mine and found it precious. I conceded the self-possession and composure and he kissed me. Any remaining mistrust melted.

He was shocked at the sound of his own laughter, as if it were an old friend he hadn't seen for years. Trapped between responsibility and enchantment, she was his last hurrah before middle age claimed him.

Chapter Thirteen

"Tell me your safe word."

I thought for a moment, it would have to be something intimate and relevant . . . Chapter Eight. "Your name is the safe word."

He looked surprised. "I like that. Let's break the anonymity."

As I mouthed his name silently he placed his hand over my eyes. His breathing quickened and I felt something soft and silky against my cheek. It was one of my stockings, and I knew what he intended to do with it.

She wanted to take the pain away, to touch his chest and heal him, but broken men are broken for a reason, and he had cast her as the woman in white.

Chapter Fifteen

"Do you trust me?" he said.

Reading the certainty between us, I nodded and he raised my hands above my head. "I need you to understand," he said as he tied the stocking around my wrists, "trust is more important to me than anything." This was not merely submission, it was surrender, the ultimate act of acceptance. I was about to give him something he had probably never experienced.

At that moment I finally understood the unanswered

questions in his novel. His eyes told me that what lay beneath was vast and deep and full of monsters: the sadness expressed as anger, his fear of abandonment, the euphemism for love, the extremes. He believed he was a damaged man who could not trust and therefore could not be trusted. But he was no longer unfathomable.

She was like lightning on a hot summer's night; you know you shouldn't look but you just can't stop yourself.

Chapter Seventeen

Themes of loss and isolation echoed throughout his work, his novel a conduit for unmet desires and deepest fears. I imagined his commitment was total, but absolute investment is always fraught with danger, especially in matters of the heart. I had taught myself to hold back, that final five per cent an insurance against emotional bankruptcy; it was a lesson hard-learned. Our vulnerabilities may have sprung from a different source but they inspired a mutual understanding: he had seen something in me that made him feel secure. Perhaps he knew me better than I knew myself.

That spark of optimism had gone. The laughter and playfulness died the moment she'd gone, and he felt guilty with or without her. He wanted her to miss him as much as he missed her, and that only added to the guilt.

Chapter Seventeen

"I'm going to take you to the very edge," he said, and I knew exactly what he meant. "Turn over. I want you whimpering into the pillow."

His words shot through me like a well-aimed arrow and my submission was immediate. He gently bit the nape of my neck, his mouth travelling downwards. I almost sobbed when he reached my shoulder blades: he'd found my exterior G-spot.

The muscles surrounding my spine contracted. The fragile structure that supports us and makes us human, its nerve endings so over-worked and stimulated, was now laid bare, protected only by a thin layer of skin. I begged him to stop, and he understood without my using the safe word. I was at the edge but not yet ready to fall.

There is always a confessional aspect to sex, and his was both catholic and Catholic: he allowed her as much pain as pleasure would permit.

Chapter Nineteen

He moved to the end of the bed and I resisted the temptation to watch him undress. Kneeling beside me, he said, "I promised I'd never hurt you." I knew he meant it, but I held my breath, waiting for his next move.

My heartbeat raced as his fists twisted around my knickers, the sound of fabric tearing a reminder of his strength. He leant against me, his weight pinning me to the bed. I had yet to see him naked, but he allowed me a moment of fore-knowledge when he pressed himself into me.

"Turn over," he said, and untied my wrists. I touched his body for the first time. His muscles were hard but my lips were gentle. I licked the soft hollow of his collarbone and my back arched when he echoed the movement towards my nipple. He stopped, teasing me again. I ached for his mouth and begged him to go on. "Suck me," I whispered.

"Bad girl," he said, and squeezed one nipple hard as he sucked the other. The switch was instinctive but he already knew the effect it had on me.

The pain was exquisite, his mouth and fingers controlling it by degrees. As his name was about to pass my lips the pressure subsided: he knew how far to go. I wanted to touch him, to feel how hard he was. My hands slid down his back to his waist but he stopped me. "Not yet."

"Please let me touch you."

He shook his head with a look that told me he was enjoying my torment. I was being manipulated by an expert: in place of resisting, I was now pleading with him.

She ran barefoot down the street calling his name, forgetting that silent is an anagram of listen.

Chapter Twenty One

I ran my nails along his back. "I'm in agony," I said.

"I told you I was going to take you to the edge." With a trail of kisses down my stomach, he pushed my legs apart. He leant back as I revealed my most intimate secret. Lost in the moment and unaware of me watching him, he looked as though he was gazing at the most beautiful work of art.

We were entranced by our separate perspectives. "So pretty," he murmured, then looked up at me. His lips grazed over me, his every move causing the current running between us to amplify. He slid two fingers inside me as the pressure of his mouth increased.

I wanted him to go on, to make me come like this but I stopped him, seconds before. I drew his face up to mine. His mouth was wet and tasted sweet as I licked myself from his lips.

He ran his fingers down my cheek, now a gesture of assurance, and lay beside me. "Touch me," he said.

A top note of compassion with a base note of cruelty, the scent of him lingered on her clothes and skin, as potent as if he were there beside her.

Chapter Twenty Three

"Leave your marks on me," he said, and I knew he needed to feel the pain as much as I did. I worked my way down his body, my nails scoring red symbols across his skin, proof of his trust in me. Almost there, I hesitated. "It's your turn for the agony," I whispered as my mouth hovered over him.

"Suck my cock," he said in a tone that was as much an order as a request. My fingers encircled him and I moved my hand down, shocked at his length. He was so hard I could almost hear the blood pulsing through him.

"I said, suck it." Both his voice and size made me shiver, knowing that he could hurt me, but never would. As I licked him, my tongue almost sizzled against the heat. I took him into my mouth and sucked him until he pleaded with me to stop.

He flipped me onto my back and held me close, whispering reassuringly as he eased into me. The momentum was cautious, measured by reading my body. When he finally reached my depth he pulled out. "Beg for it," he said, forcing the words out of me.

All self-control renounced, I begged shamelessly, shocked by my unleashed dark side. He kissed my face as his cock thrust into me harder and faster. I couldn't hold back any longer and he knew it. "I want to hear you come," he said, grinding into me.

Seconds later, I let go and heard myself come louder than I ever had before. The volume increased as he came with me.

Holding me tight he looked into my eyes and said, "I want to take you to Devon."

I smiled. "You already have."

He had reached inside her and written his name on her heart. In return she negotiated with his demons, shook hands and made a deal. The settlement was not taxing, it just took a little acceptance and a lot of love.

from a story by the Editor

The Author's secret life was not so secret after all. The walls he had so carefully constructed were made of paper rather than bricks and mortar, and the Editor's touch sealed the fissures.

As for her, she no longer lived vicariously. Editing was a frustrating business, knowing she was interfering in another's dreams. The Author's words had set her free, and despite the battle of wills, released in her the confidence to submit her own work. The mutual debt of gratitude was complete: he was no longer so angry at the world, and she no longer hid behind her title.

The reviews of his novel were mixed: few critics grasped its complexity, choosing instead to focus on what they could not hope to understand. He almost forgave them their shortcomings. When he read her stories he basked in her forthcoming glory, and said, "You will eclipse us all, including me."

The Editor's collection is about to be published. The Author allowed her to steal moments from their time together, many of which appear in this story. They often travel to Devon, by car and by metaphor.

Monkey See

Matthew Branton

March

He looked at people getting it on all day and hadn't got one
on for his wife in four months. Not while she was there,
anyway.

He had a list like a film censor – a table he'd knocked up
in Claris Works at home – that ran to six sides of A4. One
pile of each page filled a six-shelf tray next to the PC: top
shelf for couples, second for threes, third for fours-&-
mores, fourth for pain, fifth for toileting, ground floor
for children and animals. He ordered it that way based
on the frequency of what he saw, so that the most frequently
used sheets were on the top. He meant no pecking order by
it.

He'd had to draw up the lists himself because no one had
done this job before him. He was the only one in the nick who
knew much about PCs so he got it. The PC in front of him
only had room to run Quicktime these days and the printer
beneath his desk had taken one scuff too many. The lists he'd
had to do at home had been xeroxed so many times the
gridlines looked like they'd been drawn in his step-daughter,
Lori's eyeliner. The pen in his left hand moved up and down
the boxes as his right hand clicked.

DI Sturgess put his head over the partition and said,
"Derek, mate."

"Two secs," he muttered, not looking up.

Sturgess glanced at the screen, turned his mouth down and ducked back.

Fran rang before lunch, told him to pay the gas. The bill had come in that morning and there was a £7.50 credit for prompt payment. She told him to make sure he did it before he left. He asked about her day and she said her team leader was trying to do her head in.

It brightened up in the afternoon and he had to swivel his screen away from the low sun, turn his cuffs back over his freckled forearms. He was working down a stack of page twos, a rush-job – the case against the hard-drive's owner had to go to the CPS by the end of next week, the sticky had said – and he stroked six boxes with his pen even as he hit control-W, revealing the picture behind the one he'd just ticked off.

His eyes shifted focus and saw a woman taking one man in her mouth and another up her front – what he'd come to term a spit-roast – squatting on one with his feet towards the camera: he'd named this the cross-bow, because if you drew it with stick figures it looked like one. He checked the box on page two labelled SR and the box labelled CB, ran his eye over the other options to see if any applied: did any of the participants appear to be under eighteen? No. Were any of the male organs unusually large? And if so, was there pain involved in the penetration? Borderline. The guy underneath had a girth on him, no barney there: but the girl was looking up at the bloke she was blowing, which suggested – to Derek at least – that she was maybe halfway into it. He left the box blank. Was the grouping mixed race? Possibly – the girl looked a bit like Jennifer Lopez, and he wrote "F-PR?" in the box next to the I/R designation. I/R meant inter-racial, PR, Puerto Rican. Since most of it came from the States he'd learned a lot about the ethnic mix there, saw it himself last September in Florida. Pointed them all out to Fran, not that she'd been interested. She'd said she didn't want him bringing his work home but he'd had a sense there was more to it than that.

He remembered the gas as the tea-trolley came round. He got a custard Danish that had sat around too long and a cup of builder's, ate the cake while he waited on hold for the bank. The girl who eventually answered was Manc, though the bank was in Leeds: he gazed vacantly at a woman with a wolfhound while the Manc girl took him through security. He couldn't remember his memorable fact – it was usually his mother's maiden name or his first wife's birthday – and he had to ask for a hint and then think hard for a moment to get it.

He never knew whose computers he was checking. Most of the time, he was aware, they were just looking for leverage: *had a look on your hard disk, Short-eyes: you can talk to us or you can talk to Vice and I'll tell you for nothing, you don't wanna talk to Vice*. Fraud collar, he bet, silly sods. He didn't have to be told to know: fraud was the growth industry, and the hardest to pin without some help from the suspect. So 14-gig tapes piled up through the internal mail; he took one off the top every morning, set it to upload onto his own, 20-gig drive, and picked up a butterscotch-with-sprinkles from the canteen while it was spooling. He liked to get his breakfast down before he started.

There were several ways to do it. He could run the Yank app. that looked for picture files, then check those files for the percentage of flesh-tone pixels: but too low a setting picked up holiday snaps, too high missed the latex and leather, or the close-ups. It took ten minutes just to pull files for you and crashed your machine more often than not. He hardly ever used it.

Better was to search for file names that would lead to the folder you were looking for. Hardly anyone was stupid enough to leave filetype identifiers on the end – jpg, .rm, .mov – and most of the time they renamed them completely, so you searched for naming systems. BJ was always a good start. CS for come-shot, or MS for money. FCL. DP. WS. Eight times out of ten you got a result.

If you didn't, you had to work harder, try and think like them. People kept it buried in their hard drives, usually the system folder, in his experience, where there were thousands of plug-ins and extensions to lose their collection amongst. But they wanted to get at it fast when the urge was on them: at the fag-end of the day, when the wife had gone to bed scowling about work; when they were lonely and tired and needed to feel like part of the human race again. They didn't want to be opening a dozen folders to find the good stuff, so there was usually a shortcut near the surface that would take you in deep: a folder alias hidden behind a document icon was a common one. You had to get a feel for the way they liked to organize; then think like them, say to yourself *where would I put it, if this was mine, if this was what I needed?*

He'd got good at it, hit paydirt inside two minutes almost always. He was only meant to be doing it for three months to begin with, but no one else in the nick had any talent for it. Three months turned to six, then to nine, now to fourteen. He heard the uniform call him Bitchfinder General around the canteen till he put a stop to it. He was proud to be good at his job but once you'd found the stash the rest was monkey work. Open the pix, tick the boxes: monkey see, monkey do. He knocked off at five-thirty while the uniform went through till seven. Who was the monkey there?

He took the commuter train home, had to pull his warrant card every few months or so – pissed-up city boys, school kids with screwdrivers, office girls getting humped in the toilet. One asked if he wanted to join in once, cheeky tart. She didn't know he'd been on the slack since three weeks after the computer detail started. Fran did, but she'd got it all wrong. Did she want this marriage to work, after her last one? Yes, she did. Did she want him back in uniform? No, she didn't. He loved her, but she broke his bollocks sometimes.

He walked home from the station, mile and two clicks by his dashboard clock and he needed every step. Fran didn't understand why: he rented a tape about airtraffic controllers he saw on Discovery once, tried to tell her afterwards how he felt the same as those guys: when they finished their shift they pulled up a pew to the canteen fishtank, sat and monged out in front of the guppies and whatnot till they felt ready to go home and deal with their wife's day. All she'd said was that he was hardly an airtraffic controller and maybe he'd stop giving her colds all the time if he let her pick him up in the evening.

The streets around the station were terraces: a paperboy's dream, doors fronting straight on to the street, walk along with your sack and bang-bang-bang – no driveways, no dogs, no problem. As you walked, you could look straight in, out of the corner of your eye, bang slap into the middle of other people's quiet time. The rest of the way home you could only do it in winter, in the hour between people turning on their lights and remembering to close their curtains, but round here you could do it all year round. He smelled coal smoke, wet brick, drains, walking slowly, frowning, like his eyes were moving because he was thinking, like the last thing on his mind was seeing what people were watching.

There was no one downstairs when he got home. The TV said NO MESSAGES [PRESS MENU TO EXIT], white on blue like MS-DOS: pre-Windows, when his job hadn't existed. He called "Hello", trying to make it sound less like a question than an admission. There wasn't any answer, so he put the kettle on, went to the foot of the stairs.

"Fran? Sweetheart?"

"Min the bath" came muffled back from upstairs. "Joo pay the gas?"

"Yeah," he called. "Cuppa tea?"

"Nye get out." Irritably.

There was a time when he could've taken the cup into her – soaped her back, whatever – while she talked about her day. But he hadn't fucked her in four months and he didn't have to see it to know that the bathroom door was closed. The kettle was starting to rumble. He went back into the kitchen, made the tea, cupped his hand under the spoon while he carried the bag to the Addis in the corner. Then he sat down at the table, started on the post.

Two for Fran, both handwritten, wonky stamps: Mount Pleasant and N4. Three for him, printed, C-thru windows showing mailmerge type, return addresses on the back to Southend, Guildford and Leeds. When he'd split up with Charlie and got his transfer, he couldn't get arrested by a bank. Two years down the line, new mortgage, new PEP, new wife, and they were practically buzzing his house with helicopters. 7.9% till August! £250 cheque back! As a valued customer . . .

Fran came down, hair up in a turban, body wrapped in the pink fuzzy bathrobe and matching slippers he'd got her last Christmas after she'd said absolutely no more underwear this year. She went to the kettle without looking at him, so he said, "You smell nice," to her back.

"You don't," she said, pouring the kettle on to the bag he'd left in her Far Side cup.

He sniffed theatrically at his armpits as she pulled the belt of the robe tight, dropped the bag in the sink and turned to look at him, cradling the cup in both hands.

"I smell like a man," he said, Captain Caveman voice.

She didn't crack a smile. "Lori's back tonight," she said, looking at him over the rim of her cup.

He frowned. "She allright?"

Fran hitched her shoulders. "She broke up with that fella."

"The black guy?"

"He was Nigerian."

"Right." The guy'd said his name was Echo, the one time he'd met him – he'd thought it was either a street name, or it was some art-college joke he didn't understand. You ask someone a question, they come back saying Echo. Some student thing. But Ekow, it must've been. He'd only seen it written down before, had thought it was pronounced like the green binbags at Sainsbury's.

"I'll pop round Londis, get some more Persil," he said, trying to show he was a parent here too. When Lori was here he felt like a lodger in their family, and he'd wanted that to change for a long while.

"She's upset actually," Fran said. That "actually" sounded like "back off", but probably just meant her Sloggis were up her arse about something.

"When's she get in? I could go and pick her up."

"I think she's making her own way."

"No trouble," he began.

"She's making her own way," Fran said, like that settled it, put the cup down and shuffled out into the lounge. Twenty seconds later he heard her hairdryer start, and that was it, couldn't get a word in if he'd wanted to.

Didn't get the chance later, either. Lori's connection from town got in at eight-fifteen, crafty little cow: too late for tea at home, just in time for her mum to treat her to a Harvester. Feeding up disguised as girl talk: Fran was a good mother – a good woman – and he tried to remember that. He cooked up a Sizzle and Stir with a microwave nan, took it to the sofa, forked it off his lap with the TV on. They'd both been through the let's-make-an-effort-to-eat-like-a-family in their first marriages and sometimes – most of the time – talking was the last thing you needed. When you had his job you wanted to leave it in the locker room, not come home and run through it all again. Even before the pictures.

And after them, as soon as she found out about them, all she wanted was him off the job. He told her that'd mean uniform, and did she know what uniform was like after all the balls-ups in the papers? Pensioners to puberty-dodgers call-

ing you racialist, couldn't do your job without everyone
getting their oar in.

But that wasn't where this was coming from: this was
coming from they hadn't fucked in four months, and if her
first husband hadn't been such a tosspot they wouldn't have
a problem. Him and Charlie, his first, had worked through
the three-times-a-day to the once-a-fortnight-if-you're-
lucky, then sat down and agreed that if one of them felt
like it they should just say it, and the other should accept
that they'd both feel better afterwards, even if a Typhoo and
Trio was more in the way of what they fancied. That was
what you did when you were married. Fran's problem was
she'd got fucked too much along the way, one-nighters no
repeaters, expected to be chatted up, fawned over, flattered
like men in clubs do when they're after a swift bunk-up.
Marriage was supposed to be different from that, wasn't it?
Not for her it wasn't; and instead of talking about it she
blamed it on his job.

He wiped the plate with the nan, watched a nature show
about a skeleton in Africa, a twelve-year-old boy dead of a
gum abscess way back when. Kept showing him howling in
the bushes to cover up the lack of facts – he was supposed to
be the missing link or something, the first one they'd found
with a skull big enough to worry about a mortgage. Homo
Erectus. He went upstairs for an empty-house wank after,
but couldn't get the hippy egghead from the show out of his
mind; turning over the dead boy's vertebra in his fingers,
showing the opening for the spinal cord: *the aperture is wider
– see? – than that which you or I have*. The boffin said the
Neanderthals thought with their spines as well as their
brains. That made him feel weird, wondering if the spine
in his back was thinking, if it had memories he wasn't aware
of. His cock seemed to: its mind was elsewhere tonight, like
so often lately. He tried the usual – armpits of Fran's dirty
workshirts, face in her pillow, business end of her vibrator –
but no cigar.

He put his trousers back on, found a raw silk shirt from an

Orlando factory outlet year before last, let it hang down over his strides, Florida-style. Twenty bucks – he never forgot what he paid for clothes – and made you feel like a million; the sensation against his shoulders made him long for warm air and he was hooking the ladder down from the loft before he remembered *ER*: screw it. Wasn't the same since Clooney left anyway. He took the steps gingerly, ridged aluminium cutting into his bare feet, but he took the weight on his arms till he was out on the nailed chipboard and heading for Fran's binbags by the cold water tank.

It was Florida up there allright, the spring's central heating thermals supplemented by the sun on the roof all week. There wasn't room to stand up straight as you got towards the tank, and he stooped low, hands dangling down by his knees. The stuff he wanted was underneath the bags, in the suitcase. He took a careful note of the position of the black bags, then eased the case out from under, doing the magician's tablecloth trick in slo-mo and not making a bad job of it. He undid the belt around it, checked his watch – still be making trips to the salad cart, if he knew those two – and opened it up.

The Dolcis shoebox he passed over: letters, postcards, stuff he knew he shouldn't read. Similarly the Saxone: Lori's baby pics, family snaps from Fran's marriage to Marc, the wanker. He took them out and placed them side by side on the hardboard. Underneath was the Dudley box file, lifted from some stationery cupboard years ago and home to Fran's personal snaps ever since. He cross-legged on the floor in front of it, glanced once over his shoulder at the top of the ladder – like a kid up a treehouse with a grot mag – told himself not to be so stupid and got on with it.

The trick was to remember the order they came out of the box. He lifted off the top layer, put it flat on his left; took out another handful, put them next to it. When they were all out, he started anti-clockwise, the pics from the bottom first: trikes, paddling pools, Southend; feeding a peacock on

Canvey Island. Her frown, at five, was the same at forty-five. He loved her, wanted to put them all back in the box now and go down, get a round of Irish coffees ready for when they got back. Instead, he replaced them carefully into the bottom of the box, set his face as he picked up the next pile.

But it was still recs and Jungle Gyms, lions at Longleat, ponchos, tartan-trimmed flares. Grinning at the camera with her first blue eyeshadow and shiny pink lipstick, little bumps under the chest of her V-neck T-shirt. He'd been in his room above the pub then, wanking over Richard Allen paperbacks, lifting Number 6 from the newsagents when old Farnsworth was still groggily marking up the *Express* and *Mirrors*. Number 6 or Navy Cut, for the push-up pack: suave in Shoeburyness, thinking someone – some girl – would notice. He'd had his first *Knave* from Farnsworth's too; skimmed it off the return pile round the back one morning. No wanks were ever like your first ones. He still remembered the big, felt-tip "X" on the cover to prevent resale, could still see this one girl from it, apple-tits, had a hat with a veil on. A way of looking at the camera. His cock was rearing out of his fly and sliding between the folds of the shirt before his brain – or his spine – caught up. It felt fucking marvellous.

When it was over, his temples were thumping from the heat, the cooked air, the sudden exertion. He thought he'd better sit still a moment, not get up till the blood had rushed back from its day-trip. He took the shirt off, dropped it in a smeary puddle behind him and sat, breathing slowly. He only turned over the next pile because it was there, started leafing through the pictures, feeling bad about it because he'd just come. Lots of red-eye in these, and Fran wearing make-up for real now: weddings and birthdays, back gardens, Margate, Dymchurch, Clacton, Terry bikini sets; I'M WITH STUPID through to FRANKIE SAYS and a full set under the cotton. A noise downstairs made him snap his head round, see what he was: a forty-year-old squatting over his second wife's teenage snaps, toss-rag festering on the floor behind him. He was down the ladder – shirt wadded up and thrown behind the water tank – and halfway down the stairs before he saw the pizza and ruby flyers feathered on the doormat. Some kid doing the rounds after school, whacking them through the letterbox, that was all. Did it pay better than papers? The hours were better, though you'd miss that feeling, dawn to drivetime, that the world was your own, shiny and clean, that this was your turf. He didn't know if people even had papers delivered any more. He went into the bedroom for a shirt.

They wouldn't be back for an hour at least, by the bedside clock. Stupid to jump like that, could've given himself a heart attack. Wanking on the sly put ants in your pants the moment your tackle was back in them: he bet it was the same for everyone, the kid in the toilet to the scrapheap geezer in his allotment lean-to. The guilt was like riding a bike, you never forgot it.

He went down to the kitchen, put the kettle on, found the Bushmill's and the squirty cream for the round of Irishes. The trick was to load the coffee with sugar, two or three spoons a head, or else the cream – even squirty – started to sink and you just got mush. He spooned Gold Blend into a jug, lined up the wine glasses. Everything ready, so the moment he heard the car he could get cracking, come through with a tray just as they sat down in the lounge. Everything ready, nothing to do but wait. He went back up to the loft to get the silk shirt, give it a rinse, hang it behind the boiler where – if Fran found it – she'd think it'd hung there since last summer.

He'd forgotten about the photos, still 52-card-pick-up'd on the chipboard floor; he knelt down, started gathering them up, putting them back how they were. He had to turn over the untouched piles to do it, stopped himself before he started going through the boyfriend-era again. Why was he doing this? He'd seen them all before. It made him feel bad to pry like this, and he was always off with Fran after. After four months without sex, off was what they didn't need.

Spotty herberts in hair gel and patterned jumpers: why did he need to look at them? They made him feel sick somewhere, even the first few as he turned them over. He could tell just by looking at them that they'd had horrible cocks – turkey-necks, or wonky round the bell-end – had he been looking at too many bell-ends lately? This particular train of thought had never come upon him when he'd looked at these pictures before.

Five gets you ten that was what it was. He hadn't asked for this job and it wasn't his fault he was conscientious at it: he had his pension to think about, and you never knew what was around the corner, most likely uniform again. You kept your nose clean and showed willing, so the day some Volvo who'd read too many *Guardian* specials tried to hang one on you, you had nothing to show but white space on your sheet. It was hard being married to a civilian. Say what you like – and he loved her – but they could never really understand. And as for Lori . . .

She'd have been telling Fran about her course all night. Art, she called it. What he had to look at all day every day she chose to make pictures of and called it Art. The art bit came in because she took the cocks out – spit-roast, doggy, cowgirl, crossbow, the men airbrushed out pixel by pixel, mouths and holes yawning wide but empty – called them things like *Nature Abhors a Vacuum*. Horrible things they were. Her tutors said she had real potential. Real potential for fucking her mum's marriage up, the selfish little mare. And him paying her course fees, expected to be grateful for the privilege. He stuffed the photos back in the box, any which way, shoved it all back in place, went downstairs and made the kettle boil so many times that when the car finally pulled up he had to trip the cut-out himself, slosh it still bubbling into the jug with the coffee grains.

The trick was the sugar.

September

He had a bad moment as they pulled up and saw the house, feeling like he was out of his depth here, feeling like he was flushing the last six months down the pan. He told himself not to be stupid – this was the pay-off, the watershed, he was convinced of it. Do this and get back on track. He followed the line of cars parked two hundred yards along the verges – 4 × 4s, Hyundais and Daewoos, the odd Jag, had to be a good sign – and pulled in at the first space, let the engine idle a moment before cutting it.

"You ready?" he said.

"Yeah," she said, looking at the house. The tip of her tongue came out, put a fresh gloss on to the wine-dark lipstick. "You?"

"Ready and willing," he said, trying to keep it light. She didn't ask about the able.

There were two bouncers in DJs under the too-bright carriage lamps, took their twenty quid and membership number, directed them to a room off the hall for their coats. They made him feel like the greeter at the swank hotel in Orlando had, the first real night of his honeymoon with Fran, welcoming him effusively back into the restaurant every time he'd stepped out for a slash. He took her shiny black mac off her shoulders, put it on top of his own on the piled-high sofabed in there, looked at her standing there in her boots, sheer tights, mini and tight top, her eyes done dark as Dusty's. The dress-code for the party was fetish, but mail-order took three weeks even with the web, and she'd drawn the line at going uptown to some perv shop. He'd offered to go himself, but she'd pointed out that he'd never yet got her size right, and in more forgiving fabrics than rubber as well. She'd said that what she had would do – they were only going to test the water, see what it was about, after all – but if he wanted to look like a deep-sea diver himself then he was welcome. He wore black slacks and a black silk shirt he'd found after a long hunt, hanging behind the boiler in the airing cupboard.

"I look all right?" she said.

"You look fantastic," he said, trying to mean it with his eyes.

She tugged at the scoop-neck on her top. "Yeah?"

He growled, made to paw her. She slapped his hand away playfully but when he went to kiss her she turned her head.

"My lipstick," she said.

They sat on a window ledge in the lounge, sipping warm Red Bulls and avoiding eyeballing anyone. In front of them a bloke in accountant's glasses and a Hard Rock café T-shirt was getting tossed off to Celine Dion by a naked woman whose tits put Derek in mind of a couple of snooker balls dropped into a pair of nylon socks. They'd been there an hour and these were the most active people they'd seen: a couple in their thirties had been there at first, dressed up to the nines like a rap video, but they'd not seen them again; everyone else looked like pub landlords and nail salon pro-prietresses, and they all seemed to know each other, talking about their holidays. There were people wandering around down the garden but Fran hadn't wanted to go down there until they knew what the score was. The bloke in the Hard Rock shirt kept looking at Derek like he was asking him for something.

"You all right?" Derek asked Fran.

She nodded, pursing her lips and looking away as the snooker woman sank to her knees. Hard Rock groaned and jerked his hips, and Derek had to look away too. The size of the house had promised so much – he'd remembered that Christine Keeler film, men in DJs around a swimming pool – but inside it looked like it hadn't had so much as a J-cloth run over it in twenty years, fag burns making their own counter-pattern in the carpet.

"It's smoky," Fran said, in a tone he couldn't gauge.

"Yeah," he agreed, and gave it a second. They'd both seen the big magic-markered sign Blu-tacked to the hall wall by the stairs: ABSOLUTELY NO DRINK OR CIGGIES IN

THE PLAYROOMS. NO THANKYOU MEANS NO,
THANKYOU. HAVE FUN!!!!

"You want to stay?" she said.

"You want to?"

"It is a bit smoky in here," she said.

He felt like he had in a bus shelter twenty-five years ago,
telling Sarah Mitchell that it was all right, he had three in his
jacket. The memory didn't seem to come from his head. "It
said no smoking upstairs," he said.

"Did it?" she replied, turning her head towards him.

There was a blue bulb in the landing light, a Rasta
propping up the wall underneath it. He grinned at Fran as
she led Derek by the hand to the top of the wooden hill. They
saw four white-gloss bedroom doors, two shut, two ajar. A
rope hung across the landing beyond them.

"Y' all right?" the guy said.

"Do you just go in?" Fran asked.

He grinned, wide. She pushed open the first door, and led
Derek in.

The only light came from a TV, playing blue and grey light
over the bodies packed in there. It took Derek a moment to
get his bearings, concentrating on covering Fran's back as he
was: what he saw when his eyes adjusted was a master-size
bedroom, three queen-sizes packed into it, three couples and
an Asian girl on the beds, couples lining the walls. Everyone
was wanking, or wanking someone else off; no one was
talking, just moans and *yeahs* and wet sounds. Fran led
him to a space against a wardrobe, stepping carefully over
feet, discarded shoes and bags. He slipped into the space, put
his back to the veneer, and she scooched her bum up against
his groin, let him put his arms around her waist and watch
over her shoulder.

The TV showed a silicone blonde in a classic cross-bow,
two black guys doing the honours. No one was watching:
they were watching each other, or what was being done to
them. After a while he was hard against his wife's bum and
felt like he ought to be doing something, so he smoothed his

palms across Fran's hips, the front of her thighs; she put a hand on his, but instead of lifting it off her she pushed it under her skirt, let him feel where she'd cut the gusset of her tights out. He tried to do it surreptiously but she pulled the front of her skirt up and he thought, what the hell, go with the flow; he was the only guy in the room with his flies done up, after all.

He was concentrating so hard on what his fingers were doing that at first he didn't notice the women either side running their hands over Fran's Wolfords. It was only when she gasped the third time in a way he'd never heard before that he looked down: she had each hand wrapped around the guy on either side, holding them there in what he called the parallel bars – a rare one, but you saw it in the artier stuff – while their women knelt before them working the heads while they ran their nails inside Fran's thighs. He kept his fingers moving, not knowing what to do, sweating hard with Fran's body pressed against him. The woman on the left looked up and smiled around the thing in her mouth. It all escalated very quickly.

He couldn't remember after how they'd got on the beds. No one was behaving like people, and you probably had to go a few times to get used to that. In the meantime it'd just been hands, everywhere, curves connecting, no one thinking or talking. His shirt was off while Fran was sucking him and a woman ran her hands over his back, said "ooh, you're sweating", and licked it off his bare shoulder blades, ran her tongue down his spine making him buck hard and Fran squeal in protest. A guy started playing with Fran's bum while she knelt but she just sucked harder, going to town with it until she had to just clutch his thighs and gasp at what was being done to her. When he knelt down to help her with her clit he felt the guy going into her, and while he was still registering that, suddenly there was another guy filling her mouth. He stood back, not knowing what to do; he couldn't object, no one else was, and the guy getting blown by his wife was *smiling* at him, for fuck's sake. Grinning. He turned away and a woman in brown stockings and what looked like one of Charlie's trademark white Doreens, nothing else, pulled him further onto the bed. She was soft like a lilo and gasped like a puncture whenever he pushed: he fucked her next to the guys fucking his wife, listening to her lose it, unable to see her face. The bed was too soft and it took him a long time to come. The woman was about ready to spit in his eye by the time he finished: Fran was still going strong as he left the room, he wasn't sure where for.

They posted pictures from the party in the members-only section of the website later in the week. There weren't any with him in. The three with Fran – from the back, all the women were from the back so you couldn't see their faces – were from after he'd gone back downstairs. She'd enjoyed herself a lot more than he had, but that had to be a good thing. The only thing she'd said after was that she'd had her cap in so it ought to be all right, medically. Daewoos and Hyundais, he'd thought, driving back under the orange lights, Jazz FM on the stereo. The odd Jag.

He couldn't help himself, saved the pictures out of IE5 on the computer at work, built shortcuts onto the desktop so he could get to them when he wanted to. Looking at the pictures was a way of not thinking about it, or of processing the information outside of his head. That felt like the best thing to be doing.

He'd never looked at her back so much before, the curve of her spine. The party had shown him a kind of competence in her that he didn't seem to have: he'd know what to do better, now he knew the lie of the land. The location came as an e-mail Friday nights, was the way they liked to work it. He got through the week, same as everyone does. Friday afternoon she rang. He turned away from the screen to take the call.

"I said yes to Dave and Angela for tomorrow night," she said. "That's all right, isn't it?"

"Tomorrow night?"

"Barbecue. They asked us August Bank Holiday, remember?"

"August."

"I just found it in my diary. So I rang her and it's still on."

"OK," he said.

"Is it?" she said. He glanced at the screen, reached out, hit control-W.

"Yeah, course," he said and changed the subject, stretching out his shoulders as he talked. His back was killing him.

Bahn

Zoe Constantin

From the cool darkness of the train station, Sarah emerged into the harsh sunlight of August. *Germany was never this hot*, she thought. The air shimmered; already, a gloss of sweat covered her skin. And yet, the immediate difference revived her. When an elderly woman prodded against her back, Sarah gave way with an apology in her best German.

The woman narrowed her eyes, glanced over Sarah. No words, but her face clearly expressed her amusement at Sarah's accent.

Sarah shrugged. So, some things had not changed. She would not let one encounter spoil her plans. Spotting a bank kiosk, she let the crowds sweep her in that direction, past throngs of chattering schoolchildren, wearied travellers, and untidy students.

No help for that, she thought. Even before she found a hotel, she needed to change money. She'd changed ten dollars in New York, but that would only buy her a cheap dinner.

A shadow crossed over her shoulder. A man brushed against her, then spoke. She ignored him, until he spoke again.

Sarah turned, shaded her eyes against the sunlight, too surprised at first to understand his fluid German.

Immediately, he smiled and said in English, "You will have a long wait, I fear. The lines for summer tourists . . ."

Then his expression changed slightly. "Are you American? You could use dollars in most hotels, you know."

Again the instant recognition of her nationality. She bit her lip and did not answer.

The man continued to smile, undaunted. "However, if you do want to change money, you could take a streetcar to the town centre. The banks there give a much better rate." He appeared to accept that she wanted his directions. "Take the number one streetcar to the Friederich-Ehebert-Platz," he said. "There you will see a Deutsche Bank on the corner. Not far. Do you have a ticket for the streetcar?"

Sarah kept her expression friendly but her eyes neutral, something she'd learned over the years. She deflected his questions politely, nodded or shrugged, until at last he departed.

She waited another moment. No stranger returned. With several more nervous glances, she threaded her way to the streetcar station. She boarded the number one, where she made a passable exchange of German with the conductor. "Sehr gut," he said when she gave him the correct change. He was grinning carelessly.

It rankled Sarah that the first man had spoken English, and that he'd known she was American. *Some things never change,* she thought again. When she had lived here before, she'd tried to escape her American identity, without success. Though she studied the accent and memorized pages of vocabulary, her face – with her direct eyes and expressive lips – betrayed her nationality even before she spoke. At best, she convinced a few shopkeepers she was English. For an American, her accent was good, they told her.

The loudspeaker announced a stop, interrupting her thoughts. "Stadt Bibliotek," she thought she heard the conductor say.

Two stops more, maybe three, until the bank. Reading the map, she noticed a few changes in the route. Perhaps it was better she'd accepted the man's directions.

Sarah watched the line of stores blur past as the streetcar

sped through a long stretch without stops. *Bahn*, she thought. *Strassenbahn, Eisenbahn.* Variations of the word for train, the first word she'd learned in German. The streetcar's rhythm conspired with a ripe, August sun to rob her thoughts of clarity. She shook her head to disperse the cloud of sleep. Exhilaration alone had carried her from the airport to the train station in Heidelberg. There, she bought a newspaper and soda and felt remembrance slip beside her, whispering memories of ten years ago.

I want it to be different this time, she thought.

At the kiosk outside the station, she made hotel reservations, then lingered, drinking her warm soda and translating handwritten signs in a collection of languages. Most were from students travelling across Europe. She knew – she'd been one.

"Friederich-Ehebert-Platz."

The streetcar stopped abruptly in the present. *You will see the bank on the corner, near the Bismarkplatz.* She remembered the man's clean English, spoken with an accent neither German nor American, and she wondered where he'd studied English.

Memory and language followed Sarah through the summer afternoon, from the bank where she changed money to the hotel by the train station, where she listened to the shriek of trains until sleep came to her at last. From sleep, she drifted into the unsheltered territory of dreams.

Dreaming, she walked the main street of Heidelberg, moving like a swimmer against the pulsing heat. Sunlight brushed her with sweat. *Too hot*, she thought, turning down to the river.

At the intersection of street with an alley, a man appeared. She decided, *I'll start with him.*

Sarah tapped the man's shoulder. "Fuck me," she said in cool and perfect English.

The man nodded as if he understood perfectly. He led her into the narrow alley, to a doorway littered with newspapers and cardboard boxes and the rich, lingering scent of decay.

Sarah leaned against the door and raised her skirt. "Do it hard." She kept her voice level, only her lips trembled.

With a practised motion, the man opened his pants and lifted a stiff organ to her naked sex. "Wet," he growled. "Oh, yes."

He entered her smoothly. She stifled her cry, though a quick pulse of orgasm penetrated her body. She wouldn't cry out, not yet. "Fuck me harder," she said.

At her command, he slid her into a corner of the door-way and braced himself with one arm against the frame. His body moved in a steady, rising beat against her, as if he wanted to break through the barriers of her flesh. "Is this what you want?" His voice grated in her ear.

Short, scattered sensation broke through her orgasm – the heavy musk of garbage, a sharp clatter of traffic from the upper streets, the chiming of bells from the nearby church. The only emotion she let herself feel was determination. At last, the man gave a tremendous thrust and strained against her, crushing her into the soft wooden frame, releasing his flood into her body and over her legs. Loosed from her waking prison, she cried out in pleasure.

A train whistle broke her dream.

Sarah sat bolt upright in bed. *Oh, God. Not again.*

A trickle covered her thighs and fingers, a sharp, musky scent that collided with the bitter, salt sweat coating her lips. Through the open window, she heard the announcements of departing trains from the train yard below. Shaking vio-lently, Sarah pulled a robe around herself and stumbled to the shower.

That's not what happened, she tried to remind herself. *It's just a dream. I didn't do anything. Not this time.* Still, she scrubbed her arms and legs, as if she'd lain for hours on a public street coupling with a stranger. *I'm not like that, not really,* she told herself and dressed quickly.

When at last she'd regained her composure, Sarah took the bus to the old quarter of town, to a small jazz club near the University Square. Sensing her fluency return, she hailed a waitress in German and ordered goulash and wine from the scant menu. The last, hazy sunlight of the day filtered through the smoky windows, illuminating the outer rooms of the club. On the tiny corner stage, a quartet adjusted the microphones and made other, tentative preparations for their performance. Afternoon tourists of several nationalities crowded the bar; Germans populated the tables, waiting for the evening show. Sarah tasted her wine and considered what to do next.

"Is the seat free?" A familiar voice, soft and clear, spoke behind her. *In English*, she realized, turning around.

The man from the train station pointed to the empty seat beside her. "May I sit here?"

Sarah remembered the custom that let strangers share a table. A list of German phrases, the legacy of a distant classroom, echoed through her mental speech. Out loud, she answered in English. "Of course."

He signalled to the waitress. "I heard you order," he said to Sarah. "Your German is quite excellent. Where did you study?"

"Here, at the university."

"Then you were an exchange student."

When the waitress arrived, he gave his order, quickly, and with a rich tone that skated effortlessly between the impersonal accent of pure High German and the myriad dialects of Southern Germany. It was Sarah's favorite accent, the one she had set as her goal ten years ago. In her mind, she found herself memorizing a new phrase he used, hearing it spoken in memory with his intonation.

And yet, even to her uncertain eye, he did not look German.

"Möchten Sie auch etwas zu trinken?" The waitress asked if he wanted something to drink.

"Ja, ich hätte gern ein Pilsner."

He ordered a beer, then turned back to Sarah. "So, you must tell me. Do you want that we speak German or English?"

"It's been ten years since I lived here. You might prefer my English."

He laughed. "I should be gallant and say you speak perfect German. But it's true – I heard your hesitation. Though your mistakes are not many."

"Now I know you're not German."

His eyes were dark, almost black. "Why do you say that?" he asked quietly. Despite the music and the crowds, his voice carried to her.

"Every other German tells me how beautifully I speak their language. They must be surprised an American would know anything other than English."

"True. The Americans even walk with an accent. No," he said. "I was born in Germany, but I am not German."

The waitress returned, carrying his beer and her goulash. "Bitte schön."

Throughout her meal, the man kept silent, and Sarah assumed their conversation would not continue. No matter, she'd come for the music. Wrapped in the summer evening, she listened to the saxophone echo blue notes through the smoky room, and her mood lifted to serene. She'd ordered a second glass of wine when the man spoke to her again.

"Did you know I followed you here?"

Sarah held still at his words, her complacency gone. She thought quickly of the hundred ways she knew to end a conversation like this, but somehow her American methods seemed inadequate with this man. "Why?" she said at last.

"I have a proposal for you."

Despite the apprehension that chilled her, she kept her voice indifferent. "What's that?"

He lit a cigarette and blew the smoke toward the ceiling. "You are careful," he said, as if she hadn't spoken. "I noticed in the train station – you didn't smile. You spoke very quietly. No up and down, no emotion. But you do this only when you feel danger. Is that not true?"

She tried to smile. "Why should I be afraid of you?"

"I did not say afraid, exactly. But you are, and because I'm a stranger." Casually, he tried to take her hand, but she snatched it away. "So, you don't allow touch."

"I don't touch people I don't know. Why did you follow me?"

"Because you are pretty – black and white and pink." His eyes wandered over her face, and his mere glance felt intimate. "And you know the town. You aren't here to see the museums, the castles. You came here for memories. I would like to make these new ones for you."

He spoke as though he'd read her plan, imperfect and undecided, from her soul. She nervously placed her empty glass to one side and looked for the waitress. "Who are you?"

"Call me Jack. Jack of all trades." He delivered his answer in that perfect, flat accent.

Sarah glanced at him, then away from his dark, smoky eyes. "That's not your name."

"No, but it will do." This time, he caught her hand before she could avoid it. "You don't like me, I can see. You want to run away. Do you like only girls?"

"No." Her pulse answered the heat of his skin.

"Then why not? I'm good-looking, they tell me."

She laughed, shakily. "And they tell me I speak perfect German."

With his free hand, he ran light fingers along her arm, still holding her fast. "Yes," he agreed. "Sometimes, they wish to be nice. Perhaps they lie to me."

He was a mosaic of dark. His eyes, his hair were both painted with shadings of brown verging to black. His skin was a dusk deeper than tan, and his cheekbones that might have been German, but which were not, lifted to an angle that spoke of countries farther east.

"No," she admitted. "They don't lie."

"Then I tell you my plan." Still he stroked her arm, raising currents of warmth through her skin. "We leave here and go with the bus to the Strassenbahn – excuse me, the streetcar. We ride across the river and look at the moonlight. Perhaps you still don't like me. Then I leave.

No problem." He called to the waitress. "Rechnung, bitte." He motioned that he would pay their bill.

A remnant of sanity clung to Sarah, despite his fascinating voice and beautiful eyes. But just a remnant. "Why should I go with you?"

Jack turned back to her. "Because I think you want to. Though perhaps you don't know why."

He could be Mephistopheles, she thought. The devil who trades in secret desires. He was right, she did want to go with him, despite the warnings from her rational self. Perhaps this was her plan after all. She stood to follow his challenge.

They took the bus from the University Square to the Bismarkplatz, then changed to a streetcar bound across the river. "Vorsicht bei der Abfahrt," called the conductor, ringing a bell. The streetcar staggered into motion, slowly at first as it rounded the corner of the Platz, pulling straighter and faster once it turned onto the road to the bridge. Sarah stood by the doors, watching the streetlights flash by, letting her body sway to the rhythm of the car. *Bahn*, she thought.

Jack stood close behind her. "I was not lying," he said. "I think you are very pretty." Gently, he kissed her bare shoulder.

She jumped. "Don't do that."

"Why not? I like to kiss pretty girls." Jack kissed her other shoulder. "Skin like silk and velvet," he whispered, grazing her cheek with his lips. Gently, he ran light fingers down her arms to cup her hands in his. Sarah shivered, remembering her dream. *Oh, yes, said the stranger* . . .

"Bergstrasse," called the conductor. "Nächste Haltestelle."

"This is our stop," said Jack, pushing the button to signal the conductor. "From here, we can walk to the river."

When his lips abandoned her shoulders, she felt momentarily bereft.

For several blocks, they walked in silence past the rows of old-fashioned storefronts, yellowed plaster and red-tiled roofs, broken here and there by the sheer glass window of a modern café. "You're an interesting girl," said Jack. "So timid. So careful. And yet, you decide to walk with me."

"Don't you want me here?" She kept a scant foot separate from him. Still in control, she thought.

"Very much. But I would like to know why you came back to Heidelberg."

"It's not important."

"Not quite true. I saw, also in the train station, you wanted something. That's why I followed you."

They'd reached the small plaza marking the bridge. Sarah walked past Jack to the stone pillars of the bridge. It was full evening, and moonlight cast strands of light over the rippling waters of the Neckar River. Along its bank, the dark mantle of a riverside park separated Heidelberg from its river. "I don't think you could possibly understand," she said, making her voice cold and distant.

"Of course not, since you will not talk about it. But I have a string of guesses. Did a man attack you? Is that why you are afraid of sex?"

She flinched. "I'm not afraid."

"Yes, you are. A blind man could see this. And yet you want it, very much."

The dark mongrel of Satan stood behind her, quoting the secret text of her life. Sudden anger twisted the words from her mouth. "How could you ever understand? I had a baby—"

She stopped her mouth with her hand, horrified she'd said what she never permitted herself even to think. She spun back to face Jack.

Jack lifted his chin, his eyebrows arching to make new shadows in the lamplight and waited for her to continue.

"No," she said. "I can't. I can't tell you."

He nodded as if he did understand, after all. "I have my own secret," he told her. "Not so big, perhaps, but I will tell you what you guessed earlier. My mother, she is German, but my father is from Turkey. My name I use in public is Jehan, but my real name, the one my father gave me, is Kemal. Please call me that if you like."

Small confessions eased the tension between them. Sarah leaned back against the stone pillars, listening to the calm wash of the river against the tiled shore. "Why are you telling me this?"

"Perhaps to say that I do understand." He hesitated. "Do you know the word *Gastarbeiter*? My father was one. It means guest worker, a very pleasant word you might think. And yet I have heard Germans, good Germans, shout that word as if it were a bomb that could explode my soul. I was born here, and yet I will always be outside the others. Like you."

A rivulet of breeze ran over Sarah's skin, stealing away her anger. "I had a plan," she whispered. "I came to make new memories. I thought, if I spent a week here, and nothing bad happened, then I could forget what happened before. I could go on with my life. Stupid, isn't it?"

"Not so very stupid. Can you tell me what happened?"

"I was young," she said. "Young and reckless. I met someone here – another student – and I wasn't careful. Not the first time, not any time we made love. When I found out I was pregnant, I went back to America." She spoke faster to let the words escape. "I gave the baby up for adoption. It was a little boy –" Her voice broke into tears. "I don't know where he is. It's not allowed."

For a moment, she pressed her hand against her mouth, kept her brimming eyes fixed on the ground, waiting for his reaction.

Kemal sighed. "A simple story. It cannot begin to describe the complications. I'm sorry for you."

Sarah wiped her eyes. "I don't know why I told you that. I must be crazy."

"It is the night. It makes the secrets harder to bear. And perhaps, you begin to trust me, a little." He stepped closer, to brush the hair from her face. "Cry a little. It will make you feel better."

She let the tears spill from her eyes, over her cheeks. "Call me Sarah. That's my name."

"Sarah." He spoke with quiet satisfaction. "A pretty

name, for a pretty girl. But you are wrong, Sarah. You want
to erase something with nothing. There are the days I think I
should leave Germany, I should go to İzmir, where my
family now lives. And yet, I remember it is only some
Germans who hate me, who would put me in a cage. I have
friends here and memories I would not lose."

From the lamp and moonlight, Sarah saw the answering
sheen of tears on Kemal's face. Astonishing. Her own grief
dissolved at the sight. She stepped lightly to him and put her
arms around his shoulders. "Kiss me," she whispered.

He brushed her lips softly, a light caress, as if he couldn't
believe she let him. "I wanted to kiss you at the train
station," he whispered. "So soft, so sweet. Like a dove."
He marked each word with another kiss, each longer and
more demanding, until he wrapped his arms around her and
held her to his chest.

Sarah listened to the strong rhythm of his heart against her
own. Her plans shifted to new patterns, and she realized they
were simply a recognition of her desire. "Kemal," she
whispered. "I want to make love to you."

"Sarah, Sarah . . . What are you saying?"

She started to tremble, this time in anticipation. "I want
new memories. Good ones. Ones that make me smile."

Kemal kissed her forehead. "You might shatter, and what
then? I don't want to hurt you. What about the last time?
What about the baby?"

He wanted her to tell him his doubts were wrong – she felt
his own desire shimmering through his clothes. "I won't
shatter," she said. "And we'll be careful, both of us. Kiss me
again, Kemal. Once more, then we go."

"Yes, we must go."

Breathless, they rode the streetcar through the city to
Sarah's hotel. Sarah clung to the pole by the door, letting
the rattle of the car shudder through her body. Its muffled,
clattering rhythm lifted the absence of years. Kemal pressed
against her back, his arms wrapped around her waist, his
cheek against her hair. Bahn.

Once at the hotel, Kemal went to the restaurant and returned with a bottle of wine. "Quickly, quickly," he said, as if she might change her mind. In her room, he kissed her greedily, tenderly, stopping just once to pour the wine. "Sarah," he whispered. "It's so good to be here. Are you certain? Are you afraid?"

"No, it's wonderful." She nearly sobbed.

"Hush. We've been too impatient. We have all night to kiss, make love, whatever." Kemal led her to the bed and gave her the wine. "Drink slowly, and remember this. Remember everything we do." Taking a drink from his own glass, Kemal set his lips to hers and let his wine pour into her mouth. The crisp, light wine calmed her. "You are delicious," he said. "I want to kiss more."

Anticipation ran taut throughout her body as he laid her across the bed. Slowly, Kemal parted her legs and kissed the back of her knee. "I like this very much. Do you, Sarah?" He lingered over the syllables of her name, then moved his lips over her skin, kissing first one knee then the other. Then his tongue skimmed her thigh. Sarah moaned.

"My poor, little girl. I but kiss you and you are coming."

"It's been so long."

"Yes, I know." He kissed her foot. Ran a staccato of kisses from her ankle, past her knee, under her skirt to her panties. "These must go." He lifted her bottom, slid her panties from her, and tenderly kissed her sex. "You are very, very wet," he observed.

Sarah moved as if to protest.

"No, I like this," he said. "I would like to think you are always wet. If not, I would like to make you so." He nuzzled her belly, then dropped his mouth over her sex. "A treasure."

Sarah felt as if they'd always been here, had always made love. She ran her hands over her breasts and down her body, to run wildly through Kemal's hair. "You're beautiful," she said. "I can hardly believe it."

"Tell me a story, Sarah, while I feast on your body."

Her tears threatened to return. She ordered them away, but said, "All my stories are sad ones."

"Then tell me a sad one, and we will try to make it better."

Maybe we can, she thought. Sarah picked the first story, the oldest one of her life.

"When I was ten years old," she said. "I read a story about a little girl who slept without her pajamas, so I decided to try this myself. It was wonderful – the sheets were like a great, cool hand laid over my body. I'd never felt anything like it. I wanted to laugh, and I think I did, but suddenly, my mother opened the door to my room. She pulled the covers away and shouted, 'What are you doing?'" Sarah curled a lock of Kemal's hair around her finger. Kemal's slow, tender kisses spread a warmth through her belly.

"She told me I'd been wicked – she used that word, wicked – and she told me never to do that again. But three years later, when I was thirteen, I dreamed I stood at my window, watching a boy who stood in the street. In my dream, I lifted my nightgown over my head and stood there naked, hoping the boy would see me.

"He did. He turned around and looked at me with very serious eyes. I felt cold, then hot. I didn't do anything else, I just stood there, knowing he could see my breasts."

Softly, Kemal drew a line of kisses down her thigh. He crossed to the other leg, travelled back to her sex, up to her belly. "I love this part of you," he murmured.

"I had this dream again and again," she continued. "Each time in a different place, each dream more exotic and daring than the last. One time, I was standing in a room with floor-to-ceiling windows. Outside, on the sidewalk, people passed by, looking at me. This time, I pretended I didn't know they could see through the glass. I undressed very slowly, making certain I kept my eyes to the floor. I walked from one side of the room to the other, as if I were looking for something. I felt their eyes on me, but I pretended to be indifferent."

"You didn't want responsibility."

"That's right. I wanted to be wicked, but I didn't want to

be punished. I thought, if I were like a picture, they couldn't blame me."

"And who are *they*, Sarah?"

"People. I don't know."

"People like your mother?"

"I guess."

"Do you still believe you are wicked?"

"Sometimes."

Kemal lay his head on her belly and drew caressing circles over her skin with his fingertips, kissing the silver web of scars that marked her pregnancy. "When you had the baby, did you feel wicked then?"

"I felt – oh, god, I felt a thousand different things, all miserable – but yes, I felt wicked. As if God had punished me for taking pleasure."

She felt the warm pressure of Kemal's head, and the rumbling of his chest when he spoke. "Americans are ashamed of so much," he said. "All day long, they scream sex, sex, sex. And yet, they are afraid when someone notices. Sarah, there is no god in heaven that would call pleasure wicked. Only the unhappy do this, when they try to deny others what they dare not feel." He ran his tongue over the lips of her sex, easily recalling the warmth of her first excitement. "Listen," he kissed her shuddering belly. "It is now almost nine-thirty. The next train comes from Frankfurt. It will have at least a hundred passengers – I know this. I want to make you scream from pleasure." He pressed a kiss inside her thigh. "I want everyone to hear."

Sarah's resistance faded with each kiss. Her throat hurt now, and she was panting quickly. Kemal covered her sex with his mouth and sucked. "You are delectable." He slid hands over her hips to her waist, driving his mouth against her. The edge of teeth tickled her, then his tongue, thick and firm, reached inside.

"I'm coming . . ." Her throat opened in relief. She wanted to ask him where he'd learned this. Each caress was practised, as if he'd studied her for years. Then, he pointed his tongue deeper, and she couldn't think anymore. "Fuck me," she cried. "Oh, please fuck me."

"Not now. Not yet."

Through the window, a thin, rising whistle announced the approaching train. *Hundreds of people*, she thought. *Listening to me scream in pleasure.*

"You are coming again," said Kemal.

"I haven't stopped. Lick me faster."

He obeyed, with an expertise that nearly frightened her. Now she couldn't hold it back. The moan rose from her belly to her chest, travelling through her aching throat to burst out, savage and incoherent, until she lost the ability to speak and could only howl. Dimly, through the window, she heard the train pull to a stop, its brakes shrieking against the rails.

"Sarah, Sarah . . ." Kemal chanted her name like a song he'd just discovered.

"Don't stop, Kemal. Please don't stop."

"Dear Sarah, we've just begun to make love . . ."

Bottomless on Bourbon

Maxim Jakubowski

He had often promised to take Kathryn to New Orleans. But it had never happened. They had spectacularly fallen apart long before the opportunity arose. In fact, the travel they had managed to do in between feverish fucks had proven rather prosaic. So much for promises. They hadn't even visited Paris, Amsterdam or New York either.

So, whenever he could, he now took other women to the Crescent City.

For sex.

And fantasised about Kathryn's face, and eyes, and pale breasts and cunt and more.

New Orleans was for him a city with two faces. Almost two different places, the aristocratic and slightly disheveled languor of the Garden District on one hand and the hustle and bustle of the French Quarter on the other, contrasting like night and day. The touristic charms concealing darker, ever so venomous charms. The heavy placid flow of the Mississippi river zigzagging in serpentine manner through the opposing twin shores of Jackson Square and Algiers. The gently alcoholic haze of New Orleans days and the enticing, dangerous attraction of fragrant New Orleans nights. Nights that smelled and tasted of sex.

He loved to see the women sweat as he made love to them, enjoyed the feel of bodies sliding against each other, in moist, clammy embraces as sheets tangled around them. He took unerring voyeuristic pleasure in watching them shower after, washing his seed away from their openings, cleaning away his bites, the saliva that still coated their nipples, neck or earlobes which he had assaulted with military-like amorous precision.

Those were the memories he treasured. Stored away for all eternity in his mental bank vaults. The curve of a back, the soft blonde down slowly being submerged in a small pool of perspiration just inches away from her rump, highlighted by a solitary light bulb, as she kneeled on all fours on the bed and he breached the final defences of her sphincter and impaled himself in her bowels. The sound of a moan, of pleasure, of joy. Ohhh . . . AAAAHHH . . . Chriiiiiist . . . The tremor that coursed through the girl's taut body as he discharged inside her or as she rode the ocean waves of her oncoming orgasm.

Yes, New Orleans, his city of sex.

Endless walks through the small streets between hotel room episodes. Invigorating breakfasts of beignets and coffee and ice-cold orange juice at the Café du Monde; oysters and thick, syrupy gumbo at The Pearl off Canal Street; loitering hand in hand in the farmer's market full of the smell of spices and seafood, chewing on garlic-flavoured pistachio nuts; obscene mounds of boiled crawfish at Lemoyne's Landing; hunting for vintage paperbacks through the dusty shelves at Beckham's; po'boys at the Napoleon House; zydeco rhythms at the House of Blues; a routine he could live on for days on end. Until he would tire of the woman, because she bored him once past the mechanics of fornication, never said the right thing or talked too much or simply because she wasn't the woman he really wanted to be with in New Orleans.

There had been Lisa, the software executive; Clare, a lawyer who looked like Anne Frank had she ever grown up, and liked to be handled roughly; Pamela Jane, the investment banker he had met at the hotel bar who wanted to be a writer and Helene the biology teacher from Montreal. He didn't feel he was being promiscuous; four women in six years since Kathryn. Some he had found here, others he had brought.

But somehow none had fitted in with this strange city and, even though the sex had been loose and fun, and the company never less than pleasant, there had been something lacking. Even at midnight, buckling under his thrusts on bed or floor or sucking him off under the water streams of the shower, he knew they were creatures of the day, anonymous, predictable; they had no touch of the night, no share of darkness. And darkness was what he sought. In women. In New Orleans. What he knew he had once detected under Kathryn's fulsome exterior.

He had high hopes for Susi.

She was Austrian, in her late twenties, and worked in a managerial capacity for a travel agency in Vienna, which made it easier (and cheaper) for her to jump on a plane for purposes of pleasure.

They had met in New York some months earlier. It was Spring and the weather was appalling for the season. The rain poured down in buckets and all Manhattan was gridlocked like only New York can manage. He'd been in town promoting a book and negotiating the next contract with his publishers there (he never used an agent) and was booked on an evening flight back to London. He'd been staying, as usual, at a hotel down by the Village, off Washington Square. He had booked a car to JFK and it was already half an hour late. They had checked at reception and found out that the driver was still blocked in traffic near Central Park and Columbus Circle. He had promptly cancelled the car and rushed with his suitcase to the hotel's front steps to hail a yellow cab. They were few and far between and he wasn't the only hotel guest heading for the airport. Both he and the tall, slim red-headed woman went for the same cab which declined the airport ride pretexting the conditions. They agreed to share the next cab to come along. She was even later than him, as her flight preceded his by twenty minutes.

"My name is Susanne, but my friends call me Susi with an

i," she had introduced herself as the driver made his slow way towards the Midtown Tunnel.

Despite clever shortcuts through Queens, the journey took well over an hour and a quarter, so they had much opportunity to talk as they inched towards their planes. She had been in town for a week, visiting her parents who both worked as diplomats for one of the big international organisations.

She did miss her flight, while he caught his with a few minutes to spare. E-mail addresses were exchanged and they had remained in touch since.

They had quickly become intimate. He'd sent her one of his books and she had remarked on the sexual nature of many of his stories and confessed to some of her own sexual quirks. She was an exhibitionist. Would sometimes take the subway back in Vienna dressed in a particularly short skirt and without underwear and allow men to spy on her genitals. She was shaven, so they had a full view of her naked mound. She was also in the habit of masturbating in parks, where she could be seen by passers-by, actually encouraged voyeurs to do so and knew that, sometimes, men were jerking off watching her just a few metres away.

She would pretend her name was Lolita. He asked her why.

Because she had little in the way of breasts and her bare pubis evoked a child or a doll, she answered. She was submissive by nature, she told him.

She sent him a series of photographs taken by an ex-boyfriend she had broken up with shortly before the New York trip. He found them wonderfully provocative in a tender sort of way. In the first, her long, skinny frame stood in contrast to the sluttish, traditional black lingerie of embroidered knickers, suspender belt and stockings almost a size too big for her. Yes, she had no breasts, barely a hillock worth of elevation and no cleavage and, he imagined (the photographs were all black and white), pale pink nipples like a gentle stain in the landscape of her flesh. Her hair was a bit longer than when she had been in New York, her eyes dead to the world. In the second photograph – he could guess the sequence they had been taken in, pruriently imagined what the boyfriend in question had made her do, perform, submit to, after the camera had been set aside – she was now squatting only clad in suspender belt and stockings, her cunt in sharp focus, lips ever so ready to open, her head thrown back so you could barely recognise her features. Photograph number three saw her spread-eagled over a Persian carpet and parquet floor, one arm in the air, both legs straight, holding herself up by one arm, like a gymnast, her face in profile, a most elegant and beautiful vision of nudity with no hint of obscenity at all, her body like a fine-tuned machine, a sculpture. In the fourth, she was standing and the photographer had shot away from crotch level and her body was deformed like in a hall of mirrors by the skewed perspective, the focus on her enlarged midriff. The one thing that struck him as he kept on examining the photos on his laptop screen was how her sex-lips didn't part and how he wished to see inside her. The final photograph she had sent him (were there more? more explicit or extreme? she had answered that others were just out of focus but his imagination as ever played wildly on) was both the sexiest and the most vulgar. She was on all fours, her arse raised towards the camera in a fuck-me pose, long legs bent, rear a bit bony, the line of her cunt-lips straight as a ruler and continued by her arse-crack and darker hole. Every time he looked at this one, he couldn't help getting hard. And he knew that she enjoyed knowing that.

He told her about the delights of New Orleans and invited her to join him there one day.

To explore possibilities, he said.

Initially, she only said maybe.

But he persisted, courting her with a modicum of elegance and she agreed. It took a couple of months to find a week when both could free themselves from previous commitments (ah, the sheer logistics of lust!) and arrangements were made. Flights to New York were coordinated – her job came in useful – and they both arrived in Newark an hour or so apart. Neither flight was delayed.

Curiously enough, there are no direct flights between New York and New Orleans and their connection went via Raleigh–Durham.

As they emerged from the airport luggage area, Susi smelled the heat that now surrounded them like a blanket and turned towards him, kissed him gently on the cheek and said: "I just know I'm going to like it here . . . Thanks ever so much for bringing me."

By the time the taxi dropped them off at the small hotel he had booked on Burgundy it was already dark.

It was summer. Moist, no wind from the Gulf, the air heavy with the powers of the night, the remains of the day lingering in patchy clouds, they were both sweating, their bodies not yet acclimatised.

They dropped their bags and he switched the air-conditioning a notch higher and suggested a shower.

He undressed her. Now she was no longer black and white. The nipples were a darker pink, closer to red than he imagined and darkened a shade further when he kissed them. Her pale body was like porcelain.

Long, thin, exquisitely supple. Since Kathryn, none of the other women, here or elsewhere had been anywhere as tall. He escorted Susi to the shower cubicle and switched the water on. She looked at his cock, growing slowly at the sheer sight of her nudity. He soaped her with infinite delicacy and tenderness and explored her body under guise of washing, refreshing her from the transatlantic journey and its grime and tiredness. He fell to his knees and wiped the suds away from her crotch. Her gash staring red against the mottled pinkness of her pubic mound. She hadn't shaved there for a week or so; they had agreed she would let him shave her clean. A delight he had long fantasised about. He parted her thin lips, like opening a rare flower and darted his tongue inside to taste her. Susi shuddered.

The first time was good.

They were shy, affectionate, slow, tentative, testing pleasure points and limits with great delicacy.

She was extremely self-conscious of her lack of opulence breast-wise and he lavished particular care on her there, sucking, licking, nibbling, fingering her with casual precision until he caught the precise pulse of her pleasure behind the gentle swell of her darkening nipples.

They came closely together. Silently.

The later days filled quickly between wet embraces and ever more feverish fucks as they grew used to each other's quirks and secret desires. She had always wanted to take a riverboat down the Mississippi and they spent a day doing so, passing the civil war mansions and lawns and observing the rare crocodiles still lingering in the musty bayous. Just like tourists. Which they were. Sexual tourists with, so far, no taste for the local fare. Breezing down Magazine Street in mid-afternoon as the antique shops reopened for business.

Taking a streetcar to the Garden District. Lingering, with verbose guides, in the atmospheric cemeteries, with their ornate crypts and walls of bones. Visiting the voodoo Museum, trying to repress their unceremonious giggles. He, covertly fingering signed first editions at the Faulkner House.

Susi never wore a bra – she had no need for one – and neither did she slip knickers on when they would go out walking. Long, flowing, thin skirts revealing the shape of her legs when she faced the sun, only he knowing how unfettered her cunt-lips were beneath the fabric, sometimes even imagining he could smell her inner fragrance as they walked along hand in hand and conjuring up the thoughts of other, lubricious men passing by had they known of her naked vulnerability. It turned him on, this constant availability of hers, this exhibitionistic desire to provoke. Walking along Decatur, passing one of the horse-drawn carriages waiting there for tourists, a dog held in leash by a small black child wagged a tail frantically and brushed against Susi's leg. He smiled. She asked him why.

"He could smell your cunt," he said.

"Do you think so?" she remarked, her eyes all wide.

"Yes," he told her. "You smell of sex. Strongly."

Her face went all red, approximating the shade of her short bob, and as he watched the flush spread to her chest and beneath the thin silk blouse.

"It turned him on," he said.

"Oh . . ."

"And me too, knowing how naked you are under those thin, light clothes," he added.

She smiled.

Later, back in their hotel room, she insisted they keep the curtains open when they made love, knowing any passing maid or room-service staff might see them in the throes of sex as they walked past on the steps outside the window and, as he moved frantically inside her, he saw she kept her eyes open, was actually hoping they would be seen. The idea excited her.

The same night, a few blocks before Bourbon, she suddenly said:

"I have to pee."

They'd only left the hotel a hundred yards or so ago, so she must have known the need would arise. He offered to go back to the room.

"No," she said. "The side street there. That will do."

It was dark, no one around, although the risk of passers-by emerging off Toulouse was likely.

Susi pulled her long skirt upwards and bunched it around her waist, her thin, unending legs bursting into pale view, the plumpness of her cunt in full display under the light from the illuminated wrought iron balcony above them and squatted down. He watched, hypnotised, as the hot stream of urine burst through her labia and splashed onto the New Orleans stone pavement. Her eyes darted towards the main street, almost begging for someone to come by. None did. Her bladder empty, she rose to her feet, the skirt still held above her waist in insolent provocation.

"It's a bit wet," she said to him. "Would you dry me?"

He got down on his knees, wiped her cunt-lips clean with the back of his hand then impulsively licked her briefly. Her clit was hard, swollen. Susi was in heat.

"Fuck me here," she asked him. "I don't mind if people see us."

"I can't," he said. "We've only just got out of bed. I don't think I could get hard enough again so quickly."

Susi glanced at him with disapproval.

She dropped the folds of her dress.

They began talking.

"Does it turn you on?" he asked.

"Yes."

"What is it? A feeling of control over people, men, that they can see you but not touch?"

"I don't know," Susi remarked. "My body is nothing special, but I love to show myself. Gives me meaning. It's a bit confusing."

"Your body's great. You shouldn't underestimate yourself," he answered. "But you must be careful. On the nude beach outside Vienna, with your girlfriend along, there's an element of safety, but elsewhere it could be risky, you know."

"Yes."

"Some people could read other things into your need to exhibit yourself. You could get yourself raped."

"I know," Susi answered, with a slight sigh in her voice. "Sometimes, I even imagine what it would be like. Several men."

"Really?"

"Yes. Five of them. First they fuck my every hole, then I am made to kneel, still naked, at their feet and they all jerk off and come in my face and hair."

"A bit extreme . . ."

"I know . . ."

He tried to lighten the mood. Already feeling anxious in premonition as the darkness neared.

"The ultimate facial treatment. Better than soap!"

Susi laughed and led the way back towards Bourbon Street.

He described how Bourbon Street would be when Mardi-Gras came. The noise, the coloured beads, the floats, the beer, the wonderfully hedonistic atmosphere that gripped the whole French Quarter, the fever that rose insidiously as the alcohol loosened inhibitions and the music from the bars of either side of the street grew in loudness, competing rhythms crisscrossing on every corner, clouding minds and bodies.

How the revellers on the balconies would bait the walkers below, sprinkling them with drink, offering beads for the flash of a nipple or a quickly-bared backside to massive roars of approval from the wild crowds.

He could see Susi's eyes light up. Yes, she would enjoy Carnival here. No longer requiring an excuse to bare her parts to one and all and the more the merrier.

"And what happens behind doors?" she asked him. He shuddered to think. He'd only ever stayed in New Orleans for the first night of Mardi-Gras. Had heard mad rumours of uncontrollable excess, of sex in the streets. He'd once come across a range of video cassettes in a 7th Avenue porn joint in New York documenting the sexual side of Mardi-Gras here year after year. But, like with wine, he was unaware which were the good years or the bad years and had never sampled any of the cassettes in question.

His mind and imagination raced forward. To a clandestine video cassette in a white box and Polaroid cover shot of Susi's porcelain-white body, face covered with come, labelled "SUSANNE 'LOLITA' WIEN, MARDI-GRAS 1999". A vintage performance, no doubt.

Bourbon Street night deepened as the beer flowed ever more freely, spilling into the gutters from plastic cups being carried up and down the street by the Saturday night-revellers. The music surging from all around grew louder, the lights more aggressive and the crowds swayed uncertainly. Young kids tapped away for a few cents or break-danced outside the bars, the neon signs of the strip clubs entered battle, pitting male strippers against female ones, topless joints against bottomless ones. A row of mechanical legs danced a can can from the top of a bar window, advertising further displays of flesh inside.

Susi was curious.

"I've never been to a striptease place before. Can we?"

"Why not?" he acquiesced.

They entered the dark bar. A woman down to a shining lamé bikini was dancing around a metal pole at its centre. A few men sat by the stage desultorily sipping from half-empty glasses. They ordered their drinks from a sultry waitress and watched the stripper shed her bra with a brief flourish. The performance was uninspiring and the most exciting thing about the dancer for him was her gold navel ring which gleamed in the fluctuating light. His mind went walkabout as he tried to recognise the rock and roll tune she was, badly, dancing to.

Several shimmies and swirls later, and a liberal shake of silicon-enhanced mammaries exposed, the song (some country and western standard given an electric and gloom Americana twist) came to an end and the stripper quickly bowed, picking up a few stray dollar notes thrown onto the stage by the isolated punters on her way off.

"Is that all?" Susi turned to him, asking.

"I think so," he said.

"But it's not even bottomless. She didn't even show her cunt!"

"Maybe because it's a bar. I don't know," he said, "there must be some local bye-laws or something. Don't know much about the rules in American strip clubs," he continued, surprised by Susi's interest.

Another stripper, black, stocky, took to the stage and a soul number burst out of the speakers. The previous performer was on the other side of the dance area, soliciting tips from some of the men. One whispered in her ear as she accosted him. She nodded. The man rose and he followed the woman,

who now wore a dressing gown, to a darker corner at the far
end of the bar. Susi nudged him and they both peered in that
direction.

They could just about see the stripper throw back her
gown and squat over the lap of the man who had now seated
himself.

"A private dance," he said to Susi.

"Wow! Cool!" she said, one of the more irritating man-
nerisms he had picked up on when they chatted online back
in Europe.

There wasn't much to see. The stripper moved in silence.
The man appeared to keep his hands to himself but the
darkness engulfed the couple.

"I'm turned on," Susi said in his ears.

"Really?" he said, finding the atmosphere in the bar quite
unerotic, the black stripper now strutting her square rump a
few feet away from his face.

"Yes," Susi added. "I don't think I'd make a good stripper. No tits, as you well know. But I sure could lap or table
dance. I'd like to do that for you . . ."

He grinned.

"Sure. Later, in our hotel room, I'll look forward to your
demonstration."

"No. Here," Susi said, a deep tone of excitement in her
voice.

"Here?" he queried.

"Yes." He could see that her right hand was buried in he
folds of her dress, that she was fingering herself through the
material. "Can you arrange it? Please. See the guy at the bar,
he appears to be in charge. Get him to agree. Please, pretty
please?"

He shrugged.

It cost him fifty bucks and some haggling.

He walked back toward the stage where Susi was downing
the rest of her Jack Daniels.

He nodded.

"It's yes," he said.

She rose, a mischievous glint in her eye. She took him by the hand and led him to a chair, nowhere near the darkness that offered shelter further down the bar but in full view of all. She pointed a finger, indicating he should sit down, which he did. Sensing what was to happen now, the bar attendant stationed himself at the door to Bourbon Street to prevent further spectators and a possible loss of his licence. Susi camped herself facing the chair he now sat on and pulled her dress above her head. You could hear a pin drop as the barman and the few spectators dotted around the stage witnessed her naked form emerge from the cocoon of the fabric, whiter than white, shaven mound plump, and so bare, like a magnet for their disbelieving eyes. A couple of the attendant strippers peered out from the dressing room on the side of the bar counter.

The music began and he had no clue what it even was, his mind in such turmoil.

Susi began writhing a few inches away from him, knowing all too well how much she was the centre of attraction.

She danced, wriggled, swerved, bent, squatted, obscenely, indecently, her hands moving across her bare flesh in snake-like manner, her fingers grazing her by-now erect nipples, descending across the flatness of her pale stomach and even, although he hoped he was, because of his close proximity to her dance, the only one to notice, lingering in the region of her cunt and actually holding her lips open for a second or so.

He felt hot. Even though he, by now, knew every square inch of her skin, this was a new Susi, a creature he had only guessed at.

It was quickly over.

He held his breath.

A few people clapped in the background.

Susi's face was impassive but flushed.

She picked up her discarded dress and slipped into it.

"That was good," she said. "Can we go, now?"

On their way to the door and the muted sounds of Bourbon Street, the barman handed Susi a card.

"You're quite a gal," he said, as she brushed past him. "My name is Louis. If you're seeking more serious fun, just call me."

Susi slipped the card into her side pocket without even acknowledging him and emerged into the twilight.

"I'm hungry," she said.

One of the nearby hotels had an oyster bar. They shared a plateful each of oysters and shrimps. She smothered each with a generous helping of tomato-flavoured horseradish as she gulped them down.

"One of your fantasies realised?" he asked her.

"You might say that," Susi answered. "But there are others."

"I have no doubt." He smirked, still uncertain of the path they had embarked upon.

"Don't look so glum." She smiled. "You did say we would come to New Orleans and explore possibilities, didn't you?"

"I suppose I did."

The rawness of their sex that night was compelling and savage. She sucked him with hungry determination and wouldn't allow him to withdraw from her mouth when he felt his excitement rise. Usually, he would hold back and penetrate her, which prolonged the pleasure. He came in her mouth. She let him go and he watched her tasting his come before she finally swallowed it.

"You taste sweet and sour," Susi said. "Must be all those oysters you've been eating."

The following day, she insisted they visit a place called The Orgy Room. On Bourbon, of course. As pornographic films were projected on the walls, a group of people pressed together like sardines in a can were force-fed into an exiguous room and allowed to jostle and play on pneumatic fun-fair carpets, or were they water beds? Most were drunk. The constant movement was, he felt, somewhat unpleasant, and far from arousing. Soon, he was separated from Susi in the swaying crowd but could still see her at the other end of the room. She deliberately exaggerated her movements and rubbed herself against others, often pulling her short black leather mini skirt up her thighs so her genitals were fully visible to those closer to her. He observed as various men took notice and soon congregated around her. He could see her face flush amongst the laughs, and the human wave of bodies soon directed her against the back wall where she stood motionless, her skirt now bunched at her midriff and a couple of men frantically fingering her as she pretended to ignore them. He watched from afar, not quite knowing what he now felt. Eventually, the siren rang and the crowds thinned and made for the exit. As Susi reached him, trailed by the puzzled men she had snared in her net, she took his hand in hers. The men observed this and interrupted their progress towards her. Sweat poured down her forehead, her thin red hair plastered down against her scalp. They walked out.

He looked up at the sky. There was a storm brewing.

"I came," she remarked. "Jesus . . ."

"Susi . . ."

"Take me back to the hotel," she ordered. "Tonight, I want you to fuck my arse."

The next morning, she expressed a desire for breakfast in bed. They had woken up too late for the hotel room service. He volunteered to fetch food from a nearby 24-hour deli. The night rain had swept away the heat momentarily and the cool air came as a welcome relief as he walked the few hundred metres to the shop and back.

When he returned to the room, Susi was speaking on the phone. She put the receiver down as he walked in.

Maybe he shouldn't have asked, but he did. Force of habit. He'd left the hotel number with a few friends back in London, in case of sudden business, magazine commissions.

"Was that for me?" he asked Susi.

"No," she replied. "It was Louis, from the bar."

"I see."

"I wanted to find out about the . . . secret places, the real New Orleans, so to speak . . ." She looked down as she spoke, the white sheet lowered down to the whorl of her navel. There were dark patches under her green eyes, from lack of sleep and the intensity of the sex. He'd never found her as attractive as now, he knew.

He set the bread, snacks and fruit juice bottles down on the bedside table.

"And?"

"And he's given me a few addresses. Said it's his night off, offered to show us around."

"We barely know him. Do you think it would be safe?"

"You always told me that New Orleans was a city of sex. Not vampires or voodoo. That it was constantly in the air, you used to say, remember."

"I did."

"Well, it would be silly not to find out more, wouldn't it?"

"I suppose."

"He's picking us up from the hotel lobby around nine tonight. He'll show us beyond Bourbon."

They walked through the market at midday. Beyond the food area full of cajun spice mixtures, chicory blends, pralines, nuts and colourful fruit and fish, there was a flea market of sorts, stalls selling souvenirs, bric à brac, clothing, counterfeit tapes of zydeco music, hand-made bracelets and all the flotsam that draws people to a tourist town. On a previous visit on their second day here, Susi had spotted a black felt table where a long-haired superannuated hippy was selling fake body jewellery, which could be worn without the need for piercings. She selected several pieces.

Late afternoon, back in the room, she retreated to the bathroom for a shower. She emerged half an hour later, splendidly naked and scrubbed clean, her dark red hair still wet.

"Do you like it?" she asked him.

He looked up from his magazine.

She took his breath away. How could her body be so damn

pale and so heartbreakingly beautiful? She had rouged her nipples a darker shade of scarlet and accentuated the bloody gash of her sex-lips with the same lipstick. A courtesan adorned for sexual use.

She had also strategically placed the small rings and clips she had purchased in the market across her body. A ring hung from her lower lip, stainless steel clamps from her hardened nipples and a stud appeared to have been pierced into her clitoris from which a thin golden chain hung, which she had until now worn around her wrist.

"Like a creature from a dream," he said. "From a very dirty dream, may I add. You look great." He could feel his cock swell already inside his boxer shorts.

"Come here," he suggested.

"No," she said. "I have to dry my hair. Anyway I also want you to conserve your energy. Your seed . . ." she concluded with a smile.

"As you wish," he said, unable to keep his eyes away from her jewelled cunt.

"This is my fantasy night," she said.

It felt like a stab to his chest.

He already knew what she had arranged with Louis.

It was a very private club on Ramparts, at the other end of the Vieux Carré. From outside, it looked like any other house, slightly run down and seedy. But the moment you passed the door, you could almost inhale the familiar fragrance of money and sin.

"You sure you still want to?" Louis asked her as they walked in to the lobby.

"Yes," Susi said.

Louis guided them into a large room full of framed Audubon prints and a fake fire-place and asked them to make themselves comfortable. And left through another door after showing them the drinks cabinet.

Alone with her, he said nothing at first. Then, sensing his unease, Susi said:

"It's not quite the fantasy I told you about. Just the second part, really . . ."

"Oh . . ."

"And I want you to be one of the men . . ."

"I'm not sure I . . ."

"I'd feel more comfortable with you there," she interrupted him. "You'll enjoy it, you'll see. Anyway, you knew what I am, what I like, when you suggested we come here. You'll get a kick out of it. You like watching. I see it in you. Even when we fuck, your brain is like a machine, recording it all, storing every feeling, every tremor, every moan away. Memories that will last forever."

Before he could answer her, the door opened and Louis came through with three other men. Two of them were black, tall, built like football players, the other white man was middle-aged, stocky, silver-haired.

"Here we are, Susanne," he said, without introducing the others. "You're in charge now . . ."

The thought occurred to him he had called her Susanne. "Friends call me Susi," she had said back all those months ago as they caught that New York cab. So Louis was not considered a friend!

Susi indicated the centre of the heavily carpeted room.

"A circle around here." There was something more Germanic than usual in her voice as she ordered them to clear the heavy chairs away from the room's epicentre.

The circle soon emerged, as the furniture was set aside.

Susi stationed herself there and undressed.

"You all stay dressed," she said to the five men. "Just cocks out, okay?" She positioned herself and as the men's eyes followed her every movement she opened her legs and stuck a finger inside herself. She was already visibly very wet and there was an audible squishing sound as the finger penetrated her. Louis unzipped his jeans and pulled his cock out. The others followed his example. One of the black guys, he noticed, was enormous, at least ten inches and thick as hell. He discreetly examined the other cocks, and was reassured that his was still reasonably sized in comparison. Joint second biggest, he reckoned, not without a wry thought.

Susi now introduced a second finger into her cunt, secretions now flooding out and dripping down the gold chain.

There was both a sense of the ceremonial and a sense of the absurd about them all. Six human beings masturbating frantically. Five men with their cocks out, fingers clenching their shafts, rubbing their coronas, teasing their glans, heavy balls shuddering below as the woman in white at their centre teased her cunt in a parody of lovemaking.

"Not yet," she warned. Had one of them intimated he was close to coming?

Time felt as if it had come to a standstill, swallowing all their halting sounds of lust.

She adjusted her stance, now kneeling, her hand buried deep inside her crotch, almost like praying, and indicated she was finally ready for her baptism of come.

The men came, one by one, spurting their thick, white seed into her face, as she leaned forward to receive them. He was the third to orgasm and noticed the arc of his ejaculate strain in the air separating him from her body and the final drips landing in the thin valley between her muted breasts. Soon, she was covered with the men's seed, like syrup dribbling across her thin eyebrows and down her cheeks. He didn't think she herself had actually come, although all five men had.

There was a long silence as they all stood there, the men with their cocks shrivelling already, the drenched woman in quiet repose.

Finally, Louis spoke:

"Well, Susanne, just the way you wanted it?"

She nodded as the men began zipping up.

"Care to move on to your next fantasy?"

What next fantasy? he wondered. What else was she after?

"Yes," she said, rising to her feet and picking up the green towel Louis had previously left on a nearby chair and wiping her face clean.

"Good," Louis said. "There's quite a crowd out there waiting."

Still not bothering to put her clothes on again, Susi asked him: "Can you give us a few minutes alone, before, please?"

"Sure, Susanne," he said and the four men trooped out of the room.

"So," he asked her the moment after they had closed the door. "What else have you planned for the menu, Susi? It must be a fantasy I am unaware of. You're so full of surprises."

"I know," she answered. "I should have told you before. I'm sorry. It'll only happen once and then I shall return to my boring life, you know. Maybe the time will even come for me to settle down, marry some decent guy and even have kids. A nice Hausfrau."

"What are you talking about, Susi?"

"I want to be fucked in public . . ."

"What?"

"Just one man, that's all. But I have to know what it feels like with people watching, you see. You said this was a city of sex; I'll never have the opportunity again. Just this once. We're miles away from home, no one knows us, we are not likely come here again. Only you and I will ever know . . ."

"You mean with me?" he asked.

"Yes. If you wish to be the one."

"I . . ." He was at a loss for words.

"It's all arranged with Louis. We'll even get paid five hundred dollars."

"It's not the money . . ."

"I know . . . I understand if you don't want to. Arrangements have also been made for another man, if you decline. But I do want you to watch . . . really . . ."

His thoughts were in turmoil. This had all gone too far. He had played with fire and the flames were now reaching all the way through to his gut. As they always did. He never learned the lessons, did he? Long before Kathryn, he'd been going out with a woman who was avowedly bisexual and it had planted a bad seed in his mind. Not for him the common fantasy of watching two women together, no. The idea of bisexuality had preyed on his mind for months and one day, curious to know what it must feel like to suck a man's cock, from the woman's point of view (after all, they never minded sucking his, did they?), he had agreed to an encounter with another man. He distressingly discovered he enjoyed sucking cock and had been irregularly doing so for years now, in secret, whenever a woman was not available and the tides of lust submerged him. He had never told any woman about this. Feared they would misunderstand. Blamed his insatiable sexual curiosity. Even Susi wouldn't understand, he knew. Not that this was the time to tell her. He always went that step too far. And paid for it. Emotionally.

"I just can't, Susi. I can't."

"But will you . . .?"

"Yes, I will watch."

There was a crowd in the other room of the house on Ramparts. They had been drinking liberally for an hour or so, it appeared. There was a heavy air of expectation about them. Louis led Susi in. Like a ritual, holding the thin gold chain secured to her clitoris, her eyes covered by a piece of dark blue cloth. This is how she had wanted it to happen. She didn't wish to see the audience. Just feel it and hear it around her as she was fucked.

They had cleared a low table in a corner of the room and Susi was taken to it, carefully installed across so that all the light was focused on her already gaping and wet red gash and positioned on all fours, her fake jewellery taken from her body and was helped to arch her back and raise her rump to the right level.

The man who had won the quickly organised auction came forward. He looked quite ordinary, late twenties, an athlete's build, not very hairy, he had kept his shirt on but his cock already jutted forward as he approached Susi's receptive body. He was uncut and his foreskin bunched heavily below the mushroom cone of his glans. He was very big.

The man found his position at Susi's entrance and bucked forward and speared her. A few spectators applauded but most remained quite silent. From where he sat, he couldn't see Susi's face, only her white arse and the hypnotising sight of the dark, purple cock moving in and out of her, faster and faster, every thrust echoed by a wave of movement on the periphery of her flesh, like a gentle wind caressing the surface of a sand dune.

It lasted an eternity, much longer he knew than he would have ever managed. The guy was getting his money's worth. And the audience, many of whom were blatantly playing with themselves in response to the spectacle unfolding before them. She would be very sore at the end of this. Sweat coated Susi's body like a thin shroud as the man dug deeper and deeper into her and he watched her opening enlarge obscenely under the pressure of that monstrous cock.

Shamefully, he couldn't keep his eyes away from the immediate perimeter of penetration, noting every anatomical feature with minute precision, the vein bulging on the side of the invading cock as it moved in and out of sight in and out of her, the very shade of crimson of her bruised labia as they were shoved aside by the thrusts, the thin stream of inner secretions pearling down her inner thigh, and neither could he prevent himself getting hard again watching the woman he knew he had fallen in love with getting fucked in public by a total stranger.

That night, she curled up against him in the slightly exiguous hotel room bed, drawing his warmth and tearing him apart inside.

They had packed and waited in the hotel's lobby for the airport shuttle they had booked earlier that morning. One suitcase each, a Samsonite and a Pierre Cardin. They hadn't discussed yesterday night, acted as if nothing had happened. They had the same flight to Chicago where they would part. He on to London, she to Vienna. Now he knew, he would want to see her again, in Europe. It would be easier. They had come through this crazy experience and he realised how much she had touched his heart.

The blue mini-coach finally arrived, ten minutes late and he picked up the suitcases and carried them to the pavement. As he was about to give her case to the shuttle's driver, Susi put her hand on his arm.

"Yes?"

He had never realised how green her eyes were.

"I'm not coming," she calmly said. "There's nothing for me back home. I'm staying in New Orleans."

"But . . ."

She silenced him with a tender kiss to his cheek. When he tried to talk again, she just quietly put a finger to his lip indicating he should remain silent.

"No," she said. "No explanations. It's better like this."

The driver urged him to get on board.

As the shuttle moved down Burgundy, he looked out of the window and saw Susi walking to a parked car with her suitcase. Louis stood next to it. The shuttle turned the corner and he lost them from sight.

The short drive to Moisan was the loneliest and the longest he had taken in his life.

He would, in the following years, continue to write many stories. That was his job after all. In many of them, women had red hair, green eyes and bodies of porcelain white. And terrible things happened to them: rape, multiple sex, prostitution, drug addiction, even unnatural forced sexual relationships with domestic animals. But they all accepted their fate with a quiet detachment.

He would continue to occasionally meet up with strange men and take uncommon pleasure in sucking them off. This he did with serene indifference, because in his mind it didn't count. It was just sex, meat, it was devoid of feelings.

He never visited New Orleans or saw or heard of Susi again.

The Heart in My Garden

Carol Queen

These days there's a lot of money to be made if you're in the right place at the right time, if you keep your shoulder to the wheel. That's how Mike and Katherine got their nice house, their cars (hers with that new-car smell still in it), an art collection, and a healthy nest egg. The house is close to San Francisco. Her car is a Mercedes. The art is mostly modern, up-and-coming painters you'll read about in *Art Week* any day now.

They're young enough that they don't have to worry about kids yet, so they don't – if you asked them, both would say, "Oh, kids are definitely on the agenda," though they'd sound a little vague. They're old enough that the honeymoon's over, neither of them quite remembering when it ended.

Seven years is a long time to be married. Still, aside from that, things are sweet. The rhythm of their weekdays, long-familiar now, has them clacking along toward the weekend like they're on a polished set of tracks. They fill weekends with rituals of their own.

It dawns on Katherine very, very gradually that she can't remember the last time they made love. She knows they did when they spent that weekend in Monterey – Mike's last birthday. In that romantic B&B, how could they resist the impulse to fall into each other's arms? And it's always a little exciting to be away from home. But they had to break it off in time to get in a day at the aquarium – the whole reason they went – so Mike could see the shimmery glow-in-the-dark jelly-fish, delicate neon tendrils floating in the black water. He had seen a special about them on the Discovery channel, had to see for himself. She lost her heart to them too: she and Mike stayed in the darkened room for almost an hour, silent, side by side with their hands clasped together so lightly that for minutes at a time she lost track of the sensation of his skin against her palm.

That's what she likes about being with him. It's so easy. They can drive together silently, not feeling as if a conversational black hole has swallowed them; they can spend Sunday mornings reading the paper and trading sections with a touch on the arm; they fill each other's coffee mugs without being asked and hand back the steaming, fragrant cups accompanied by a little kiss. After that they work in the garden, sometimes side by side, sometimes like her grandparents used to: Granddad in the vegetables, Gram in the flowers. She can imagine the next fifty years passing this way.

They must have had sex since Monterey – that's four months ago – but she can't remember it. Mostly now they do it late at night, right before sleep, but it's not on a schedule like practically everything else. Neither is it very predictable, tied to watching the Playboy channel or *Real Sex* on HBO; lately they don't watch those shows much anyway. If you asked Katherine, she'd probably say she doesn't really notice, nor does she notice being turned on, wanting sex, thinking about it very often. There was a time when she lived in almost constant arousal, but that was years ago. She and Mike had just met; she was so much younger then. She's always too busy now, tired all the time, except when they get away for a few days. And they haven't had time to leave town since that weekend in Monterey. Katherine's lawyer; Mike's software company will go public early next year. And if you asked Katherine whether her friends have more sex than she and Mike, she'd probably tell you not much – everybody's so busy now. Everyone has to concentrate on reaching for the brass ring. How else could you afford a house with a garden, two cars, the basics?

Katherine masturbates sometimes after Mike has fallen asleep. Lines of code lull him into light snoring, while Katherine's legal cases keep her awake. She goes over arguments, making mental checklists of every point she'll have to hit when she's in court the next day. She considers this productive time, until she has it organized in her mind – then the arguments begin to repeat themselves and she's so wound up over them she can't nod off. When she gets to this point, she pulls her vibrator out of the nightstand. It's one of those quiet vibrators, barely audible – even though Mike sleeps right next to her, once his breath has evened and slowed she won't wake him.

If you asked her, Katherine would admit that this proximity feels erotic: a little illicit but comfortable too, like the comfort of being with him while they weed or watch glowing aquarium fish in companionable silence. She sometimes slows down her breath to match the rhythm of his, a lingering synchronicity within which they are alive, alone, together – it doesn't matter that he's not conscious of her; it calms her down. Her climax, when it comes, drifts up on her gradually, and its power always surprises her.

Sometimes she gently places herself against him: pressing against his back when he's turned away from her, or reaching out with just her toes to make contact with his soft-furred calf. It's funny that she doesn't necessarily think of making love with him during these times, but in a way she *is* making love with him. If you asked her, Katherine would say that Mike knows she's doing it, knows it in his sleep. (When she first developed this habit she used to ask him if he had dreamed about anything in particular, but he could never call up sexual dreams. Or if he knew, he never said so.) Katherine respects Mike's sleep too much to thrash or buck, and really this is more about her own tension than about passion. And a tension-tamer orgasm can be quiet, an implosion that rocks her to sleep without rocking her world.

She wakes up refreshed the next morning and goes to court.

*   *   *

Mike has his own private time a couple of days a week, after Katherine leaves for the courthouse. He works a flex schedule, a perk of having stayed at his job for over five years, and two days a week he works at home. He's just as efficient at the home office as at the one downtown, even though this one overlooks his and Katherine's garden. In fact, he's *more* efficient at home, getting at least as much work done in less time. He takes one if not two breaks to jack off, the first in the still-rumpled bedclothes right after Katherine leaves (she accepts without question that Mike will make the bed on the days he stays home).

The first one is his favourite, especially because the bed still smells faintly of Katherine; he buries his nose in the pillow and lets the scent keep him company as he strokes himself hard. It's his way of keeping her comfortably close, even though she's already halfway to work by the time he begins. He takes plenty of time, a slow hand-over-hand on his cock while his mind wanders; he's in no hurry. His eyes closed, usually, he drifts through a lifetime's worth of mental images until he finds the one that sends a jolt of heat through his cock, maybe makes it jump a little in his hand. That's the one he'll use, embellishing it into a fully fleshed-out fantasy. If you asked him, he'd say he doesn't feel that he guides the fantasy. He feels like he's along for the ride, almost like the folio of erotic images riffling inside his brain has a life of its own, each separate image, in fact, a separate reality that he's simply stumbled into the way Captain Kirk is thrust into a new dimension if his crew doesn't set the transporter controls just right.

For half an hour twice a week Mike drifts in and out of dreams that take him to all sorts of places, sometimes even out of himself. When his orgasm comes it almost always swells up like music at the climax of a movie, the place in the plot where you're supposed to just give yourself over to the story, cry if it tells you to, or clench your fists in fear. When he's done he almost always writes code for two or three solid hours before even thinking of making himself some lunch.

When the weather permits he takes his sandwich out into the garden.

He doesn't always take a masturbation break in the afternoon. Sometimes he's on a roll and wants nothing more than to work – Katherine comes home at six or seven and finds him still at it, though on those days he falls asleep really early. But once every week or two he gives himself an hour or two to surf the Net.

He has his favorite sites bookmarked. On the Net he always travels with a tour guide, the sensibility of all his favourite webmasters leading him into cul-de-sacs of sexual possibility he hadn't even known existed. Katherine uses the Net for e-mail and shopping at Amazon.com – for her it's just a handy extension of the local mall – but Mike goes to the bad neighbourhoods and stays there as long as he can.

He thinks about going in and never coming out. Only his work ethic stops him from spending all day in this perpetual peepshow. If he overindulges, he knows, he could get his telecommuting privileges yanked, so he doles out his Web visits, perks he allows himself when he's done a good afternoon's work.

In Mike's mind there's no infidelity in exploring chat rooms and cybersex sites as long as he stops before Katherine gets home, as long as she's busy doing something else. He's never told her about it but he doesn't think she'd mind, as long as he gets his work done and their marriage doesn't suffer. For all he knows, she has her own favourite bookmarks on her computer at the office. He wouldn't mind that; it's just play, nothing real. Virtual.

It isn't often that Katherine comes home early. Once in a while she can get out at midafternoon on Friday, usually because she and Mike have decided to go up to the wine country or to a spa weekend. In the eighteen months Mike's been working at home, she's never arrived home before 5:30.

He makes sure he's zipped up by then, either back at work on his code or in the kitchen starting dinner. They often cook together, and sometimes Mike has dinner waiting when she has to work late. She pages him and dials "7:30" – he knows that's when to expect her. He doesn't even call back unless he needs to ask her to swing by the store for bread or a bottle of wine. They shop on Saturdays, though, so usually everything he needs is waiting in the kitchen. Mike likes to cook. So does she, though she rarely makes dinner by herself.

Today, though, the judge continues Katherine's case because a prosecution witness didn't show up. She's out of the courtroom at noon. She usually eats with the rest of her team on court days, so they go around the corner to the little Italian place. It's so close to the courthouse that Katherine almost always recognizes most of the diners – judges, other attorneys, people from the jury pool.

She's working with Marla today, the newest member of the practice. Marla's just married, still trying to balance an intense work life with being in love. She's never late, but Katherine has seen her come to work breathy and flushed – if you asked her, Katherine would say she remembers those newlywed days when once in the morning and once at night wasn't enough, when she and Mike would sometimes skip dinner because they were on each other the minute they got home, when once Mike even got them a motel room at noon.

Marla fishes around in her purse and shows off the set of cufflinks she's gotten Bill for Valentine's Day. They're porcelain ovals with tiny pictures painted on them: one has a bottle of champagne, one a can-can girl with her ruffled skirts thrown high. "Wine, women, and song!" says Marla gaily. "And I got him a really good bottle of French champagne, and I'm taking him to see *Cabaret*. Katherine, what are you doing with Mike?"

Katherine hasn't planned anything special with Mike because she's forgotten that today is Valentine's Day. Jesus, wasn't it just Christmas?

"Ummm, just a really nice dinner and some private time." This is the best Katherine can come up with without notice, but it satisfies Marla, who has very few brain cells to spare for thinking about Katherine and Mike. She's probably too busy imagining the way she'll tug Bill into an alley when they leave the theater, and give him a sneaky handjob right there in public, Katherine thinks, only a little sniffy about Marla's single-minded focus. You're only young once.

Still, with the afternoon suddenly free, Katherine decides to give Mike a Valentine's Day surprise. He's probably forgotten it too – he's been just as busy as she has – but thank goodness it's a holiday that lends itself to last-minute planning. Katherine detours by Real Foods on the way home, picks up a good wine, some big prawns for scampi, a couple of cuts of filet mignon. On the way to the register she passes the bakery and adds a little chocolate cake to her basket. "Strawberries too," she thinks, "if they're any good yet." The store has a heap of huge ruby berries that look like they were grown in the Garden of Eden. And right next to the flowers stands a card display. She picks one that looks like a handmade Martha Stewart crafts project, a slightly-out-of-focus heart against a sapphire-blue background, blank so she can customize its message. She stops at the coffee shop downstairs for a latte and writes "Dearest Michael, you are the heart in my garden. All my love, Kath."

She thinks about using the pager – "3:30" – but decides against it, decides instead to slip in and surprise him. If she can get into the kitchen via the back door, she might be able to start dinner quietly without interrupting his work. She parks the Mercedes a couple of houses down from theirs.

Her grandparents' house and garden were in Idaho: at this time of year the garden would be cut back and mulched, maybe even buried under a drift of snow. Katherine loves living in California because even in February the garden blooms with life. The roses are finally gone but the pink ladies, tulips, and irises are starting; in the corner calla lilies burst whitely out of a clutch of huge green leaves. When she picks them she always includes one of those big leaves in the vase; otherwise the sculptural, curved callas almost don't look like flowers.

Passing the window of the room in which Mike works, she glimpses him, so riveted to the screen that he doesn't see her. "Must be on a roll," she thinks, but then she sees that he is moving in a way that she wouldn't expect to see from a man writing code. Though his body is partly obscured behind the desk and monitor, it almost looks as if he is masturbating.

Katherine noiselessly lets herself into the house and heaps her shopping bags onto the kitchen work island. She lays the store-bought roses carefully on top, drops her purse and briefcase beside them, slips off her shoes. She makes it to the door of Mike's office without being heard.

He's on a roll, all right: onscreen Katherine sees not lines of code but a tiny movie looping repeatedly, a naked man in a blindfold lying on his back, a woman in a shiny black catsuit – it looks like it's made of rubber – crouching over him. The suit encases her body completely, except for her crotch, which is naked, shaved bare, and she engulfs the man's hard, upstanding cock over and over with the shockingly exposed pussy – at least, Katherine finds it shocking, but not in a bad way, more like a shock to the system, cold water in the face, waking her up to feelings she barely remembers.

Clearly, Mike has not forgotten anything. His hand pumps his cock rhythmically, eyes riveted on the miniature tableau as the catsuited woman thrusts down and down and down. He times his hand strokes to the woman's down thrusts, just as Katherine herself times her late-night strokes to Mike's slow and even breaths.

If you asked her why she isn't upset, discovering him like this, she might tell you it's like her own late-night forays, only so much hotter: she's never seen Mike jack off in the daylight; she hasn't seen his cock this hard in years; she's erotically attuned to his deep breaths from all those nights lying next to him, vibrator or no vibrator; she's fascinated by the tiny couple on the screen, smaller than Barbie and Ken; and the fact that Mike finds them so compelling makes her pussy wet. That her pussy is wet in the middle of the afternoon is such a welcome surprise that all she can do for a minute is touch herself through her fine cotton stockings, the black fabric clinging to her almost as tightly as the tiny woman's shiny catsuit, Katherine's mind spins, looking for a way to incorporate this unexpected scene into her surprise Valentine's Day celebration. Silently she begins to unbutton her grey rayon suit.

Mike's erotic reverie has advanced him so close to orgasm that when he feels a hand stroke his thigh and replace his own hand on his cock, it could easily be a part of the virtual connection he's having with the woman onscreen. For a second he doesn't even look to see who is holding him. Then he's recognizes Katherine's hand, a touch he knows almost as well as his own, and sure enough, when he glances away from the screen, she is crouched beside him. She wears nothing but her black bra, which snugly cups her breasts, and her black tights.

Smoothly she stands up, pulling him by the cock, and pushes the office chair across the room. "Lie down, Michael," she whispers. "So you can see the screen."

The rug, fuzzy against the back of his neck, gives him just enough cushion. When Katherine stands over him the screen is obscured, but that doesn't matter because she is taking the crotch of her tights in both hands and sharply ripping, tearing a hole like the one in the woman's catsuit. Katherine's pussy is pink, swelling, her arousal beginning to form visible moisture like dew on the callas' broad leaves. Mike strokes her thighs, reaching for her.

Katherine crouches down over him, and as her pussy makes contact with his rigid cock the woman onscreen is visible again. Katherine's tight wet pussy sucks at him. He's aware of the rug under his back, Katherine's weight poised just above his pelvis, her thigh muscles pumping as she matches the catsuit woman's thrusts, again, again, again. Mike's hands rove her body as he climbs again toward the climax she had interrupted. Her hands rest on his chest for balance, for contact with him, and he feels their pressure through his nipples. On the screen, the blindfolded man is completely under the catsuited woman's control.

Mike thrusts up into Katherine, his eyes wide, flashing from her to the screen, from her to the screen. He slips one hand through her brown hair, pulling the clip that holds it back in its demure professional style. The thick silky hair falls through his fingers, into her face, curtaining eyes that are getting wilder and wilder. Her breasts fill his hands; he squeezes, remembering their ripeness. Now their pelvises grind together, his cock thrusts up into her as deeply as it will go, both of them climb toward climax: maybe not together, but close. She has slipped to her knees, straddling him, her weight on him now, and he lifts her like she's riding a bucking pony when he thrusts into her. Onscreen the catsuit lady and her blinkered paramour have not changed; their fuck can never escalate. But Mike and Katherine are leaving them behind.

Almost. Without warning Katherine moves her hands. She puts them over his eyes, a moist, fleshly blindfold.

"Fuck me, Mike!" she hisses. "Hard!"

If you asked him now, Mike would groan that he has missed her, missed this, before bucking involuntarily into a come that she has taken from him, imperious and powerful in her ripped tights, that he could not hold back from her, that she demanded.

He has barely stopped shaking when she slides up his body, threads from the torn stockings tickling his nose, her hot, swollen pussy at the tip of his tongue: the catsuit woman demanding service, Katherine demanding pleasure, letting him drink from her. He laps like a cat until she yelps, convulses against his tongue, collapses on him. For a few seconds he rests under her body like it's a tent and he's a kid hiding from everything.

They walk into the kitchen naked and steamed from a long shower. It still isn't quite 5:00 – on an ordinary day she wouldn't even be home from work yet.

She'd intended to make him dinner, but he insists on helping like he usually does, and begins rinsing the prawns

while she runs water into a crystal vase, slices an inch off the
stems of the roses, arranges them. They're red for Valentine's Day; the store hadn't even bothered to order any other
colour.

"Put a little sugar in there," says Mike. "They're wilting."

By the time the filets are on the grill the roses are perking
up.

"Look," Katherine says. "You were right about the sugar.
Hey, what's that beneath the vase?"

He opens the card, reads the message, kisses her, and sets
the blurry heart up against the vase. After dinner they put on
jackets and take their wineglasses out to the garden.

Les Jardins de Kensington

Justine Dubois

Her pale eyes flutter, as all thought deserts her. She holds his hand, a hand more rough and ready than the rest of him. He is otherwise all elegance; the eloquent drape of his body in a low slung chair, the tilt of his tall, handsome head, a look in his features chiselled by intelligence and self-deprecation. He is the eminence grise of her life and of his own.

No one knows that she still sees him. Her friends never approved. And yet, they wonder what secret it is that makes her so very happy. He smiles down at her, his sweet curvaceous smile, joyous, rhythmic across his features. They stride, hand in hand, through the park. His eyes are opaque until they glance at her, whereupon they dance with blue animation. The circle around his pale iris is cornflower blue.

They should be jaded with love. They have broken all its rules. And yet, passion remains, like a curious personal blessing between them, the most reliable, the most courageous thing they know.

Kensington Gardens are deserted. A rough wind plays through the trees. The Orangery, where in summer they take elegant lunches, is like a space wiped clean, its distempered walls grey with shadowed light, a graceful husk and mausoleum, surrounded by the dot-dash of fat topiary. Leaves scud across the gravel.

Her lover leads the way, his long stride longer than hers. There is a bleak glamour of winter about the place. It is about to rain. He is undeterred. He makes his way to the formal gardens just beyond the topiary dance sequences, gardens surrounded by tall hedgerows, where, in summer, fountains play modestly against banks of flowers, primary cacophany, such as Gertrude Jekyll refused to recommend. The round pond is beyond, just visible through the toothless bushes, the blind windows of Kensington Palace behind them.

He checks his watch. It is 3.25 pm. They have just lunched together at The Royal China, where old Hong Kong meets old Queensway. They have drunk tea with blossoms floating in it.

"What are you waiting for?" she enquires gently.

"A client of mine. He said he would be here," he replies distractedly, his tall neck scanning the fragmented hedgerows. "I am selling him the Kandinsky."

They hear the light pace of a foot on gravel. A young man approaches. She has seen him before somewhere. At a private view maybe? Her lover smiles. The young man nods in acknowledgement. He looks serious. His dark eyes scan the familiar features of her lover briefly and then dwell more completely on her. He perceives her shyness, her modesty, her amiability.

She smiles at him and then looks up at her lover trustingly. The young man perceives her love, but is not deflected. His eyes sweep her features. She is dark-haired, Italian maybe. She has the figure of a young girl. Everything is just enough, but at no point too much. Her waist is slender, her hips rounded, her breasts high and pert. Nothing about her is overblown. Best of all, in her face is both sadness and joy. It makes her more desirable. He understands his friend's passion. They shake hands and her lover laughs. "Why did we meet here?" she asks. The two men smile. "Business. Let's walk some more."

They walk on comfortably together, she walking easily between the two men. They chatter nonchalantly. They discuss painting, Der Blaue Reiter. She glances at the young man. His looks, like hers, are darker than those of her lover. He too is Latin, or maybe Scottish, with some of its Latin ancestry. They reach the exit to the gardens. His features are almost too lean, too spartan, for someone so young, and yet their lines speak of beauty. There is something crisp about the curtailment of his nose, something proud about the shape of his head, with its tall shock of hair en brosse. He is less tall than her lover, closer in height to herself. He too has a beautiful smile, flashing, immediate, and his body is a wand, not of elegance, but of secret, sinuous strength and compactness, a feline economy of suppressed movement and emotion. His eyes dance in approval as they range over her.

Beyond the park gates, they cross the road, at the point where all the busy tedium of Kensington High Street begins. To their right is the Royal Garden Hotel tower, opposite is the old fashioned pedantry of the Kensington Hotel. "How do you know this place?" she asks, as they pass through its greenery-yallery conservatory coffee shop to the foyer, bypassing the side street entrance. "I don't. Key number 44," demands her lover.

"You have never been here before?"

"Only this morning to arrange this meeting." She looks up at him surprised, but still trusting. They mount the old, tired Axminster carpet, with its connotations of respectability, to a suite of rooms, which overlook the park and the walk from which they have just come. Kensington Palace and the round pond are framed in the distance.

The colours of the suite are dark and dismal and expensive; dark polished wood next to brick red counterpane, next to beige carpet, next to sage green curtains, and chiffon lampshades.

"What a hideous room," she says.

"Warm nevertheless," replies her lover appreciatively. A knock on the door and a trainee hotel manageress arrives with a tea tray of miniature cakes and sandwiches and pots of Darjeeling tea and slices of lemon. The men's eyes follow her as she moves around the room adjusting the curtains, the phone by the bed, the counterpane. Her lover tries to tip her generously. She declines, looking at him strangely. She calls him "Sir". She hesitates and then leaves to check the other rooms. They hear the click of a door.

The three of them exchange glances. "Why are we here?" She puts down her bag. For one faint moment, the look in her lover's eye is imperious, greedy. "I want to watch you make love to someone else." She blushes. The young man feels her embarrassment like a stab of pain. Instinctively, he puts out his hand to reassure her. Her lover throws himself into an armchair, draping himself in elegance and comfort. She turns towards him in panic. From behind her, quiet-voiced, the young man asks, "Do you agree to this?" His eyes scan hers carefully. She witnesses his concern.

"I don't know," she answers shyly. "Why would you want to?" she begins to ask. He takes her hand.

"Let's try, let's take it slowly," he says. "If you change your mind . . ." His sentence trails unfinished. But she feels reassured. He removes her coat and gently lays it on the bed. She steps from her shoes. She glances back at her lover sprawled in the armchair. His eyes are bright blue. He smiles back at her, a mixture of reassurance and daring.

The young man casts him a look of contempt. He removes her skirt and throws it at a distant chair. She glances back at her lover. His head is turned away, as if distracted by some distant sound. She raises her hands dutifully above her head, like those of a baby girl having her jumper removed. The young man watches her intently. He traces a tear on her cheek. Beneath her clothes she is dressed demurely, not like a seductress at all. She wears a long satin slip, embroidered and embellished with panels of cream lace. She looks curiously old-fashioned.

The young man's breath catches in his throat. Instinctively, he reaches for her. Her lover coughs. They glance at him. He is smiling. The young man holds her narrow shoulders tenderly in his fine splayed hands, hands more elegant than those of her lover. He kisses her brow and the side of her neck beneath her ear, kisses her startled eyelids closed, and then, lastly, her mouth, a gentle, hesitant flutter

of a kiss, a soft measurement of warmth and pillowed softness. He allows a moment of adjustment to the new perfume
between them.

Her eyes remain closed. Against the dark screen of her
mind, she thinks of her lover. His mouth explores her neck,
forcing her head backwards, arching her frame to his hold
over her. She begins to enjoy the idea of being watched, of
pleasing him. Will her lover be aroused? He lowers the straps
of her slip and bra and kisses the tenderness of her girlish
breasts. The folds of her slip collect softly around the
narrowness of her waist. She is beautiful, exquisite in her
simplicity. Her eyes open briefly. The young man meets her
gaze. Her eyes are suddenly focused on him, tender with
appreciation. The look between them is long and considered.

She hears the sound of a door opening. And then his lips
again seek her mouth and tenderness is replaced by passion.
He draws her towards the bed. He pulls her towards him, at
one moment stretching his lean body against her, gathering at
her softness, and then, at another, arching himself above her,
in order to control and pleasure and enjoy her. They are like
dancers.

She now responds to every nuance of his touch. Her eyes
remain closed. All is feeling between them. A light touch of
pressure on the side of her waist and her body moves,
opening to his. His hand beneath her waist inspires the
greedy raising of her hips to him. Is her lover proud, watching her? He enters her, and it is as though she had always
been his. She opens her eyes briefly, in astonishment, sees
her own feelings reflected in his. Was this what her lover had
intended, that she should fall in love? She closes her eyes, her
mind. Her body racks with sweet pleasure.

The young man's arms cradle her, watching, waiting for
her. She does not remember his name. And then his limbs too
race against hers. She feels the fullness of his love. He calls
out in a soft muffled sound of surrender to the moment. His
body folds into hers in tenderness. All is familiarity and trust.
They open their eyes briefly to look at one another. Nothing

but smiles and serenity between them. They shut them again, and then, simultaneously, they remember. They sit up in unison and turn towards the chair, but it is deserted. Her lover is framed in the doorway, his head turned from them. He wears his jacket and tie. His trousers fold like loose chains about his ankles. The young woman manageress kneels before him, as in a devotional painting.

Ignored, they watch every passionate move.

Sodomy and Sorcery

Mark Ramsden

For a while sex with strap-ons became such a thrill that I wrote two versions of this scene for my next novel without noticing. I'm too mean to throw anything away so here is narrator Matt describing some passive anal sex. Along with transvestitism and various visualisations and invocations this was once part of a forbidden form of Viking sorcery known as Seithr or "seething" (that was their excuse, anyway). It was of course forbidden because warriors weren't supposed to do such things. It wasn't "manly". A thousand or so years later it's still thought "manly" to bash each other up at the footie or get drunk but some real men like to be fucked. Matt does, anyway . . . Sasha is a short American Dominatrix and Matt is her business manager (don't say pimp). Time Out *thinks they are a transgressive version of* The Avengers. *But that nice Emma Peel would never do this . . . Would she?*

Sasha places carrots, celery, menthol chewing gum and water within easy reach. The E is coming on. We can push my limits. And I do feel like a good servicing. Fore and aft. Truly, madly and deeply. And, for once, I don't even have to ask. Or beg. Or plead. Or wheedle. Sasha straps Little Sasha on, looking very determined. There's actually nothing that minuscule about this prime specimen of dick-shaped silicone. (Silicone conducts body heat. *So* much better than horrid plastic and rubber.)

"Come on!" I tell her. Although I did promise myself I wouldn't beg.

"Wait!" she tells me. "And it's easier on your back anyway."

For once I do her bidding. Anything to encourage her to get a move on.

"Look at you!" she says, rubbing it in before she sticks it in. "You're gagging for it!"

"Yeah, yeah. Well, maybe I got tired of servicing Madame. Keeping up with *her* unreasonable demands. It's time someone looked after *me* for a change."

She smiles enigmatically. Can I really have had the last word? Is this a dream? I hook my heels above her shoulders. She rummages inside me with a cold dollop of Vaseline that liquefies and warms and spreads itself just where it's needed.

"Shush, now! You little slut!"

The tone is affectionate, warm as buttered toast, sweet as her breath on my face. She rubs a finger inside her pussy and rubs it just beneath my nose, then smiles as some greedy little pig or other keeps moaning and groaning.

"Do it!" says the eager one.

"Wait!" she says. She rubs lube down the shaft of her purple prong.

We're not using Marvin today, the black dick-shaped one with realistic veins. Little Sasha is anything but petite, a phallic model in regal purple. Sasha thrusts her (him?) skywards. It sways lewdly as she swings her lovely hips to and fro. Women do like playing with those things. So much so, that you might even think there was something in Freud's penis envy theory.

At last it looks as if she is ready but she makes me beg once more, smiling as she does so. It's cute watching Sasha's tongue lolling out of her mouth as she aims her prong. And soon I really know what it is like to be a woman, as some vigorous but clumsy thrusts go everywhere except the orifice in question.

After some very unladylike swearing we have lift-off. It's in. And it's a big one. Good. Golly. Miss. Molly. Ooh-ee. But I'm not the only one chewing the duvet. Sasha is grunting like a drunken hog. It's a power thing, maybe. Or maybe the reverse thrust is scrunching her bits the way she wants them scrunched. Something is afoot and it's more than holding hands at the movies, more than a middle-class dinner party, more than reheating last night's soap operas.

Keri Pentauk calls the prostate the "he-spot", the male G-spot. It certainly likes being touched. And as the bliss-waves spread outwards even I don't feel so grumpy any more. Sasha's good at this. She's thorough. Industrious. I like the cut of her jib. Academics who never do this stuff see chicks with dicks as a metaphor for women taking control of their lives. Because they only look at pictures of it. But what it *feels* like is a thoroughly good stuffing. Meat, roast potatoes and all the trimmings. And, what's even better, you can have passive anal sex without having to do it with horrid men with moustaches. You don't have to listen to Barbara Streisand or House music, neither do you have to screech hysterically at the Eurovision Song Contest. You don't have to listen to singer Tom Robinson either. Although I'm not alone there. There's a lot of people not listening to him.

I digress. After a considerable period of filthy horrid swinishness there is an exchange of Tantric multi-orgasms. Holding my own sperm in shoots the energy around my body and leaves me gasping, swearing and praying for mercy. It's almost *too* good. Don't believe me? Well this sort of thing isn't going to be written up in the *Guardian*. Or on *Eastenders*. Or in lifestyle mags. But I don't like to preach. Getting drunk and watching the footie is of course an equally valid option, as is twittering on and on about mythical ideal husbands.

Some time later, after the big hugs, we give each other a sheepish smile.

"I only do it because you like it," I say.

"That's all right, babe," she says, patting me sympathetically. "It's so considerate of you to keep on trying to please me like this."

Not too much later we cuddle up for the drift sleepwards,

all spooned up. My blood feels like warm champagne. She has her arms around me, purring and humming happily. I am turned away, looking for Kate's face in the darkness. Still restless. Still searching.

Do What You Love

Susannah Indigo

Sitting up here on the kitchen counter with my blue plaid skirt up over my hips and my legs spread open, I watch him slice carrots for the soup. He likes me to sit here and tell him stories about my day in school. Especially about boys. When he walked in he lifted me up onto the counter without a word, pulled my panties off, spread my legs and propped my knees up. He watches my bare pussy and cooks while I talk. This may be the kinkiest Daddy I have ever had.

"Eddie Burke pulled my skirt up again after math class, Daddy," I begin. I know he loves this, and it's a true story, just a very old one. "And then he said I was a slut because he looked at my panties and they were blue and not white. I hate him."

Daddy comes over and kisses me, stroking his fingers across my clit. This is part of what makes him so kinky, those damn fingers. I've never seen his cock in the daylight, but he drives me wild with his fingers.

"Those little boys who tease you in school don't even know what a clit is, do they, baby?" he says. His fingers are everywhere. It's his fingers and the spankings that get to me. This Daddy can spank me like nobody else can. I think it's because he makes me wait so long – always talking about what he's going to do, talking about how my ass looks when I'm over his knee, about how deep his finger is going to go up my ass if I don't hold still for him.

The only time I ever feel his cock is in the middle of the night, long after he's brushed my teeth and read me a bedtime story and dressed me in the soft pink ruffled nightgown he bought for me. Then, when I'm sound asleep, I'll wake up on my belly with his weight on top of me and the nightgown raised to my waist and his lips against my ear, whispering, "It's OK, baby, Daddy's here, it's OK, Daddy will make you feel better, just lift your bottom up in the air for Daddy, yes, baby," and his hard cock forces its way all at once up into my pussy and Daddy whispers and rocks his hips hard into me and I cry a little bit because I'm not ready and it hurts and that makes him fuck me harder and harder until I'm more than ready and Daddy comes hard and fast up inside of me and he falls back asleep with his full weight pressing me down into the bed, whispering, "You're such a good little girl, you're so good to your Daddy. You make your Daddy come so hard."

It really does hurt, in an intensely erotic kind of way. But he's not the Daddy that worries me.

A book got me started in this, one of the dozens of motivational ones I read back when I worked for a corporation and thought I needed it. "Do What You Love, The Money Will Follow" was the name of it and I liked that one because it told me what I wanted to hear: that you could make money having fun. I already knew what my kind of fun was – painting, feeling sexy, and getting well fucked.

Money and energy underlie all our dreams, no matter what those dreams are. They said I was a good painter back in college but then real life and two babies – their father is long-gone – took over my energy and priorities. I started my own graphic design business on a surge of energy, but it exhausted me trying to make ends meet.

Not long after I read that book, I found myself at a charity masquerade ball at the Black Palace Hotel. I wasn't planning on going, but my friend Cheryl dragged me there at the last minute. All I could find to wear was my high school cheerleader outfit.

*   *   *

"Katie," Cheryl whispered to me over by the bar where I was spending most of my time. "See that man over there, the one with the silver hair and the black cape?" I did. "He's so toasted! You won't believe this. He pointed to you and said, 'I'd give anything to fuck that little cheerleader.'"

I turned and smiled at him. I smoothed my little green-and-white pleated skirt, which has the same effect on men that it had on boys in my senior year of high school.

"Tell him I have my price."

"What?"

"Ask him what it's worth." I could blame it on the wine if I had to, but I was really tired of being so straight and working so hard.

Cheryl had been drinking enough that she marched over to him without hesitation. She came back in a few minutes, laughing. "He says a thousand bucks, cash."

"You're kidding." I looked down at my tennis shoes and bobby socks. "Tell him he's on – to bring me the cash and a room key and he's in for a fantasy night."

Cheryl likes to be adventurous through other people – she works for the biggest bank in town and doesn't get around too much. "I'll check the room number, just in case I never see you again," she said.

When my pink-nightgown Daddy leaves in the morning he tucks the sheet up around my chin, kisses me chastely on the cheek, leaves the thousand dollars on my dresser and closes the door softly. That's all he wants – to tease me mercilessly all evening in my schoolgirl clothes and then fuck me hard and fast in the middle of the night. There are worse ways to earn a living.

I kept the name of my graphics business, Ariel Design, and still use the corporate identity just as though I was spending untold hours at my Mac producing work for clients to pick apart. I think of this as my Little Girl Slut business, delivering dreams to men with plenty of money and fantasies. I'm even thinking of writing one of those motivational books of my own – "The 7 Habits of Highly Effective Sluts." I pay taxes on all of this, of course. I'm not an unethical person. I just happen to be illegal in this state.

That first night dressed as a cheerleader was wild. He treated me like a bimbo and I loved it. I was so tired of being smart all day long. He told me to keep my long dark brown hair in the ponytail, stripped my letter-sweater off of me, and made me lay across the bed while he lifted my pleated skirt. "This," he said, "is for every girl who ever snubbed me in high school." He started to spank me with his bare hand. I had no idea how much I would like being spanked. He made me perform a cheer for him naked. The fucking afterwards was ordinary after the intensity of the spanking, but he did pay me the thousand dollars, cash.

I spent weeks afterward sliding between feeling cheap and getting so hot I had to masturbate several times a day. I loved it, but I could never tell anyone except Cheryl about it.

I called the cheerleader-fuck man up at his office a month later and told him how much I enjoyed our evening. He told me if I really liked it he knew where I could get lots more.

My first real "trick" – such a cheap word – called me beforehand and explained what he wanted. I was nervous – I had Cheryl run a credit check on him, as though that would help. Now she does that for all my new Daddies. Running unauthorized credit checks was a walk on the wild side for her, so of course I started to kickback some of my tips her way.

"Katie," my first real Daddy said, "I want you to call me nothing but Daddy when I'm with you." That's what they all want. Daddy fantasies run deep and they're not so uncommon. My name is carefully passed around to certain men. "And I want you to wear a little girl dress – deep green taffeta. Petticoats, white cotton panties, little white socks, patent leather shoes. Your hair pulled back in two white barrettes. No make up, no nail polish. The suite's reserved – see you on Friday at seven."

It was hard to find just the right little-girl frilly dress for a size ten woman, but I did, and as I dressed before the full-length mirror and slipped on the patent leather shoes and wiped the lipstick from my lips, I got a little scared – I actually felt like a little girl. I wanted to sit on the floor of that luxurious hotel suite and wait for my Daddy to come home and take care of me.

Which is exactly what I did. When he arrived, this man I now call my petticoat Daddy, he stood in front of me in his expensive suit and shining loafers and told me to stay where I was on the floor and to be a good girl and kiss his feet. Just those words made me wet. I bent over and kissed each foot slowly.

He took off his jacket and walked across the room near the full-length mirror on the wall. "Crawl to me, baby. Crawl to Daddy."

I stayed on my hands and knees and crawled to him, unable to take my eyes from his. He stood me up in front of the mirror, lifted my stiff petticoats and began to examine me. It took a long time. He pulled off my white cotton panties and told me he expected my pussy-hair to be completely gone by the next time we met. He approved of the white plastic barrettes in my hair and said the size of my breasts was just perfect for little-girl clothes.

He explained that I could never wear a bra because little-girl nipples were meant to be seen at all times.

"Yes, Daddy," I said obediently.

He pushed me back down on my knees. "Unzip my pants, little girl. Daddy wants his cock down your throat."

I opened my mouth and he wrapped his fists in my hair and fucked my mouth like it had never been fucked before. I could see the image in the mirror – a little girl serving her Daddy. He stopped before he came and threw me down on my belly, lifted my petticoats, spread my legs and knelt over me.

"Daddy wants your ass, little girl."

My first Daddy fucked me until I couldn't move that night. My mouth, my ass, my pussy, my breasts. I never got off of the floor or even took the green taffeta dress off. It was covered with come when he left.

"Say 'thank you, Daddy'," he commanded before leaving. "And get that dress cleaned before next time."

I was torn between being glad he was leaving and begging him to stay to give me more. But I knew he'd left the thousand dollars on the table and that he was done with me for the moment.

"Thank you, Daddy," I whispered as I kissed his feet again before he walked out the door.

I looked at myself in the mirror after he left. I was a mess, but I loved what I saw. I was in business.

I had lunch with Cheryl at our usual table at the health club one day and noticed she was reading "What Color is Your Parachute?"

"I'm pretty sure my parachute's black," I told her.

Cheryl laughed and put the book down. "How can you do it, Katie?" she asked.

"By specializing."

"No, I'm serious."

"How can I do which part?" It's a good question to ask of anyone who doubts the value of selling your body. "Which part bothers you? That it's illegal? That I'm making serious money?"

"I don't know," she admitted. "Maybe the little girl part. What if you make these guys want real little girls? You could make them perverts."

I laughed. "No, I'm pretty sure they come to me as full-blown perverts. You know what they say about the correct conjugation of the word 'kinky' – I am erotic, you are kinky, they are perverts. We're all adults, and we're certainly all consenting."

Cheryl sighed. "You can never do anything simple.

Couldn't you just fuck them straight and skip the abnormal psych stuff?"

Of course not. The secret is that it turns me on as much as it does them. "I don't think my petticoat Daddy knows how to fuck straight, Cheryl. I can barely sit down after he leaves."

"Katie. I'm worried about you."

I told her not to worry. At least not about the sex I was having. But I carefully explained how she could make some extra money and help me if she wanted to – taking messages, clearing introductions. I promised not to call her my pimp on my business records – officially, she would be freelancing for me as a fact-checker.

Everything seems possible in this life. I can paint, I have time to bake cookies for my kids' classes. I can dream, I have time to hear myself think. I follow the natural rhythms of my body and stay up at night in my studio painting and sleep while my kids are at school. It takes time and space and focus to create dreams. But it's working – my paintings have started to sell, and I'm talking to the owner of a gallery about the possibility of my own show there in the spring. Henry Miller said it best – "Paint and die happy." All I have to do to get the time I need is to live out my sexual fantasies.

"You know I screen some by e-mail nowadays, Katie. Wait 'til you hear this one."

I always smile at the vision of Cheryl in her business suit and floppy bow tie sitting in front of her computer at her desk on the third floor of the bank, pimping for me.

"It's a woman. I told her no, women weren't your thing, but she says she's a Daddy too."

"Really? A female Daddy?" My imagination had stretched so far since I redesigned my business that everything seemed possible.

"Yeah. And a kinky one too. Look what she sent for you."

Cheryl slid me the folder with the information. On top of

the papers was a faxed photo of a well-known childhood doll. Except this doll was blindfolded, half-naked, and had her wrists and ankles tied together with bright pink ribbons.

"Oh, my." The doll was making me wet.

Cheryl looked at me in surprise and maybe a little bit of satisfaction. She seemed awfully interested in this woman.

"Well, you know," I finally said, wondering when my mind slid so far down between my legs, "maybe I can do it if she's a Daddy."

My doll Daddy rattled my brain from the first minute she arrived. She was tall, with black cropped hair, ruby red lipstick and a wicked grin that said she was ready to play.

She brought me a doll. I was already wearing a little girl pink leotard outfit, per her instructions, and now here I sat with my plastic twin. "Play with the doll for me," she commanded.

I knew right away that this Daddy and I had the same kind of girlhood. While some girls were making cute little prom dresses for their dolls, some of us were stripping her down, checking her out, making her the slut she was meant to be. Let's face it, that doll is built to get fucked.

She tied me up with pink satin ribbons just like the doll. She stood over me and fucked with my mind and then let me go to work on her body.

"Suck Daddy's breasts," she ordered, leaning down close to my mouth. "Yes, sweetheart, yes, suck Daddy's nipples harder."

I learned something incredible that first night with my doll Daddy. It didn't matter that I had no experience with women. My kink has nothing to do with gender.

"Lick Daddy's pussy, baby," she said, and she was straddling me and riding my mouth and I was tasting her juices and she was hard and I was soft and she was completely in control of me and taking me down where all good Daddies take me. I was her little doll and I was serving her and she made me bring her to orgasm over and over until she finally wrapped the pink ribbons loosely around both of our bodies and we fell asleep breast to breast, her knee pressed up hard against my own untouched pussy.

The doll sits on my office shelf as a reminder. Cheryl begged me for every single detail afterwards. I gave her the high points the best I could remember. I swear she's going to ask me to videotape it all before I know it.

The only problem in my big business plan is my charm-bracelet Daddy. He came into my life six months ago. My charm-bracelet Daddy took me to the amusement park on our first night together. He held me tight on the rollercoaster, ordered food for me and when we left he bought me a balloon and tied the string around my wrist. We went back to the hotel and spent the night together. There was no sex, and I just slept wrapped in his arms. It was intensely erotic. This Daddy not only rattles my brain, he rattles my heart. Nobody's been allowed to do that in so many years I'd forgotten how it could be.

In the morning he fastened the heavy silver charm bracelet around my wrist. There was just one charm – a silver Ferris wheel. "I know you, Katie," he whispered softly. "You'll wear this bracelet for me, and only for me." I did.

This Daddy gets to my heart like no one ever has. His name is Jeffrey and he's a writer. I know all their names, of course, but he's the only one I think of by name, since I'm not supposed to call them anything but Daddy. He ties me to the bed and tells me stories.

Sometimes he unbuttons my blouse and ties my hands behind my back and reads to me and I close my eyes and enter the warm and loving childhood I never had. A few times he's even tied me up and talked about baseball. He says he likes the captive audience.

He tells me it's all about power. He takes my control away little by little until it's all real and it's all new and it all matters. The sex is spectacular when he gets me like that – it's like I enter another space, another realm, where only the sensual and the artistic sides of life can be seen. This Daddy knows some secrets about me that even I don't know and it scares me more every time I see him.

There are ten charms on the bracelet now. Some of them are reminders of the places we've gone to – the Ferris wheel, a little sailboat, a rollerskate, a Rockies baseball cap. One of the prettiest ones is a little silver and gold pair of ballet slippers, a reminder of the night he took me to the ballet and we went out dancing afterward and he held his hands on my hips in just that way that only certain men know, making me beg him to take me home and fuck me.

The other three charms are a little more intense, from different kinds of nights when we never set foot out the door. There's a baby rattle, a miniature dildo, and a baby bottle. I could never explain them to anyone. It's enough to say that I was definitely doing what I loved when he gave them to me.

He's on his way over now. He's the only Daddy I've ever let come to my house. The kids are at Cheryl's and my upstairs studio is locked up. I've put on the outfit he requested – red halter top, blue jean short skirt that shows my ass if I bend over, bare feet. The charm bracelet weighs heavily on my wrist.

He brings dinner, a big bouquet of my favorite orange roses, a new Van Morrison CD and a small wrapped box. I sit on his lap to open it. His hand high and hard on my thigh makes me almost forget about presents.

I open it and it's a new charm, of course, signifying what we're going to do tonight, just as all the others have. I hold it up to the light. "It's beautiful, Daddy, thank you." A tiny silver paintbrush and palette. "It's very pretty. But I don't understand?"

Daddy kisses me like I'm his. "Take me upstairs, Katie, To your studio. It's time."

Nobody ever goes in there except close friends. "No."

Daddy finishes fastening the charm on my bracelet and

wraps my legs around his waist. "Yes, baby, you're going to let me into your life tonight. From now on, no more secrets. You're mine."

Only for tonight, I feel like saying, and only for a price. This is just business.

He stands up and carries me like a child up the stairs, pausing to get the studio key. "I know what you need," he whispers.

I don't stop him. Maybe it's the weight of the charms or maybe it's just the way he's holding me with my face buried in his neck. Or maybe it's the love I forgot existed.

He carries me around my studio and looks at every single canvas, admiring them and commenting in detail. He even seems to know something about art, thank God. But not as much as I do. I like that. He stops for a long time at the painting I made of a headstone with my imaginary epitaph on it:

KATHERINE ELLIS
PAINTER
MOTHER
DANCER
LOVER
WHILE ALIVE
SHE LIVED

I don't think I can stand it – it's making me cry. I don't want this closeness, not here, not yet.

"Katie, it will all be OK. You can trust me." He lays me down on the hardwood floor and begins to make love to me softly, gently, with his tongue, with his hands, and the kisses, the kisses, the kisses that I know will never stop until they reach down into my soul and bring me all the way out for him. Daddy unties my shirt and starts in on my nipples, teasing, twisting, biting, staying there until he knows I will feel him hard on me tomorrow. I cry softly, so softly that it feels like joy and Daddy wipes my tears away with his cock.

He straddles my face and caresses it with his cock, stroking my lips, my eyes, my cheeks, until I can't see anything but my Daddy.

"You belong under me, baby, always." Daddy rolls me over and lifts my skirt and enters me hard, laying his full weight flat out on top of me, pinning me to the floor, holding me down, keeping me still, giving me the force I need. When he begins to move into me, slowly at first and then harder, rolling his hips into mine, I give way to his power and I cry for my Daddy, I cry and I come and I pray that he will never stop, never release me, never let me be anywhere but here.

I fall asleep curled between his legs with his soft cock in my mouth and his hand wrapped in my hair. This Daddy knows how to hold me down, how to own me, and how to lift me, back up and give me wings.

In the morning he stands before me. "I'm leaving, Katie. The money is on the dresser. But it's the last time."

Oh, God, he's never coming back.

"I'll be here next Friday night, same time. I'm not anything to you any more but your Daddy. If you want to be with your Daddy, it has to be for love, not money." He pauses to give me a look that melts me back into the bed. "Do you want to keep the appointment? Do you want to move forward, Katie? I'm your Daddy. I'll take care of you."

This is not in the business plan. But taking risks is. I rise from the bed and kneel before him, nipples tingling and heart fully awake. Do what you love. Do what you love.

"Yes, Daddy, I do."

What will Cheryl think? Maybe she's ready to take over the business and find out what she loves.

How to Write an Erotic Story

Bill Noble

She nibbled her way up the back of his thigh, then whispered little kisses into his crack. She loved the way the dimples in his butt hollowed when he clenched.

"Tricia, cut it out!"

Grinning made it hard to use her lips for tickling.

"C'mon, Tricia. I'm trying to write." Garroll rolled over on the blanket, his broad face scowling down at her.

She nuzzled his pubic hair, intoxicated with the thick perfume of sex and sun. "What're you writing?"

At Garroll's shoulder, the screen of his laptop went black. "I'm trying to write a dirty story."

"Really?" She traced a long line around his scrotum and watched it tighten. Penises do look like elephant trunks, she thought sleepily. She flicked the tassel of his foreskin with her tongue and eyed the response. "What about?"

"About two people lying outdoors and teasing each other."

"Just teasing?"

"Yeah."

"You mean, no actual fucking, no orgasms?"

"Yeah. I thought it'd be fun."

"Who'd read a story where nobody gets to come? That's the whole point of dirty stories."

"No. The point of dirty stories is to get turned on."

"Bull pucky, Garroll." She started to catch the hairs on the inside of his thigh between her lips, working her way downwards.

"Can I read it to you so far?"

"Sure." She put her mouth over his knee and licked. He flinched.

He rolled back and hit a key. The screen flickered to life.

Steve couldn't decide what he liked best, Tricia's freckles or the perfect pink Mount Fujis of her tits—

"Tricia?!"

"I can change it if you want, but 'Tricia' turns me on."

"And you should call them breasts, not tits." She let a big, warm river of air loose in his butt crack.

— the perfect pink Mount Fujis of her breasts — "No, see, that doesn't work. 'Tits' sounds small and perky."

"Like mine," she murmured, trailing them over his sun-warmed shoulder blades. She pressed her puss against his tail bone.

— or her long tapered thighs that were wrapped around his head. Tits or freckles, he thought, licking her sweet snatch and looking up at her dreamy grin. Even her dreamiest grin had a hint of mischief in it, he decided. Maybe it was her grin he liked best.

"That's really sweet. It's sexy. But he's licking her puss. She's gonna come."

"No, she's not."

"She's not?" She liked the out-of-focus red-gold dazzle as her hair cascaded over his brown shoulder. She French-kissed the side of his neck. He turned his face and she let their mouths melt together. After a while the screen went black again.

She pushed him over on his back and spent several minutes licking her way down his chest and belly. She took his wally in her mouth. It was just that blend of plump and soft she thought was so yummy. She sucked him way in and made swallowing moves on his wallyhead. He sighed.

"Tricia?" He was swelling, pushing past the point of resistance in her throat.

"Mmm?"

"I really was trying to write."

"Mmm." She started to move her head up, then down.

"Mmm," she said, projecting the vibrations through her lips. Amazing the things you could learn in church choir. Amazing. She wondered idly what she might know how to do if she'd played the tuba as a child. She moved faster on him. In fact, she took him right to the edge, his thighs knotted and shaking, his head twisting back against the blanket.

Then she stopped.

"What . . .?"

"Maybe it's sexier if you don't come." She smiled sweetly up at his startled face. His thick, dark eyebrows stitched together. She loved the way he looked when he was pissed.

He sat up and took a shaky breath. He grabbed her and rolled on top. He horsed her arms beneath her till they were trapped against the small of her back. She giggled. With her legs clamped between his, he ground his wet shaft against her clit. She struggled until the sensations overwhelmed her, then relaxed and began to mew.

"Like it?"

"Yeah. Yeah, I really do." She felt like she was melting. Her voice was an unsteady whisper.

"Good," he said, and reached up to tap the space bar on the laptop. His fingers began to click over the keys. She tried to kiss some of the sweet, slippery taste of his wally into his mouth, but he would only let her reach his chin.

How long can you turn a woman on without letting her come? Steve wondered. What happened if you just kept her right at the edge? Would she lose interest, or would she go into orbit? In the interests of science, he was going to find out.

He never stopped sliding against her, even while he was whispering the story in her ear. It was breathtaking, the detail her senses could resolve: the ridge up his underside, his kidskin balls, the taut, twin cylinders in his shaft, that little lurch as the cleft of his wallyhead slicked over her clit. She struggled halfheartedly to free her hands. The midday heat sluiced them with sweat; their bellies made a loud sucking slurp that turned her frantic.

Would he relent eventually and put his prick in? Tricia didn't have any way of knowing. Steve was such a strong-willed guy.

"Garroll?" Her voice trembled.

"Yeah?"

"Just come lie beside me, would you?"

He rolled off and stroked her hip tenderly with his fingertips. "You okay, Trish? I was just teasing."

In a flash she was on top of him. She stuffed his sturdy wally into her puss and sat up. His pupils dilated. She flashed him a crooked grin, pinched his nipples.

"Hey, I thought you were really unhappy."

"Might've been." Her hips started a slow undulation. She watched him staring at her belly muscles. That had always been a big turn-on for Garroll.

She took him right to the edge once more. Then stopped moving. The laptop had blacked out, but lit up when she began to peck at the keyboard.

Once she got Steve's thing n her snatch he forgt about teasing, though. Mn were loke that onceyou got them trned on you could do anythingg

She'd let Garroll do the spell checking later. She sat up, still holding him tight inside her, and began to use her typing finger to stroke herself. He tried to thrust, but she settled her weight onto his thighs and held him still. She began to vibrate her finger sideways across her clit. Her eyes clouded up. She clenched her muscles just often enough to hold Garroll right at the brink, but not often enough to let him come.

The laptop went black. She clicked the cover shut, and came like a stampede of butterflies. And came, again.

She aimed a mile-wide smile at Garroll's astonished face. She slow-waltzed his wally until she felt him not quite spurting, lifted – his mouth flapped open – and then slid down hard. *Poor boy.* She came like the World Series. *Got a thing or two to teach him about dirty stories.* She came like a custard bucket. Came again. Came like Julia Roberts on IMAX. Like the 1812 Overture twice. Like nine hundred nuns in Vatican Square. Like starbursts. And higher, further, vaster still, like the bright bloom of creation opening over the void.

And again.

Pull Me in the Pullman Carriage

Helen Lederer

Karen glared resentfully at a couple of girls wiggling their way up the Edgware Road towards her, their minuscule knickers outrageously visible through the chiffon of their summer dresses.

She pulled herself together. Just because it was Bank Holiday and most other people were having barbecues in strappy vests and shorts or sex with their partners somewhere conveniently close to the M25, didn't mean she had to curl up and die. Well not yet. Something would happen to her. It would. But then she remembered the last time Positive Thinking had brought a result.

She had noticed her friend's brother looking at her out of the corner of her eye in the car on the way back from Ikea. The more he looked at her, the more she had re-arranged her mouth to resemble what she thought was a Michele Pfeiffer pout with wide startled-looking eyes.

Then suddenly he said, "Karen?"

"Mmmm?" She looked at him apparently casual.

"Do you know what you remind me of?"

"No," replied Karen expectantly, opening her eyes wider and puckering her mouth like the clappers.

"A goldfish."

"Thanks."

*   *   *

Yes. She had good reason to be depressed. And last night with her flatmate hadn't helped.

"When was the last time you had sex?" Cora had wanted to know. She was only bothering to talk to her because her boyfriend was out experimenting with male company and beer, "in case their own relationship got co-dependent", and also because Coventry was playing Munich.

Karen made the mistake of telling her.

Cora screamed incredulously. "Five YEARS? – There's something wrong, Karen." And then she offered, "Have you thought about the Wrens?" after a few pitiful looks.

Instead Karen thought half-heartedly of the vibrator that had been left behind in the flat. But she knew that she couldn't bring herself to actually use it. In any case, Cora had told Karen not to, since they didn't know where it had been. Actually, Karen could well imagine where it had been, which was an even better reason to leave well alone.

No, she'd hang on for the real thing. Bank Holiday had to be got through with or without sex – and since it was without, she might as well catch a train.

"We all know about you and trains," said Cora derisively. Karen bitterly regretted a previous occasion where after a few cranberry vodkas she had rashly confided that she always got turned on in a train. She couldn't exactly account for it, but it might have something to do with the regular vibrations which seemed to speak to her vagina and get it purring. Once, on a particularly long journey, she'd even had to find a loo to go in and give herself a seeing to before she exploded.

Instead of being impressed at this account of rather original sexual display, Cora had been disappointingly horrified.

"What, in the loo?" she'd asked, amazed. "On public transport?"

"It wasn't public," defended Karen. "That's the point."

"You're weird," confirmed Cora.

"I'm not," said Karen. "Look at those male commuters – have a look at what they're doing to themselves under those tables. They're not tapping the Formica underneath I can assure you!"

But Karen could see this was not a subject to dwell on with Cora, so she justified the train journey as merely a necessary mode of transport to get her to her "friendzzz" in the country for Bank Holiday – rather than any surrogate sexual playground of orgasmic possibilities. Perish the thought.

"Is that the friend whose brother thought you resembled a goldfish?" Cora needed to know.

"I can't remember," said Karen. Cora really was a pain. She'd be buying a *Time Out* at the station to start auditioning for other flatmates as well.

"Great," said her friend Frances when Karen had invited herself over the night before, making out she wasn't desperate but could she come down the next day, please?

"As long as you don't mind sharing the bed," Frances stipulated.

"No," said Karen truthfully. "Who've you got in mind?" she joked.

Frances didn't laugh because she'd been married to Brian for a few years and had therefore lost the art of repartee.

"You've met her before?" said Frances.

"Not that woman from Cornwall with the caring personality?" Karen asked.

"She's a homoeopath – well, she's training to be anyway and–"

Karen cut her off, bored already. "Anyone else?"

"Her kids."

Great, thought Karen, *a homoeopath from Cornwall and kids as well*.

Impulsively for a second she toyed with an alternative plan. Perhaps she could get herself booked on a last-minute "water-sports" weekend. She'd seen it advertised on afternoon television: a group teamed up at a man-made lake and learned about being wet and cold with some sailing thrown in. But what if all the men were accountants? Or worse, what if there weren't any men at all? She could always do what that weekend Life Skills workshop had recommended – hang out in Hyde Park talking to trees. But to be honest she didn't want to attract any more unkind attention. Cora was enough.

No. She'd chosen the only course of action available. Even if Frances *was* married to Brian, at least it was a known quantity and she knew she'd hate it marginally less than staying in London.

The train was hot and crowded as she bumped herself along the carriage with her carrier bags of women's magazines and a rather phallic-looking brie baguette. Her overnight bag was lolling off her shoulder, which meant she had to raise her armpit to straighten it, which meant in turn that the faceless grey men at the tables might spot her armpit stubble or, worse, get a sniff. God, summer was a worry.

Oh, for the camouflage of winter, when velvet-tailored jackets hugged themselves tightly over unsightly body parts. But no. Her Ghost dress with matching cover-up cardi was falling off with the strain of her ill-thought-out baggage and smelly cheese.

This was getting increasingly annoying, as three carriages down she *still* couldn't find a seat. The only "possible" was an aisle seat next to a man whose lap-top, phone and spreadsheets had been staked so obviously across the table. She wasn't in the mood to squeeze in and balance her carriers on the two centimetres left. Nor was anyone else, which she could see was an effective use of the territorial imperative but, really, who gave a fuck. Obviously she would if she could, but not with him.

Finally Karen spotted a seat opposite a woman and baby. The seat next to them was piled high with baby bags, toys and general nappy paraphernalia, which explained why the whole area had been given a wide berth.

As Karen set about committing herself reluctantly to the seat, the woman smiled in a rather fixed way at her, clearly enjoying the sucking of the baby at her nipple. Karen really didn't know if she could stomach such a sight for long. But it was between "lap-top" or "breast". Bank Holidays brought them all out, it seemed.

The woman's eyes seemed to glaze over as if in a sexual reverie, which looked ominous. Karen decided if the woman got near a climax she'd turn tail and go, carriers or no carriers. She'd sort of suck it and see, as it were, before moving on.

Karen distracted herself with the weekend ahead. Perhaps they'd do that drive again to the nearest Ikea where you bought small candles and tiny noticeboards and paper-clips, having looked at the garden furniture and decided against. Sensible in her case, given she had no garden. Or perhaps they'd stay in and have a take-away. A far cry from when they were at school. She remembered nostalgically how Frances and she had been allowed to go away together at eighteen and catch the ferry to Calais. If only their parents had known what had been in their minds they'd never have been allowed out of their rooms.

But then, in those days, if you wanted a snog you just went out looking for it. Why wasn't it possible now? She was just as keen to get one but somehow looking hopeful seemed to put men off once you turned thirty-five.

Or was it the fact that they'd both been virgins which seemed to open so many doors? Not theirs, per se, but did "Virginity" offer more pleasure possibilities than the "lone penetration" of the future? Karen pondered on these pro-fundities as she watched the baby twitch and guzzle while the woman smiled unashamedly.

Her Life Skills weekend workshop had advised her that if she thought of those moments where things had gone really well, she could re-create the mood and make them happen again – more or less. Karen set to on an early memory involving a penis.

Here was one. She remembered Frances' sister had got them both tickets to a hockey club disco in Sidcup. A drink in one hand, she could remember looking around pleasantly at the men, none of the insecurity of the present day with, "Do I look attractive, are they committed and does my breath smell?" tattooed across her waistband. It was simply, "Here I am, in my nice white rosebud Biba cotton dress – take me I'm yours and we'll deal with the virginity factor later."

She remembered how a real-life Wimbledon player who had been deseeded (as he was fast soon to become again) asked her if she'd like to go out for a walk. She did, and very soon found herself snogging him against a wall. She felt it was necessary to tell him about the virginity thing, since it was quite interesting to her and she assumed it might be of interest to him, but he didn't seem to be listening – a rummage around her breasts and a fingering up her pants seemed to be more pressing. After a lot of heavy breathing Karen knew she had to take action to prevent the usual cross and sulky riposte. This was the lot of an active virgin. She leaned down to oblige him but he'd already got there before her, waving it about as if to say, "Ready!"

She had become quite efficient at seamlessly hoovering up, like a cat with a saucer of cream. A neatening up of house-work really, thought Karen fondly.

Then she had reported in to Frances about exactly what had happened with the tennis player and received general approval before they were driven home by the unwitting sister.

As the train journey continued Karen busily went over other penis occasions and started to wonder how often Frances had similarly reported in to her? The thought suddenly struck her: had it just been Karen who'd gone round doing the "plating", as it was then called. What had Frances been up to in the meantime?

She knew Frances liked to *talk* about it a lot and remembered when she first met Frances' husband Brian, he seemed to like it too. She found him staring at her mouth in a rather odd way. Eventually she asked him what was up and he replied, "I'm just imagining that little mouth round all those dicks. Hope you don't mind."

Well, she did, but as usual she didn't say.

"Tell him about the chewing gum," Frances had instructed.

"No, I can't," said Karen, "I really can't." Not sure if she liked being in the company of Frances and Brian together.

"Let me then," begged Frances.

Karen had allowed the telling to go ahead, since at that point in her life talking about sex wasn't as painful as it had become. Talking about it now just reminded her how easy it had once been and would she ever remember how to do it again? "Your hole will heal up at this rate!" Cora had cheerfully remarked recently.

Frances duly got into her stride about the chewing-gum incident, which had involved a tall Australian. He had been allowed to take Karen to a beer cellar near Charing Cross and it was here that he had suggested kissing Karen "there", which was indeed a new one on her – so much so that she'd thought she'd misheard him at first. But when he dropped her back home, she soon realized she hadn't. They went into the play-room upstairs – which had been re-named the "piano room" for obvious reasons. (They had cut out Formica flowers and stuck them over the piano since it was the late sixties and the room needed to reflect its time. Frances always liked using background information to embellish a scene.) A lie down together on the Mexican rug was followed by the usual routine of "Hey, I'm a virgin but you can play with me" type of thing. Frances then described how, at bedtime, Karen couldn't get her knickers off. They were stuck and she simply couldn't think why. She pulled and she pulled, until she bent over and had a peek. The Australian was obviously partial to a bit of gum and, rather than break off proceedings with Karen, he had chosen to deposit the gum – perhaps as a personal signature, like the flag left on Everest. Karen, however, wasn't that impressed at the time since much scissor work was required to free her from her pants.

Brian had clearly enjoyed the gum story and insisted on a re-play of just exactly *where* the gum had been, and *when* did she discover it, and *how* did she remove it from her – you know . . .

Karen had started to get slightly uncomfortable then, about how much pleasure they both might be getting at her expense.

"Why don't you tell Brian about when we went camping in Brittany then?" suggested Karen. "You know, when we had to go in the tent and you ended up with Robert and . . ."

"You ended up with Patrick," finished Frances.

Brian had started to shift about in his chair stiffly.

"When was this then?" he asked.

"Oh," Frances said airily, "it was ages ago. I think it was more to do with Patrick and Karen though. Do you remember when you got in his tent and he came before you even got to lie down!"

"Yes," said Karen, not sure whether to pursue how Frances and Robert's goings-on had all got a bit ugly because Robert had been one of the few blokes who *wasn't* keen on the virginity thing at all. Karen remembered having to find her torch – which wasn't easy because she had to slip about over Patrick before finding it in her rucksack and go and calm him down. Amazing what the offer of a plating can do to placate an ugly scene, she mused. Then they'd packed up and left the next morning without reference to it again.

Brain had changed the subject after that and suggested quite a strict game of Scrabble which didn't allow people's names. Which ruled out Dick, of course.

Karen was just beginning to doubt the real usefulness of going down to see her friend at all, when there was a commotion opposite. A woman was lurching down the carriage with a bottle heated up in a tumbler. She screamed when she got to Karen's section.

"What?" said Karen, nervously looking around, wondering what was wrong. "What?" she asked again.

"My baby!" screamed the woman. "My baby!"

She looked furiously at where the suckling woman was sitting – who, it had to be said, appeared to be on the brink of a massive orgasm judging by certain sounds and kicking movements of her legs against the table-top.

The new woman plucked the happy baby from a monstrously enlarged nipple and shrieked, "She's mine!"

The first woman could no longer keep the orgasm at bay as it had been building for so long and roused herself with a "Yeeees!" before sinking back into the seat with closed eyes, clearly spent.

"I *told* you," said the new woman, now apparently familiar with the situation, "I *told* you I'd be a few minutes, but it's Bank Holiday – they're short-staffed."

The baby had started to whimper without the succour, so the new woman shoved a teat from the now heated-up bottle in its mouth. Then the two women started to snuggle and admonish each other indulgently.

Karen's mouth had dropped open so much the two women turned to look at her with interest. "This is too much," thought Karen as she gathered up her bags, looking around for support from the neighbouring passengers. None was forthcoming. Apart from looking up at the louder phase of the orgasm, most of them had retreated back into their holiday reading and Game Boys.

"It has to be first class," Karen decided, and began hobbling down through the corridors again. By now several people had got off and it was easier to find an empty compartment. Karen was shaking with disbelief and settled down to ring Frances on the mobile to tell all.

She was still looking at the mobile when a man came through and sat opposite. Karen felt very exposed since two people alone in a private compartment are somehow required to acknowledge each other. She looked up quickly to see who the offending interloper was and whether there would be any more trouble ahead.

Amazingly and miraculously, the interloper turned out to

be a man of around her age, not particularly good-looking but not ugly either. Karen started to feel hot. Perhaps this was it. Positive thinking had worked. This was a man on his own in her compartment. She made herself look directly at him since the Life Skills workshop had forced everyone to look each other in the eye for at least five minutes. This had been excruciating but was apparently crucial for bonding and sexual attraction. The man soon became aware of Karen using her new life skill and finally could stand it no longer. He asked her. "Is that a Nokia?"

"Yup."

"How do you find it?"

"OK. Well except I can't plug in addresses."

"It's easy," he said, keen to get rid of the staring eyes. Karen was just as keen to stop staring because it had produced tears and she didn't want him to think she was emotionally unstable. He moved a little closer to her and said, "May I?"

"Of course," Karen replied as if they were at a tea dance.

She was starting to get hot. Hot because she liked him. Hot because he was a man and hot because, well, it was summer and her Ghost outfit absorbed the heat.

"It's hot isn't it?" The man took off his jacket and Karen noticed some sweat marks under his arms. She found this exciting and mentally worked out how long she had before her stop. Was there time to either jump on him or at least get a firm promise of a date? She tried to look attractive while she weighed up her options.

"Do you know who you remind me of?" he said.

Oh, no, she thought. *Here we go.*

"A goldfish?" she suggested, to get it out of the way.

"I wasn't thinking of a fish, no," he said.

"Look, I know this is mad," Karen ploughed in, realizing she had ten minutes left and simply had to jump in feet-first. "But I, well I'd started wanting something to happen today and now it has, so I was wondering . . ."

The man looked very interested. "Yes?" She could see his pupils starting to dilate, which was encouraging.

"And, well, I wonder, if you could just, well, could you kiss me, do you think?"

"Here?" he asked.

"Yeah, it's just a train thing," said Karen, trying to be throw-away. "It's just with the rocking motion of the train, I tend to vibrate . . ."

"Do you?" asked the man with even more interest.

"Well, I wondered if you could just, sort of test it for me, to see if I'm vibrating?"

Karen hoped this made sense to him because it didn't entirely to her but they were getting close. The man stood up awkwardly and slightly adjusted his trousers. He came over and cleared his throat, and then started very tentatively putting his tongue over her lips and then inserted it into her mouth.

It was so long since Karen had snogged anyone, she'd completely forgotten what to do. But she wasn't going to argue. She just sort of hung her mouth open to see where he was going next. Then he used his hands to prise off her cardi and pull down the straps of the Ghost shroud. People were getting off at the station and looking in with fascination. She realized that one breast had been taken out of her bra and was pointing straight at the window but she didn't care. Something was happening. She'd made it happen and it was happening now.

The train pulled out with many more curious people waving at their window. With some awkwardness he lamented that he lacked "protection" but offered to lick her if that would appeal at all? She said it would and together they moved into an even more unusual position, with her legs up against the window while he set to.

Suddenly his mobile rang.

Oh no, don't stop now, Karen thought but couldn't really give this too much attention. He picked the phone up, breaking off only to say he'd missed the stop and that he was sorry. Then he resumed the action.

Then Karen's phone rang, which he deftly intercepted and

said, "It's for you," holding it by her ear while he continued his work.

It was Frances.

"Was that your right breast I just saw winking at me through the window?" she demanded.

"Probably. Are we there already?" gasped Karen, raising her hip for a better angle.

"You *were*. I can still see the train in the distance. I forgot to tell you my brother was on the same train. He would have got you off in time. Mind you, he brought his friend down with him, who apparently went off to the loo and hasn't been seen since." She sounded annoyed.

"Ooohhh," managed Karen.

"Exactly," agreed Frances. "I was going to set you up with him. The least you can do is turn up. What am I going to say to the friend?"

The man paused to lick his lips.

"Ooohhh, sorry, can't think right now . . ."

Little Deaths

Heather Corinna

"So, how would you want to go?"

I'd thought about it for an hour now, listening to each of them in turn, thoughts of quiet calm and peace, thoughts of swift release be it by gunshot, by heart attack, by being slammed to the front of a train. We talk death over coffee, interspersed by celebrity gossip and the season's lipstick shades, compliments on my geisha sandals, sad coos over her recent divorce, her loss of such a great job, her inability to come as often as she'd like, or with whom she'd like, or just to come, period.

Women can do that. It appears to be one of our singular arts: to give as much credence to a magazine article as we do to the great tragedies of our lives.

I brush a pile of scone-crumbs from my trousers.

"Slowly," I said.

"Slowly . . . like, how slowly? From a terminal disease?"

"I don't know. Just slowly. I wouldn't want it to be any more sudden than anything else. I'd want to feel every second of it, right down to the last."

This was cause for much uncomfortable chuckling.

"And I suppose you'd want to be teetering on the verge of an orgasm at the end, right?"

I hadn't thought of that. Not a bad idea. "That'd be good. I wouldn't want to come, though."

"We should have expected this kind of answer from a professional masochist."

This is almost true. Yes, they should have expected that kind of answer, but I'm really a professional sadist. Hey, it's a job, pretty much like anyone else's, and besides, I'm good at it. It affords me hand-tailored Armani suits, I get to get my rocks off while I'm doing it, and it's legal. Barely, but then, so is going five miles over the speed limit and everyone does that all the time.

Definitely slowly, very slowly. Just thinking about it made my nipples stand at attention.

"So what, you'd want to order death to do you slow like you order everyone else?"

Stereotypes. One might expect better from artistic, feminist circles. I know better. "Not at all. I'd want it to be the one time where I wasn't in control."

Breathe. In and out, in and out. Focus, centre, that's it, girl.

I turn the blow dryer on the damp fishnet, reminding myself it's uphill from here. Five minutes of peace, but then I've got Alex, not the damn idiot who just threw up on my knees.

I broke the golden rule with Alex months ago: never, never get attached to a client. He broke the rules first anyway, coming to me when he never really wanted to be dominated, when he wanted to have a battle and win. Trouble is, in all the time it took to get him to stop glaring at me and trying to squeeze my ass and to start licking my boots and kissing my rings, I got a little attached to the guy. It's a funny thing about a lot of these people: they come begging to be dominated, ordered around, the whole wash, and the truth is, most of them want to be me. Maybe that's what got me so much about Alex, that he wasn't afraid to show it.

It didn't hurt that he had money to burn and the most gorgeous ass I'd ever seen to carry his wallet around on.

I roll the stocking back on, examine my face in the mirror, look for the little lines around the red lipstick, under the eyeliner, knowing they're there, but choose to live yet another evening in denial. That'd make me good old (emphasis on old) Christina Maria Mendoza, and Ms. Mendoza never really got us very far. Besides, it's Mistress Tina who has to answer the door, and there's no one here to get it but me when it rings.

And ding dong, what do you know. Maybe I was really meant to be a psychic.

Breathe, honey, in and out. Say your mantra: I am the Mistress, and I must be obeyed.

I am the Mistress and I must . . . answer the fucking door. I must answer the goddamn door.

Look through the peephole, God knows who it could be, but there he is. Look over that sweet pout, those green eyes, that body you know is twenty years younger than yours, even if no one else would. If there's a God, his name is surely Doctor and you don't go see him when you have a cold, either. I often wonder if liposuction is considered a sin or a salvation by the Hoover people. Only a client, Chris, and don't you forget it.

While you're at it, unlock the goddamn door, huh?

Unlocked, and I walk back, settle my ass on the stool; waiting, watching. He comes in, looking at the floor, and for a moment it almost breaks my heart I broke him in this well. Just a second of that gaze would knock me flat, and I'd love every minute of it, even for the loss of face it'd cause.

"Mistress Tina, how may I serve you?"

So, here I am, and I'm thinking. You could knock me flat on my ass for starters, I ponder, grab me by my hair and fuck me senseless while I pleaded with you to stop, for starters. You could make me come more times than I wanted to, suck my cunt even after I ordered you to stop, and drive me freaking nuts with the agony of an overstimulated clit and a million dead brain cells, but I don't say that, don't ask for that. This guy is a client.

Instead I ask him to shine my shoes, kiss my fingers, kneel at the stool and sing my praises. This is work, not play.

While he's doing all of this, of course, I imagine he's doing what I want him to be doing, I'm organizing my third dresser drawer in my head, figuring how I can get both to lunch and to the sale at Betsey Johnson tomorrow and still have time to get my nails done.

While he's doing all this, of course my mind starts to wander and I'm thinking about this morning with the coffee klatch, I'm thinking about dying slowly, I'm wondering how sweet it could be to have to surrender, to have no choices, to be laced to this stool with nothing to do but die.

And I'm dripping wet just thinking about those ropes around my ankles.

"Tie my feet to the chair."

There's a long silence. Oops, I crossed a line. Regardless, I am the Mistress and I must be obeyed, for crying out loud.

"I said tie my fucking ankles, slave. Now."

There is that scurrying sound (I know this one well), and then the ropes move slowly around my feet. His fingers should be trembling. His fingers aren't trembling. I should hear his breath breaking, but it's as even as if he were doing dishes. I can almost see a smirk on his face.

"Tighter. I want my toes to tingle."

The fibres tear into my skin as I pull my ankles to see if he's done it. He's done it. He could push this stool back and I'd fall. If I tried, I could stop the fall with my hands, but I wouldn't be able to get up by myself unless I united the binds. He could near do anything he wanted to do me right now, and he'd be in control. But then, I'm in control even if I change the rules and there isn't shit he can do about it.

"Stand up. Look into my eyes."

Another moment of silence: I don't breathe, I don't blink, I don't say it again or reach for my crop. I let it hang in the air until I know it stings harder than any whip could.

He stands, lowers his eyelashes, and he looks, deep. I am assaulted by this bright green gaze, fire behind the pupils, hot breath on my upper lip, the scent of him. I can hear his nostrils flare. Silence is a wool coat after a cold downpour; heavy and damp and stifling. He leans forwards; I can feel the tremor between our lips. I have never once kissed this man. If

I leaned a quarter-inch closer, I could, and it'd be exactly what he wanted, for me to fall sway, lose my hold. I could and I'd be able to feel that half-open mouth all over mine, and God knows it'd be what I want.

His hand is on my knee.

"Leave," I tell him.

I am heavier than strong silences.

Riding the subway, late at night, but it's busy nonetheless. There must be a million people on the train. The lights from the top of the car are flickering on and off; I am annoyed by this, annoyed by the clatter of the children in front of me, annoyed by the incessant display of affection of the couple beside me. Love and affection makes me nervous and neurotic. I know this because my therapist has pointed it out enough times, I've taken to writing it in the memo section of each check I dutifully sign off to her. I am annoyed, but that doesn't keep me from watching.

They both need a shower, I think, and the girl needs a trip to her stylist to get rid of those split ends really badly. I contemplate telling her this, decide not to, my eyes drawn past the hair to the hollow between her breasts where I watch her lover's hand wantonly go, in plain view of anyone on the train, including me. I can hear his smirk, I'm suffering some sort of *déjà vu*, but his fingers pull out a pink nipple from a half-buttoned sweater and roll it between them, pinching it hard as he catches my eye.

I don't look away; I suppose I'm too seasoned to care. He turns and whispers into her ear and she smiles, leaning down, biting the button from his trousers (which are fabulously cut, I'm thinking potentially Armani, but probably some knock-off) as she winks at me. I stare back, hoping she isn't issuing some kind of invite, since I've never been real big on trains and, to top it off, whatever my proclivities may be, sudden threesomes with two people who aren't my type when I'm off-duty just isn't on my menu. Maybe she's not, maybe she is, who can say, but if she was she got over it fast. I seem to be the only person on the train who notices she's got her hands wrapped around his cock and her lips poised like an arrow in a quiver. I seem to be the only person on the train who can hear him telling her what to do in a voice that isn't his, in a voice that is distinctly mine. No one else is seeing his hands pulling her hair back and forth, sliding her mouth up and down the length of him as the train rumbles underground and the lights flicker. I'm the only one hearing my voice from his mouth ordering her to slide her hand under her skirt and slip her fingers inside her warm cunt, the only one seeing her smile as the tears flow from her eyes, the only one who sees her lift her lips from between his legs, smile at me through running mascara and say,

"Drop it."

"Drop it?" As I'm asking this, my handbag falls to the floor (my prized red Coach bag which, as it vanishes, I remember easily ran me a cool six bills). As the train turns, I watch as a thousand plastic cards fly out through the now open doors, and she says it again.

"Drop it."

Then my shoes are gone, then my coat, and rings scatter in every direction. Lipsticks, hairbrushes, my whip, crisp green bills are floating out the door, but I can't move. My eyes are glued as she sucks him harder, as he pushes her head violently, as she moans, sliding her fingers back and forth through the thatch I can barely see, my voice barking orders beyond my control.

"Drop it," she says once more, through lips covered in come, and I watch my own hand fall away, and pieces of my hair fly off like uncaged birds, and they both smile at me as my skin sheds, and my bones begin to clatter against the windows like xylophone pieces, and I remain, but everything, everything is gone, and now she speaks in my voice instead of him as she flutters into the air out into the darkness of the underground tunnel.

"Now you're free."

I have this dream three nights in a row, and it's identical, nothing changes, not even what I'm wearing or the faces on the train. So, I take up drinking again. I've got news for Freud: tequila is stronger than the subconscious.

"Why?" he asks. I answer with my whip, sure, straight and sharp as a thousand knives, and he cries out and slaps a hand over the welt on his shoulder. I don't need to remind him it isn't his place to ask questions with anything but a single flare of leather.

He ties the ropes without questioning again, smart boy, even though he isn't being particularly nice about it. His fingers are rough around my wrists, and the knots on my ankles were tied tight enough to make my toes tingle. I watch the whip fall from my hand and onto the floor.

There is something strange and ironic about this: my being bound and completely in control. He sits there on his knees, like a dog deprogrammed from attack training, the fury still in his eyes, but he waits on my word.

I envy him, and that is truly surreal. In some way, I realize, I want as badly to be as broken to him as he is to me, but that isn't how I played the game, so that just isn't possible.

In some way I'm sure would be over-analyzed by all of my cronies and delved too deeply into by my therapist, some part of me just wants to (drop it) let it go, and in another bigger way, I hate him for having that fire in his eyes that makes that clear, and I want to see him suffer, just like this, perched between my knees, my legs spread wide open, cunt gaping, with no permission to touch it, no matter how much the bulge in his pants says he wants to.

"Stay put. I'm going to take a nap. You can leave when I'm asleep." I smile, and it is so false, I swear I can feel my teeth rot.

Thank God for booze. I sleep, maybe not safely, but soundly.

Shit. Dammit.

I try and kick myself for this, only to wind up on the floor with a reverberating elbow.

Shit, shit, shit. It's dark and the ropes are too tight, and I am a fucking idiot. Slick, Mistress, forgetting to tell him to untie you first. If there was an award for worst performance in a leading role, I'd be fondling an eight-inch gold erection instead of these knots.

I file through my brain, flip past thoughts with my fingers. He's not supposed to be back here until Friday. I've got one client tomorrow, but he's iffy and he's new and he doesn't have a fucking key. The phone is . . . where the hell is the phone? What day is it? It's Monday. Dammit, I am going to starve to death and, to top it off, I have an appointment tomorrow it took me six weeks to get.

Isn't this what you wanted? I hear myself say, ordering myself to shut the fuck up immediately with little success. Okay: breathe in, breathe out. I'm going to go back to sleep, and when I wake up, I'll have this whole situation under control.

That's bullshit, and I know it, but I'm going to sleep anyway. If I don't, I may die of ennui.

I am in a circus ring. The auditorium is packed with people filling their mouths with popcorn and pink sugar-candy, their fingers sticky with it, pieces of it on their teeth as they cheer. There are three lions circling me as I flail my whip in the air and push at them with a stool. Saliva drips from their jaws, and their roaring bellows, echoes in my ears. I feel a trickle of sweat float down my neck between my breasts pressed tight together in the corset. A cage door locks.

I see their faces: one of my father, the same look he always had after he'd been drinking and my mother was long asleep, another of my ex-husband, his eyes as terrible as they were when he found out about the affair with Leslie. The third has Alex's green eyes, and his white teeth, which I see as he grinds them together, advancing at me. I am barking out orders, but they advance all the same, and I pass my gaze over the crowd, feeling nervous, cracking the whip on the dusty ground. I hold the thick handle between my sweaty fingers, feeling my hand tremble over it, wielding it like it were Zeus' thunderbolt, throwing its thin, sharp tail at the animals. It only stifles them momentarily: they cry out, they roar louder, pad closer, circle more tightly.

A face in the audience catches my eye, waving, smiling, mascara on her cheeks, looking at the whip with a sonorous expression. "Drop it," she mouths, blowing me a kiss: I lose my hold and Alex the lion catches the whip between his teeth and tosses it outside the metal bars.

They advance, I move backwards, trip over the stool, feel the cold iron on the back of my neck, hear the audience howl, see them gape like ambulance chasers.

A set of jaws bites into my calf, and the lion that is my father sniffs the blood on Alex's jaws, laps at it with a long tongue. They are hungry, my heart is beating, a million people are watching me lose control. My ex-husband's teeth sink into my ankle, and I start to cry, sliding down to the ground against the chilly cage. There is a loud round of applause, and the tears come harder until I cannot hear anything but my own sobbing and pleading. A long lion-tongue laps at the salt on my eyes, another set of teeth sinks into my thigh. I can feel pooling blood run along my leg, feel the scratchy tongue lap it up as another mouth sinks into my breast, blinds me with the pain of the hard bite and the ripping of my skin, and the pleasure of the slow licking across my wounds. They lick up blood and salt and sweat as the audience leans forward in their seats, hushed.

Strong teeth sink into my neck, growling as Alex's mouth clamps on my cunt, and I am stricken with a mixture of shame, pain and happiness as my vision blurs and I come, roaring as soft-clapping fills the auditorium, falling away in a pool of my own blood to the rhythmic sounds of tongues that feed on my dying body.

My mouth is as dry as sandpaper, I'm strangely damp with sweat and cream; sticky. I slide open one eye surreptitiously, bleary in the invading sunlight; see the tight knots from last night still there. My feet are a fairy-tale ingenue, set to perpetual sleep.

It must be Tuesday. Crap. I have a thousand things to do, I have a sale I have to get to, I have to get to the bank, pay the credit card bills that lay in a pile like a grotesque hill of caterpillars, I have to call the cleaning woman, I have to – shit. I have to get out of these ropes. Little did I know I had a goddamn boy scout for a client. That's what I get for not asking questions.

I fold my fingers into themselves, slide my wrists back and forth, up and down so slowly. I should know how to do this, I do know how to do this. I vow when I do get out of this I will use my hands to slap myself silly for being such a fucking idiot. My head is throbbing from frustration. It may be a caffeine-withdrawal headache, or it could be that chemical imbalance my mother was always so certain I had.

I am this close to crying after a couple hours of useless wiggling and pushing, I've only made the knots even tighter, and I hate myself for being upset about this, for putting myself in this situation in the first place. Feet pad by the doorway, trailed by ghosts of conversation, and I'm this close to calling for help, but I can't. What the hell am I going to say, and besides that, they avoid me like the plague, and I'm sure they'll just attribute my screaming to one of the many others I've ever-so-politely asked them to ignore in the past.

Fuck. I slide back into sleep. It seems like the only productive thing to do.

I wake up, sure something is growling in my flat, discovering it's only my stomach. I can't remember the last time I ate. I know I drank lunch on Monday, that extra two pounds on the scale tugging on my hair, I never have breakfast, nor do I have dinner, so it must have been that pasta salad on Sunday with the red peppers that just were soggier than a Kleenex at a funeral, as far as I was concerned. Sunday, Monday, Tuesday . . . two days. Not so bad. My stomach needs to get a backbone, I determine. Besides, it's what I always wanted: a diet I couldn't cheat on. I just have to make it to Friday.

I could swear the corset has gotten tighter, the room smaller. I'm being neurotic. I'm beginning to understand what people mean when they swear they will die of boredom. I'm sure they have no idea how awful it really could be. I try and replay in my mind the last time I was this close to getting what I wanted, and there wasn't a goddamn thing I could do about it.

I'm not coming up with anything. I do not find myself in this situation often, thank God. Come to think of it, I've ordered my life so this can never happen, so that not only my hobby, but my profession circulates around getting exactly what I want, exactly when I want it, regardless of what the hell anyone else wants. This shouldn't be happening.

This isn't what I wanted. I honestly can't believe there are idiots who pay me to feel like this.

I remember now. How poetic, now I should remember, face pressed into the carpet to avoid the glare from the windows, this goddamn stool on my back like an addiction.

I must have been fourteen. I think it was thirteen, but I'm not altogether sure. Somewhere between twelve and eighteen there was some sort of rift in that infamous time-space continuum that made all of those years into a long surrealistic episode right out of a Wim Wenders film. Luckily, I stayed awake through most of them, which is more than I can say for my experience with Wim Wenders films.

Summer Camp, upstate, 1980. That awful camp my parents sent me to every year just to prove we were wealthy and almost white enough to afford it, with every debutante known to man prowling around the grounds, most of them away from their parents for the first time. Stupid bitches. First taste of freedom and half of them spent most of it blowing off the junior counselors. I was the only spic there, and with a name like Mendoza, nobody gave two shits which family in Germany my father came from. I was a spic, plain and simple. I was also the only one there smart enough to know giving head to fourteen-year-old boys didn't get you the nights out and liberty; eating out the head counsellor did. Besides, Jennifer was prettier.

The price to be paid for that of course was that everyone hated me with a vengeance.

I woke up one night to giggling, found myself tied to my bunk being poked at by Adriana-Stewart-Jones (of the Binghampton Stewart-Joneses, as was pointed out enough to make you homicidal), who had a lock on my bare nipple with her fingers tight enough to bring tears to my eyes. The whole squadron of Winters, Schwartzes and Windsors were in attendance, flashlights in my eyes, the putrid scent of adolescent venom in the air.

"So," Adriana jeered. "We've got ourselves a real live lezzie, here, girls." I remember thinking then that she could have a house in the Hamptons if she wanted when she grew up, but that disgusting nasal voice had her branded a Bronx hairdresser no matter what she did.

I managed a laugh. "I'm not a lesbian, you idiot." Tried to wriggle from the brassières that tied my hands and ankles, but the hands over them got in the way.

"Bullshit," she said. "Jane followed you and Jennifer last night and watched you stuff your face between her legs for half the night, and besides, we all knew it anyway, freak."

"I'm not a lesbian, you idiot." I said again, flinching as she pinched at my nipple, watching an acrylic nail hit the floor.

"What the hell would you call it then, dyke?"

"Opportunism." This bought me about a minute of bimbo-time. Not long enough to get out, and there was no way I was going to get through that throng of society's finest anyway.

"Whatever. You're a lezzie in my book, and that's all that counts, bitch. Jane told me what she saw, and I know what I know. I think we ought to find out for ourselves, don't you, girls?" A ripple of nervous laughter erupted into a full-

fledged war cry. I felt my stomach turn. I watched as the
queen bee undid her front-hook and wiggled out of her
cutoffs with a jeering grin.

"See?" she called out. "She's staring at my tits. Lez." She
leaned forwards and shoved her breasts in my face, overripe
with the scent of Loves' Baby Soft and Hawaiian Tropic.
"You like my tits, Tina? They as good as Jennifer's?"

The laughter rippled again, and tears of shame stung my
cheeks. I bit the nipple near my lips, hard, and she
screamed.

"That bitch bit me! You little shit!" Her hand cracked at
my cheek, but I could feel her breath more shallow, feel her
heart beating faster. The throng moved closer. My fists
curled up into themselves, cold and hard as rocks.

"Give it to me, Lindsay," she squawked, grabbing an
object from her comrade's hand. "She liked it at Jennifer's,
she's going to like it here."

Shit.

Jennifer's vibrator whizzed into action, cradled in the hand
of Leona Helmsley in training. I kicked with my feet, only to
bring on another raucous row of giggling and laughter, and it
didn't do shit except to cause two of the bunch to climb onto
my feet. Adriana crawled over my stomach, wielding the
thing like a weapon, grinning over her shoulder, the grin I
can only see beyond her ass poised inches from my face
floating in the air like a hallucination. I could smell her cunt
from there, musky with sleep, sweaty with girlish nervous-
ness and the adrenaline rush of inflicting suffering on someone else. Close enough to smell, too far to reach.

The rest all swims in and out in flashes: roars of laughter,
hands on my hands, hands on my feet, Adriana's crotch
swaying back and forth in front of my face, the vibrator
rolling over my cunt by unskilled hands that didn't even
know where to put it. I shouldn't have come, I shouldn't have
been able to, I didn't want to, I tried so hard not to, but those
hands were everywhere. The thing was whirring, the scent of
girl-sweat filled the air, I was helpless. I had a cunt inches

from my face, felt it drip once onto my neck. I was helpless, I was watched, I was crying quietly with shame, silent as a stone, and I completely got off on it.

I even stayed quiet when the other counsellors were marched into the cabin and found me, laced like a holiday turkey, Jennifer's vibrator stuffed deep between my legs, salt staining my face. I stayed quiet when Jennifer ended up fired. I stayed quiet when I laced Adriana to a table in the woods and watched as Jennifer licked her clean, while I watched tears streaming down her cheeks, and listened to her moan, saw the venom in her eyes as I stared at her, unflinching, knowing she knew what I knew, and knowing she completely got off on it. Just like me. I never broke my gaze, not even when I slipped my tongue between Jennifer's legs, and she slid her face between mine. I stared like an ambulance chaser as Jennifer slid her clit back and forth on Adriana's mouth. Never broke my gaze, not even after Adriana's little boyfriend came to see the show and I rode the asshole until he thundered, pubescent hormones in a frenzy watching his girlfriend and fucking me, and I came with his hands full of my brown spic tits, silent and staring and smiling at that little bitch, even as we got dressed and walked away.

She never said a goddamn word about it either, and at that moment my love of being helpless got lost in my love for making someone else suffer.

I might be awake. I might be asleep. There is an itch on my back and goddammit, I can't scratch it. I'm thirsty, I'm hungry, it's too damn dark in here too see. I might be in a room, I might be in a womb.

I decide I am asleep. My body follows suit.

There is ringing in my ears, too loud. I shake my head, trying to exorcise sound, the ringing continues. I'm sure I am going completely fucking insane.

It won't stop. I'm dizzy. Ring, ringing.

Telephone.

Oh, my God, the phone. I twist to look for it, my eyes dry as sandpaper, and my limbs feel like lead pipes. I inch around the floor a speared seal, hear the rasp in my throat that was supposed to be a scream of annoyance, hear my voice filling the room.

"You have reached 212–6549. You want something, or you wouldn't be calling. Say please and I might call you back."

"Tina."

Alex. Oh, God.

"I came, but you looked so sweet sleeping all tied up, I didn't want to disturb you."

You bastard.

"You can get the phone, Tina." I can also get a million diseases I never will, you goddamn-idiot. Where the hell is it?

"Just look by your hands. It's right there."

I looked across the carpet at the thing. Too bad I busted my ass moving over here. Get back to the phone, across the carpet, have to go slow, can't feel my damn fingers, click it on, roll down.

"You sonofabitch." I sound like shit. My throat hurts.

"You don't sound good . . . thirsty maybe. I'll bring water on Friday." Friday. It's – what day is it? Wednesday? There is a silence on the other side. Friday, two days, oh, God.

"Alex!" More silence. "Alex!"

"Why did you want me to tie you up and leave, Tina?"

"Get over here and untie me, now. Now."

"You'll answer me first, and in case you haven't noticed, you're hardly in the position to order me, or anyone, for that matter, to do anything . . . Mistress." Sonofabitch.

"You didn't answer, Tina. Nothing to do with the conversation you had with Liz on Sunday, perhaps?"

How the hell did he – shit.

"I'll be over in an hour."

End of conversation. That bastard.

*　　*　　*

48.

49.

50.

51.

52: 59, 58, 57, 56, 55, 54, 53, 52, 51, 50, 49, 48, 47, 46 . . . I can't decide if this is nausea or excitement. It might be homicidal frenzy.

Counting minutes until I'd meet him out back behind the dumpster in high school, counting times I'd run that brush through my hair waiting for the phone to ring, hating it and loving it all at the same time; forgetting about it completely when it was over.

Key in the lock, door a crack open, hand around the latch. My lungs rasp with the sigh of relief that echoes in my ears.

Hand in front of my eyes, lifts the lids, a tongue clicking over lips.

"You thirsty, Tina?" Blurry face in front of my eyes. Alex's voice. I nod my head.

"Vision blurry, feeling nauseated at all? Maybe a little bit tired?"

I try to speak and nothing comes out, clear my throat, start again. "Untie me, you bastard."

Calm, deep voice, fingers on my wrists. "Fasting hypo-glycemia, at a minimum. You drink before you started this game? Not the best idea. Dangerous games you like to play, Tina."

The heels click away, I close my eyes again, relief tittering on the edge of a ramshackle bridge.

The faucet runs, turns off, the feet pad back, the hands slide behind my head, put the glass to my lips. Water: I pull a mouthful in ravenously, and it fills my mouth like toxic waste, burning my throat, and I'm this close to vomiting as I spit it out on the floor.

He tugs on the ropes at my ankles; my skin itches furiously at the pressure.

"Tell me you don't like this. Go ahead, lie to me and tell

me this isn't what you like. What was it she said? Bound,
slowly, on the verge of orgasm. Is that right?"

"How did –?"

"Twice a week, 4:00. She talks about you quite a bit, not
surprisingly. You'd be amazed, Tina, how many women
entertain notions of dominating, at how fascinating they find
you and others like you. Amazing to me what they perceive
you are, and how the men who see you are."

Confusing, this talk.

"The only people who know anything about what happens
in this town are therapists, Tina."

Jesus fucking Christ.

Jesus fucking Christ: a wave of common sense. I've been
dealing with a goddamn shrink. Maybe I really am a masochist, not a sadist, after all.

"You're a fucking shrink?"

His hands tugged at my hair, his fingers pulled a nipple,
his lips were in my ear.

"At night, when you sleep, you are most likely little
Christina Mendoza, at lunch with the Stepford Wives,
you can be Chris, scare them all with your prowess, with
your red lips, with the power they think you have and
they don't; when you work you are Mistress Tina, to be
obeyed and never denied. If you have a scalpel in your
hand, you're a doctor, a paintbrush, you're a painter, a
whip, you're a Domme. Costumes, names, roles, Tina
. . . some of us, like you and like me, can play more than
one.

"I'm not a shrink now." His hand slid down my cold chest,
slid between my legs, I quivered in fear and then in pleasure
as the hard pinch I anticipated delivered a soft circling over
my clitoris that made my head spin.

He licked my ear, whispering, fingers circling, another
working slowly in and out of my cunt. I bit back sound, bit
back breath.

"I am whatever you want to call me: Master, Father,
Angel, Demon, God. But whatever you call me, right now

. . . slave, I'm your salvation, and I'm exactly what you want, and I'm all you have.

"I put my trust in you from the first time I came here. Now you have to return that trust. Really, you don't have a choice.

"Really, you don't want one. Do you?"

Adriana's ass over my face, too far too reach, close enough to smell.

"Do you?" He slid his lips down over the corset laces, through the thatch under the garters, teeth on my lips, tongue sliding between, lapping juice from his fingers as his mouth locked over my clit, and a voice that must have been mine said: "No."

My tongue felt like a piece of felt in my mouth. I might die here, like this, I think I could starve to death, feel my throat dry out like a spoiled piece of fruit, tied up like a victim, under someone else's hand, under someone else's power, with the walls spinning like this, unable to move.

I could die like this, completely out of control.

A moment of fear, a moment of anger, another of shame, and my skin is on fire, turning fast, and pulling the air in is impossible. Panic. This isn't what I want . . .

"Alex." It rings out, a cobweb of hushed, panting sound.

"Yes . . ." I feel the tip of his tongue move with infinite slowness, dragging over my skin, making me shudder.

"This isn't . . . I want it to go slow."

I can hear him smirking. "Who asked you to speak?"

The flare of anger and pride that rises up burns out as quick as a match blown out by surrender.

"Alex . . ." He cuts me off.

"You may speak."

"I want it to go slowly. And I . . ." His tongue flickered over my clit again, sharp as a knife. I bite my tongue, but I can't really feel it, all my sensation is where his mouth is.

His voice is soft. "Yes . . .?" I can hear myself smirk.

"I changed my mind. I don't want to die like this."

"I wasn't about to let you. Not after I finally broke you, Tina."

Broke me – I . . . oh, fuck it.

"There's something else."

"Yes?"

"I do actually want to come."

His voice got stern, teeth on my clit, room spinning. "You actually want to come . . .?"

I know this game.

"I want to come, now, please . . . Master."

I can't hear him smirking any more, but I can feel it, a soft smirk wrapped around my lips, working a rush of frenzy and expiration from my skin, a smirk that mouths, before I allow myself a different death than I anticipated:

"Yes . . . Mistress."

Demeter's Garden

Catherine Sellars

A Cautionary Tale for Plant Lovers

Ian Ramsay first became acquainted with the botanist, Dr Demeter Pride, through his work as a buyer for a chain of north eastern garden centres. He had to inspect some new varieties of indoor-flowering lilies that she had been working on. She was apparently something of a recluse, choosing to live alone and work from home. Few had ever been privileged enough to visit her house and garden. The strange plants populating her large Victorian terrace were her only society.

When Demeter opened the door to her honoured guest, he was immediately struck by her air of restrained fertility. She was taller than average, full-bosomed, with what his mother would have described as breeder's hips. There were no straight lines to her form; she was all curves. The pot of trailing jasmine that she carried wound around her figure to further accentuate its voluptuousness. A crisp white shirt and full skirt could not disguise her physical opulence, and the blue ribbon in her hair was unable to contain its glossy abundance.

She had led Ian through the house. Each room was its own continent with a carefully controlled climate. They voyaged through the desert in her back bedroom, the rain forest in the bathroom, to the tropical paradise of her conservatory. As they moved through the house she tapped thermostats, and checked sprinkler systems, stooping to pick up fallen leaves and stopping to congratulate favoured plants on their blooms and foliage. In the kitchen she disentangled herself from the jasmine's embrace and offered Ian tea with toast and honey. The honey was from her own garden. She called it rent from the bees that lived there. Ian had asked her if she had baked the bread herself and she had laughed, asking him, who did he think she was, Jane Asher? It was at that moment, laughing and eating honey with her in the walled privacy of her beautiful cottage garden that Ian had made up his mind to marry her one day.

One warm evening in July, Ian entered Demeter's garden uninvited. Blooming with health and glowing from hours in the sunshine, she was gathering roses, taking the strain from the laden branches, but she dropped the flowers in surprise at Ian's sudden arrival. The urgency of his approach caused her to take a step back, and then another. He moved towards her, his mouth watering, his eyes wide, and he grabbed her, like a hungry man grabbing a piece of ripe fruit.

Demeter fell down before him. On the flower bed he spread her legs, and found her lips amongst the lavender and savoured their ambrosia, then released her bosom from her blouse and to let her breasts spill over his arm. The weight of their bodies crushed their couch of flowers, releasing a wonderful scent with each fervent thrust. Ian ground Demeter like barley and squeezed her like grapes, releasing her juice till he was drunk with pleasure. The moon was high in the sky before Ian took leave of her naked body. He left her in a state of exhaution and disarray, searching for her knickers amongst the hollyhocks.

Returning from their honeymoon, they found Demeter's garden in full bloom. Lavender bushes hummed with perfume and bumble bees. The pergola groaned beneath the weight of huge bunches of grapes and enormous rose blooms. The clematis garlanding the trunks of ornamental fruit trees were in full flower. The gem-like blooms shone in the shade of their drooping branches, laden with apples, plums and pears. Moths and butterflies fluttered between lilac, laburnum and honeysuckle, while sparrows and thrushes took turns at singing or bathing in the marble bird bath at the garden's centre. As they sat amongst the verdant splendour, fanned by balmy summer breezes, they discussed their plans for the future. She spoke of children, of many children, but Ian had his career to think of. He could not allow family commitments to interfere with that. And then of course, there was the cost. They had very different priorities, but agreed to compromise. They would discuss the matter again in a year or two, and in the meantime, Demeter would have to get herself sorted out. So she agreed to visit her doctor and, as a cloud threw the garden into shade, the conversation ended on a sigh. Walking back into the house, Ian noticed a limpness in the rose-blooms and felt that there was a sulki-ness in the way that the clematis closed up their flowers for the night.

It was the middle of winter when Demeter returned home from hospital after a miscarriage. A problem with her IUD had resulted in this, her first and only pregnancy. Ian found it hard to conceal his relief at the outcome of this unexpected turn of events, but his relief turned to impatience and frustration when his grief-stricken wife remained inconsol-able. He had followed Demeter into her frozen garden with her coat and slippers one night, when she had run barefoot from their bedroom. The black skeletons of the fruit trees were frosted with silver in the moonlight, and gliding amongst them was the spectre of his distraught wife, her feet invisible through the freezing mist which covered the ground.

Pale and thin, she had lost that lustiness he had loved so much. She seemed unreal, ethereal, like a deranged phantom haunting their barren garden. She was gazing at an apple hanging frozen from a bare branch, marvelling at its arrested life. Ian ran to her, crashing through the beds of hibernating flowers and, in his hurry to reach her, caught his dressing gown on the thorns of a rose bush. Cursing, he tore himself free, shattering the last of the late-flowering roses in the process. Demeter threw herself at him, accusing him of murdering her garden, before collapsing into tears. And that was the moment, as she sobbed in his arms amongst the empty rose bushes, that Ian realized that he no longer loved her.

With Spring, Demeter seemed to regain her spirits. By the time that the blossom was out on the fruit trees, the colour had returned to her cheeks. But things would never be the same between Ian and herself. He tried hard to make the marriage work. He was motivated by guilt and pity, but the more attention he devoted to Demeter, the more she lavished on her plants. Every daylight hour was spent in her garden. He tried to help her with the weeding, propping up the iris or knotting the stems of daffodils after they had flowered, but she did not trust him in her garden and resented his presence there.

In early summer, a Japanese student started her work placement with the garden centre. They began to go out for lunch together, and then for a drink after work. Soon they were seeing each other on a regular basis. She was cool-natured, emotionally disciplined and serene. Being with her was a relief from the traumas and obsessions of the drama queen he called his wife. She massaged away his domestic troubles with essential oils. Her lipsticked kisses covered his body with delicate pink Os of delight. Love with her was perfectly choreographed, beautifully controlled. She made an art form out of the act, filling it with ritual and mystery. Ian could not resist, and besides, what Demeter did not know could not hurt her.

Demeter barred Ian from her garden. Entry was strictly forbidden. At first he did not mind, but he became intrigued at the comings and goings of various workmen and numerous deliveries of stones, plants and earth. By the middle of August, he could no longer contain his curiosity, so one evening while Demeter was busy with her ferns indoors, he broke the new lock on the gate to her walled garden. The gate swung open and he gazed in shame and disbelief at what greeted him. The cottage garden was gone. Its rambling, trailing riot of colour had been replaced by subtle shades of green. Before him was a perfectly ordered, Japanese garden. Pots of tiny firs and maples were arranged on wooden slats and benches. Little bonsais of all shapes and sizes were placed around a pool of Japanese coy carp. A small footbridge spanned a tiny waterfall where the bird bath had once stood, and in place of the cornflowers, hollyhocks and poppies were camellias and Japanese lilies. This domination of nature through art was totally out of character for Demeter. She had somehow found out about his affair.

Ian had dragged Demeter, screaming, into her garden. They drowned out the gentle murmuring of the water with their crying and yelling for almost an hour. Ian could not understand why she had felt the need to create this garden. Why had she not discussed her suspicions with him face to face? He refused to end his affair and insisted that Demeter give up her gardening. It had become too much of an obsession. He had promised to stay with her if she agreed to get medical help, and Demeter had told him that she would get rid of the Japanese garden, put every thing to right and give up her garden for good in the winter.

Ian could not end his affair. He made plans with his lover to marry once he had rid himself of Demeter. They would buy a flat, without a garden, and start a family. Demeter seemed much calmer. She spent a lot of time finding homes for her houseplants. Ian was so relieved to see the removal of the little footbridge and bonsais that he gave Demeter a free hand in the landscaping of her last garden. All autumn she worked at it. Visiting nurseries all over the country. Plants and seeds arrived daily in the post from all over the world. Ian tried to guess how it would look in the spring, but the season kept its secrets.

One morning in February, after staying out all night with his intended, Ian came home to find the house deserted. Barren of houseplants, it had seemed a cold and lonely place for some time, but this morning there was an extra chill in the air. He walked out into the garden. A solitary magpie was cawing mournfully, a blackbird pecked viciously at a frozen slug amongst the rotting leaves. Demeter had been busy, for scattered around the garden were the most grotesque statues, frozen in bizarre contortions of depravity, their marble as cold as the day. Ian called out for Demeter but only the walls answered him. At last he found her stretched naked on the frosted flags, her twisted corpse recording the agony of her death, her fingers still clasped around the empty can of weed killer.

Ian took his new bride for a Caribbean cruise to get over the trauma of his first wife's death. It was July before he returned home once more. No one had entered the garden since Demeter's suicide, so he expected to find it a little overgrown, but nothing could have prepared him for what he was to find.

Ian noticed the stench even before he opened the gate. The garden stank like the Amazon. As he forced himself along the overgrown pathway, struggling through the tangle of creepers and ivy, sap dripped from the breaking stems, and the sticky orange pollen of huge waxy flowers stained his skin. He could see a clearing ahead of him. He could just make out one of Demeter's vile statues, disquietingly life-like in the pale green light. It was a satyr raping a nymph. Frozen in lust, the satyr's eternal erection, perpetually primed and ready to fire, was aimed ominously at the exposed rear of the unfortunate nymph.

Above the statue was the most gorgeous plant that Ian had ever seen. Great scarlet bells hung amongst the emerald leaves. Long yellow stamens beckoned like fingers from the centre of each flower. The beautiful blooms seemed to illuminate the whole clearing. He thrashed through the thick growth to reach the flowers, heedless of the thorns and nettles of unfamiliar plants that caught at his flesh. It was becoming difficult to breathe for his lungs were filled first with the rancid stench like rotting flesh and then with the heady scent of powerfully perfumed blooms. He could feel his skin crawling, a rash began to appear on his arms and his head started to throb with pain.

Ian reached the garden's centre and filled his aching lungs with the sweet scent of the huge red flowers. He watched fascinated as a shiny black beetle fell dead from one of the blooms. He tore his attention away from the captivating blooms and studied the Elizabethan knot garden set carefully at the clearing's centre. He gazed at it in terror, for the strange herbs planted there did not form the geometric patterns usually found in such ornamental gardens. Instead the plants spelt out his fate, for they formed the letters of the words, "Thou art poisoned, Murderer!"

Jack

Cara Bruce

I was thirteen the first time I met Jack. It was one of those stifling-hot Virginia days, the kind when the air smells like Budweiser even if there's no one drinking. All my carefully applied make-up was running down my face and dripping onto my faded blue cotton halter top. The beige streaks got caught up in the lacy neck and I was just about to pull the top off altogether when Jack came up behind me.

"Hey," he said, his southern drawl heavy, like he wasn't opening his mouth at all, just sort of pushing the words out with his tongue. "Sure is hot."

"Yep, sure is," I said and looked at him. He was scrawny. His white undershirt was soaked to the bone and sticking to him – you would have been able to see all his muscles, except for the fact that he didn't have any. "I'm Jack," he said, rubbing his sweaty palm across his chest before offering me his hand.

"I'm Ceilia, but everyone calls me Sissy," I told him. I used to hate the nickname but nobody ever paid mind so I had no choice but to get used to it.

"Sissy," Jack said, smiling. "I like that."

Suddenly we heard voices. I recognized the high, shrill laugh immediately – it was my older sister Janice. I crouched down behind the fence and Jack did the same.

Janice and her boyfriend came up the path, stopping just a few feet away from us. I held my finger up to my lips, signalling Jack to be quiet. We sat there hunched down and watched as they began to kiss. He was sticking his tongue down Janice's throat and she was making these awful moaning sounds.

Jack and I had to clamp our hands over our mouths to keep from bursting into laughter. They lay down on the grass and the guy rolled over on top of her. Janice started saying stuff that I guess was supposed to be sexy; Jack and I just sat there and watched. After a few minutes they were done and gone. I looked over at Jack, who was even redder then before. His eyes were as big as the dishes hanging on my Mamma's wall.

"You ever done that?" I asked him.

Jack shook his head no. "Have you?"

"Nope," I admitted. Then we both fell over laughing. We laughed so hard tears rolled down our faces, mingling with droplets of sweat.

"Oh, Jack, you are a man," I said shrilly, mimicking Janice's heated cries. Jack made a bunch of kissy noises and we laughed until our sides hurt. That's how Jack and I became best friends.

It wasn't until many years later that Jack and I ended up having sex, and I fell in love with him. Poor Jack, he never really filled out like his brothers or most of the men we knew. Maybe that's why he thought he had to act macho, always bossing me around: "Sissy do this, Sissy do that, Sissy girl, come here and get on your knees."

Oh, sure, there were times I hated him, but for the most part I just couldn't help myself – I was in love with the man. Jack was bossy, and he was rough in bed. It just made me feel sorrier for the poor guy – always feeling like he had something to prove.

Life was good. I made up names for the kids we were going to have and made plans for our wedding. Then one day out of the blue Jack seemed to lose interest. He'd come over and just sit there staring at the TV, watching soap operas and talk shows. Maybe it was because we were best friends before anything else – but a best friend never would have done what he did to me. I woke up on our wedding day and there was nothing in my bed except a letter on my pillow telling me he'd gone. He didn't write another word to me until the other day, when I got a letter telling me he was coming home and needed to see me.

I was sitting on my porch thinking of all the things I wanted to tell him: that he was a rotten bastard, that he'd messed up my life for years. It was a hot day and I held a glass of ice water to my forehead. The longer I sat waiting for him the angrier I got, until I'd almost made up my mind not to talk to him at all, just to give him a big smack across the face.

An hour later his big old truck came rumbling up the driveway, spraying dirt every which way and sending my flowers flying. Just like Jack – not even out of the truck and already messing up everything in sight.

The door to the cab opened and I saw his boots hit the ground. He stood behind the door for a moment and I walked over to give him my hand in greeting. He looked up at me and smiled. It was still Jack, except for one major difference: he was a she.

My mouth dropped open and I took a few steps back, almost losing my balance stumbling on an old tyre.

Jack's head dropped. She stared at the dirt and said, "I'm sorry, Sissy. I should have told you but I was afraid you wouldn't see me."

I didn't know what to say. Jack was a beautiful woman. His cropped hair was now long and curly. He still had the same slim build, only with tits. There was no way I could hide my shock. I walked up to her and wrapped my arms around her 'cause I didn't know what else to do. Jack pulled me close and held me. Her new body fit perfectly against mine. She smelled like musky sweat. I laughed to myself, thinking of all the heartsick nights I had spent imagining Jack with another woman.

"Sissy," she started slowly, "I know this is probably a shock but I'm happy now. I had to leave."

I held my finger to my lips. She looked up and met my eyes. I smiled at her.

We went into the house and I fixed her a drink. She sat easily in the chair, her legs spread open in tight blue jeans. I wondered if the operation was complete. I wanted to pull down her pants, more out of curiosity than lust – or maybe even out of anger.

"Have you been to see your family?" I asked, keeping my cool.

"No, I wanted to get your reaction first," she said. "You know, Sissy, I really did love you."

"I know," I said, forcing a smile. "I loved you too."

We made ourselves comfortable in the living room and talked about old times. After a while I came over and sat next to her on the couch. Jack looked at me tentatively. Man or woman, I supposed the brain was the same – I used to be able to turn him on like a light switch. I didn't think it should be any different now.

"You want to take a shower?" I asked. "You know, to cool off?"

"Sure, Sissy, that would be great." I led her to the bathroom and handed her a towel.

"Do you mind if I join you?"

Jack looked a little uncertain but I didn't leave. She slipped off her sweaty tee-shirt and black bra. I was surprised at how nice her tits were. She was hesitating, though, and I didn't want to give her time to get uncomfortable, so I stripped and stood waiting. Jack unbuttoned her jeans and slipped out of them. I looked at her crotch and smiled; I couldn't see any major differences between hers and mine – but I also couldn't wait to get down on my knees and find out. We got into my small shower stall.

"Let me rub you down," I offered, soaping up the wash-cloth and sliding it down Jack's back. She kept her back to me so I had to turn her around to get at her front. Jack kept her head down – the poor girl had no idea what was going on. I lifted her chin with my hand and brought her lips to mine.

The kiss was soft and sweet. I opened her mouth with my tongue, a mouth I had known once before but without lipstick. Jack moaned: her voice was higher. Slowly I drew my hands over her round, wet ass. I groped it, pulling her closer. I pushed her back against the shower door and knelt before her.

My hand reached up between her legs, pushing them farther apart. My fingers slid easily up her dripping slit. She arched her back and leaned on my hand. If she were truly a woman then I knew what she would like; I thrust another finger into her and felt her created cunt tighten around me.

"Oh, yeah," she murmured as I knelt before her. My tongue went from clit to cunt as my fingers pumped. I felt her knees weaken as she grabbed my hair.

"Do you want my dick?" I asked her, my fingers never ceasing.

"Your dick?" she asked, her voice surprised – but I detected a twinge of hope.

I led her out of the shower and pushed her onto the bathroom floor, then ran into my bedroom and got the harness and dildo I had gotten as a joke for my twenty-first birthday – which Jack had missed.

I strapped it on and sauntered back into the bathroom, feeling like a cowboy with my gun drawn. If she wanted to be a woman I was going to fuck her like one. She looked at me wide-eyed; I smiled as if this sort of thing happened to me every day, and lay down on top of her.

"How does it feel to be a woman?" I asked her, guiding my plastic prick into her hot hole.

"Good," she whispered. "It feels so good."

"Do you like my big cock?" I teased with the old Jack's own words. "Do you like my big dick inside you?"

"Yes, oh, yes, I do."

I thrust it in a little farther and began to pick up the pace. "Tell me. Say 'I like Sissy's cock.'"

"I like Sissy's cock," she whispered.

I brought one hand down and slid a finger up her tight ass.

She bucked her hips against me and groaned. I fucked her hard and rough, the same way she had fucked me years before. Jack was clenching at my shoulders, digging nails into skin, trembling and whimpering.

I got my angle perfectly so my clit was being hit with each thrust. Her legs began to shake.

"Oh, yes, Sissy, fuck me, oh, yes." I pumped her harder and faster until she came, calling my name and writhing on the floor. My only regret was that I couldn't come first and leave her unsatisfied.

We got up off the floor and showered again. Jack looked at me now with those big post-orgasm doe-eyes. I fixed up some dinner and we sat down to eat.

"I'm really sorry I left you, Sissy," she said. "I've always loved you."

"I was sorry you left too, but I got over it," I told her with a smile. I had her right where I wanted her – still in love with me, and now in love with my dick.

"Maybe things could still work out between us?" she asked, resting her hand near mine.

"I don't know Jack, it seems like we've both been through a lot of changes." She laughed until she realized I was serious.

"Oh Sissy, you don't even know how much I've missed you," she gushed, tears forming in her eyes.

"Why don't you spend the night?" I said. "I've got a little game we could play."

I led the horny Jack into my bedroom and brought out my handcuffs. Once she was securely fastened to my bedpost I began to dress.

"What are you doing?" she asked, frightened.

"I thought I'd go get dessert," I said. "Don't worry, I'll be back."

I took the keys to her truck and walked out the door. Who knows – maybe I'll come back someday.

In The Pink

Isabelle Carruthers

She had another name but she called herself Camille, after the hurricane of '69. "It looks good in neon," she said. "Besides, I'm just blowin' through this town anyway."

Camille was a burlesque dancer who worked the southern coast, from the Texas Gulf as far south as Tampa. She placed herself at the whim of Greyhound, having long ago decided that random destiny had nothing useful to offer.

She dressed only in crimson, her signature colour, and her hair and nails wore the same deep hue of red. When she took the stage she always kept her back to the men until the end of her routine, teasing them with brief glimpses of her generous breasts and rosy nipples. There was an added advantage to this tactic, for by the time they saw her face and realized how old she was, their hands were already stretched out to offer money. Camille had good reflexes and was able to snatch the bills before they had a chance to get away. Sometimes, if the tip was good, she would lean close and press her breast against the man's cheek, leaving behind a trace of colour from her rouged nipples.

In her youth, Camille was one of the best around, renowned for her beauty and exotic stage presence. She had done well for herself, having stashed away several thousand for the day when she might want to call it quits and buy herself a little trailer and an acre of sandy beach. But she wasn't ready to retire yet.

Camille was almost forty-three now. Her dancer's body was still lithe, her skin still soft, but her eyes were careworn and tired, her illusions long ago blown to sea. In the harsh lighting of the dressing rooms, the lines on her face were accentuated by the layers of make-up she wore to look younger. Girls were what the men wanted now, but she did not look like a girl, not even when she stumbled into good lighting.

She was no longer making enough money. Camille needed a new gimmick.

The idea first came to her as she danced the midnight show at The Casbah, a club near the waterfront frequented by dockworkers and merchant marines. The Casbah was a nondescript dive, just a big room with a circular bar and flashing neon signs in the window.

Nightly Floor Show!!!
Topless!!!
Bottomless!!!!
Live Nude Girls!!!

Camille pranced in her crimson stiletto heels on the scarred mahogany surface of the bar, always careful not to squash the bartender's fingers or topple neglected highballs. With many years of experience, she had developed a flawless sense of balance that aided her in such precarious situations.

On this night, Camille was dancing to a raunchy blues set, her hips gyrating languidly and her arms entwined with the heavy smoke of cigarettes. She had just stripped down to her crimson bra and thong when she felt a hand stretching along the inside of her thigh. Looking down she saw a twenty-dollar bill waving at her, and beneath it a sweaty face that leered from the depths of drink.

She reached for the money but he pulled back with a frown, motioning for her to come lower.

". . . inside your panties . . ." His hand moved toward her crotch.

Camille shook her head emphatically while she continued to rotate her hips, holding up four fingers. "Forty," she said. "No one gets to see pussy for less than forty." In reality, she operated on a sliding scale, but the man held a fat wad of bills in his hand and she knew he could afford to pay more.

Nodding, the man peeled off another twenty, and Camille eased down so that her knees were level with the man's ears. She opened her thighs and placed her hands on his shoulders for balance. He hooked a finger in the crotch of her panties and gave it a tug, stuffing the bills in the gap with his other hand. Several men stood behind him, craning their necks, hoping for a glimpse of what lay beneath the filmy red satin. The sweaty man's knuckles pressed deliberately into her flesh.

"You didn't pay for that," she scolded, pushing his hand away as she rose. Undaunted, the man smiled broadly and clapped his hands. She continued her slow gyration around the bar stage, picking up the lesser denominations that were her usual fare. Camille rarely got tips bigger than a twenty since most men seemed to hold onto their cash for the younger dancers.

When Camille made her way back around to the sweaty crotch-stuffer, she found him again waving an arm in her path, with many men crowded close behind. He beckoned her closer and Camille leaned down to hear his proposition. ". . . inside your cunt . . ." he said, his fingers holding a fifty-dollar bill in front of her face. The man rolled the bill into a cylinder and held it out casually, as if merely offering her a cigarette. The other men pressed smaller amounts of money toward her from all directions, hoping to persuade her to agree.

"Oh, what the hell . . ." she said.

Taking the bills from their outstretched hands, Camille squatted and spread her thighs as before, bracing her arm on the man's shoulder. She pulled the fabric aside, revealing her crimson-furred pubis, and shuddered as rough fingers opened her and pushed the money upwards. Before she could rise, the man quickly shoved in a finger to more firmly lodge his contribution in place. The crowd of onlookers roared their approval, slapping the man on the back enthusiastically as if he had just won the lottery. Camille smirked and got to her feet, annoyed but more than $50 richer for her trouble.

At the end of her dance, Camille returned to the dressing room and found a private corner. She felt gingerly inside and retrieved the bill, still rolled but not as tightly. It was damp and full of the musky scent of her body. As she unrolled the bill and laid it flat she noticed that it smelled vaguely of the strawberry douche she used the day before, but otherwise was no worse for wear.

Camille laughed to herself, pondering how much money she might make in an evening's work like this, all of it stuffed neatly inside her, like a bank. And the idea suddenly seemed not so very incredible. After all, everyone had their own thing. There were dancers who dressed like schoolgirls and some who dressed like nurses. Some were French maids, and others wore animal skins and prowled the stage like tigresses in heat.

Camille had found a new gimmick of her own.

She quickly gained infamy on the strip circuit as the dancer who let men stuff her with money. Her earnings quadrupled, and although every locale had rules against intimate touching, the club owners almost always looked the other way. Kink was good for business.

The clubs where Camille usually danced were small, limited to crowds no larger than forty or fifty patrons. At best only half would pay to play, so she never made as much money as she would have liked, not more than $800 or so for the night, minus what she had to kick back to the club. Camille dreamed of hitting it big just one last time, making it back to the top before she retired. This was in her mind when she managed to book a three-night engagement at The Pony Club, a working man's bar on the south Texas coast.

The Pony Club was a huge warehouse, on weekends routinely filled with as many as two hundred oilfield workers with bulging pockets and crotches. They wanted hard liquor and naked women and they weren't too picky about the quality of either.

Camille took the stage at 11.00 p.m., and the men began to crowd around, many of them having heard the rumors of her risqué floor show. She danced briefly at the smoky edge of the stage while she stripped down to red leather lingerie. She dropped to her knees and then eased into a sitting position with her arms braced behind her on the stage.

Scooting to the edge of the platform, Camille placed one spike-heeled foot on the shoulder of a lanky man to her right and the other foot on the shoulder of the man to her left, her long legs stretched wide before the now attentive crowd.

"How would you boys like to make a deposit in my bank?" She lifted her hips suggestively. The lanky man nodded wildly and began to lick his lips, having already heard about Camille. He had carried a crisp new fifty-dollar bill in his wallet just for this purpose. The other man looked stunned and swallowed convulsively, staring at her crotch. As far as the eye could see, hands began digging into pockets.

"I only take deposits in denominations of $50," she admonished.

"But . . ." She smiled. "You all get to take advantage of my convenient drive-thru . . ."

With a flourish, Camille tugged at the customized crotch of her garment and the fabric gave way, exposing her freshly depilated womanhood. She had taken care to lubricate herself well for this experience and hoped her shiny and fur-free look would be even more enticing.

"Roll 'em up tight now," she cautioned. "Don't want the vault to fill up too quickly!" The audience swarmed into disorderly lines, fights breaking out as men jockeyed for position. The waitresses stood gaping in shocked disbelief as the place descended into chaos.

The men filed past with their contributions, rolling their bills into neat cylinders under Camille's watchful eye. One acne-mangled youth, who appeared considerably under the age limit of 21, positioned his bill hesitantly, leaving it to hang awkwardly from the lips of her femininity.

"Don't be shy, just push it in!" she crowed. The boy looked at her exposed sex in terror, his hand trembling fiercely.

"Let me help you out there, kid." Two long fingers dipped forcefully inside her, pushing hard enough to dislodge all obstacles and draw a moan from Camille.

"Oh! Thank you!" she said.

"My pleasure, ma'am." An attractive man in a dark cowboy hat withdrew his hand from between her thighs and tipped his hat before stepping back to allow the next in line.

Camille lost count of the deposits as she lay on the stage. It seemed fitting somehow that these men were paying into her body since it was, after all, her body they were paying for. When the crowd around her was finally reduced to grinning onlookers who jabbed each other in the ribs and joked about stuffing her cunt with rolls of quarters, Camille pulled her knees together and announced, "This bank is closed, gentlemen. Thank you for your business, and please come again."

She rose to her feet, feeling as if she had just stuffed herself on a Thanksgiving dinner. The handsome cowboy stood watching and tipped his hat to her again before she disappeared behind the curtain.

The other dancers gave Camille a cold reception when she entered the small dressing room. They were jealous of her stage antics and all the money she had made, far more than any of them could expect unless they engaged in the same undignified behaviour.

A chunky young Latina blocked Camille's path as she made her way to her small space in the corner. "You're a disgrace to the profession!" she spat, full of indignation. "Exotic dancing isn't sitting on the stage with your pussy spread open in front of the whole fucking room. That wasn't dancing! I've studied dance for over ten years and . . ."

Camille laughed and tossed her head.

"Hah! You think these guys come here to see you dance? You're some kind of 'dance diva' or something? Sorry, honey, but they come to see tits and twat. If you can manage to stumble out there in your underwear, then they'll pay to watch you take it off. There's no art in that. It's the pink you show that makes the money flow. Now, I'll thank you to get your fat ass out of my way."

Camille's adversary shrieked a response and stomped from the dressing room, slamming the door behind her. The other dancers quietly resumed their cosmetic endeavours, pretending to be oblivious to the heated exchange. When a knock sounded at the door, no one else got up to answer it, so Camille did. The cowboy who had watched her show stood in the corridor outside the dressing room.

"Yeah? Need something?" she queried.

"It's about my deposit," he said. "I didn't get a chance to make one yet." He lifted his hand to show her four $100 bills.

"Thanks, but no thanks," she retorted, turning to leave. "I'm no hooker."

"No, wait . . ." the cowboy said, reaching to grab her arm. "That's not what I want. That's not what I had in mind. I just thought perhaps I could negotiate something special with you, for a fee."

"Yeah?" Camille eyed him suspiciously. "Like what?"

"Well. You might need some assistance retrieving all that money," he offered. "After all, some of it was stuffed in there pretty deep. I should know."

Her eyebrows raised.

"I was thinking that maybe for the right price, you might let me . . . help you out."

"You'll give me four hundred if I let you help me take the money out?"

"Yes, ma'am. Or to watch you do it yourself, whichever you prefer. I'm not too hard to please."

"Just to watch. No funny business. No fucking, no sucking."

"Why, no, ma'am, of course not." He clutched his hat to his chest and seemed genuinely shocked at the suggestion.

"Wait here." She joined him five minutes later.

The man, who said his name was Harry, walked with her to her room at the Capri Arms Motel a couple of blocks away. As they entered her room, he sat down in a chair by the door and waited politely.

Camille ran her hand over her belly with the pride of an expectant mother, plumped up by the fortune tucked inside her.

"Would you like me to lie down on the bed?"

"Yes, ma'am, that would be fine," Harry nodded, handing over four crisp $100 bills.

"Naked or lingerie?"

"Well, naked, if you don't mind."

Camille complied, kicking off her shoes with a sigh. She stopped a moment to rub her feet before stripping bare and lying down on the mattress.

Harry moved his chair to the foot of the bed and motioned her to scoot down, and down further, and then further still. She was reminded of her last trip to the gynaecologist. Finally he grabbed her by the hips and pulled her all the way to the edge of the bed, his hands pressing her knees apart. Even to Camille it seemed an undignified position.

Harry tossed his hat on the bed beside her. "I'm ready when you are." He grinned.

As he watched, Camille began to extract the bills, one after another, unrolling them and tossing them into Harry's hat as she did so. The strawberry-scented musk of her body permeated the room.

There was a lot of money.

Soon, it became difficult for Camille to retrieve the bills. She could feel them with her fingertips, but they were too deep to grasp.

"I'll get them," Harry assured her. "Turn over and get up on your knees."

Camille complied, resting her forehead on the mattress and lifting her rump high enough to allow him easy access. Harry rolled up his sleeve.

Camille realized quickly that he was using more than just two or three fingers, and she began to regret her decision to accept his assistance.

She whimpered as his fingers wiggled around blindly, gathering up a few bills. Finally, he withdrew and tossed them into his hat.

"$300 more. Now, that wasn't so bad, was it?" he queried.

"Holy fucking christ!" she moaned. "This is too weird. Just hurry up would ya?" Camille didn't go in for the kinky stuff, but she knew this was necessary. She didn't want to end up in an emergency room with some kind of blockage.

"Yes, ma'am."

Harry pushed his hand inside her again, and Camille yelped at the impact as his fist bumped up against her womb and felt around, as if he was digging for buried treasure without a map. He gathered more dollars and pulled them out, discarding them into the hat. By now Camille was almost in tears and cursing, ready to get this agony over with.

"Just one more time should do it," he said, sliding his hand again inside. His fingers roamed freely, moving left and right inside the cavity of her body.

"Okay, all done," Harry pronounced, finally withdrawing his hand from her with another wad of bills. He had the demeanour of an auto mechanic. She half expected him to present her with an invoice for labour.

"Oh, thank God," she whimpered.

"My pleasure," Harry said.

"I wonder how much money that is?" She guessed she

might have made as much as $2000 tonight. Adding to that the $400 from Harry, she was positively rich. Camille smiled, exhausted and sore, but happy with her new fortune.

"It does look to be a considerable amount, ma'am," Harry said, placing a sticky, strawberry-scented hand on her still upturned bottom.

"And I'm sorry to have to be the one to give you bad news, but . . ."

Camille looked back over her shoulder as Harry stood and retrieved a small pistol tucked inside his boot.

"This is a stick-up. Please keep your ass in the air and no one will be hurt."

Camille did as she was told. Her cooperation was rewarded by a $50 bill, which he tucked carefully between her legs on his way out.

After her self-proclaimed $2000 haul, Camille became something of a legend on the club circuit. She continued to dance for two more years and amassed a tidy sum to see her through her old age, although she never hit it really big again.

On her forty-fifth birthday, Camille moved to a sleepy seaside town in Florida, where she bought an acre of beachfront property with a trailer, and a chihuahua she named "Pink."

All the townspeople knew about Camille and her risqué past, and some teased good-naturedly that she probably had a few hundred dollars still stuffed inside her. Camille always laughed and tossed back the same response.

"Yeah, but I'm saving that for my dowry. No one gets in my bank without putting a ring on my finger first."

After a night of heavy drinking, some local thugs decided to see for themselves if there was any truth to the rumour about Camille's buried treasure. They went to her trailer on a moonless night and pulled her out onto the beach in her pajamas.

Pink, barking viciously in a valiant attempt to protect her mistress, was hurled bodily into the ocean by one of the assailants, a former star quarterback on the high school football team who was later heard to brag that it was the longest pass of his career.

When interrogated later, the culprits admitted that they had in fact recovered money that night, but only a lone twenty-dollar bill. Camille was very unhappy to hear that someone had managed to slip a twenty in the pink.

It made her feel so cheap.

Usherette

Jacqueline Lucas

Sweet Kill
(aka *The Arousers*) (Curtis Hanson, 1971 US)

I'm on the late shift so I mosey down Portobello to the Electric
in my black leather hot pants which'll be wasted on the morning
kiddies. They call me the sweet lady. They get dropped in for
the double bill by their upper class parents who wander down
Portobello for the antique shops. But it's a mixed crew really
and I used to think they thought *I* was sweet. I mean, *me*. I can
be really slow. In this case I should know cause it's *my* job to lay
out the nosh. We have Liquorice Allsorts and Marathon bars.
Curly Wurlys and M & Ms. Ripples, Rolos, Revels and Opal
Fruits. KP Choc Dips, Lion Bars and Milky Ways. Rowntrees
Fruit Pastilles as well as Jelly Babies and Wine Gums. Mun-
chies, Maltesers, Mars Bars, king size Double Deckers and
Fizzy Chewits. And Cadbury's Chocolate Buttons. Toffets,
Nerds and Dweebs. Bought in specially for the Saturday
morning crew. And I'm the one who gets the ice creams out
last minute so they don't go soft, and the popcorn maker, which
is no joke, I can tell you. And the cakes from down the road,
three types which I lay out, and nosh, always the staff helping
ourselves, it goes on all the time. But you get tired of them.
There's a walnut loaf type, a carrot cake and a chocolate shaped
like loaves of bread and you have to be careful: if you don't take
care, like Ian, they end up all dried out. I take pride in keeping
them going and not wasting a poorly cut slice.

The Man in the Glass Booth
(Arthur Hiller, 1975, US)

Michael's in the box and gives me a friendly wave, we tell each other everything and share snacks, always egging each other to help ourselves to stock. Ian's not even awake tearing tickets. Michael looks at me with a touch of interest and fear – like a parcel that might detonate. But Ian looks at me with complete bewilderment – in fact we eye each other up like two species meeting in a forest, not knowing if a curious noxious substance might spring from the rear end or tail. Michael is sort of camp but seems to like girls and black and an artist and we have a sort of understanding. I think it's sexual chemistry. We've never done it but it's always there. The fact we've never done it.

The Company She Keeps
(John Cromwell, 1950, US)

Ben comes in for one of his spurious visits which everyone looks at distrustful – from Lucy now parked all sullen in her booth to Michael and Ian pinning up posters. After all they've seen the results and they're not pretty and we all know he only comes on the odd occasion like a doctor to his mental patient, all solicitous. I pretend to be consumed with laying out my sweets like I can't really have visitors when everyone *knows* I'm not done up like this for nothing and by the end of my shift there'll be twenty odd "friends" who'll have stuck their head in down the Portobello Road.

Goin' Down The Road
(Donald Shebib, 1970, Can)

I nip out regularly so I almost feel I'm one of *them*, socialising down Portobello market on a Saturday afternoon. But it beats that job I had hawking secondhand books on the corner, always watching your back and far less cachet. I mean, all the others here have film degrees or art ones. I'm the only one with "O" levels.

Driving Me Crazy
(Nick Broomfield, 1988, GB)

Ben gets the message that everyone thinks he's a spineless slimeball who's screwed up in every department so he leaves in a cloud of contempt which follows him to the door and he's not said when can I see you with red eyes from crying, he's in self-preservation where's this going guilty mode. I take some pleasure in checking out his spots, he's really going off the boil. I take out my anger on the popcorn machine which burns my fingers as I load in the kernels, exploding in unison as I have a "what-am-I-doing-behind-this-counter-on-a-Saturday-with-my-life" panic attack. So when the kids arrive it's all I can do to get the confidence to peddle my sweets.

In The Best Interests of the Children
(Elizabeth Stevens/Cathy Zheutlin/
Frances Reid, 1977, US)

My favourite is a blond called Rupert, I could wrap him in my arms and take him home, he looks so vulnerable. And you can see the haves and have nots. The ones who buy Loseley ice creams even parents wouldn't go for, or Ritters at a quid a go, and the ones that can hardly buy Curly Wurlys. I give them stuff but I have to be careful and make out like I made a mistake. No wonder they like me.

During Bugs Bunny I go in half a dozen times cause there's a bit of a ringleader called Bruce who gets them all going, crying and running about the aisles. But that's what *I'm* here for. I wouldn't let them come to any harm. When Anna Paquin takes her flight with the geese when Jeff Daniels get wounded I'm so choked up I can hardly speak. Just as well cause the owner arrives and he likes an usherette in the movie house. I hate the word. Usherette. They almost had us wearing ice cream trays but I said no way.

Love in the Afternoon
(Billy Wilder, 1957, US)

What's he doing here? And he hangs about for ages and pretends to need a stocktake on ice creams but I smell a rat and reckon it's the hot pants. I feel his eyes on my arse all the way to the deep freeze like in *Short Cuts* where the husband follows his wife to the diner and watches men admiring her arse as she bends over to scoop ice cream but when they slag off her fat arse he puts her on a diet. From the Raymond Carver story; it's my favourite. He gets her on such a strict diet and when he catches her noshing he makes her spit up her food. It's awful.

Anyhow this is all going round in my mind in a split-second sort of way as I bend over when he asks me to count all the flavours we carry: stem ginger and acacia honey; traditional butterscotch; country fudge with almonds; flaked milk chocolate; peaches and double Jersey cream; old-fashioned vanilla; rich chocolate; strawberries and double Jersey cream. And still I can hardly contain a scream when he puts his hands on the waistband each side of my hot pants.

Body Heat
(Lawrence Kasdan, 1981, US)

And the worst thing is that this middle-aged bearded slightly fat Rolls Royce-driving entrepreneur summons a thrill like those corny flowers opening they use in art movies that's supposed to remind you of a woman's vagina and I'm only on 3.85 and the odd shift. Time stands still which is another of those corny film metaphors, I'm learning a lot here after all, and I mustn't turn round or he'll have his dick in the opening of my leathers and there's no one on my sweet counter and the cash box is out. Luckily he gets embarrassed or cold feet and his voice breaks into a shaky *Great hot pants* and I turn round and pass him an armful of stem ginger with an awkward smile. This way I flatter him that he doesn't repulse me which he didn't when I couldn't see him but let's face it. I follow him awkwardly into the foyer and his wife's waiting with a quizzical look that says *Since when are you dishing ice creams with usherettes!*

My Name is Nobody
(Mio Nome e Nessuno)
(Tonino Velerii, 1973, It/Fr/W.Ger)

The kids are off with barely a look at me like they've forgotten I was the centre of their world when they came in. This is the bit when I sweep in, binliner in hand. I don't want the kids seeing me doing this, I have more dignity behind the counter. This is when I feel I'm only a cleaner and not an aspiring film student. But everyone knows I'm well over thirty and only at an access course.

Sudden Impact
(Clint Eastwood, 1983, US)

Me and Michael start bagging, I get a needle would you believe. I knew *those* two weren't into *Fly Away Home*. There's more sweeties here than the kids bought, like bubble gum wrappers and gobstoppers half digested. We meet in the middle and that's when I get a sense that my slimmed-down arse from nerves and black coffee is being weighed like old-fashioned sweets. You know. The sherbert fountain when the flying saucers are already in the bag. That's how I feel. A curiosity but a fear that it'll ruin things. After all Michael knows everything from my ex to Ben to all the characters in between including the actor that keeps coming in to hassle me – no doubt of the out of work variety and into medication.

Between Friends
(Donald Shebib, 1973, Can)

Michael knows it all cause we sit round for hours guilty that we ought to be catching *The Magnificent Ambersons* or *Lawrence of Arabia* but when your head's crowded it's an effort to get ice creams never mind a refill for the coffee machine. Instead we sit in the foyer pissed off at the inconvenience of filmgoers and anyone who has the temerity to turn up late and want coffee . . . I won't mention the stock take till the memory of my response to that fat git wears off. It'll do the rounds. Anyway, back to Michael and I in the middle of the aisle with a bin liner apiece and a look that says I'm curious. I could *do* you. Just for the hell of it. As well as one that flashes. Not clever.

We head back to Lucy who's come over all deputy manager so I restock my table for the Patrick Keiller double bill and look diligent while visitors from abroad stick their heads in for a peek at the architecture of the oldest cinema in London us lot don't notice.

Interlude
(Douglas Sirk, 1958, US)

This man comes in enquiring after his little boy. A little late for that I reckon. My voice goes up a few notches cause I think we've a drama on our hands, a child stolen by a woman like me. The wife must have been, he says. You can tell they're not together.

Dogs in Space
(Richard Lowenstein, 1986, Aust)

He's got an amazing dog in tow and once we establish the kid's not abducted I lavish my maternal untapped energies on the black and white four-foot mutt who slobbers all over me, and Michael and Ian give me that look like I'm on the make with a thirty-nineish wealthy-looking dog-owner with almost no hair and kind blue eyes that are misleading cause you can tell he's never kind.

I straddle Oliver in my hot pants in a way that makes Lucy feel like cutting my shifts. I make a mental note to give her more time on that bitch of a girlfriend. And Keith brings down flyers and joins the dog love-in. Keith talks ten to the dozen and gives us a minute to pass a look back and forth that's more than downright friendly and more than the curious one me and Michael share. This is the full McCoy and as I'm dragged into the chaos of Portobello Oliver's owner says, I'm Ralph. See you next Saturday no doubt. And I say hope you find your kid! with such a huge smile it's embarrassing, and pretend not to notice Michael, Ian and Lucy slagging me off, they're such bitches, even Ian isn't as mealy-mouthed as he appears.

Telling Tales
(Richard Woolley, 1978, GB)

We all know each other's business. Problems with love and money. Paranoias that come out on late night shifts waiting for *The Tenant* and *Repulsion* double bills to stagger out round 3 a.m., when it's beyond pizza and guzzling ice cream and it's down to not being able to hang on to our fears another second. That was when I heard Lucy's girlfriend flaunted her latest blowjob in the loos of Heaven and told Lucy to get a grip, she wasn't getting any younger, and Ian's girlfriend was maybe off to India, and Keith. He's all over the shop and drags in the strangest types. And Michael's ex who was seeing his best mate at *his place*!

The Misfits
(John Huston, 1960, US)

Graham's the big secret, but all projectionists are odd, we've had plenty here. Couldn't tell *him* about the bad moments.

When they did the music one-offs even the bouncers joined our shrink sessions then came in like it never happened cause each dodgy story explains why we'll sit here till 3 a.m. for frumpence on Saturday night and walnut cake. We've all got specialities. Lucy loves guided tours for foreign visitors, she knows her art history, and Keith likes little boys and handing out posters down Portobello, and Ian likes a trip to the shops and Michael loves it when it's chaos for a special event, keeping the lid on double bookings, and me, well I'm developing an unwelcome reputation for turning up in outlandish outfits, for being the sweet lady and discussing life's problems, and for having my feet in both camps.

Posse
(Kirk Douglas, 1975, US)

But that's largely down to the cookie crew who pop in regularly with people like Hanif or Anish or Harry (E) in tow, talking Lisson Gallery and Cobden Club en route to 192. My new gang take me up though they'd never dream of tearing tickets when they could be ambling down Portobello with their artist and writer shags who only acknowledge me on account of *them*. I strain to be twice as attractive and entertaining but I'm too old for this. Not quite married and not quite divorced and not yet educated and not quite penniless. No one can make me out.

Half Life
(Dennis O'Rourke, 1985, Aust)

We hardly get a soul for *Robinson in Space* and it's another one I *ought* to see instead of sharing gossip about the cinema's takings while pocketing coins that slip the cashbox. Occasionally I sit in the booth and get the odd phonecall. No sooner am I here than that actor comes by and sidles up for a chat. My heart leaps and drops as I spot Ben slide past trying not to look on his way for his coffee and bagel ritual. At least I

vary my intake. Today it's half a slab of Ritters milk chocolate with crispy flakes of corn. A spoon or two of the hot
veggie takeout I give to Michael. The potatoes and pasta with
cheese bit. A handful of popcorn and a fizzy orange and half a
pack of KP original salted.

No Man of Her Own
(Mitchell Leisen, 1949, US)

I look at the actor with a tired smile cause after my boss, the
dog man and Michael's new attentions, I'm worn out and it
only reminds me that the wimp who's just passed by is happy
without me. Relieved. Dying to spend his Saturday night
with his ritual hot dish and TV. It's that anal retention I find
so fascinating. The actor looks strung out and I can't remember how I encouraged his little habit passing by. I'm
almost ready to give up the weekend outfits when Lucy turns
up and I excuse myself to work in the office.

Sunday Too Far Away
(Ken Hannam, 1974, Aust)

We all know there's no office, it's an airless box the manager
pretends to do her books in but *he's* not to know. It's
starting to drag, changing from bright and noisy to rotting
fruit and vegetables. The boys turning up with boxes of
over-ripe plums. I'm ready to ask if I can sit in for the next
show. After London comes out I rearrange my goodies for
Breaking the Waves. But no sooner than I tell Lucy there's a
problem, cause Keith wants to see it and he ought to mind
the coffee.

Alone in the Dark
(Jack Sholder, 1982, US)

I stand my ground and in no time I'm making more noise
than the entire audience once her husband gets paralysed and

particularly the hand jobs she gets in to please him now his bottom half won't work.

Someone arrives halfway through and wants me to show them to a seat. I can hardly look at them. Can't they see I'm in the middle of a fucking movie? And I lose it after that. It's broken my concentration and now when she talks to herself like the Virgin Mary it starts to grate. Keith has joined me and he's taken over my crying jag. By the time I come out the day's over and now it's the long drag of the late shift. I don't want to call a friend and be reminded some people have a social life.

The Desperate Hours
(William Wyler, 1955, US)

I feel like calling Ben and putting the phone down. It's that time of day. Michael can see I'm getting low and that attraction thing has gone and we're back as mates on a shift. And he starts to ask me my news, which means has Ben called but it's not like he cares. He's got that look of concern I don't trust. Lucy slinks up with that same look. I've been here since eleven, it's not authentic. I share a butterscotch ice cream and a coffee with Ian to kickstart me for *Hamlet*. We all know the types that'll be in for this one. Notting Hill and Holland Park dressed for movie and dinner with friends.

The Line
(Robert J Siegel, 1980, US)

I see friends of friends and that makes it worse, they think I've fallen on hard times and so do I. And we don't *need* to tear tickets cause they know *I* know they've bought their ticket, it's stupid. We slag off culture vultures. Michael can get really nasty and the giggles get us through to *The Big Blue*.

The Last Movie
(Dennis Hopper, 1971, US)

My actor again would you believe, with an odd-looking companion. I think he's a dealer. But I'm doing it again, offering free coffee and an end slice of carrot cake. I'd kill for a veggie hot dog. Instead we spend our wages on pizza delivery, even Graham who normally nips out for a Chinese takeout, and it's the one with the egg on top and spinach even though I'll have one bite and give my share to Michael. Still they're not into sweeties like I am. I've got that much Ritters at home it's embarrassing.

The Day of the Dolphin
(Mike Nichols, 1973, US)

There's a bit of action with police chasing a black guy down the road and they look like they're about to shoot except we don't do that here. And Keith runs out of the auditorium, well he would be watching fucking dolphins, and tells us the film is down and Lucy's in her element cause she's in charge and has to give an announcement and Michael does his drama queen and rushes up to Graham to find out the film's snapped.

We offer free coffee, guess who's first in line, and it's up and down to fill the machine, get out ice creams and more demand on cake. By the time the dolphins are cavorting again me and Michael are run off our feet and sharing a fag when guess who walks by with his dog.

Cornered
(Edward Dmytryk, 1945, US)

And it's so awkward cause Michael's not moving and he asks if we fancy stopping by for a *nightcap?* First, I've never heard of nightcaps, second I never take them and I tell him Michael and I were going to have ourselves a nightcap when we come off, which is a downright lie cause we're not members of an all night drinking club.

1 + 1 = 3
(Heidi Genee, 1979, W.Ger)

It's fucking dead to the world at this hour and Michael looks intrigued. Why don't you both pop by? Michael's in there like a flash he only wants to see the pad.

Nightcleaners
(Berwick Street Film Collective, 1975, GB)

Well, I'm busy packing up my sweets, emptying coffee dregs and generally getting sorted. I won't have the next person on complain. It's awkward when Dustin Hoffman brushes past me binliner in hand. I make out I have highfalutin plans, binliners to fill and I do. But this time me and Michael joke around cause he can't wait to see what Ralph has up his sleeve and I touch up my make-up while Michael finds a condom though it doesn't look used. Can't they restrict themselves to handjobs? This gives Keith more ammunition to tell us where the world's heading when Bella comes for Lucy and she's got that look that says she's been on the make and happy to have had her evening free. You know the minute they're in the car, Lucy'll start whining at her in the worst possible way. She can't wait to hear out Ralph report so she books me and Michael for Tuesday and another late weekend.

After Hours
(Martin Scorsese, 1985, US)

We head towards the smart end of Elgin Crescent and he answers the door with Oliver. The dog. I ask about the kid but he says he's with his mother. Where is she? I ask, like I don't know they aren't cohabiting. And we head up so many flights I lose count. Michael and I sit opposite each other on matching leather sofas and we start to get the giggles which is him and I to a tee. He comes in with glasses and a bottle of champagne and I see a line of coke on the table.

Before I can signal, Michael is helping himself. I've no luck with drugs but I do it just for the hell of it. I get an immediate kickstart and then there's the champagne and not much in my stomach and I see we're heading somewhere when Michael looks at me again. It's that curious look taken up a few notches and Ralphie wastes *no* time getting down to business.

Let's Get Laid
(James Kenelm Clarke, 1977, UK)

I find you really attractive, don't you, Michael, he asks. Now I have two of them looking at me with that dumb look of desire – it always makes you foolish. What's going on guys! I say cheery but Ralph's on his way over and kisses me and touches my breast. Well he knows how to touch them and I see Michael and he's passed from foolish clown to horny bugger.

Man on Fire
(Elie Chouraqui, 1987, Fr/It)

Shall we fuck her Michael he says as he drops his hand to rub the crotch of my hot pants and slide his hand up inside. Come here Michael he tells him and Michael comes over like an obedient pup. I can feel his hard-on while Ralph has moved behind me and is sliding his hand down the back of my shorts. I hate my arse and don't want him to feel it but what's happening in front with Michael is amazing and I wish Ralph wasn't there. Particularly when I feel that his hands are enveloping Michael from behind me and touching his face. What did I fucking tell you I hear myself thinking.

Signs of Life
(Lebenszeichen) (Werner Herzog, 1968, W.Ger)

I wonder if Michael had a clue to his intentions. Ralph heads to the windows to draw the curtains and on his way back takes his cock out of his trousers and Michael finds this as good a moment as any to take his prick out too. Well this is the moment *I* would if I had one and I can hardly *believe* it when Ralph turns down the lights and straps a dildo on me. I feel a darn sight better fully clothed. He's telling me to ram my cock up Michael's arse he's such a pretty arse and I've got a beautiful cock and to be honest I've forgotten most of his choice phrases, as you can imagine I've not found the opportunity to pick Michael's brains.

Three Into Two Won't Go
(Peter Hall, 1969, GB)

He's naked now and he's wanking himself off while he tells us what to do and me and Michael are a touch inhibited till Ralph rubs some cream on his cock and tells Michael he's going to coat his pretty little arse with it and he spreads some on my cock too and pulls both of us over to suck at his, only the taste is all hand lotion and it's making me gag and when it's Michael's turn he seems to enjoy it and looks up at me with his mouth full.

Take It Like A Man, Maam
(Ta' det som en Mand, Frue!) (Elizabeth Rygard/ Mett Knudsen/Li Vilstrup, 1975, Den)

He holds my cock and guides me to Michael now on all fours who squeals pure pleasure when I ram it in as far as it goes. Now Ralph's behind me pushing me in and out of Michael for what seems like ages with Michael crying and Ralph grunting and knocking my thighs till he says we're going to come we're going to come we're going to come. The sounds they make are horrendous and I can hear Oliver scratching at the door to get in.

I've got Michael having what looks like a fit on the ground beneath me and hot come jetting between my legs which must be Ralph's and two men in a heap and a dildo with nowhere to go. I unstrap the dildo while the boys return to planet earth and sit on the soft leather couch. And with what appears like synchronicity both of them start lapping at my pubes like there's money to be found. I'm already thinking stains on leather.

Not For Publication
(Paul Bartel, 1984, US)

Now we're talking cause their tongues are sort of French kissing while they're exploring my clit and it's as exciting watching them snog as it is to feel them and Ralph jumps up and returns in no time interrupting Michael's skills with a vibrator like a fighter jet and before I know it I'm moaning with pleasure. They're urging me in unison, come baby come, let it out, let it go, sweet pussy, beautiful cunt and when it finally happens I multiple orgasm into the back of the expensive leather sofa and it's enough to fill a coffee filter and I'm ready to sleep but I've two stiffies awaiting action.

Let's Do It Again
(Sidney Poitier, 1975, US)

Ralph flips me over and now I'm too tired to follow the details but it feels like they're taking turns. I soon wake up when I feel Ralph's cock in my arse he's directing again and getting Michael to lie on the couch underneath me. It doesn't take long till he's turning him over and I hear myself encouraging the boys though I'm ready to drop.

Spot
(*Dogpound Shuffle*) (Jeffery Bloom, 1974, Can)

Ram your cock up his beautiful boy arse I chant repetitively do it do it do it. Michael's screaming now and Ralph is riding him and Oliver is yelping in tandem with Michael and somehow manages to push open the door to find the three of us in a compromising position. I feel more embarrassed than I ever did with Michael or Ralph. The show's over. Oliver is sniffing at us, particularly the boys and to be honest I find it a bit disgusting sharing body fluids with a dog. I start pulling on my clothes and let's face it, it's hardly the night to spend cosied up in bed, all three. Michael follows suit only he looks disappointed like he wants something. Scrambled eggs. Fresh coffee.

Two For The Road
(Stanley Donen, 1966, GB)

We've all gone quiet and Michael asks if I want to share a cab. He's sleeping at Ian's. I wonder if he'll tell him. I can hardly look at him. Ralph asks us to come by again but we know he doesn't mean it. He's after one-offs is Ralph and there's always the dog. Are you allright asks Michael which is his way of acknowledging we've made a poor choice. When I see him Tuesday there's no curiosity looks, just a false sort of upbeat hello.

A Cry in the Dark
(Fred Schepisi, 1988, Aust)

I go to the loo when there's a lull and have a good cry for Michael, and particularly Ben who should be out there making sure I don't get into these messes. And for Oliver. I feel like I've only had pure affection for dogs and now they've been sullied and I blame myself really cause of all that cavorting in the foyer. And the worst thing is Lucy when she quizzes, cause we describe the house and the coke, the champagne and the decor, but come over all vague like it was so boring. And when we order a pizza I don't give him my share but get an appetite of my own for a change.

Fade To Black
(Vernon Zimmerman, 1980, US)

Deathrocker, Sex Boy, and Fuck

Thomas S. Roche

It is Walpurgisnacht. But then, it generally is.

Deathrocker and Sex Boy float like avenging angels or haunted death spirits. They wander through the legal/illegal smoke and smart-drug B.O. of the Orphanage, the club where they hang. The Orphanage: the Orphanage is littered with spirits, orphans, junkies, water-nymphs, download losers, upload pricks, former Catholics, urban soldiers of fortune, punk rockers, goth rockers, fallen new-agers, fashion victims of poorly executed Exile-on-Main-Street chic, and other assorted rejects. Basically the club fills up each weekend night with anybody fucked up enough to waste their time there. Lingerie-boys dance in indiscreet abandon suspended above the dance floor in cages, wearing manacles. Strap-on girls writhe on platforms to either side, flashing trendy blue-black modern-primitive tattoos at the edges of rolled-up sleeves on tattered Fruit of the Loom T-shirts copped from their fathers or, maybe, their boyfriends. The club is filled with machine-gun drum machine mixed with guitar feedback and samples from the Black Mass played backwards, the Ave Maria, Russian Orthodox services, obscure William Burroughs albums, and Pavarotti. The flowers of evil scatter their petals on the winds of the approaching apocalypse.

Deathrocker cocks her head, tosses her hair, feigning indifference.

"There's Fuck," she says.

Sex Boy's snappy retort: "Fuck?"

"Yeah, Fuck. You know."

"I thought that poser spent his time at the Gallery. Or the fucking Institute."

The Gallery is the Gallery of despair, perhaps the only club in town, maybe anywhere, with a more pretentious clientèle than the Orphanage. The Institute is strictly for kids as far as Sex Boy is concerned.

"She," sneers Deathrocker. "Fuck hangs here now," she says. "She got kicked out of the Gallery. They told her never to come back. Something about a bouncer and a twenty-dollar blowjob."

"Fuckin' A, twenty dollars. That's a lot to pay for a blowjob. I thought Fuck was a he."

"She," says Deathrocker. "Look at those tits."

Look he does, oh, yes. It is certainly something to behold. This is the good part; keep your hands out of your lap. Fuck wears a tight spandex dress stretched across shoulders and tits and flat belly and bulging crotch, boneframe angled and dangerous. She has knife-edged eyelashes, razorblade earrings, thick blackberry lips in an eternal pout. Bleach-white hair scatters like Niagara Falls over her broad, unblemished white shoulders. Her tits are big and silicone-firm. Her long legs stretch into heaven or hell (depending on your particular wish). The legs are unstockinged, bare, beautiful. Fuck wears high-heeled deathrock boots, the buckles recycled from chalices used by the Pope when he had his little breakdown and said the Black Mass in public a few years ago – you remember. No one seems to know, in the stories they tell about Fuck, whether Fuck is a he-fuck or a she-fuck. But rumour has it that under that tight spandex Fuck harbours the yin and the yang, the princely pestle and the bearded clam, the pride and the prejudice, John Thomas and Pussy Galore, both of 'em in eternal synchronized interaction. It's called "G.O.D." on the street, short for Genetically Operative Doctoring, but that term is, according to the Faustus and Pangloss article in last week's New England Journal of

Medicine, no longer considered scientifically accurate. Living tissue splice is now the preferred medical term for the technique. But it's still theoretical, never even tested in the chop-shop labs in Amsterdam. The operation is strictly the thing of urban legend, even if you hear stories all the time in the drag bars and whorehouses.

The chick responsible for spreading most of the Fuck stories is a burned-out designer drug techno-child whom no one trusts anyway. But she claims to have sucked Fuck's cock, down on her knees in the little girl's room, and fingerfucked her pussy at the same time. That's enough to get my hormones flowing, I dunno about yours. Everyone knows it's unlikely that Fuck's the androgyne the stories say Fuck is. But from the looks of those tits and the bulge in the front of that dress, it might be true, and some of us prefer to dream. Wonder about it for the next couple pages, OK?

"I'm taking Fuck home tonight," says Deathrocker. Right into Sex Boy's ear.

Sex Boy laughs. "Taking Fuck home. You think you're taking Fuck home. Gonna fuck 'im?"

"What else?" shrugs Deathrocker. "Wanna join in?"

"I don't waste my time on cheap-perfume posers."

Deathrocker doesn't respond. She slides away towards Fuck.

Goth girls and B&T dance-club whores crowd around Fuck, aching for a feel. Fuck remains distant, aloof, untroubled, untouched. No one at the Orphanage will grace that multiply endowed form tonight. Then catch sight of Deathrocker, dancing, swaying through waves of blue-grey smoke, smelling of cloves and whiskey. The crowd dissipates.

"Pleased to meet you. I'm Deathrocker."

"Fuck." Fuck pouts at Deathrocker, shoulders back. Her nipples poke through tight spandex. Fuck does not offer to shake hands. Instead, the two wordlessly head for the dance floor.

The two become ghosts in the strobe lights. They engage

in a dance-floor grope session, rubbing against each other and whimpering. Sex Boy haunts them from the shadows, watching. Stretch jeans stretched more than previously.

Deathrocker and Fuck make their way to the front of the dance floor. A circle forms quickly, ghoulgirls and wraith-boys watching the show. Whispers travel through the crowd. Deathrocker, anonymous black-clad bitch, is putting the moves on Fuck, the coveted thing of many sexes.

Deathrocker gets down on her knees in front of Fuck. The dance is an excuse for Deathrocker to mimic cunnilingus/fellatio with this creature of Hindu divinity. Sex Boy watches from beneath the strobe lights, touching himself surreptitiously.

Fuck gives Deathrocker a significant wink, then turns, stalking in those heels through crowd of silent deathrockers who part for her like the Red Sea for Moses. Deathrocker kneels there bewildered, thinking about it. She follows Fuck out the door. Sex Boy is not far behind.

Fuck is waiting outside. The trio climb into Sex Boy's rusty sixties Cadillac, and Sex Boy gets the top down and hammers the car into gear. Fuck and Deathrocker play the tongue game in eighty-mile winds up Third. Fuck gets her hand up Death-rocker's skirt and slips the middle finger in there.

The apartment is not far away, and the triumvirate don't waste any fucking time making a pot of coffee.

The three of them get down on the stained black futon. Fuck's black dress comes down hard around his/her tits. Her nipples are pierced with 14-gauge rings. Sex Boy's always had a thing for pierced nips. He gets his hand on the left one, and his mouth on the right. He nibbles at the silver ring as Deathrocker slides to her knees and gets Fuck's skirt up over her spread thighs, around her waist. Deathrocker gropes for the hard shaft of Fuck's living-tissue manmeat, which pops out helpfully in eight-inch thick-headed splendour.

Sex Boy, French-kissing Fuck, reaches down and wraps his fingers around the base. He guides the cock into his girlfriend's waiting mouth. She sucks it down hungrily.

Deathrocker pulls at Fuck's tight white panties until they come off over her ankles. Sex Boy and Deathrocker reach Fuck's crotch at the same time with their fingertips, groping to discover what generations of two-week trendies have tossed and turned in their beds at night wondering about.

They gasp, as one, as they feel the softness of Fuck's cunt giving way to their probing. Sex Boy prevails. He bats Deathrocker's hand aside and slips two fingers inside. The cunt is wet and ready. Sex Boy slides his tongue deeper into an eager Fuck's mouth.

Deathrocker swallows Fuck's cock again and again, then sucks on the balls. Her tongue snakes down to flicker across erect one-inch clitoris just below. Sex Boy has his fingers working overtime inside Fuck's cunt. Deathrocker reaches out, smears her fingers with lube from the 16-oz pump dispenser on the nightstand, and goes to work on Fuck's ass.

Fuck's ass gives way eagerly, clean and slick, more eager and open even than the cunt. Deathrocker gives it two fingers. Sex Boy's tongue has become a whirlwind, a horny thunderbolt, Fuck whimpering in unholy abandon as she/he takes it multiple times and feels the two pairs of hands working their dark magic upon his/her high-tech body. Fuck begins to recite the Lord's Prayer. The threesome explodes in a whirlwind of sex and sensation – fade to black.

Faint stream of light through the window, first thing in the morning.

Sex Boy has cut his tongue on one of Fuck's razorblade earrings. He gets up, puts his jeans on, brushes his teeth, takes a piss, washes the blood off his lips.

It is not quite morning.

As dawn breaks through the windows in streams of apocalyptic brilliance, Fuck's flesh begins to decay.

Sex Boy thoughtfully reaches up and pulls the blinds closed.

He bends over the stereo. With the flick of one switch,

three disks begin to play simultaneously. Skinny Puppy, Diamanda Galas, the ubiquitous Pavarotti.

It's a wake-up call to the not-yet-dead.

Cock bulging against stretch jeans.

Sex Boy unzips and starts for the futon.

Da Da

Toby Litt

It is 1976. Brighton, The Grand Hotel. An as-yet-unfamous pop group from Sweden has just won the Europrism Singing Contest. They are called DaDa (pronounced as if referring to a lickle baby's daddykins rather than to a dubious European art movement of the early twentieth century). The song with which they have triumphed is called "Stalingrad". It likens the joyful terror of knowingly beginning an abusive relationship to the encirclement by Wehrmacht forces of the Russian city of Stalingrad. The chorus goes: "Stalingrad! / You beat my sister up really bad. / Stalingrad! / I never knew you were such a cad. / Stalingrad! / Meet me tonite at the helipad. / Stalingrad! / I want some more of what sissie had."

After the awards ceremony, DaDa retire to one of their two matching penthouse suites at The Grand Hotel.

The members of the band are two foxy chicks, A1 and A2, and two horny guys, B1 and B2.

A1 is wearing a blue chiffon jump-suit trimmed with yak fur, knee-length suede boots and a knitted Peruvian menstruation hat, with symbolic ear-flaps (ie, whatever you say, I won't fucking listen).

A2 is dressed in a more fireside-porno look: *crème-caramel* coloured silk blouse under an I-read-books-sometimes cardigan, fitted-by-a-gynaecologist spray-on blue jeans and Scholl-but-sexy clogs.

A1 has long blonde Aryan hair; A2 has a tight chestnut perm.

As for the guys, B2 looks like he is seeking political asylum from the Glitter Band; whereas B1 is sporting the latest designer-Serf outfit (complete with encrusted faecal traces) by international Swedish designer Sprog Max Borgstern.

B1 and B2 both have big bushy beards.

A1 and B1 have been married for three years but manage with effort to combine being recovering alcoholics with being on the rocks.

A2 and B2 are an item: Lot 69 in the Stockholm I'll-Be-Your-Sex-Slave-For-The-Long-Winter-Months Auction, September 1975.

Unbeknownst to B1, A1 is having an affair with B2. A2 is fully aware of what's going on – in fact, she encourages it, because it allows her to pursue her illicit flinglet with B1. A1, of course, is completely ignorant of A2's affair with her beloved husband.

That is the situation, as they burst triumphantly back into the second of their two direly decorated hotel rooms. The wallpaper is a Touch-Me TM velvety effect, just, in a way, as Austria mimicked Germany during the inter-war (1918 to 1939) period.

B1 turns on the headboard radio and a stiltonesque- Bontempi-organ and Electro-zither track begins to play, in C minor.

B2 strokes the dimmer-switch with practised forefinger (he has one of these, a dimmer-switch, not a forefinger – urrh, you silly dur-brain! – amongst the myriad gidgets and gazmos in his batch-pad back in Stockholm).

A1 says, "I feels so hot and am really turned on by the winning we have dome of Europrism, no?"

A2 replies, "God, here below I am such of a wet pussy, you know . . . I drip and I am horny, so I want taking hard and now, baby."

(Being Swedish, DaDa talk like a porn movie all the time, of course, yah? Until now, however, they have never acted in a porno way, too.)

B2 says, "As you say, the idea of all those pretty girlies

from all over the Europe, just with the hots for me, it makes me hard in the pants like a stick of the famous Brighton rock, but much more wide."

B1 replies, "You are correct in that I feel as long and rigid as the pier penetrating the womanish sea that I am seeing outside this very window here."

A1 says to B1, "I cannot wait for privacy in a room of one's own. Take me here and now, in a rough manner, from behind."

As she speaks, however, A1 winks at B2; B2, pretending to smoulder at A2, but actually directing his linguistic lust back at A1, says, "My hot-rod of throb will in the very next moment be riding down your sticky-Tarmacked highway of desire."

B1 rips off his sheepskin jerkin and begins to unlace his mediaevo-flies. At which point, A2 looks at designated fuck B2 and says, "All this bad horniness is making me of the very same persuasion. I am here for you to take me wherever we want to go."

With this declaration, A2 flings her cardigan across the room. It lands on the textured mini-bar, knocking over the six assembled bottles of Babycham. (One of which is suspiciously empty. Oh no! Could someone else be in the room, hiding somewhere?)

B1 continues to struggle with his immensely complex crotch-fastening arrangements.

A2 finds it equally hard to remove her the-world's-your-speculum blue jeans.

By contrast, A1 pulls the rip cord on her jump suit and "has it off" in a mere demi-hemi-semi-trice.

And B2, once the sparkly shoulder pads are ditched, nudifies himself with utter celerity.

As she has very little else to do, A1 kneels down and starts to find out just how sugary sweet B2's stick of Brighton rock really is.

Oh, no! A divorce could be in the offing.

But the sight of their co-band members getting down on it

merely inspires A2 and B1 to redouble their efforts of fashion escapology.

"I am to you a microphone," groans B2 to A1. "Show me the technique you are having."

Finally, B1 says, "Have you a pair of scissors in your possession?"

A2 replies, "Good, Batman." Her handbag is very handy, and soon she is snipping her way through his twenty leather-look pant tighteners. They ping and they pung, and soon his Palace Pier is being lapped by the incoming tides of A2's saliva.

But more (and other) is to come.

A2 reaches across and, in a post-Global-telecast frenzy of Sapphic lust, tweaks A1's bright red nipple.

"The fans," she says. "They are wanting us to be do-be-do-be-doing this to each other for the longest day."

A1 groans and, removing B2's lurve-microphone from her imminently million-selling larynx, says, "I am a waterfall of wanting this dream to come true. Let me 'visit with your close family'."

With which rare Swedish lesbo-idiom, A1 muff-dives across the room like a Furby on heat. (If you'll excuse the anachronism.)

In her delight at being so pleasured, A2 releases B1's schlong from its dental clamp.

The massive Euro-penis strafes the room with heavy threat, like a Sherman tank about to liberate Paris.

He puts his hands on his lithe hips and says to song-writing chum B2, "How about you and me, here and now, melodic big boy?" Big-beefy-beardy B2 needs no further RSVP. He is suckety-sucking before you can say Roger Wilco John Thomas.

All of top Swedish pop band DaDa are now naked as the day they last sauna-ed together. (Wednesday.)

Gay *fellatio* and dykey cunnilingus last for a long while.

Then A1 says, "Now give it to me up where the sun ain't gonna shine any more."

B1 and B2 look at each other confusedly. In order to do this, B2 has to make a small centre parting in the afro-bush of B1's public hair. Neither of them knows which of them A1 meant. All they are sure of is that A2 wasn't the addressee.

So, how do they solve this tricksky problemo?

Well, surely, by pulling themselves apart and then by pulling apart A1's pert bumcheeks.

"I'm to die for it," she says. "I ache like a tooth."

The Swedish are a polite people.

"After you," says B2.

"No," says B1. "After you."

Eventually their prevarication annoys A2 into taking action, she turns her soon-to-be equally unit-shifting shitter ceiling-wards and says, "Last one in's a cissygay-boy."

And so, B1 slams his schlong into A2 and B2 buries his hatchet in A1.

Swedish ugghs and mnnns sound much like English ones.

The ex-backing-singer nymphettes, side by side on the chocolate counterpane, ride the hard cocks of what will, in twenty years, be widely acknowledged as the greatest song-writing partnership since Lennon and McCartney.

Hands reach out from one coupling to touch the humping humps of the other.

Now the shit really hits the fan, who has been hiding half under the bed all this time. (After celebrating the band's success by quaffing a bottle of their Babycham – Aha!)

She is sixteen, a virgin, but very obviously up for it; viz she is wearing an ultra clingy DaDa T-shirt and a pair of hot pants that would make even the Turin Shroud's eyes water.

She can no longer remain anonymous.

The squits of superstar bum juice in her flaxen hair are just too much for this little fuck-kitten's neurons to process.

She crawls out on hands and knees, much to the popta-bulous quartet's surprise and delight.

Her yellow-butterflied bunches swing as she says, "Make me depraved like you guys."

The fan's pert titties jiggle beneath the DaDa logo like two heads giving blow-jobs.

B1 and B2 immediately pull their un-Trojan stallions out of their particular siege situations.

The fan seizes her opportunity, in both hands.

Her cutesy-girl clothes are ripped from her soft English flesh. And, pretty damn soon, A1 and A2 are collaborating in holding her spread-eagled on the floor whilst B1 and B2 unite in de-hymening her Limey love-passage.

"Your songs mean so much to me," the fan yelps. "They helped me get over my break-up with Derek."

With their free hands, A1 and A2 begin to twist her beehive-shaped, honey-sweet nipples.

"Ow," she says. "That hurts in an unexpectedly nice way."

"Hold her in a still position down," A1 demands. "While I fetch the equipment."

A2 sits her fanny on the fan's face.

"Tongue my wet parts," she says. "That's an order, corporal. If you don't, we won't be doing no Christmas Message on your stupid Fan Club flexidisc this year."

B1 and B2 are banging into the fan like the rhythm section on "Nympho Hippo, Hunky Monkey", which is to be the follow-up single to "Stalingrad".

("Nympho Hippo, Hunky Monkey" concerns the attempts of a grossly overweight Norwegian girl to seduce a particularly well-hung orang-utan in Oslo Zoo, one dark and windy night.)

A1 returns from the beside table with her King Dong KlassiK vibrator – twelve inches of throbbing battery-powered silicone.

"Let me coming through," she says.

Miraculously, B1 and B2 part – like the Polish populace in 1939 for the invading German Panzer tanks.

The fan faces the black fucksimile of a porn god.

"Pierce me like an ear," she shrieks. Clever B1 and B2 are soon giving her a taste of the wonders of stereo, stud-style.

A2 is feeling left out of all the fun, and so she fetches her own unmatronly orgasmatron – it's a "Holmes", and pretty soon it's installed in front of a roaring fire, having a bit of crumpet, up her own personal Baker street. "Aaaagh," A2 shrieks, like an out-of-sync disco violin.

At this moment, both B1 and B2 have an idea for a follow-up single to "Nympho Hippo, Hunky Monkey". It will be called "What's Yours Is Mine (and What's Mine is Yours)". The subject of the dead-cert gold-disc song will be the transfer of the herpes simplex virus from a Belgian child prostitute to a senior member of the Royal Family of Luxembourg and thence, by stages, in each succeeding verse, to an English butler, a Spanish opera singer and finally – in a delicious irony – the child prostitute's own grandmother. The chorus will go: "It's cold, it's sore / It's really rather raw / From poor-oh whore-oh / to Euro bore-oh / from Tea-at-four-oh / to Toreador-oh / to At-Death's-Door-oh! / What's yours is mine / (and what's mine is yours) / Oh!"

The thought of creating such a musico-masterpiece makes B1 and B2 simultaneously ejaculate in such an extravagantly creamy fashion that the shag-pile carpet of the penthouse suite of The Grand Hotel, Brighton, will need a shampoo and set before the room is once again fit for human habitation. But the fan-gangbang night has many more hours and many, many more pervy permutations to get through before Dawn spreads her rosy cunt-lips. (Dawn being, of course, the chambermaid.)

Downtown

Hanne Blank

Adult Books flickered the neon sign, hanging behind grimy glass. Katie hung back a little bit as her lover opened the door to the place, which she did without reticence. An even five feet of fireplug-stocky, fire-engine red-haired, freckle-faced stone butch, Mick looked a lot like Opie Taylor. Opie Taylor with D cups and a strap-on, and a boyishness that was probably the quality Katie liked best about her.

The shoppers inside were few, and uniformly male. Mick's presence seemed not to trip their radar, but then Mick passed, more often than not. She usually used the men's room.

Katie was another story. You just don't walk into a porn shop when you're an expensive-looking five-eight brunette and expect heads not to turn. The boys don't know, and don't care, that you sleep with girls when you look like that . . . in fact, if they knew, they'd think it was the answer to a prayer. The hungry glances that strafed Katie's body made her nervous as hell.

Eyes down, she walked past the racks of cheap plastic dildos and grubby-looking magazines, watching Mick's short, firm legs, feeling a little tingle of excitement smoldering somewhere below her belly button. She would've sworn that she didn't know how she'd let Mick talk her into this, but her swelling clit would've called her a liar.

Katie liked sleaze. Secretly. She never came right out and said it. Not even to Mick. But it didn't matter. Mick knew

how to read between the lines. And Katie liked it dirty, and
rowdy, with a scintillating edge of danger. She wasn't about
to cop to it, but then that's just not something you do when
you've got pearls from Tiffany, a briefcase from Coach, a
birth certificate that says Grosse Pointe, Michigan, a law
diploma that says Harvard, and a business card that says
Junior Partner, McMicken, Hunting, Daniels, and Smith.
Not even when you're wearing a nipple-less bra from Fre-
derick's underneath your Chanel suit. It was the unspoken
contract of their relationship: don't ask, don't tell. Just
pursue.

And pursue Katie did, following in Mick's footsteps past
the Swedish penis enlargers, past the copies of "Shaved
Pregnant Oriental Twat" and "Barely Legal Lesbo Teens",
past the rows and rows of video covers that showed every
conceivable orifice and every conceivable thing with which
an orifice might be stuffed. They walked straight to the back
and turned right, Katie catching up with Mick as she paused
before the doors.

Booth number three was small and dark and barely big
enough for the two of them when they closed the door and
slid the bolt home. The dim light overhead reminded Katie
of the light in Mick's beat-up old Toyota, yellowish and wan.
Without preamble Mick's hands were under Katie's blouse,
silk tugged from her waistband, breasts spilled from under-
wires, rough thumbs pinching nipples, rolling them over and
over. Katie whimpered, kittenish, into her lover's mouth,
already telegraphing her urgency though they'd hardly begun.

The booth wasn't comfortable, but that wasn't the point.
Fortunately the floor wasn't sticky. Katie breathed a sigh,
then shivered and sucked in her breath, her long, red-tipped
fingers anxiously fondling the short soft fuzz of her lover's
brush cut as Mick's tongue and lips and teeth fastened onto
one already-hard nipple. The tinny whine and thud of the
disco music coming through the wall accompanied their
grinding embrace, doing nothing to mask the raspy groans

that limped out of Katie's throat as Mick bit and chewed and licked and sucked.

"Whaddaya want, cutie? You sound like there's something you want," Mick coaxed as Katie squirmed.

Katie blushed, the scarlet in her cheeks as obvious as the unconscious grinding of her hips. Mick slid her hand down, sneaking it under Katie's hem, and stroked the soft skin just above her stocking top.

"Good girl, Katie," Mick growled smokily. "Hose, not pantyhose, just the way your Micky told you to. Did you do the other thing Daddy told you had to do if he was going to bring you to the peeps?"

Katie nodded shyly.

"What's the matter, girl? Cat got your tongue? Did you do what I asked you to do or not?"

Katie's voice was a hoarse whisper. "Yes, Daddy. I did what you asked me to."

"Show me."

Her cheeks and ears red, conservative pageboy falling forwards to cover only some of her embarrassment, Katie leaned forwards and pulled up her skirt, hitching it up slowly. Black garters descended to tan stocking tops, and between her thighs . . . nothing. Not even a scrap of pubic hair remained to hide the puffy cleft of her pussy. But that was the way it was supposed to be. Daddy told her she should be bare. So she was.

"Oooh, Katie. What a nasty little girl you are, no panties on, getting felt up in a peepshow both like some trailer-trash slut," Mick snarled, stroking one fingertip up and over the arch of Kate's silken-smooth mons. "I think you should reach in Daddy's pocket and find out what I've got in there for you."

"For me, Daddy?" Katie asked, her voice little-girlish. Mick could feel how hot she was, could already feel the slip of girl-juice as she stroked the edges of Katie's cunt.

Mick nodded as Katie's long fingers slipped into the pocket of her 501's, withdrawing the roll of shrink-wrapped quarters. "What are the quarters for, Daddy?"

"Well, we are at the peeps," Mick said, leaning Katie back against the wall and teasing her nipple with her thumb and forefinger as she nudged her knees apart. "But these quarters are for you."

With that, Mick grinned wickedly and slid a finger into Katie's cunt. Her wetness, gratifyingly copious, let her slide right in, all the way to the knuckle as Katie's eyes closed reflexively.

"That's right, baby," coaxed Mick, "you just love the way your Daddy fucks you, don't you?" Working her fingers in and out several times, Mick waited until Katie's hips were rocking in anticipation of the next stroke. In slid the roll of quarters, right alongside two of Mick's fingers, and Katie's eyes flew open, surprised.

Don't worry, baby," Mick soothed, "I've got more quarters for the booth. Don't you worry. Daddy's gonna take care of everything."

With that, Mick fumbled in her pocket with her free hand, then slapped two coins into the slot in the wall. The rickety creak of the metal shade accompanied the arch of Mick's hand as she ground her fingers and the quarters deep into Katie's sopping cunt, forcing her to arch and muffle a squeal.

The gel-covered lights that surrounded the peepshow stage lent an odd blueish-purple cast to the light in the booth, like a television screen. Opening her eyes in an strange mix of perversity, pleasure, and the frantic fear of exposure, Katie could see the reflections of eyeglasses behind other windows. Men were watching. Could they see her and Mick? Or were they watching the dancer? She could somewhat see them. Were they? What if . . .?

And then Mick was biting her nipple. And then Mick was grinding the roll of quarters in and out of her sopping cunt, mashing her clit with her thumb. And then Mick's mouth opened wide and she tried her hardest to take Katie's entire breast inside, and Katie gasped and Mick moaned and thrust into her with four fingers, the cunt-juiced roll of quarters hitting the floor of the booth with a thud.

"Tell me how good it feels to have your greedy little pussy full of Daddy's hand, Katie," Mick demanded, grinding Katie's G-spot as her thumb relentlessly circled her clit. "Tell Daddy how much you like being his peepshow whore."

Faltering, partly from embarrassment, partly from desire, and partly from the searing knowledge that she did like having Mick's hand in her to the knuckles as she bucked and moaned like a porn star in booth number three of a sleazy peepshow in a sleazy porn store in a part of town she would've never been caught dead in, Katie did, spilling out the words interspersed with the sharp sweet noises of impending orgasm. And Katie forgot to try to figure out whether anyone could see her, or Mick, or not.

Blouse tucked in, hair hastily combed, Katie followed Mick back out of the store, pausing for a moment or two to look at the magazine rack, tall and cool and femme next to short and butch and boyish.

"God, that's so fake," Katie laughed, pointing at a typical "girl-girl" spread, the teased hair and fake nails, silicone tits and neon-painted lips frozen in the industry standard blow job pucker. Considerably less anxious now, neither Katie nor Mick noticed the few glances of the few men who lurked in the store as they stood, backs to the counter, pointing and giggling.

Suddenly a male voice boomed from the counter, half the length of the store back. "Hey, lady!" it shouted, and Katie turned around, alarmed. Mick, of course, never responded to "lady".

"Hey, lady," the cashier repeated, his voice a perfect match to his burly, stocky, hairy-armed Sicilian frame, "you can't bring that kid in here."

"Kid?" Katie murmured, looking at Mick, then at the shopkeeper.

"You can't bring the kid in here, lady," the shopkeeper yelled. "You're gonna haveta leave. I don't care if you come in here, but don't bring the kid."

Katie looked at Mick, who arched an eyebrow eloquently. Lifting her hand to her mouth, she licked one finger as she gestured her tall, well-groomed girlfriend toward the door, smiling at the lingering taste of Katie's juice on her skin. "C'mon, little girl. You heard the nice man."

One in the Hand, Two in the Bush

Lauren Sanders

"Hold it!" Alexis commanded. A click and the cameras stopped; all eyes turned to her. Bodies stilled off set as if she'd pressed a pause button. On set, a man relaxed his grip on a woman's thighs, which had been posed missionary-style, making her look somewhat like a roasted chicken. Her legs dropped to the bed. He took a few steps back, glaring at Alexis as he stroked his erect penis. But for the alacrity of his hand-cock motion, he looked like some kind of sex zombie.

Having arrived just a few minutes earlier, I took the opportunity to move in and claim a camouflaged spot behind a couple of leafy floor plants, going for my usual fly-on-the-wall routine. Alexis sighed, "Billie, you've got to get the light in closer." Without a word, the woman standing behind a massive eyeball of a light dollied forward. I held out my microcassette recorder. "That's it, on top of her, I want to see her pussy glow. And can we get some glitter make-up on her thighs?" A woman with enough unguents to paint the cast of *Cats* came running. As if she were a gynecologist, she sat down in front of the star's legs and began her cosmetic doctoring. "Beautiful," Alexis said. "We're going for broke here, boys and girls, the fucking of the gods." There were a few giggles. Alexis turned to the naked man. "Mark, don't look at the camera so much. Use your tongue for a while, then pull back and pick up the crystal. Okay, heat 'em up and action!"

Mark, tongue jutting lizardlike from his mouth, moved along the woman's thighs. Two video cameras hovered close to their bodies. The woman moaned, giving what seemed like a virtuoso, *"Oh, baby, oh!"* I tried to remember her name. It began with a T, Tessa something . . . Tessa Toupee or Tepee or Tempe. And he must be Mark Vladimir, the featured male lead on this latest Zipless Pictures project: *One in the Hand, Two in the Bush*. It was already being hailed by the Alexis acolytes as groundbreaking erotic cinema.

I took my reporter's notebook from the pocket of my blazer, slipped the ball-point pen from behind my ear, and wrote down a few fragments: cameras. Smoke machine. Attractive young people with props; clipboards, cell phones, beepers, headphones. Everyone watching. Me watching them watch. The sanctioned voyeur.

Indeed it was like watching the trials I'd covered before the strike, and just as I'd been conscious of researching every case to the last detail I'd come prepared for my virgin viewing of this sex shoot. I'd seen a few videos, skimmed through insider magazines with names like *Skin, Video X-tra*, and *The Bondage & Discipline Tour*. I read selections from the classic texts, everything from Freud and Krafft-Ebing to *The Filmmaker's Guide to Pornography*. Going on-line, I logged into the appropriate newsgroups, gleaning information on new releases, industry feuds, HIV rumours, while familiarizing myself with the jargon. I could tell you the difference between meat and money shots, tout the industry's preference for Astroglide over other lubricants, and delineate scenes by their reductive categories: the boy–girl, the girl–girl, the boy–girl–girl, and so forth and so on.

The category of the moment was boy–girl, the action, post-insertion with sex toy, as Mark moved a thick, conelike crystal in and out of Tessa's vagina, stopping every few minutes to roll his tongue along the clear, wet stick. As they spoke I jotted down their dialogue.

> *Tessa says: Move me, fuck me with the light of God.*
> *Mark says: Baby, I'm here. I am God.*
> *Tessa says: Oh, I want you inside me now!*

Mark took a step back and ripped open a condom wrapper. It was a Zipless rule that couples practise safe sex, HIV test or not, yet there were exceptions: the married couple, the long-term lovers, or women with women who outright refused to work with those silly dental dams. But Mark and Tessa were a nonexception couple. That even I noticed this couldn't be good. No wonder Alexis looked dyspeptic, as if she were on the verge of bursting into bitter song; if this were indeed a musical and not a sex film shoot. The rest of the crew seemed constipated, watching nervously as Mark, a hirsute figure with a penis about the length and width of the average-size banana, fixed an airhole at the end of his condom, smiling perfunctorily at Tessa, whose face, though done up like a side-show gypsy, conveyed a fuck-me-yes-but-I-don't-have-to-like-it quality. Was it me or did she appear sorrowful beneath her rough and tumble exterior? I couldn't stop staring at the bottoms of her feet. Black from stomping back and forth on the dusty wood, they would need a touch of air brushing in the edit suite. The condom wrapper fell to the floor, sounding a light slap. Then came a collective sigh of relief as Mark, penis erect and snugly encased, put his palms on Tessa's thighs and pushed them upwards. One camera clung to their torsos, the other moved to Tessa's face. Mark took his penis in his right hand and guided it inside of her.

"Okay," Alexis said, "pick up with the other camera, keep going, on their faces. Good, good . . . shit! Tessa, be a goddamn martyr if you have to, but don't look like one. Cut!"

As from the sudden burst of a water balloon, frustration splattered in every direction. "We're going to be here forever," a guy in faded jeans, with headphones and a boom mike mumbled to nobody in particular.

"Shut up," Tessa snapped at him. "He smells like onions. I mean once or twice, but this is too much, and he's all soft again. You try smiling about fucking a slinky."

"You think you smell so great with all that flowery crap

you rub on," Mark said. "She wonders why I lose my concentration."

"I thought the onions were supposed to help," Tessa whined, as if she were a Class A tattle-tale. I wondered if she had older brothers.

"What is it with the onions?" Alexis asked.

"He says they make him more vee-rile," Tessa sneered at him.

"That's not what I said, you little . . . uh!" Mark jerked his head back in disgust, ran his right hand through his hair, and then glowered back at Tessa. His Adam's apple bobbed up and down as he started to speak. "I said they make my come more milky."

Alexis quickly moved between them, taking Mark by the elbow. "Look, we're wrapping today, and I absolutely refuse to be here all night. So go brush your teeth and no more onions. What do you do, eat them raw?"

"Like an apple," he said.

Alexis shook her head. "Honey, next time you're worried about the plumbing, try zinc capsules like everyone else. Now, you want to clear the set?"

"That's not the problem."

"Yeah right," someone murmured.

"Okay, enough from the peanut gallery. If you want to help, do a private little rain dance for Mark, and you," Alexis turned to Tessa, "go use your vibrator a few minutes. You're being paid to fuck a slinky if you have to."

Alexis sighed, leaned back in her director's chair. She caught my eye and motioned for me to join her. I did as instructed, like everyone else. For, as plagued by perfectionism as Alexis was, when she said cut, no matter how long they'd been shooting, everyone stayed with her vision. I got the feeling they all believed they were doing important work, trekking beyond the traditional porno métier . . . where no *man* had gone before. Women worked cameras, carried cell phones, and swung mikes. Yet even for these millennial years, it veered toward parody. A vision of Lesbos within the drab fascism of California porn.

And where on the Left Coast would you find a director who treated her actors and crew as if they were her own children? The other day I heard her on the phone asking Mark if he'd taken his Cs – he had a cold coming on; now she was pained by Tessa's phallophobia.

"I just don't get it," she was telling me. "I love using her because she doesn't have implants and her tits aren't that big, it's a different kind of aesthetic. It says something. You're recording this?"

I nodded.

"Don't," she said, rubbing two fingers on each of her temples. "I'm too riled, I have to think it through."

"Why are you so upset?"

"Why? I have a feature star who flips out when a man gets near her and you ask, why? Girl–girl scenes she's the best, but this isn't a lesbian company, that's not all we do. I've been telling her she doesn't have to feature, which would be a shame because every time she's on screen, it breaks ranks. She's not what a porn star should look like, blah, blah, semiotic bullshit maybe . . . but it's true."

"Because she's flat-chested?"

"Yes, of course. But if she won't do men, it's less powerful. Women don't have the tit fetish, most of them anyway. And that's not the point here. She made such a big deal about not wanting to be pigeonholed, not wanting to be an industry dyke. A lot of women are like that, they'll only do girl–girl scenes. It's safer, they feel less pressured with women."

"Less pressured, that's a laugh," I said.

Alexis looked at me, her brow furrowing inquisitively. "Are you a lesbian?"

"No."

She eyed me suspiciously and within seconds I was ten years old again, running to confession for a crime I didn't commit.

"Really, I'm not," I said.

"I'm sensing something, a sort of karmic sound bite. Are you in therapy?"

"Been out a few years, thank you very much." That question was easily answered. As far as I was concerned I'd fulfilled my quota on shrink time with Sam in Miami.

"Then you must have hit on this?" Alexis said, eyebrows raised as if she were waiting for a salacious disclosure. I became conscious of my tight-fitting blazer, the double-breasted wool jacket that wasn't exactly power suit material, but had been conservative enough to get me through the courts. Here it felt constricting, and heated up the back of my neck as if I were hiking the Stair Master. Besides, all the lights and cameras and action had made the set extremely hot.

Think journalism, I told myself. I am a journalist. My job is asking questions. Ask a question. I squeezed into my reporter's face, the one where my brow caverned in between my eyes and my lips pursed downwards. "So what happens if Tessa won't do it?" I ventured.

"Oh, she'll do it, she just needs a little tender loving care. Anyway, forget her for the moment. I want to know what's got you so flustered."

"I'm not flustered."

"You are too. The second I asked if you were a lesbian your entire face changed."

"It did not."

"You should see yourself, your cheeks are all red."

"It's hot in here, aren't you hot?" A bead of sweat dripped down the side of my face.

"Heat is an emotion."

I laughed out loud. "That's ridiculous. Heat is a physical condition."

"Brought on by emotion."

"Or temperature."

"The temperature in and of itself is irrelevant. Unless you're moving through it or self-combusting, you don't feel the heat. This is basic physics. So what's got you all worked up? What's making you feel the heat, so to speak?"

"I don't know, maybe the goddamn klieg lights."

"And why?"

"Because they're hot."

"What if I told you the lights were shut off ten minutes ago?"

"Were they really?"

"Immaterial."

"Of course it's material, you just said what if. I have the right to know whether we're speaking hypothetically or not."

"That is exactly my point. We're not talking about the lights, we're not talking about the heat, we're not talking about any physical characteristic of the set. We are talking about why when I asked if you were a lesbian you got flustered."

"I am not flustered!" I shouted, heat brimming beneath my skin, a mockery of my argument. Whatever argument that was. Confused, and embarrassed by the force of my words, I turned my head the other way. Across the set, a group of young women sat laughing and smoking cigarettes. Their easy communication made me angry. So free and libertine they were, working on a radical porno film. I felt even more isolated, more protective of my own world.

Alexis put her hand on my shoulder. "I didn't mean to upset you. I have too many freaked-out people around here already."

"I'm not freaked out." I turned to face her. "It's just that this ghostwriter thing won't work if you keep asking the questions."

"But it's only fair. Yesterday I talked for three hours about my adolescent masturbation to *Playboy*. All I'm asking for is a little reciprocity."

"The more you know about me, the less you'll trust me. I lose my authority."

"You have no authority, Rachel, you work for me."

I stared at her eyes, the folds around them conferring an air of wisdom earned the hard way. Times like these she looked her forty-two years, distinguishable from the rest of her cast and crew, from me, too. She took her hand from my shoulder and tapped my thigh twice, letting her palm linger a moment on my leg. The gesture wasn't at all sexual; it was, in a word, maternal. "All I'm saying is stop being so rigid, this isn't some dumb news story – no offence. Whatever you lose, who cares? Look at what you might gain." Her voice was a combination of brass and silk, it was a *Penthouse* spread transported to the New York Philharmonic, and it provoked the same mesmerizing power I'd felt upon our first meeting, the baptismal belief that my life would be incomplete were I not her ghostwriter. What I hadn't realized was just how unfulfilled I'd been until then. Something like a ghost.

"I really don't want to talk about me," I said finally.

"Oh, I think you do, you've just never been able to. You haven't felt safe."

"You know, I can get this kind of self-help crap anywhere. I didn't have to come to a porno film."

"Say what you like, but it's true. Do you know how many times I've been called a pervert? And practically anytime anybody reviews one of my films I'm mistaken for a whore, but this is what I do, it's who I am. When you're honest with yourself, it makes no difference what anyone else says."

"Just measure it in inches, right?"

"Pardon me?" She studied me as if I were speaking a different language. I'd forgotten how sensitive this industry could be about measurements.

"That's . . . uh . . . Warhol," I said, my ears tingling at the silent valleys in between my words. "He . . . you know, he said you shouldn't read your own press . . . just measure it."

"I've been saying that for years and I never even knew him. Some of my friends did back in the seventies, but how did you know that? Did you know him?"

"No!" I almost laughed out loud, imagining Andy Warhol coming to Bay Ridge for Thanksgiving dinner.

Alexis tilted her head back and forth. Watching her, the weight of my own hair grew heavier. I tucked it back behind my ears, one side at a time. "Rachel," she said, "if there's one thing I know – well, of course, I do know more than one thing – but I'm an expert on people." She took a deep breath, and I thought if we were part of the movie she would have taken a drag from a cigarette for effect. Instead she made a quick surveillance of the set. The young women were still laughing, a miasma of shimmering hair and cigarette smoke, the man in jeans fiddled with the knobs of a sound mixer, a woman with a clipboard sipped from a paper cup rimmed with big cherry red lipstick stains.

"You can see how being a student of human nature helps in this business," Alexis said, still scanning the set as if we were sitting together at a basketball game.

"No doubt." I feigned sophistication, but my words reverberated self-consciously.

Alexis pivoted toward me. "What I'm saying is, I've been watching you. You hide behind your one-liners, your facts and pithy insights. Believe me, I know irony feels like a safe space, but it's not. You're entitled to your emotions, Rachel. Especially the heated ones."

I felt a disabling sensation, like gas pains. In just a few minutes, Alexis Calyx had managed to disrupt the entire journalistic relationship. If anything, a reporter was supposed to remain emotionally disconnected. Alexis should know better. She'd been interviewed hundreds of times before, even once by Kim Mathews, the doyenne of TV interviewing and perhaps the country's most recognizable journalist, though I use that term loosely . . . I stopped myself, for I was indeed making light as she'd accused me of doing, but also because I realized just how flimsy my credentials were around here. I felt like Tessa Tureen, splayed with my dirty feet in the air.

Any real world concerns had spilled out into the East Village streets, while within the studio's sound-proof walls was a greenhouse of possibility. I could have known Andy Warhol. I could be gay. I could be anything I wanted here.

I clutched the back of my neck, wet with perspiration, and stared at Alexis. Our faces were indeed similar, oval shaped, with dark brown, hard-to-manage hair and black coffee eyes; just two little girls from the biggest of boroughs. We shared the ineffable bond of a Brooklyn childhood, just as Aunt Lorraine and Kaminsky together conjured ghosts of Nazi-occupied Poland. In spite of my anger at her invasiveness, as well as her reckless disregard for the tenets of my profession, I was drawn to her. A sensual telotaxis I could barely contain, let alone control.

"I'm too old for this," I said.

"Please, then I'm a dinosaur." She tapped once more at my thigh, and I wanted to tell her about the time Neil locked me in the handcuffs. How I was more afraid of telling on him, of what he might do next, than I was of the restraint. Before I could say anything, however, Alexis and I were interrupted by Alia the A.D. Everyone was set to go. Alexis stood up and winked at me, "Watch closely, this is the take."

My eyes trailed her as she walked toward Tessa, all dolled-up in her red teddy and G-string combo. Alexis leaned her elbows on the star's shoulders. Their eyes locked, Alexis talking and occasionally slipping a couple of fingers through Tessa's strawberry blonde hair. The doe-eyed porn star looked almost innocent, an admirable feat given her attire. Again, I felt the encumbrance of my own clothing. Next time I would wear jeans and a T-shirt like everyone else.

Tessa's bare arms locked around Alexis' crisp, white V-neck. Alexis towered over her, stroking her hair. They could have been mother and daughter. Who else would hug her half-naked child that closely? I thought of my own mother, and how I couldn't remember her once putting her arms around me. All my life I'd been waiting for the repressed memory that would prove me wrong.

I felt slightly put off. A little bit of sibling rivalry. Or perhaps the roots went deeper. For they could have been mistaken as lovers, Alexis and Tessa, their bodies entwined in what seemed a comfortable power imbalance.

Alexis gave Tessa's butt a light tap the way football players do after a huddle and then clapped her hands: "Okay, let's get on with it." Tessa flashed her a final adoring look, and I wondered if she was a lesbian. I remembered reading that lesbianism among women off set was as common as men with plumbing problems on it. Somehow, this made sense.

Yet we were all soon shrouded in the shadows of heterosexuality. Only the white of Mark and Tess's skin shone in cones of amber light. Even Alexis had stepped back as the scene fell into formation. Mark, his limbs sparkling as if they'd been dipped in a barrel of glitter make-up, had no erection trouble. Tessa, too, was more accommodating, her face a blush of lust and satisfaction, her body in tune with Mark's thrusting. Their rhythm was a modern ballet for an unknown audience.

You could smell it, too; the soured lotion, the sweat, the onions, the sex. It came to me in a craving so ignited, so aching, so incomprehensible, I felt myself blush. And I was pulled towards Tessa, this woman with her body arched and head thrusting back and forth. A clump of hair snagged across her mouth, and Mark without taming their beat moved his fingers to her face and gently pushed it away. His touch was so private, so spontaneous, and the way they eyed each other, as if love might be the by-product of sex and not the other way around, made me envious. Seeking solace, I looked around the audience as if staking out the faces of fellow movie-goers, trying to gauge . . . what? If anyone else was moved by this? If anyone was aroused by it? Ashamed of it? Part of me wanted to giggle childishly . . . *these people are fucking!* Yet another part wanted to jump into the scene, to lick Tessa's nipples, to suck Mark's penis, and sandwich myself between them, the three of us thrashing and burning until we all collapsed in a nest of exhausted arms and legs.

Mark, sweat dripping from his rosy face, shouted, "I'm going to come." Tessa screamed back at the top of her lungs. No words, just a series of loud grunts that had me leaning forwards with my eyes shut, slipping into the heat, the motion, a desire so palpable it dripped down my limbs. I could barely catch my breath. Mark screamed, "Oh baby,

I'm coming!" I slipped backwards, my eyes shot open. Mark fell on top of Tessa and his breathing slowed . . . and her breathing slowed . . . and my breathing slowed . . .

Alexis, face glimmering proudly, screamed, "Cut!" I leaned against a folding chair, still captivated by the naked bodies on set. So at ease in the aftermath, they gave the impression of being a long-married couple. Next to them I felt almost prepubescent.

Mark jumped up and shook out his hair. "That was so hot," he said, giving Tessa's forehead a light kiss. "Did you want to come?"

"In front of all these people, are you kidding me?" Tessa stood up and purred a round of thank-yous to the crew parting beside her with coos and compliments as she retired to her dressing room. A job well done.

And she didn't come. And nobody found this strange or incomplete. Nobody questioned her womanhood, suggested analysis, or stomped with iron feet back and forth, trying to resolve those issues that would set her orgasm free. She walked off the set even more of a diva for not coming. The next time anyone complained about me not coming I would say I was a porn star.

The idea stayed with me as I waited for Alexis amid the end-of-day collapsing of the set. Before today I would have thought my breasts too small, but they weren't any smaller than Tessa's. Maybe I wasn't as skinny as Tessa, but I wasn't exactly fat. Actually, I was in pretty good shape for a woman just over thirty who hadn't been to the gym in a few weeks. I would work out more. I would also need a few glasses of wine, or – who am I kidding – I would need a couple of Quaaludes before I could take my clothes off in front of all those people. No wonder most porn stars used pseudonyms. Perhaps, then, it was someone else people were ogling at, panting with, masturbating over.

Alexis herself had adopted a whole new identity upon entering the industry; few people were aware her real name was Patricia DeFabio. If I were to take a name, I would keep something of myself in it: maybe Rachel Silver or Rachel Slipper. No, I liked the word silver, its prurient shine, the way it bit back when you had it in between your teeth. And it was all mine, the name I'd chosen myself on my eighteenth birthday. Silver . . . like the chrome of the klieg lights, the glint from Hi-8 lenses, the beams, the rays, those silver rays . . . oh, yes, Silver Ray . . . sweet sobriquet. *One in the Hand, Two in the Bush* staring Mark Vladimir, Tessa Touche, and Silver Ray.

Yes, I could be a porn star if I wanted to.

I whispered the name Silver Ray until Alexis came to fetch me. Though giddy with my new identity, I was silent on the way back to the office where Alexis said she had a few "special" videotapes for me.

"I'm looking for my favourite girl–girl scene," Alexis said, pulling tape after tape from the shelf. Apparently, she thought she knew my sexual secret, although I had neither confirmed nor denied it myself. Oddly enough, I didn't mind. Having lesbian tendencies seemed an asset among this crowd. "It's an important theme for us, subversively that is," she said. "Time to steal it back from the boys and their computer-generated fantasies – it's like they keep remaking the same triple-X version of the Victoria's Secret catalogue. All of those shaved pussies and long red fingernails, please . . . and then they Vaseline the lenses to make everything so soft and dreamy. Have you ever seen women fuck each other? I mean really fuck each other, it's –" She paused, turning her head over her shoulder as if to make sure she still had my attention. Caught in her stare, I felt the heat of the set return to my cheeks, only this time I was more fed-up than embarrassed. I wanted to tell her I'd had enough, tell her I'd grown weary from her little theories on feminism and film and sexuality and shaved pudenda. I wanted to go home.

Perhaps she sensed my discomfort, or she'd fallen upon her own internal censors, for at that very moment she said she didn't want to prejudice my thinking *before* I watched the film. She swung her head back around and continued with the tapes until she found a box with the title *X-posure* scrawled along the spine.

"Here's my baby." She handed me the tape, along with a few others. I took them in exchange for the four tapes I had in my bag.

"You don't mind if I hold onto *Sensurround?*" I asked. The truth of it was Aunt Lorraine wanted it. She said it made her laugh, brought back memories. Memories? Nobody had those kind of memories, but I couldn't ask her to elaborate.

"Ah, *Sensurround*," Alexis sighed theatrically. "It's brilliant, isn't it? Robbie's swan song."

"Really?"

"Well, he still acted, but . . ." She leaned her hand on the doorway and looked up in her thinking-woman's pose. "They say it's dangerous for an artist to know success too early. And that's what he was back then, an artist. He wasn't like the others, never a one-day wonder man. After *Sensurround* they all called him Orson Welles; then they crucified him for it." She turned to me, a faraway gaze in her eyes as if she were vacationing in the seventies. "I fell in love with him because of that movie. Bastard."

"Is he?"

She smiled slyly. "Show me a man with a twelve-inch cock who isn't."

"Jesus, that's bigger than Barbie."

She shut off the light, led me out of her office, and although only a few minutes earlier I'd been eager to leave, the way she spoke of her ex-husband had roused my curiosity. Yet as much as I wanted to keep the conversation going, say something more about measurements perhaps, I experienced the strange sensation of stumbling down a dark street and coming to a well-lit diner, but as I went for the door a hand turned the sign from Open to Closed. Alexis Calyx and I were through for the day.

Before *X-posure*, I'd been looking without touching. But I did get aroused, omnivorously so. There was no telling which scenes might catch my fancy: boy–girl, girl–girl, girl and her large electronic appliance . . . Pleasuring myself, however, seemed disrespectful to Alexis. She was my employer, her videos part of my research.

Yet, by handing me a film she believed was tailored to my specific desire, Alexis Calyx had in fact given me permission to indulge myself. Twisted logic indeed; perhaps the residue of my two or three weeks as a practising Catholic.

So it was with the explicit purpose of having an orgasm that I took home *X-posure*, poured myself a glass of Chablis, dimmed the lights, slipped the tape into the VCR and myself into something more comfortable, and lit . . . goddammit!

Cut!

All I had in the apartment were those skinny, Chanukah candles, the result – along with a silver menorah – of a rare burst of sentimentality one holiday season back in Miami Beach when I decided to show Sam something about Chanukah. After we broke up and I moved north, I kept the menorah around for any future religious awakenings.

Providence, for here it was with *X-posure* cued and the room just crying for candle light. I retrieved it from the closet above the sink and set it on my side table, sticking a candle in every hole, and lighting them all with a bic lighter. Flame after flame fuelled a mango-orange glow. The warm sheen enveloped my studio, as the candles roared irreverently against the black window pane. I pulled down the blinds, lest some zealot spot the sacred candelabra and bust in throwing stones.

I built a sanctuary of pillows on my bed and climbed aboard. Streams of light from the TV blending with my profane fire, I felt like a temple prostitute; numinous, on a quest for a new religion, seeking the wisdom of Silver Ray.

On screen: the scene.

Two women pretzelled in and out of each other's limbs; kissing, sucking, caressing. They were gorgeous, both with short, dark hair, nimble bodies, no implants, and even some cellulite, which I adored. Each was a mirror for the other.

Together, they formed a kaleidoscope of feminine desire. I thought of Alexis watching me watch. Then she became Shade.

My right hand slipped inside the elastic band of my sweat pants. My left hand held tight to the remote. I twirled my pubes between my fingers, spread my thighs further apart against the bed, let my fingers travel down and up so deep.

Meanwhile, on TV they were going at it furiously, one woman probing and pummelling the other with her fingers. Bring on the moan & groan track . . . *uh* . . . *uh* . . . *oh, god*. Silver Ray circles her clit with her middle finger, breathing bigtime, breathing in circles. She's going to come with them, she's sure. Come like she's wanted. Like she's needed. Into the fray, the fire, by the light of the glowing menorah, alongside this terbium orgy of tits and ass, she's pulsating to her toes, shucking and jiving like a mad bongo player . . . strumming on the old banjo, singing . . .

. . . Ringing!

A goddamn fire alarm chimed through the walls. *No, don't stop, don't stop . . . ignore it!* Another long, flat ring.

I jumped up and checked the menorah, which flickered innocently. The ringing continued. It was Yossi the doorman. I gave a breathless, "Hello?"

"Yes, it's Shade, she's here."

"What!"

"I send her to you."

The next few seconds were surreal. I stumbled up nervously, threw on a long-sleeved, black T-shirt, shut off the movie. My heart was beating as if I'd swallowed a double espresso with extra sugar, my thighs were damp inside my sweat pants. I felt slippery when I walked.

The doorbell rang. Before answering, I killed the fading glow of my early Chanukah celebration. I shouted, "Just a second!" and cursed myself for not spending the extra three hundred dollars a month for a one-bedroom. In a studio you were on display like a caged animal. I opened the door and

Shade barrelled past me, a breeze of musk and sulphur. "How dare you not return my calls, I'm way too insecure for that shit – what's that smell?"

"Smell?" I asked, horrified.

"Something's burning." Her eyes roved left, right, bouncing from the silent images on the TV screen to the pile of pillows on my bed and landing finally on the smoking gun. "Is that a menorah?"

"Yeah," I shrugged, playing it oh-so-cool given the ubiquitous thumping in my temples. Her eyebrows lowered skeptically. "It's a candle holder, I didn't have any other candles."

"I thought you hated that new-age garbage." She stared at me, oddly. "What are you watching?"

"It's just background noise."

She took off her jacket and fell down on the couch with a loud, "Huh!" I sat on my bed perpendicular to her, watching as she quickly discovered the pile of videos Alexis had given me. She beamed her lowered eyebrows at me again. "Don't tell me, you've joined a Zionist sex cult."

"It's not what you think."

"I knew something was up, you haven't been you lately."

"I am the ghostwriter of Alexis Calyx."

"Great," she nodded. "Who's Alexis Calyx?"

Shade sat quietly as I explained just who Alexis was, describing with theatrical élan our first few meetings, playing up today's scene on the set. As it turned out, Shade knew of her; she'd once been to a feminist film festival where they banned one of Alexis' movies.

"Probably *X-posure*," I threw out, suggesting intimate knowledge of the Alexis Calyx canon. I wanted to appear hip, to talk about porn stars and sexual fantasies and Vaseline lenses. "There's some pretty hard-core fucking between women, even better than the boys do it."

Shade curled her upper lip and squinted.

"It goes beyond the usual girl–girl suck-fest."

"Girl–girl what fest?" She saw right through me. I shook

my head and smiled dumbly. Shade said, "Okay, you fembot, who are you and what have you done with Rachel?"

"She went out for a quart of milk this morning, I haven't seen her since."

"And back in Miami I couldn't even get you to go to that stripper movie."

"You and your Hollywood porn."

"You know me, I'm a high-concept kind of girl."

I bit the inside of my lip, wishing for a bit of Silver Ray. She would know how to spin the situation, just as Alexis had twisted our conversation this afternoon. The best I could do was empty the rest of the wine into two glasses and sit down next to Shade on the couch. We laughed, bantering about the weather, the strike, other freelance possibilities, and just about everyone we knew. I would have forgotten how frustrated I'd been by her unexpected visit had I not found myself mesmerized by her pupils, the centre of her gaze enlarged, encased in gold marbles; and her nose, her cheeks, her thick, fleshy lips jumped out at me, animated, as if they'd been properly lit for the first time.

Shade smiled, half-laughing. I folded my right leg further into my body and pulled my hair back. I would have sworn she was staring, too, although I was operating under the influence of pornography. They should put warning labels on those boxes. Like cigarettes. *Caution: Viewing may result in excessive fantasizing and skew sexual perceptions.*

"All right," I ventured. "What are you doing here?"

"I was trying to be mad at you. You're never around the picket line, so I'm stuck with the rest of those goombahs, and then you don't call me for three days, not even a message . . . you can't do that, Slivowitz. Nothing's stable anymore, I feel disconnected, like I'm all alone out here."

"What about Tina?" I said and immediately wished I hadn't. Saying her name out loud gave her too much importance.

"Oh, I can't talk to her. She's not about that." She stared at me so deeply that for the second time that day I felt as if I'd been stripped naked by the gaze of another woman. As much as I tried to look away, I kept coming back to her, smiling too much. Shade was so beautiful. Of course I'd always known that, but it had been more of a two-dimensional, fashion model sort of beauty. I felt as if in all the years we'd known each other I'd never really looked at her until now.

"You're making me nervous," she said. "The way you're looking at me, stop doing that."

"Doing what?"

"You know what." She rested her elbow on the couch and leaned her head against it. Our faces were almost touching.

"Are you really trying to seduce me, Slivowitz?"

"Yes," I said. Then, as if in slow motion, I watched myself bring my right hand to Shade's face. My fingertips burned against her chin. She shut her eyes, grazed her teeth against my fingers. I couldn't breathe, felt the world flash by in song lyrics. Birds do it, bees do it. Between the devil and the deep blue sea. Like a virgin.

I brought my lips to hers and we kissed a slow, soft kiss. My arms fell around her body and we were making out on my couch. The words reverberated in my head: *Shade and I are making out on my couch!* She twisted her hips slightly and pulled her head back. My lips slipped down to her neck. I kissed it. Still holding me, she whispered, "We can't do this."

"Yes, we can," I said, but I didn't want to talk. I kissed her again. This time, she grabbed a tight fist of my hair and pulled me close, kissing me longingly, lusciously. Her tongue travelled over my teeth, her lips riveting mine as if her own survival depended on it, and I remembered that Mark and Tessa hadn't kissed much. They were slamming and bamming like nobody's business, but without kisses? No wonder Tessa didn't come. At that moment I would have given anything to spend the rest of my life with Shade's tongue in my mouth.

But she pushed me away, stopping midscene. I had a newfound respect for Mark's frustration. This flicking on and off of desire was maddening.

I covered my face. My eyes felt dry, but I was afraid if I blinked I might start bawling. "I'm sorry," Shade said. She clasped her hands around mine and brought them to her lips. I remembered where my fingers had been earlier. Could she smell me? Taste me?

Without letting go, Shade brought our hands down to the couch. "Listen, we can't just kiss each other like that." I kept staring at our fingers, criss-crossed like a backgammon board. Connected. "Slivowitz, look at me." She lifted my chin. "I have real feelings here, this is no joke."

"I'm not joking, Shade."

"Okay, wait . . . look at it this way, I come in here and you're talking all of this sex talk and watching porno, and really, how do I know it's me you want? I could be anybody walking through that door."

"Oh, yeah, it was either you or the Dominos man. Luckily you showed up first."

"Don't start with your sarcasm, not with me."

I huffed, averting my eyes, thinking how much Shade reminded me of Alexis, both of them lecturing me, talking down to me. How was it that everyone but me seemed to know everything about my desire? If only I had some sense of what was going on behind Shade's stony face, beyond those eyes, which despite their discomfiting scrutiny made me want to hold her tight enough to cut off her circulation. Was I supposed to tell her about the porn? Tell her that, yes, just before she'd come, I was hot, I was horny, I was the phantom Silver Ray ready for anything and anyone, but in my Rachel Silver reality I wanted only Shade. I could tell her that I'd been thinking of her throughout *X-posure*, but I wasn't sure how she'd take it. If it were a compliment or an insult.

"This is too crazy," she said. And we carefully avoided each other's stares as we spoke a litany of innocuous little phrases until she angled over my shoulders to grab her jacket. I was flooded by waves of sadness and desolation; that left-alone-on-a-dark-desert-road feeling.

She stood up in front of me. I leaned back against the couch, hugging my knees into my chest. The lower corner of my left eye twitched.

"You're really leaving?"

"I can't stay, I'm scared."

"So am I."

"Please." She held out her hand. Begrudgingly, I took it and followed her to the door, more anxious than Tessa the porn star before her boy–girl debut. Whoever said sex was less pressured with women ought to have a lobotomy.

In the doorway, Shade put her arms around my shoulders, hugging me in the Alexis Calyx role. I moved in closer, slipping my hands inside her jacket, folding myself into her body, feeling through her sweater her shoulder blades, her ribs, the rough bumps of her spine, the hook of her hips. And her fingers were stroking me, her body on mine, our legs intertwined and breasts swept up against each other. How could she touch me like that and then leave?

"We'll talk tomorrow, okay?" she whispered, almost directly in my ear. I wanted to say don't go, but couldn't. Honestly, I wasn't sure which was more frightening: her rejecting me or changing her mind.

She pivoted on the lush carpet. I watched her glide down the hall, this electrified figure in my hospital-clean corridor. I wanted to run up behind her and take her to the ground in a girl–girl version of the *From Here to Eternity* wrestling scene. I wanted to say something important. But even more than that, I wanted her to come back here and tell me everything was going to be all right.

At the elevator bank, she turned and smiled. "By the way, you kiss good."

"Watch your language."

"The neighbours?"

"No, the grammar. You mean, well."

"No, I mean, *good*." The elevator rang and Shade stepped inside. The doors whisked shut behind her. I felt dizzy, off-balance, and slid down against the moulding in my doorway.

I'm not sure how long I was sitting there when I felt Freddy push her nose up against my face, meowing. She smelled like candle wax. Her face, I discovered, was covered with it: my little waxed pussy. What was it they said about you and curiosity, my furry friend? It hardly mattered, for I knew what they never said, that whatever doesn't kill you leaves you a complete and total mess.

New York, NY by way of Taos, NM

M. Christian

Vi called it "spaghetti western weather" – a cinematic weather pattern highlighted by periods of near-cliché: dust-devils spinning against a too-blue sky; a solitary mesquite bush; tumbleweeds chasing each other down cracked streets; screen doors knocking open-shut, open-shut in a rhythmic, lazy hot breeze – followed by gusts laced with eye-stinging dust, dirt, and crisped leaves.

"All it needs –" Vi would say, part of a ritual worked up in the year they'd lived in the tiny trailer, "– is a dog looking for somewhere to die."

For a couple only three years together, they had a lot of rituals. In more thoughtful moods, Clarette would expound in a tired voice, about how the desert was perfect for such things – beads on a wire of routine that made the heat, the dust, the boredom, tolerable for just one more day. When she was in a less thoughtful mood, she didn't say anything – she'd just sprawl on their mattress in an old T-shirt and threadbare panties and try to think of anything except for heat, dust, and the boredom.

The electric clock over the stove made a gentle hum, loud if you tuned your ear to it – as Clarette did: a gentle reminder to herself that Vi would be home in just a few minutes. The hum was another of those Indian beads on a wire, a little ritual she did without thinking.

Sometimes, when she did think about it – the hum of the clock, the sun being just so close to the horizon, the obnoxious newscaster on their little B&W TV who always said "we'll be right back", all the things that happened just before the truck pulled up, the door opened, the jingle of Vi's keys in her denim pockets – she called it *her ticket.*

Because when Vi came home, it was a chance to leave the dry outskirts of Taos, New Mexico – at least for a little while.

The sun was gone, the movie over. A curtain of deep night – as only the desert can make it – was over everything. The moon was gone, new – so the sky was only lit by hard points of starlight. It was a warm night, and for that Clarette was grateful: she didn't like the desert cold, the way it seemed to cut through her.

Next to her, in their big bed, Vi was radiating sensual heat – her big breasts soft against her back, her strong legs casually draped over hers.

They stayed that way, curled around each other, for quite a while. Finally, her breath growing even warmer as she spoke, Vi said, "Where do you want to go tonight?"

Clarette was quiet for a time, letting the earth spin through her mind. The day, the Sergio Leone weather, made her think of the movies and one thing, and one thing only, came to mind when she thought of places that seemed to only exist on their little television.

"New York," she whispered, taking Vi's hand and pulling it around herself tightly.

"On the subway, late at night," Vi said, her voice low and theatrical. "The city that never sleeps is dozing, so it's just you and me sitting on the hard plastic seats, watching stations flash by through the graffiti-painted windows. Sometimes the train comes up from the tunnels and travels through the night-time city – buildings mixing bright windows with dim stars, blocking out the clouds high overhead. Brilliant signs as big as . . . well, as big as anything you've ever seen: all the colours of the rainbow, spelling out big company names.

There's a liveness to the air, like there's electricity running through it. There's so much to see, so much that your eyes can't take it all in.

"Yeah, we're on that train, travelling through it – together, holding each other. We're feeling the rumble of the rails, the sway as the car bends through the steel and concrete canyons."

Vi's hand moved, softly, gently, till she cupped Clarette's just-right-sized breast. "We're alone, travelling through the greatest city on earth. You're wrapped around me, your head resting on my shoulder, my hair tickling your cheek. My tits are heavy against your arms.

"You look up and see the names you're always heard of on the Transit maps: Broadway, Lexington, Manhattan, the Bronx, Queens, Greenwich Village, Wall Street. They roll past the dirty windows, flashing by as we clack and click down the tracks."

Vi's voice grew deeper, huskier as she gently squeezed Clarette's breast, cupping the conical shape. "I kiss you on the subway, breaths mixing as we roll. As I do, you feel my nipples harden, even through my sweater . . . did I mention I'm wearing a sweater? Well, anyway, you feel me get nice and hard – you know how I do –"

Clarette giggled, pulling Vi closer, feeling her own nipples respond.

"I unwrap you and push you back into the hard seat, kissing you hard. You feel my breath coming into your mouth, my breathing matching for a moment the sway, the rumble of the subway car. My tongue touches, then pushes hard against your own – and everything, all of you, gets that much warmer, hotter.

"My hands are on your tits –" and they were, cupping her, squeezing her hard nipples between long fingers "– kneading them, working them. You moan – in that delightful way you do – and arch your back into the hard plastic. I get down off my own seat, and kneel between your legs, push them apart. You're wearing jeans, tight jeans, and you can feel your cunt get all warm and wet at just the thought of me being there."

Vi's hand slowly smoothed her hip, a slow caress that started at the gentle rises of her ribs and ended at the fullness of Clarette's hips.

"Take me," Clarette said softly, pushing herself back against Vi, mixing their warmth.

Vi kissed her shoulder, then pulled her till she was lying on her back. "I will," she said, kissing around the tiny rosebud of her right nipple. "I promise."

A light suck, a gentle draw of nipple into mouth. Clarette sighed: a heavy, wind-gust sound.

Vi looked up, for no reason, and saw the alarm clock's harsh red glow – and the little statue. "We're outside now, and it's cold. The sky looks busy, filled with more than just stars: it's full of the mad glow from those famous streets. The wind is gusting around us, pushing our coats around."

Clarette spread her legs, a loving, practised motion, and Vi slipped a finger up between her very wet lips, feeling them part ever so slightly. When she got to the top, the hard, throbbing bead of her clit she stopped, feeling Clarette's furnace, the gentle heat from her cunt.

"Behind us, waves lap heavily on rocks, kicked up from the big ships coming home after months at sea. Like I said, it's cold, but we're not cold. We're hot, lover – we're very hot."

Vi rested her hand there for a moment, a heavy heartbeat, then kissed Clarette on her gently rising/falling belly.

"Where are we?" Clarette giggled, spreading her legs wide and snaking a thin hand down to flick casually at a momentary tangle of long pubic hairs.

Vi smiled, nodded to the little statue next to the glowering alarm clock. "She's there, huge and powerful, above us. Lit by brilliant lights. She's a Goddess, Clare – as green as new grass. Her face is almost invisible, lost against the dark sky, but we can see her, Clare – we can see her smiling out to sea, looking out across the world."

Vi breathed in, slowly, savouring her own excitement, the wetness she felt in her own cunt. Covertly, so as not to detract from her story, she brought down her other hand and relished in her own wetness, the hard point of her clit. She moaned, ever so slightly, and – reflexively – clamped her thighs down around her fingers.

Back to Clarette – a few deft strokes to open her up, to make her ready: downwards, from the little forest of curly hairs to the wet lips beneath. Clarette hissed, a primal sound of love and welcoming, and spread her legs even wider.

"We're looking at her face, on her island, in the middle of the bay. It's cold, but we're hot, sexy – so damned fucking hot. You're wearing this beautiful leather coat, like smooth darkness, and it feels so good wrapped around you."

Another sweet hiss as Vi's fingers dipped in, pushing gently till plump outer lips met second joints. She stayed there, moving with slow in-and-outs that made Clarette's hips gently rock and clench around them.

"We're there, beautiful –" another nod at the cheap little Liberty trinket by the clock "– we've made it that far and even farther. We're standing at her feet, looking up at her.

"I put my arms around you, pull you close against me. You feel my tits pressing into your back. I kiss the back of your neck, a butterfly graze that makes your skin dance with goose bumps, and your nipples get even harder. One of my hands drops down and takes hold of one of your tits, squeezes it through the coat. It feels like someone else, like a great leather hand grabbing you. You breathe heavy and you feel your cunt get real wet."

Vi stroked faster, harder – fucking Clarette's hot cunt with her fingers. Then she changed the pattern, allowing her own excitement, her own wetness and fire to guide her fingers: Up and down, small circles around her clit, back down past warm, wet lips, and in – to tease the tight ring of muscles, then back up again.

Vi bent, took a hard nipple into her mouth, and nibbled – adding a new tone to Clarette's sounds. Between gentle sucks – just the way she liked it – Vi whispered, adding to the scene:

"My hands rise to your face, stroking your cheeks. You kiss my fingers, suck them in – tasting my cunt on them. Holding you, I'd had my fingers down between my legs, feeling my own lips, my own hard clit, getting myself all wet and hot – for you.

"You taste me, and know that I'm wet for you, sexy.

"But there are other things to taste than just my fingers. I slowly drop my fingers down and slowly – almost too slowly – start to unbutton your coat. One, two, three – with each one your body tingles, your nipples get even harder, your cunt gets even hotter, wetter. Four, five, six – and then that's all. The coat parts and the cold slaps on your . . . yes, it slaps on your smooth belly, that spot – right there – between your tits, your thighs. You're naked, beautiful, hot and burning naked out there on that cold island. The coat hits the ground, and you're before her and me – glowing with fire, cunt juice painting your thighs. I turn you, look at my own goddess, my own Liberty. I kiss you, hard and mean, tongues stroking each other, lips hot and slick. I kiss you, and my hand snaps up between your legs –"

Between Clarette's legs, Vi's hand moved a new way: from the throbbing clit, the tiny hot bead, down to enter, full and deep, into her – past the tight muscles, and all the way till the rough spot. With each cycle, each tap of Clarette's clit and then deep down into her, Clarette's voice changed, becoming deeper, deeper – more and more bass. She was lost, somewhere else, floating on Vi's hand, her fingers and her words. She might not have been at the foot of the Statue of Liberty, but she certainly wasn't in a trailer in Taos, New Mexico.

"I'm feeling your clit, so hard on that cold night. You push down, trying to get all of me into you. There, under the shadow of Liberty, I put my fingers in you, deep and hard.

Then I start to fuck you – ending each stroke with a strong press on your magic G-spot. You moan, making sweet music. You buck down, too excited to be patient. In the distance, you hear a foghorn – and you realize that anyone floating by, anyone with a good telescope, could see us, could see you, standing there, pale and naked, quivering with excitement. You're on display, Clare; you're out there on that island for the whole of New York to see."

The motions of Vi's hand in Clarette's cunt became less focused as her own excitement started to pull at her. Vi moved a bit, feeling the silken skin of Clarette's breast slide across her lips . . . until the hard tip of a nipple was there, and then in Vi's mouth. She sucked with a shocking intensity, making Clarette arch her narrow back and put her hand on the back of Vi's head. Sucking as she stroked, and stroking as she sucked, Vi felt like she was a great woman; a chain going from mouth to tit, from cunt to hand.

Breaking the pleasant suction with a soft wet *smack!* and another punctured moan from Vi, she breathed deep (one, two, three, four), then: "You're so hot, beautiful, so wet. There, standing on the cold flagstones in front of the statue, you push down, trying to swallow my fingers with your cunt, trying to get even more of my thumb on your clit.

"But I'm nasty – right, lover? You know that. Three fingers for your tight cunt, your wet cunt, thumb for your clit, and one finger – my teeny tiny little finger, that reaches back, between the cheeks of your tight –" a kiss on her sweat-slick belly "– ass and taps (one, two, three, four) on your asshole.

"Oh, yes, your sweet ass. A few gentle taps then away to take just the smallest amount of cunt juice, and then back – no taps this time. Not this time . . .

"Look up at her, Clare – look at her. Great and green. You look up at the statue – recognizing her from photographs, movies, your little toy on the dresser, but really seeing her for the first time. Maybe you wonder – being the slut that you are

– what her great copper snatch must look like. But whatever you think, you look up at her as I work at your own cunt, and then your asshole as my little finger *slips* neatly into you.

"Oh, yes, lover – nice and full and hot, bare and shining in the hard lights around Liberty, starting up at her distant smile and the faint lights of the city beyond. You're there, you're right there and you're with me, and I'm with you –"

The come boiled inside Clarette, a rumbling body-come that opened her eyes, opened her mouth and shut, clenching, her legs around Vi's hand. The moans changed into a heavy avalanche of sounds, a growling bass escalation.

Within her, Vi felt Clarette's cunt grip her, matching for a long time the fluttering beat of her heart. Looking, smiling, happy that she was happy, Vi held her, stirring the last of her quakes with a few kind oscillations of her fingers. "Oh, yeah, come, come, *come* –" she crooned, putting her heavy arms around her.

Vi's other hand was still between her own thighs, still working the hot, wetness of her cunt. With her head resting on Clarette's belly, she looked down at her downy triangle of pubic hair. Slowly, a tease for herself as well as her lover, she inched her way down with a series of little kisses till Clarette's cunt was an inch – then less than that – from her lips. A kiss, at first, then a taste – then a lick, then many more: a dance of lips and tongue on Clarette's cunt that pushed her lover, and then Vi herself up and over. Together, they came till the quakes were nothing but a soft series of delightful tremors.

Sleep floated down on both of them – much more so for Clarette, but quite heavily for Vi after a hard day of work, and they crawled into a comfortable spoon: Clarette, as usual, facing the side, the dark window sprinkled with very bright desert stars, and Vi a warm comforter curled against her back. Before she slipped down into a dreamscape, Clarette turned her head to receive a gentle, sweet kiss from Vi. "Thank you for taking me." Clarette said, then – a beat or two of her heart later – she added: "Do you think we'll really go one day?"

Vi smiled, pulling her closer, mixing their heat together even more as sleep started to earnestly tug at them. "Why?" she said eventually said, stifling a yawn: "We can see the whole world from here."

Only Connect

Lauren Henderson

It's a truism that men can only concentrate on one thing at a time. Isn't that the stereotype, that women can juggle twenty different tasks at once, running from one pole to the next, keeping the plates spinning with a few swift flicks of the wrist? Men are supposed to be the opposite: so single-minded that if they try to do more than one thing simultaneously they end up messing up both. It's a neat little theory but it completely fails to account for what Dan is doing to me right now. One hand on the wheel, the other between my legs, his eyes never leaving the road, his index and third fingers stroking me through my silky French knickers. A stereotypical man would be completely thrown by the speed bumps; but Dan, far from treating them as an obstacle, is actually using them as a choreographic motif, working his fingers round the edge of the material and into me a split-second before the front wheels hit the first bump, then remaining frustratingly still, allowing each subsequent bump to drive his fingers a little deeper into me, like a wedge, so that I find myself grinding my hips in anticipation as we reach the next one, barely able to wait. Dan starts rubbing the heel of his hand against me, his fingers still inside me. The seam of my knickers, caught between us, chafes against me so successfully that it might have been specially designed for the purpose. I am moaning. Dan is still looking straight ahead – it's pretty much a point of honour – but his lips are curved into the smuggest smile I have ever seen on a man.

I'm the one here who can't concentrate on anything else. It doesn't occur to me for a moment to reach over and stroke Dan through his jeans, slip my fingers between his waistband and belly, rub my thumb down the coarse hairy line of skin to the hot, smooth, slightly damp and swollen-to-bursting head below. I am totally selfish when I'm being fingered, incapable of doing anything but lying back and letting out a crescendo of what I hope are highly encouraging moans. To be fair to me, I am just the same when I'm going down on someone; I don't want any interruptions, no matter how well meant. I like to give my full attention to the task in hand.

By the time we reach my flat I have come once and am looking almost as smug as Dan. Not quite, though. Dan's one of those strong silent types who loves nothing more – not even football – than seeing me go completely out of control. He gets excited too, of course, but only once he's already reduced me to a babbling, jelly-legged sex object with glazed eyes and rising damp.

Which is fine with me. Every relationship has its patterns and if Dan insists on making me come repeatedly before even so much as unzipping his trousers, who am I to complain? Early on, in the interests of balance as well as for my own enjoyment, I tried to buck this trend, but Dan just removed my hands, threw me over the sofa and slid his thumb into me as if he were testing me for ripeness, and I promptly forgot about everything else.

I manage to get out of the car without falling over, though my legs are so weak by now this is more of an achievement than it sounds. We walk decorously, which is to say without touching, up the steps to my front door and I am just pulling out my keys when Dan sits down on the stone wall that borders the flight of steps. He's just waiting for me to get the door open, but I look at him, his eyes meet mine, and I can't manage a moment longer without being in physical contact with him; dropping the keys back into my pocket I climb onto his lap, my bottom on his thighs, my feet on the wall for balance, and start kissing him. It's a dark night and as usual half of the streetlights are out, or at best flickering spasmo-dically. And the steps are high off the street, at first-floor level. We're in the shadows, a couple of closely entwined shapes, no more. What we're actually doing would be visible only to someone with night-vision goggles and a good van-tage point. I hope.

Because by now Dan has what feels like his entire hand up me and is fucking me with it in slow steady strokes, fucking me actually better than he does with his cock, which is a curiosity I've noticed before but never really have much time to dwell on because my brain is pretty much fully occupied with other things, foremost of which right now is doing my best not to scream. I have what feels like my entire fist crammed into my mouth and am biting down on the knuckles in pursuit of this good-neighbourly goal, an arrangement which is amusing Dan tremendously. His hand is almost hurting me, slamming into me like a pile-driver, but I couldn't bear him to stop. I lean fully into his other hand, on my back, balancing me, support-ing me so I can take the full force of what his other hand is doing to me without falling off the wall. God, this is good. There are so few moments in life of absolute transcendence. Or maybe that's an over-elevated way of putting it. I cannot think about anything else right now, anything at all; discon-nected thoughts rush through my brain, gone almost before I've registered them, so fleeting that they come only to remind me that there is something outside this intense sensation, to stop me losing myself to it so completely that I can never find my way back.

Dan gives a particularly frenzied thrust into me which definitely emphasises the pain aspect over the pleasure. He's losing control. We have to get inside my flat. We have to have sex. We are having sex, of course, but I mean something more specific by that. I grab Dan's wrist as he pulls back for another grind into me, though I'm whimpering with frustra-tion at making him stop, even for a moment. With a near-heroic effort of will I drag out my keys and get the door open. We manoeuvre past the ground-floor neighbour's damned bicycles – why was I trying not to make any noise outside? I should have wailed like a siren and woken the bastards up, the amount of times I've ripped my tights on their bicycle spokes. Stumbling past the second one I reach the stairs and hold out a hand for Dan, who is momentarily snagged on a handlebar. He drags himself free, grabs my hand and trips over a pedal, all at once, landing on the steps with a stumble that could send us both off-balance.

In that moment our eyes meet. We could recover; I could grab the newel post and brace myself against Dan's fall; but I don't. We don't. I let myself tumble back onto the stairs – which are carpeted, I'm not that much of a masochist – and Dan's weight comes down on top of me like the one thing I've been craving all my life. As soon as he lands we are scrabbling at each other's clothes, grinding into each other, every bit of our bodies that can wrap around the other's doing so as if for dear life; feet, knees, hands all desperate for as much contact as we can possibly manage. It must look anatomically impossible. I have a flash of intense frustration that I'm not completely double-jointed.

My skirt's around my waist, my knickers are down, Dan's unzipping himself – ah, that sound, that wonderful anticipatory sound, like a trumpet fanfare before the entrance of the key player on the scene – and two seconds later he has jammed himself up into me and we're fucking on the stairs. The relief is almost unbearable. I mean, I love everything else, all the preliminaries and the flourishes and the fanfares; I come much more thoroughly and repeatedly before the actual act of fucking than I ever do during it; but by God there is absolutely nothing like it. My eyes roll back, my hips tilt up so that Dan can get his hands under them, my feet lock round the back of his calves, I am bracing my hands clumsily against the wall and the stair riser, and we're fucking, thank God, I thought I would die if we didn't manage to fuck at this precise moment, not a second later, I thought I would actually explode.

Dan never lasts that long, which is maybe why he dedicates

so much time to all the other variations before the main theme. I can scarcely complain; he's already reduced me to a boneless sex-craving wreck, dripping with moisture – how unattractive that sounds, though it's exactly what I feel like – and now he's taking a much briefer pleasure than mine. His hipbones grind into my inner thighs, his fingers bite into my bottom and with an arch of his back and a split-second pause he sinks into me one last time, his lips curled back from his teeth in that sneer he always makes when he comes, his eyes almost closed, the slits of white glinting as eerily as if he were having a fit. He collapses on top of me. That's good too. I love the weight, and Dan isn't too big, not a great slab of meat trying to crush me out of existence. Besides, he's completely absorbed in his own sensations, overcome by them; even as I take the full weight of his body, his entire focus is on the spasms of his cock, me beneath him a collection of body parts, the woman he loves to fuck, nothing more. I hope. Otherwise I'd feel as suffocated as if he were twenty stone of loose rolls of fat.

His cock gives a couple of convulsive twitches inside me, last moments of past glory, and then everything subsides and suddenly we can hear our breathing, which is as frenzied as if we had just done a three-mile sprint. I'm always reluctant to move, even if right now the stair riser is biting into my back as painfully as if I just had sex up against an iron joist. I like to lie here, feeling the cock slowly shrink and curl up inside me before slipping out wistfully, stickily, a sad little aftermath of what was once such a proud trophy. No wonder it was a man who invented existentialism. Think of the mood swings: how important it must be to them to live in the moment. A limp, post-orgasmic cock always provokes great tenderness in me – well, if it's just done its job to my satisfaction – but one quickly learns not to use the words "sweet" or "cute" about a cock, even if you have just demonstrated how much you like getting fucked by it, tucks it away immediately, almost always insists on wearing briefs in bed. I gave up trying to understand men a long time ago. Now I just go with what seems to work. It's so much easier.

Dan braces himself against the stairs and lifts himself off me. As always, the removal of his weight is sad, but immediately makes me stretch my limbs, as if to test their new freedom of movement. He hauls me to my feet. One thought has been running through my mind for the last ten minutes, almost as soon as Dan's cock slid into me; I don't want him to stay the night. This is perfect just as it is. If he even comes into my flat it will be ruined. Tactics have been running through my brain. If I were really brazen I would just wish him goodnight firmly and continue upstairs, but I can't quite manage that.

"God, I'm exhausted," I say. "You've worn me out."

"Yeah?" He smirks, bless him.

"I'm just going to pass out. I'm shattered."

I try to look regretful, intimating that I would love to ask him in but have already been so overcome by his prowess as a lover that any further bout tonight would severely damage my immune-deficiency system. This is of course a total lie – it's Dan who couldn't manage another bout; once at night, once, if I'm lucky, in the morning is his limit. But it works perfectly.

"You'd better get some rest, then," he says, smugger than ever. "I'll see you round."

We kiss. He goes, climbing uncomfortably through the massed ranks of mountain bikes to the door. I sigh in relief and head upstairs. I don't even mind the fact that I live on the fifth floor. It's more distance between me and Dan.

My best friend David says that men adore being treated like sex objects and I should stop being concerned about this kind of thing with Dan. "Just pay him lots of compliments about the sex and he'll be fine," David assure me. I don't agree. I remember all too well the guy in college with whom I was supposed to be having a sex-only relationship who agreed eagerly the first night and then never wanted to have sex with me again. Moreover he became very bitter towards me, especially when I started going out with someone. I think this is a much truer reflection of the male psyche. Men think they want sex only, but they are only comfortable with this set-up when they're the ones after sex while the women want something more. As soon as you make it clear that you too just want to fuck their brains out on a regular basis but not have to talk to them about their families in the interim periods, they're off faster than a speeding bullet.

My body is exhausted, quite literally – temporarily worn out, used and satisfied – but my brain is buzzing. It's partly frustration; it didn't get used much this evening. Dan insists on us going out to dinner every so often. I much prefer a film, a drink, and a swift journey to my flat, as this limits the conversational necessities as much as possible. But despite the fact that we obviously have very little in common and any occasion in which we try to talk for more than ten minutes is full of laboured questions and terrible pauses, Dan still keeps suggesting dinner. God knows why. It's another reason I part company with David. Dan's constant wish to go out to dinner with me can only be explained as a need to enact what he sees as being the tableaux of a conventional relationship, the other things men and women do together apart from fucking on staircases, as if you have to have the one to be able to do the other. I plead my way out of the dinner dates as much as I can but sometimes he just won't take no for an answer. Tonight was as awful as ever. It never gets any better.

I look at my watch. Midnight. Perfect. Plenty of time for a long, hot soak in the bath. I wish now that I had made the appointment for 1.00, instead of 2.00: I thought it would be too early. But Dan and I have managed to satisfactorily conclude the evening's business in much less time than I had projected. How efficient we're getting. I have a long bath, make myself some coffee, pour myself a drink, and by 1.40 I'm wrapped in a big towel, wafting aromatic bath oil every time I move, logged on, in the chat room, waiting for my second date of the evening.

I know it's stupid, but there are butterflies in my stomach as I sit there waiting for him. I know it's stupid because he'll be there; he always is. And sure enough, at 1.56 it scrolls across the screen:

>trollfan1234: Hi! So did you finish it?

and a lovely wave of relief and happiness floods through me and I type:

lola666>sure. Disappointed though.

trollfan1234>?

lola666>it's all just the same plot isn't it? Rich boy falls in love with poor girl/waits it out for a year or so to prove he means it/ finally the family agrees. Only this time it turns out she's rich after all so it's OK. And there isn't even any tension, we know from the beginning that she's the only relative of the rich old man so when he finds that out he'll leave her all the money.

trollfan1234>OK, agreed, it's not his strongest book

lola666>Trollope should at least have made it more of a mystery, but we know that they'll get together ANYWAY so it still wouldn't have helped much.

trollfan1234>but isn't there satisfaction watching the pattern work itself out?

lola666>get more of that out of an Agatha Christie I've read 100 times.

trollfan1234>Hmmn.

lola666>he should have fallen for someone else while he was away all that time, create a bit of tension that way.

trollfan1234>Trollope does that sometimes

lola666>but you know it'll never happen, like Phineas/ Madame Goetz or John & Madeleine, the women they fall in love with in big cities are always adventuresses, then they come home to the nice girl without flashy looks, Trollope really cliched old-fashioned romantic author, why does he have an intellectual reputation?? I really don't have much to say about this book AT ALL sorry

trollfan1234>don't get started on the Joanna T v. Anthony T thing again

lola666>but it's true I really think J Trollope much more sophisticated in view of human nature, at least she sees it as protean, endlessly changeable, AT thinks everyone's personalities carved in stone

trollfan1234>do people really change that much?

lola666>oh yes I think so

trollfan1234>OK we may change opinions whatever but do our ACTIONS really change that much

lola666>Hmmn interesting maybe after lots of therapy

trollfan1234>haha

lola666>Pallisers are better

trollfan1234>well OK devil's advocate: who really changes in the Pallisers?

lola666>Hmmn I like Maud not being able to make up her mind until too late trollfan1234>yeah but it's the right thing she didn't really love him

lola666>but she'll never meet anyone else she's too old by their standards anyway! she would have been happy with Silverbridge

trollfan1234>do you think so

lola666>or at least content, yeah, she'd have been a duchess and he was v attractive

trollfan1234>funny youre arguing the way a man's supposed to & Im more romantic (like a woman) don't think Maud would have been happy

lola666>what about Lily Dale

trollfan1234>John made big mistake, he was always there like a dog, should have tried to disappear/make her jealous

lola666>so she didn't see him like the perpetual little boy

trollfan1234>exactly, women hate men slobbering over their feet

lola666>dyou speak from experience.

trollfan1234>never slobbered! teenage years had mad crushes on girls, made it too obvious, never got them, cooler now I hope

lola666>your'e right about John/Lily he really needed to go away for a long time & come back as a man – you know what I mean by that, not being sexist (he should have been masterful, etc)

trollfan1234>no its fine we agreed that we completely understand each other male/female stuff dont worry about that OK?

lola666>great! forgot!

trollfan1234>interesting we always come back to discussing relationships in AT

lola666>well I was thinking about that (am I being stereotypical woman always talking about LOVE) but youre a man allegedly

trollfan1234>yes, am looking at proof of that right now

lola666>not literally I hope

trollfan1234>no, wearing boxers

lola666>anyway I worked out that AT's political dilemmas not half as interesting as emotional ones/politics used really only to present moral choices (will X do right thing) as are emotional ones (will he marry nice girl at home)

trollfan1234>bit unfair, Maud has hard moral choice too

lola666>OK, true, and Madame Goetz

trollfan1234>God yeah, lots of them, and she gets rewarded in the end

lola666>nice idea the older/more sophisticated you get the more interesting the choices

trollfan1234>obviously I'm not old/sophisticated enough yet

lola666>me neither mine are always brutally obvious

trollfan1234>???example

lola666>no, no personal stuff we agreed

trollfan1234>?

lola666>

trollfan1234>after all, we're analysing other relationships all the time, we're not talking in traditional litcrit terms

lola666>relationships in BOOKS

trollfan1234>pretend it's a story

lola666>no.

trollfan1234>sigh

lola666>

trollfan1234>OK, enough of AT, pick another author?

lola666>I know we just finished Barchester but there must be others

trollfan1234>Minor, would annoy you even more

lola666>OK well let's do Dickens then

trollfan1234>

lola666>what?

trollfan1234>Dickens takes v long time to read, we wouldn't talk for weeks

lola666>flattered

trollfan1234>well I like talking to you

lola666>me too

trollfan1234>pick short books!!!

lola666>we could do Dickens but split up the books/discuss them every 10th chapter?

trollfan1234>Great idea they're written as serials after all

lola666>shall we do it chronologically?

trollfan1234>no one's ever asked me that before!

lola666>funny

trollfan1234>let's start with David Copperfield I've always meant to read that

lola666>OK I'll go to the library

trollfan1234>lovely library books with hard plastic covers you can read in the bath

lola666>and that dirty, musty smell

trollfan1234>I thought you said no personal stuff

lola666>funny. Not.

trollfan1234>when's good for you next time?

lola666>Monday? 1.00?

trollfan1234>five days . . . do I have time . . .

lola666>thought you were the one complaining about not meeting for ages trollfan1234>OK you talked me into it, I may be a bit behind

lola666>do your best

trollfan1234>yes ma'am

lola666>see you on Monday

trollfan1234>I wish!

lola666>TALK to you Monday

trollfan1234>sigh

lola666>I'm very disappointing you know

trollfan1234>me too we could be disappointing together.

lola666>

trollfan1234>OK, I know, I know. Want me to talk about the weather?

lola666>will it be interesting?

trollfan1234>actually no, I never know what the weather's like, I have no idea what's happening outside right now. I'm on the 8th floor, I have double glazing and my windows aren't that clean because the landlord's lazy about getting that done, also they have these catches which slip and slam back down on your hands so I'm nervous about opening them . . . sometimes I don't even know if it's raining. I'll go out into the street and feel like an idiot.

lola666>happens to me too, most of my windows are stuck, the only one I can put my head out of is the bathroom and it looks onto an air shaft. And I have five floors/no lift, it's a nightmare working out what coat to wear in the morning.

trollfan1234>my offices are airconditioned, windows can't open, etc, even more insulated. Once I was working late & there was a hurricane & I didn't even realise, got out onto the dark street and it was covered with broken glass and people with cardboard patching up their windows. Ours were fine, we're all triple-strength glass etc. More insulation. Shows how detached we are from the world.

lola666>my offices are like that too

trollfan1234>so we end up talking to each other through computers – down a modem line and bounced off a server to end up God knows where – insulation again.

lola666>that was a very neat connection

trollfan1234>thanks. I was quite impressed with it myself

lola666>have to go now

trollfan1234>OK, till Monday

lola666>bye

trollfan1234>bye

I turn off the computer and get into my pyjamas: flannel, huge, the kind of thing you can only wear when you sleep alone. A shot of whisky, to take to bed with me. And the nagging annoyance: why must he always push for more? Why does he keep asking to meet me? Can't he see that the whole point of this is this perfect, focused connection? Meeting would ruin everything. It's not that we might find each other unattractive; just the opposite. What if we did? It would ruin everything. I have everything in balance just the way I want it and I'm not going to mess with that. It's working. I'm happy. I take half a sleeping pill and wash it down with a gulp of whisky. Library tomorrow. Lovely. I'm happy. I really am.

Quiet

Lucy Moore

Tuesday night. Quiet. I am sitting in an overstuffed striped chair by the window, a streetlight spreading a candle glow over the pages of my book.

There is hardly anyone here and it is quiet except for the sound of my stockings scraping against each other when I shift my thighs, which I am doing a lot given what I am reading. My face is warm with arousal, and I am torn between raising the book to hide myself and lowering it to hide the cover, embarrassed at what I am reading but too absorbed in the stories to put it down. Not that it really matters, because there is no one here to watch me anyway, as though anyone would watch me even if they were here.

No one here except for that little earthquake heading towards me in the form of boots clicking against marble floors until he hits the carpet and becomes hard silence. I raise my eyes and peek over the top of the book at him, and snap back to the text the minute his dark eyes collide with mine. I lift the book higher to cover my face, remember the cover, drop it to my lap, remember to hide myself, and raise it again, blushing harder, breathing harder.

I can hear him pause on the carpet and turn. From behind the book I can see he has disappeared into literature somewhere around Ayn Rand.

Three pages pass, and I am wet, wide, willing. I am trying not to remember that unlike the people in these stories, I have no one to seduce but myself, and I am definitely avoiding that thought. No matter how much I make love to myself, no matter how many of those toys that should be used by a lover, the ice, lotion, beads, I bring out, knowing they will embarrass me in the morning but make me so very hot right now, no matter how many times I bring myself to the peak and hold back before I finally give in and fall, screaming so loud I cannot control it, nipples hard as I pull at them, vibrator thrumming away against my clit, thighs, stomach shaking, all this does not matter as my cunt grabs desperately, spasming, clutching for a cock – hot, hard, silky over stiff. At those moments, when I lie there in recovery, shaking, already imagining the next one because I have not satisfied anything at all, I can almost feel his mouth on my tits, his cock in my mouth.

But I am not pretty, and men do not want to do these things to me, so I settle for myself. I do not even notice that my right hand has slipped across my chest, snaked under the fabric of my blouse, and is teasing my nipple, which is pulling against my skin, puckering, aching. I shift again, the shiver of wetness, an actual drop, trickles down into my pantyhose, I pinch my nipple between my thumb and forefinger, nearly jumping at the pleasure-pain. And then there is a hand on my thigh and I really do jump.

I lower the book quickly, smacking the spine against the broad hand spreading out over my leg. The man from the literature section is squatting beside me, touching me so familiarly I should smack him for real, but instead I apologize.

"I'm sorry," I say.

He smiles, and I see an unidentifiable flicker in his eyes. "No need to apologize. I'm sorry I startled you." He is older than I am, too old for me, probably, and the muscles in his thighs push against his jeans when he shifts his weight. "How's the book?" he asks, the movement of his head only the slightest motion, his eyes locked against mine, stroking my jaw. I am blushing and stumbling, nervous.

"It's um, good," I say weakly, wondering why I can't be

normal and read mystery novels like other people do in bookstores.

"So I see," he says, smiling at my hand, my fingers still worrying my nipple.

"Oh, God," I say, and yank my hand away from my breast. I'm too embarrassed to even say I'm embarrassed.

"It's okay," he says, and his hand travels one long, slow, heavy, circle on my thigh, and when it finishes, he is further up and his fingers are pointing towards my cunt. We both look at his hand and then he removes it and stands. "Your coffee's cold." He nods towards my mug, which has ceased steaming and has evaporated into pale sludge. "May I buy you another?"

"I don't." I'm stammering, stuttering, swallowing.

He offers me his hand, firm. Don't say no. Can't say no.

Over coffee, I spill the sugar twice and my coffee three times. His name is Edward and I am right, he is too old for me, but I am not exactly overwhelmed with offers. He is an architect, or so he says, and he is reading a novel I have never heard of. I have left my book upstairs. He peers at me over his mug, which he holds with both hands wrapped around it as though he were warming them, but I can still feel his palmprint burning against my thighs and I know his hands are not cold. They are large, strong, slightly rough, and I can see the cuticles fraying and imagine the calluses against my skin.

My suit is too tight, and I shift against it uncomfortably as the skirt rides up my thighs. "Don't," he says, the third time I stop to adjust it, and he slides his hand up the back of my thigh, taking the skirt with it. He removes his hand and studies his work. I inhale, hoping that will eliminate the thigh spread somehow, but he does not seem to mind.

"What do you do, quiet Kate?" he asks me, sipping from his mug, his lips thin and broad.

"I work in an office," I say, feeling stupid and gawkish and childish and wishing I could run out. I am incapable of flirting: I know this, the woman behind the counter knows this, why can't he figure it out and just let me go?

He just laughs, though. "Do you always read erotica in public?" There is something about his phrasing that is slightly British, but unpretentious, and his voice is deep and warm around me as though I could press my palm against the broadness of his chest and feel the rumble.

"No," I say, stumbling again. "I mean, I just, picked it up."

"There's nothing to be ashamed of," he says, and I hear tenderness in his voice, though when I look up I do not see it in his face. He puts down his mug and lays his hand across mine. I jerk away and spill my coffee again. Blushing again. Make it end, make this end.

He leans forwards and his tone becomes conspiratorial. I can smell the coffee on his breath, nearly taste the cream. "I found watching you very arousing." I am shaking from the timbre of his voice and my cunt is calling out to him, and I am absolutely terrified of this man right at this very second, and more terrified because I do not know if I am more scared that he will kill me or make love to me. I jerk back again, coffee staining his arm.

"I'm sorry," I say, and I really almost am in tears this time. I grab some napkins and dab at his arm. "I just, I should go." You should have left me alone. He grabs my wrist, fingers locked, encircling the bone, the pudgy flesh. He laughs, genuine, his grip steel.

"Quiet Kate," he says. He stands, takes the napkins from my hand, kisses me softly on the forehead, the cheek, pulls back. He is holding me by my shoulders, looking down at me. "Is that what you want?"

He has a car so we take it, along rain-slicked city streets, lamps reflecting in the asphalt, sidewalks quiet with trash and recycling. I am huddled against the door. At a stoplight, he does not look at me, but his hand finds my thighs and pulls one of my legs towards him, forcing them apart. I can smell my own cunt, my own desire, my own heat, and I am sure he can too.

"Would you do something for me?" he asks suddenly.

I don't say anything. He looks over at me. "Unbutton your blouse," he tells me softly. It is an order, but it is not a command. I sit for a moment, and then, leaning forwards, I slip my suit jacket off, unbutton my blouse. There are holes in the lace of my bra and when he reaches over, again, without looking, to run the back of his fingers over my breasts, my nipple pokes through the weave, dark rose against faded white. I inhale sharply, though he has barely touched me I know now what it will feel like when he does and I want to scream, I want this so much.

But he pulls his hand away. "Could you take off your bra?" This time it is a question, but I cannot and will not answer no, though I hesitate with the hooks.

I realize that I will have to take off my shirt to take off my bra and I look outside but there is no one to see. This isn't how normal people do it, is it? Is this how people get seduced? I pull off my shirt, turning to pull the tail out from the waistband, and my naked breast brushes the cold window. I inhale sharply and I can hear Edward smile behind me. I have done this when I masturbate, held a breast against the coolness of a mirror, nipple kissing its own reflection. I love cold and ice against my skin, wanting more more more before the welcoming heat of a mouth, teeth, lips, tongue.

He pulls over to the kerb and parks the car. I am breathing heavily. He reaches over and again he trails the back of his hand over my breast, his knuckles teasing my nipples. My mouth parts. He undoes my seatbelt and then his, and then he moves towards me. He kisses me softly once, and then lowers his head to my breasts, kissing around, across my collarbone, over the flesh, and finally catching the nipples in his mouth, suckling. I throw my head back, amazed, moaning, and my hand travels automatically to plunge into my cunt, my fingers at the ready. He does not look up, he just grips my hand and pulls it behind my back as he bites my nipple gently, his teeth electric against my skin. I cry out.

"Please . . ." I beg, but he simply lowers his head to the other breast, still pinning my arm behind my back, and he sucks and nibbles and chews until I am writhing beneath him. "Edward," I breathe, and I hope I sound like a romance novel when I do. He lifts his head and releases my arm, nearly asleep. He reaches for my breasts and tugs at my nipples, pinching them between his thumb and forefinger, testing for something. I jerk again, like a rag doll, and he nods, as though I have pleased him somehow.

He comes around to my side of the car and opens the door for me, chivalrous to the last, and I fumble to button my blouse before I step onto the street. The light at the end of the block turns green and two cars drive by. He shakes his head at me and pulls me to my feet, my blouse hanging open, my nipples pouting against the night air, colder, wetter, than any mirror. I start to object.

He pulls me to him and kisses me, hard, his tongue crushing against mine, tasting my teeth, my desperation. He is hard, I can feel his cock against my stomach, and that pleases me somehow, that it is me who has done that. He pulls away suddenly and then a car passes, and I am standing there, drugged with heat, and the headlights shine on my bare breasts, stained with bruises from his mouth, his hands, exposed for anyone to see, to touch.

My cunt is so wet, so wide, so ready, that I can hardly walk, and I know, at this moment in time, I would do anything.

The elevator creaks its way up the shaft, slatted light falling across my breasts, interrupted intermittently by the floors. I look at Edward, sliding a glance through my stumpy lashes, cheap mascara long since faded. He is considering my breasts, but he looks neither pleased nor displeased. I wonder if he is thinking he has made a mistake, now that he has seen the way the waistband of my skirt folds to accommodate the swell of my stomach. It's too late for a diet now. Ashamed, I reach to pull the sides of my shirt together, and without looking away from my tits, he reaches out and slaps my hands back to my sides.

"Sorry," I say, for what seems like the fifteenth time that night.

Edward shakes his head. "Don't cover yourself unless I tell you to."

The elevator jerks to a stop and he gestures me out into the hallway. I step uncertainly, my shoes clicking against the floor. A few doors down the hall there is a man fumbling with his keys at his door. He is tall, thin, looks foreign. An orange-brown leather jacket and a newspaper folded under his arm. Spiky blond hair, small black-rimmed glasses. German, maybe. He looks up at us, and I want to move to cover myself, but I can feel Edward behind me and I don't dare. I feel very small, suddenly, between these two men. I half-expect Edward to reward me for leaving my shirt open but, of course, he does not.

The man at the door simply smiles at us as if he sees half-naked women in the hallway all the time, and then opens the door to his apartment and steps in. Edward steers me down the corridor, the floor Alice in Wonderland – black diamonds, white diamonds, checker board, chess board, checkmate, Kate. He slips the key in the lock and ushers me into a dark hallway.

Light ahead, dim yellow glow cast by an old shade, I walk towards it, drawn, moth-like. It leads me into the living room, where the only thing I notice is the books. Hundreds of them, maybe thousands. Floor to ceiling bookshelves, and then stacked along the exposed brick walls when there is no longer enough room. I run my fingers along the shelves, tasting them with my fingers, so overwhelmed with quantity that I do not even read the titles.

He walks up behind me and I turn so my back is against the shelves, spine to spine with these books. He stands in front of me, though this time I do not want to run away so badly, I just want him to take away this ache, want him to suck on my nipples until they stop pulling at my skin, want him to swallow me whole.

He pulls off his shirt and I bite my lip at his chest. Broad, firm. Muscular in that taut, quiet way that is the most masculine of all. Curls and whorls of hair threaded with grey, and I can imagine the taste of the salt on my skin. My tongue flicks out, serpentlike. I look up at his face and see the same grey lining his temples, scattered through his hair, his goatee, which has a certain sincerity about it. I catch myself wondering whether there will be grey hair, you know, everywhere, and the image of his hard cock rising up from his thighs makes me swallow hard.

I watch as he fingers the collar of my shirt and then slips it over my shoulders, letting it fall in a heap on the floor. No different than what I would have done, undressing myself. He reaches for my hands, which I am holding obediently by my sides, fighting the urge to scrape my nails down his chest to the trail of hair that disappears into his waistband, and brings them to his mouth, nuzzling the knuckles, breathing against my palms.

And then he lifts them higher, interlocks our fingers, presses the backs of my hands against the bookshelves, cool painted wood. I have to stretch to keep my hands up as high as he is holding them, pinning me against the hardcovers, and only when I am immobilized just so, he leans down to kiss me.

His kiss is soft, he tests before he attacks, tasting my teeth, my tongue with his own. It makes me start to shiver all over again, makes me forget about the ache in my arms and think about the ache in my cunt again.

Pushing my arms out, he makes me trace a snow angel in the air. He slides both our hands under my breasts and leaves mine cupping them, proffering them, a harem girl with a tray of silver fruit. He steps back and I lean to follow him, drawn by his simple existence, by the fishing line of tension he has drawn to my cunt. "You can put your hands down," he tells me, when my biceps are burning by my sides. He lets my hands drop and my fingers flicker, instinct telling me to reach for what I want, new found knowledge telling me that if I reach I will not capture it. "Would you come with me?"

"Yes," I answer, too quickly, and he turns and walks down another hallway, by the chrome kitchen, closed doors. In his bedroom, again, he has one lamp burning, this one so quiet I can see little more than outline and shadows. He leaves the door open and I stand awkwardly by the bed.

"Would you undress for me?" he asks, and I wonder why he asks me yes or no questions when I would not dare to say no. I nod, and fumble for the fastening at the back of my skirt. I hesitate, consciously nervous again. Do I take it all off at once, the skirt, the pantyhose, the panties? I cannot bear to have him see me standing in my pantyhose, my faded underwear, so I hook my thumbs inside all three and begin to pull, stumbling and sitting down heavily as I pull them off the rest of the way, glowing humiliation. It does not look like this on TV.

"So we'll work on that one," he says. He is leaning against the wall, a casual observer, his shoulder blades pressing against the doorframe, stomach and hips jutting out, he makes a taut bow with the wall.

"I'm sorry." I apologize again. He shakes his head and lifts himself from the wall.

"You'll learn," he says simply, and I wonder what he means by that. He walks towards me. "Turn around." I stand and turn, and he slips his palms under my bent elbows, cupping them in a familiar intimacy. His breath is hot on my hair and, though I cannot see him, electricity tells me exactly where he is.

I raise my hands to touch my own breasts. "No," he says sharply and grips my hand. "Not unless I tell you to."

He slips his hands up to my shoulders, his skin tough and slightly rough, sighing against my own. He rubs my shoulders for a moment, relaxing them from their tight clenching, and then he pushes down ever so slightly. I kneel on the bed in acquiescence. "Quiet Kate," he says, and breathes into my hair again as his hands move. One slides under my breast, cupping it, thumb strumming the nipple, the other along my stomach, pressing when I inhale to escape the touch, fingers lacing through my pubic hair.

"Ahhh," I moan, and at the sound of pleasure, he pulls

away. His hands skim back up to my hair, thread through so they are curled around my head, and he pushes down. I let my hands support me on all fours. He pushes again. I lower again, until I am kissing the bedding, my ass in the air, careful that my hands are balled into fists, barely touching my own skin. He lets me go and steps back.

I spin away for a moment, letting myself see what he sees, a spill of brown hair over the sheets, sun-deprived white skin glowing in the darkness, the lips of my cunt pouting and glistening, my ass spread wide. Open to him, for him. His hand traces the bones of my spine, jarring over each one, and then he trails one finger between the cheeks of my ass, down into my cunt, over it so slightly, a slight dip to avoid my clit. He pulls away.

"Don't. Move," he says. I don't. Move. I hear him, the rustle of his pants, his feet on the floor. The door clicks closed.

The silence, after a while, does become deafening. Sweat pools where my stomach meets my thighs, and the exposure of my cunt to the air does nothing to dry it. I want to touch myself, release it. If I were home, I would surely be shaking in the throes of a self-delivered orgasm, my back arching, hand pressing harder against myself to feel the throbbing, one, two, three, so hard, four, five, softer, disappearing into shame. Is this better? I move my hand, but the sound of my betrayal is so enormous I stop myself.

I lick my lips and shift, then stop myself again. Don't. Move. I cannot hear any trace of his footsteps. I picture him in my mind again, surprised at the clarity with which I remember his details. My memory has a way of slipping, so that I cannot recall the faces of even my family in their absence. Edward comes easily to me.

My tongue slips out over my lips again – a bad habit my ballet teacher tried to cure me of long ago – when I think of his chest and his arms, and I wonder at the taste of him. Salt or sweet? Hot or merely warm? I want so much to touch him. I see myself kneeling before him, his hands on my head, using my teeth to undo his pants, seeking out his cock with my tongue. I see him binding my hands and asking me to please him, and I want to. I want him to come back in here and tell me what he wants.

My cunt is still throbbing – how long has he kept me like this now – but I no longer care about me. I want to see him again, want him to lift my head and let me memorize him. Sharp eyebrows painted over dark eyes, that delicious mouth, the husky expanse of his shoulders, the strength in his arms. I fight my hands, which are desperate to pull at the eraser pearls of my nipples. I send him mental images, begging him to come inside and without ceremony, thrust his cock inside my cunt, slam into me until he comes, and take me with him, nothing but slick velvet heat. Does he know how much I want this?

My breathing is ragged, though I am motionless, I can feel the air rattle through my lungs and I moan softly, please.

But it is even later that I hear the door open, my senses heightened to his arrival. Three steps, the quiet sound of the door shutting, locking. I squeeze my eyes shut, my fists, I hear the sound of his belt zipping through the loops, and my cunt squeezes open, shut, in a tiny spasm at the noise. I cry out quietly at the sensation, frustrated that I cannot run to him.

"Quiet Kate," he says, and I do not know if it is an order or a caress. I hold my breath, waiting to hear the sound of buttons, zipper, fabric hitting the floor. It does not come. "Kate," he says quietly, firmly, the sound tickling up my spine, leaving goosebumps in its wake.

"Yes," I say, no more than a breath.

Edward moves until he is standing behind me, laces his fingers through my hair; the electricity of his touch makes me shiver, makes me nearly cry out again. I anticipate his move to pull me up, but he pauses instead, letting my hair fall from his fingers, pressing his palm against my back, tracing my shoulder blades, his fingers across my ass, and then only two fingers, in a v, across the outside of my cunt, not touching the lips, just lying there. "Don't," he says again. "Move."

When he removes his fingers, I jump, and then his hands are in my hair again and he pulls me up to look at him, my back, my muscles shrieking in pleasure from the stretch. He is smiling, and I smile back, reflexive, agreeable. "What do you want, Kate?" he asks.

What does he mean, what do I want? I want everything, I want it so badly I cannot vocalize it, I want it all, I want my tongue and my teeth and my hands all over him, I want to make him want me as much as I want him and I want to make him come harder than any other woman has made him come, watch his cock throb, let him shoot his semen wherever he wants, my face, my tits, my mouth, my cunt, I don't care as long as he lets me bring him there and as long as he makes me come and not my old weary vibrator.

"It's all right," he says, still smiling. "I know what you want." He lets my hair fall again, strokes it softly. "Turn around." I move awkwardly on the bed until I am kneeling, facing him as he stands before me. He cups my face in his hands and pulls me forwards until I am touching his chest, and he lets me explore. I spread my hands wide, touching his arms, burying my nose in his hair, letting my tongue dart out, hungrily flicking at his nipples, kissing my way down his flat stomach. When I have made a tactile map of his torso, I pull my hands back around and reach for the button on his pants. With that feline speed I have already come to know so well, he grabs my wrists in one hand, pinning them together, and with the other hand, pinches my nipple sharply. "No," he says firmly. I convulse at his touch. Still holding my hands, he reaches behind him and deftly opens a drawer, pulling out small strips of fabric. Before I can examine them, he wraps the lengths of midnight velvet around my wrists and then releases them. I pull at them experimentally, but my hands are locked together as if in prayer, in supplication.

"Now," he says, and he moves his own hands to his pants, unbuttons, unzips, lowers. My mouth parts involuntarily when I see his cock, proudly swollen, throbbing, pre-come at the tip and I am so hungry for it, it makes me moan, makes my nipples ache, makes my cunt start the drumming again. I reach for him, and he grabs the restraints. "I said no," he says, and unties me. "Put your hands behind your back," he orders, and I do, my lips moving as if to object, but no sound appearing. He steps up against me, his cock is throbbing angrily against my tits, but he has me immobilized as he reties the restraints so I cannot touch him.

"Please, Edward," I say again, when he has stepped away, and I am fixated on his cock, his balls, the muscles in his thighs, I want to lick him until he comes, let him use me, fuck my face, I don't care, but I want it so badly.

"Do you like my cock?" he asks, and reaches down and strokes it once. It throbs in response; my cunt matches it.

"Yes," I breathe.

"Do you want to suck it?" he asks politely.

"Please," I say.

"Do you want to beg me for it?"

"Please, let me suck your cock," I say, and my cunt is really thrumming now, my nipples vibrating with electricity.

"Please, Master, let me suck your cock," he says, mocking.

"Please, Master, let me suck your cock," I repeat, not caring if he makes fun of me. He strokes his cock again, catches the bead of moisture on the tip of his index finger. It hangs there, sparkling like ambrosia in the dim light, and he reaches for me. I open my mouth for it, and he lets me taste it. I suck hungrily, desperate to show him how I would suck his cock if he would only let me, working my tongue on the underside, pulling my teeth back, looking up at him.

"You want it in your mouth?" he asks, and I nod, childishly enthusiastic. He smiles at me, bemused adult. I open my mouth expectantly, baby bird. "No, no, no. Not yet," he says, taking pleasure in denying me. I sulk, and he pushes me back onto the bed so I am lying there, open for him. He moves up, spreads his legs to climb over me until he is straddling my chest. His cock throbs impatiently, and a thrill chases through me as I realize that it is for me. "Look into my eyes," he says, and I tear myself from the worship of his cock. He touches my face. "Beautiful," he murmurs. "Just like that."

He leans forwards, I keep my eyes locked with his, swirls of heated chocolate. His cock touches my chin, my cheek. I part my lips again, anticipating. "Don't you dare," he says, wagging his finger at me. I close them, he brushes the swollen head over my mouth, and I am stunned by the heat of it, hot poker, feverish, and the heat between my thighs seems just as unbearable. Over my cheekbones, my jaw, up to my hairline so I can really smell him, hot, sweat, the unmistakable new smell of a man, and I love it. The hair on his thighs is tickling my breasts and it makes me squirm. He moves back down, relaxes, his thighs rub my nipples, he leans forwards and his cock rests against my neck. "Very good," he coos. "Now what do you want?"

"I want to suck your cock," I moan, twisting my hips, rubbing my thighs together, begging for some release.

"Open your mouth," he demands. I look at him, puzzled. Like this? Not on my knees? I am stymied by geography, spoiled by jump cuts. "Open your mouth," he repeats, holding my head still. I lick my lips and open my mouth, and he slides his cock inside, hotter there than on my face. I flick my tongue around the head, tasting more of his precome, thirsty for it. He flexes his hips and begins to fuck my mouth.

The fear strikes me that I will feel as ashamed about this as I do the morning after an extended masturbatory session, waking up in sheets that reek of my cunt, melted ice dampening the blanket, my vibrator purring weakly under the bed, books of erotica lying open, their spines irreparably bent. That moment of cold separation from ecstasy, cleaning up. The morning after. But that fear is subsumed by the fact that a man, with an amazing body, true eyes, and a soft voice, wants to use me like this, and that I will not wake up alone.

He pulls out, sits back. I am gasping for air. His cock is

even more swollen, his balls tight and high and heavy. Doesn't he want to come? Was I doing it wrong? "No, baby," he says, chucking me under the chin, reading my mind. "You're perfect. But I want to taste you, and then I want to fuck you." I shudder, relieved that my orgasm is finally imminent.

He climbs off of me, bends over, takes one of my nipples in his mouth. I buck at the sensation as his hand finds my other breast, pulls the other nipple taut, pinches, squeezes. He suckles, hard, biting occasionally, pinching harder, and as hard as he does it I want it harder. I want it dirty.

I'm writhing against my restraints, miserable that I cannot pull his head to my breasts, make him hurt me with those fingers and teeth. He moves his mouth to the other nipple, slides his hand down my side, down my thigh, back up. I shiver with anticipation, feeling his cock throb against my leg and my cunt answer. His fingers tickle their way back up, tease the lips of my pussy, so swollen it hurts, and then he slips one finger inside me, thrusts, a second finger, thrusts, a third, stretching me wide, slamming in so the heel of his hand hits my clit and my body jerks in a tiny climax. He moves his head from my breast, pushes my legs apart, lies between them. His tongue hovers above me for a moment, and I hold my breath until he finds the bud of my clitoris and flicks it ever so lightly, once, twice.

I moan, struggle against my bonds again, push my hips up, and he finally humours me, stroking his tongue along my clit harder, faster, fucking me with his fingers, and I'm crying out for him. It only takes a few minutes, and I am coming, screaming, writhing, my cunt squeezing his fingers again and again, the release after such denial so perfect. He waits for me to finish, pressing his tongue flat against my clit until it stops pulsing, the aftershock of the quake settling around his fingers, and then he pulls himself up, pulls me up by my shoulders, and unties me.

"Roll over," he tells me, and I do, drawing myself up on all fours. He pushes my knees out with his, and kneels between my legs, poises the head of his cock at my weakly shuddering cunt-lips, wraps his hands around my hips, and pulls me back. I settle over his cock, so stiff I can feel it, iron-like inside me, feel every ridge of my pussy as he pushes in. He sets the rhythm using my hips, pulling, pushing. We are groaning together, his fingers are bruising my skin when we move faster, the sound of our bodies smacking together filling the air. He pulls one hand around, rubs my clit, pushes me to orgasm one more time and as I start to call out, howl into the air with my head thrown back, he pushes off me, forces me over onto my back, wraps my hand around the shaft of his cock until it throbs. I push back once, tightening the skin, and it happens, as my cunt is still pulsing from his absence, his come shoots out, the way I wanted it to, on my tits, my stomach, my face, my tongue reaching out obscenely, begging to taste it as it pools, warm and white all over my body.

Panting, we stop our movements, the throbbing subsides, recedes. I lay beneath him and watch his chest rise and fall, his face lifted to the ceiling, my hand still wrapped around his softening cock. He looks down at me, slick with sweat and his come, and smiles. "Good girl," he says softly, and I smile. Calm. Unembarrassed. Quiet.

The Little Mermaid

Cecilia Tan

When I was young, a wise old sea cow told me of the four elements: water, earth, fire, and air. At the time I had laughed, for I had never known a world other than the watery kingdom my father ruled, the softness of kelp beds and the caresses of the currents. I could not imagine what she described, her great green eyes focused on a place far away, the hardness of earth, the burning of fire, the lightness of air.

All that changed on the day I came of age. On that day I swam to the surface, as every mermaid must do when she seeks her heart's desire. I thought it a joyous day, and yet I could taste the salt of my father's tears in the water as my tail swept me from him, far and fast.

When I came upon the surface the first time, I saw the spray fly up into the moonlight like pearls. The Moon! I called out to her with a sea song, having heard so much about her as a child. She smiled down on me and I swam on my back, feeling the rush of foam over my skin. So this was air! Air tickled and made my nipples pucker where they broke the surface. Air caressed and teased as it blew this way and that.

In the moonlight I saw a great shape across the flat surface of the sea. It groaned and I swam closer to it. From my place in the water I could see its shape, so similar to one my sisters and I had found cracked open at the bottom. A ship. And then I heard another sound, shouts and voices.

Far above me, leaning on a railing, was one of the most beautiful creatures I had ever seen. He had a face like a comely merman, only his hair shimmered gold in the moonlight. He wore a white shirt with a circle of gold across his brow. He stood back from the railing then, tall and upright, and shook back his shoulders, as if he had leaned there too long. He walked then, on back flippers long and stalky, along the edge of the ship.

I waved, but he did not see me, his eyes fixed in the direction of a far-off shore.

I followed the ship as they continued towards that shore, as the clouds gathered and covered the moon, and as the storm began. As a daughter of the sea I had nothing to fear from the waves, but as the storm built, the ship was tossed. And as sea and sky battled, the ship split apart, and men spilled into the water like sand from an overturned shell. I could save but one, and I found him struggling for the surface. I calmed him with a sea song and buoyed his body with mine until the storm passed and a rosy dawn lit the sky.

When he woke, we floated near his destined shore. I lay on my back in the water, his head cradled between my breasts, humming softly to myself.

"I'm dead and gone to heaven," he said to himself as he opened his eyes. "And you're an angel."

His hands crept along my ribs and caressed my nipples as gently as the breeze. His legs hung into the water, one on either side of my tail. He blinked as if he expected to wake up at any moment. Then he leaned his head toward mine, and kissed me.

If his touch was like air, his kiss must have been fire. It started like a current of warm water, flowing down my body from my mouth to the tip of my tail. But as his lips and mine moved across each other, the warmth became almost unbearable, until I knew what I felt was burning. The sun rose then, a ball of hot fire into the sky, and I cried out with an ecstasy so intense it hurt.

"Is this a dream?" he said, then, brushing his fingers along my cheek. His arms circled my shoulders and I felt his body then, against mine, where my tail met my torso. He pulled his legs together as I turned us in a slow circle and he pressed firm against me, as a part of him became tall and upright and as hard as I imagined the earth to be. I wanted to feel him press harder, but in the water we slid past each other too easily. I locked my arms over his spine and took us in to shore.

The waves obliged and carried us up onto the sand, where I felt the weight of his body settle onto me. We kissed again, and as the sun blazed hot on my skin I held him tight. I had never felt such pleasure or agony as the way I burned for him. His eyes were closed now as his hips rocked like a boat on the waves, groaning like the ship with each sway. But this wasn't right, and I knew it. The burning was deep inside me now, where neither of us could touch. We rolled in the edge of the surf and I looked at the part of him that stood now like the mast on the ship. The yearning part of me knew I wanted to have him inside me, and I knew of no other way than to open my mouth and drink him in. He gasped as I slid my wet mouth over the hardness that was his essence, and I nursed upon him like a hungry calf at a sea cow's teat. Then came a wave of saltiness that was the taste of home.

He gasped and blinked then, and looked up into my face, then hastily down at the rest of me. He stifled a cry and then rolled to one side, hands clutching at the wet sand. "You, you're a . . ."

He said no more as a voice from up the beach came to us then. "What, ho! Who's there?"

More people on stalky legs were up on the dunes, and they began shouting as he stood. I dove into the water, then, knowing somehow that I should not be seen there on the sand. I was still full of the burning, but knew I could not stay. Does not water quench fire? I dove deep, but still I burned.

I came after a time to the cave of a sea witch, an old mermaid who had spent so much of her life at the bottom of the sea that her hair was green like kelp and her skin glowed like a jellyfish. And I asked her if there was anything she could do to ease the pain I was feeling.

"Pain, is it?" gurgled the sea witch. "What sort of pain?"

I described to her as best I could, how it felt like hunger, only it wasn't in my stomach, it was lower down, how it felt like fire, only it didn't harm me.

"And does it ever feel better?"

Here I hesitated. For I knew the one time it felt like pleasure was when I was with him. So there was nothing else I could do but to tell her of my golden-haired man from the ship.

"Man from a ship!" She cackled and schools of small fish darted away from her. "Oh, you poor thing, there be only one thing to ease your pain then." She dove into her cave and came up with a shell. She carefully pried it open to reveal a tiny blue pearl. "Swallow this," she said, rolling it into my hand.

I asked what it was, but all she would say was, "The Pearl of Desire. When you find what you most desire, you will have it. But in trade you will give up the two things that made you one of us, your tail, and your sea song."

But of course I swallowed the Pearl, because I could not know then what a price it was to pay. I swam back to the shore where I had left the man from the ship but of him there was no sign. I went along the coast then, until I came to a cliffside. In the moon's light I could see the palace built above the water, and see the flickering of firelight, dancing bright like my desire. I swam into a calm lagoon toward the sound of voices.

I watched from the water as a man and a woman emerged from the darkness of the trees. It was he, and my heart leaped in my chest to see him. He had a crown of flowers upon his head and his white shirt had been replaced by a patterned cloth around his waist. He pulled the woman down to the sand and pushed the cloth aside and I could see then what I had wanted so inexplicably before. The hard part of him, rising like a finger of coral. "Come here," he said to the woman.

"My prince, we should not," the woman replied. "If the princess finds out . . ."

"The princess is busy just now," he said, his voice liquid and low. "And I am on fire."

So he too burned. My breath came in quick gasps, the air seemed to fill my head as I watched him turn her body over, as I watched her legs spread.

I pulled myself up out of the water then, and as my body emerged from the shore I felt as though a sword were cleaving me in two. I bit back my cry of pain though, as I felt the breeze in the space where my tail had been, in the space between my legs where now there was a hungry, burning mouth.

Up the beach I heard the sound of sand as someone ran. And then a soft curse.

He was sitting alone, his arms on his knees, his jaw as hard and set as a stone.

I opened my mouth only to find I could not speak. I had no sea song to seduce him with this time. So instead I crawled towards him.

He looked up to see me and his eyebrows knit together as I came near.

I tried to remind him of the sunrise – I touched my nipples as he had, gentle like the breeze. I rolled onto my back and opened my legs to feel the cool air fanning the burning need there.

He did not ask any questions then, did not even pause to kiss me. Instead he heaved his body over mine and sank that long finger of his flesh into me, pinning me to the sand. It felt like a sword cleaving me in two, but then water flowed from somewhere in me, and the fire melted into warm pleasure, and he dove and plunged into me until we were both quenched.

While we lay upon the sand I marvelled at the creation of man. Hard like the earth, burning like fire, gasping for air and then leaking the water of the sea through his skin. He looked at me looking at him and laughed. "What is it, my darling? Are you going to scold me, too?"

I shook my head.

"No? I finally escape the cold and chill of the mountains, my father's sour temper, and the admonitions of the priests, to be married to an island princess so my father can rule the shipping lanes, and what do I find? Her people may not wear much, but they are just as afraid of lust as mine. Maybe more."

He paused, as if waiting for me to say something. When I did not, he went on. "You look familiar. Have we met before?" He squinted at me in the light of the moon, then said to himself, "Must have been a dream."

I touched him on the shoulder to prove to him I was real. He laughed again. "Can you believe I was rescued from a shipwreck? I thought I was dead, but I had this dream . . ." He looked over his shoulder toward the flickers of torches beyond the trees. "A lustful dream . . ."

He pulled me to my feet and it felt as though pins and needles were being driven through my skin. But I smiled and took a step to follow him, to be with him.

"Can you speak?" he asked then. I shook my head. He nodded to me then, smiling, and his smile made me as warm as the sunrise.

I followed him through the trees, up the hill, to a wide terrace of hard stone. "Look, everyone!" he cried. "Look what I've found!"

People came running from inside the palace bearing more torches, all of them dressed as he was, with bright cloth wrapped around their bodies. "My prince!" one of the men said, "where did she come from?"

A woman came out of the crowd and wrapped a cloth around my bare skin. "She must have been in the shipwreck also, the poor thing. What is your name?"

I could not say a thing.

"She's still in shock from being half-drowned," said a man.

"So beautiful!" said another.

Finally the prince quieted them with a gesture of his hands. "Yes, yes, she was on the ship with me. In fact, she was my maidservant, and I'd thought her lost with the rest of the hands. She will be my maidservant again, once she regains her speech. Isn't that right . . . Emerald?"

I nodded, not knowing of what he spoke, only knowing that he seemed to want me near him. And to be near him was all I wanted then.

He came to me again in the morning. The prince had his own quarters, a wing of the palace all his own. I had slept in a bed as soft as any kelp but as light as air, and then had gone to the bathhouse, where hot water sprang up from within the earth. Again I was amazed to find water, earth, fire, and air, all in one place. And again my prince came to me, and I tasted his salt with my tongue, and took him deep inside me. I could wrap my legs around the trunk of his body, and then even if we slid into the steaming water – which we did – I could still have him inside me. "My salvation," he breathed into my ear, as his flesh spear plunged into me and out, as I squeezed him hard. "And so you rescue me yet again, from my own burning need."

I wanted to tell him what pleasure he brought me. I wanted to ask him about this land. I wanted to tell him that everything was new to me and to ask him his name. He lifted me out of the bath onto the wet stone and I felt the roughness of his beard like sand between my legs. His tongue wriggled like a fish as it nestled into the soft spaces there and sparked the fire of my desire again and again. With another sudden rush of pleasure like a plunge into deep water, I clamped my knees around his head. But I had no voice to cry out with.

That afternoon I was taken to see the princess. Women came and dressd me and braided my sea-tossed hair. They were very grave as they led me to her chamber, or perhaps they did not wish to speak and remind me I was mute.

The guard there was about to open the door when my prince came running up to us.

"You must not enter, my lord," the guard said, stepping in front of the door, his arms crossed over his chest. "You must not lay eyes on the princess until the day of the wedding."

"Where are you taking Emerald?" he asked.

One of the women who had dressed me looked up with dark eyes. I wondered if this was the woman he had tried to take on the beach last night, for she fixed him with a hard stare. "She will not be harmed," she said. "The princess merely wishes to . . . inspect her."

My prince stepped back, then, and went back down the hall towards his rooms.

The princess sat upon a throne of fine polished wood, worked with gold and silver, and wore elaborate layers of cloth. The throne room was round like a cave, the slatted windows letting a sea breeze blow through. She looked over my white skin, which had only seen the sun once in my life, yesterday, and nodded. She turned to the woman who had spoken to my prince.

"She cannot speak?"

"No, not a word," the woman replied.

"She can tell no secrets, then." The princess sat back in her chair, her eyes on the far edge of the room.

"So it would seem, my lady."

The princess waved her hand, still not looking at me. "If the barbarian cannot wait a week, let him plant his seeds here. No one shall speak of it."

And then I was returned to him.

And so it went, for seven days and seven nights, during which I spent most of my time either in the bathhouse or in the air-light bed, waiting for my prince to quicken, waiting to have my newly empty spaces filled in a manner so intimate I would never have imagined it possible before. The household was busy, preparing for the wedding. The cool white halls were filled with the scent of meats being roasted on the beach, and servants with heaping baskets of fruit went back and forth. From the prince's window I could see men were erecting a roof where the wedding would take place. But my prince had no role in these preparations, and we spent long hours, lying in the bedclothes, as he would slide a finger over my shoulders, down my arm, or use a small palm frond to brush and tickle my newest and most sensitive skin, between my thighs.

On the seventh night, he came to the room bearing a basket with food for me as he always did, but he did not feed it to me as he had before. He put the basket down and took me in his arms immediately.

The torchlight flickered in his gold-spun hair, and his kiss ranged down from my lips to my neck, then to my breasts as he pulled the cloth away from me, as his lips and tongue moved hungrily over my skin. My hunger for food was forgotten as I drank in his touch instead. He lifted me off my feet then, and brought me to the bed. I lay there a moment watching him emerge from his clothing like a crab from his shell. Naked and new again he came to me then, his skin on fire and his eagerness for me making his breath shallow. I matched his hunger with mine, gobbling up his maleness as I had that day on the beach, the hard pole of him going deep into my mouth. But soon he pulled me away with a shudder, before the salt spray could come. He hooked one of my legs over each shoulder, folding me up so that the burning slot between my legs was lifted for him.

He plunged a finger into me and I gasped. "You know," he said to me then, "I had not known many women before you. I had dreamed of them, desired them, hungered for them, but had tasted so few." Here he bent his head to lick at me and I tensed with pleasure. "And the few who would give in, desperate serving wenches looking for a way to better their position. Dirty sluts. I feared their diseases and their plots for my bastards." His finger returned to the empty place in me, and burrowed there. "But then there you were, delivered to me by a magic prayer. A virgin, clean as the sea water running off your skin, and you took me in." Now he heaved himself up to lay his manhood onto my mound. I felt it there, heavy and hot, and it twitched like a fish. He seemed to have no more to say, and into me he dove. How many times had he been inside me since that first night on the beach? More times than I had digits to count. And yet I lived for that moment, when we were as close together as two bodies could be. Even as my arms clutched at his back, I held him tight, inside, and he cried out. I felt the salty flow that always reminded me of home.

He slept, then, and I would have, too, but I heard a song then borne on the sea breeze through the window. I heard my sisters singing down in the lagoon, and walking on my pins-and-needles feet, I made my way down to the water. There they bobbed, their heads just far enough above the water that I could hear them.

"Sister, sister, come back to us!" they cried.

I shook my head, unable to say anything else.

"We spoke to the sea witch," Mara, the oldest told me. "And she told us what she had done."

"But she did not tell you everything," Lara, the youngest said, salt tears welling in her eyes. "She said you would lose everything of us if you joined with him."

"Your tail, your voice . . ." said Sara, my closest sister.

"But she did not tell you what would happen if you lost him!" Mara swam closer to the shore. "Only while he is yours will you live. If he gives his heart to another, you will die."

Lara wailed. "We begged her that it not be so. She should have told you."

Sara held something out of the water. "So she told us there is one way you might be saved." She tossed the thing and it flew slickly through the night air to land in the sand near my aching feet. "Take the knife. If you cut out his heart, you will live. Let his blood drip over your legs and you will grow a tail again. Swallow his blood and you will regain your voice. And then you can come back to us."

"Emerald?" The prince's voice came from above me on the terrace. And my sisters disappeared with a quiet splash.

"Here you are," he said, as he approached. The tips of his fingers brushed my cheek and I leaned my face into the dry smoothness of his hand. I took a deep breath of his salty scent, and licked his palm.

"Hungry again, are we?" he whispered. My lips found his neck then, and the soft place behind his ear, and I felt the fire in him begin to burn again. The breeze itself was a caress on my bare flesh, the rush of the waves a seductive song of its own.

He slid his fingers into my hair and it felt as if I dove into a clear lagoon, my hair swept back from my face and my body tingling with his touch. Our lips met then, and it was like the moment when I broke the surface for the first time, his breath mingling with mine. I could feel his heart beat everywhere along his skin.

We let gravity take its course, as it so easily did on land, and soon our legs were entwined on the sand. I could feel the hard barb of him, the stone that I hungered for, sliding back and forth trying to find its way inside me. And I knew, somehow, that my sisters were wrong. In that first fateful moment when we had kissed, in that first spark of fire inside me, in the first breath of air we shared that fanned the spark to a flame, in that first embrace of the weight of the earth, I had lost the purity of the water. I could not go back. I could no longer live without air and earth and fire.

I cried out as he sank into me, salt tears tracking my face, my feeble feet drumming on his back as I tried to drive him deeper and deeper in. Tomorrow he would marry the princess and I knew, if I did not have his stone to hold me, I would float away into the air. If I did not have the salt of his come, I would burn away to ash. If I did not have his breath to fill my lungs, I would be buried alive. If I did not have his burning desire to draw me up again and again, I would drown. Tomorrow he would marry the princess but, for tonight, I was whole.

Fried Blonde Tomatoes

Robert Schaffer

What is it about burnt-out blondes? There they are, on the train to Long Island, a few too many scotches floating them along. Or out in fancy Connecticut suburbs, hair rinsed to a crisp, the financial beneficiaries of one too many divorces. And on the streets of Manhattan, with delicate perfume trailing behind them, they sashay in bewildered astonishment.

And I crave them. I crave them all.

Take the other day. I was in a toy store on Bleecker street, and behind the counter was a stringy blonde in her late thirties, skin pockmarked and eyes droopy. A drug user or ex-junkie. I got hard just hearing her husky voice, the product of too many cigarettes and sleepless nights. We smiled at each other as I pretended to peruse the plastic goods. She leaned forwards, letting her cleavage bulge.

"You know, anything you want, I'm sure I can offer you a deal."

I pretended to think about this.

"What sort of deal?"

She looked at her watch.

"Almost lunch time. You hungry?"

"Very," I said, in a voice that left no doubt what I was hungry for.

She walked out from the counter, her ass tight in a dark leather mini-skirt, locked the door, flipped the closed sign and pulled the shade.

"So," I said, "What's for lunch?"

"Oh," she breathed, and hopped up on the glass counter, "we got the blue plate special," and she pulled up her skirt and spread her panty-less crotch, "pussy on glass."

"Well, I've got the perfect side dish," I replied.

"Yeah? And what would that be, lover?"

I put my hands on her legs and bent down.

"Tongue in bush, what else?" and went to it.

She grunted as I licked. She tasted of nicotine, alcohol, and several illegal substances.

"Take your time, lover, lunch is an hour long," and she leaned back to open up wider. She didn't make much noise, just sighed deeply as I plunged my tongue this way and that.

"Make more noise," she said, in that husky raspy voice. "I want to hear you slurp!"

I slurped.

"Yeah, lover, that's it!" and she put a hand to her mouth and bit one of her fingers, making soft noises. "Kiss it, kiss it all over."

"Yes, ma'am," I mumbled, and I loudly placed big wet kisses on her moist cunt. I could feel the beginnings of her orgasm as she agitated her ass, and her breathing became jagged. She finally came with a long drawn-out sigh. She leaned back on the counter while I gently kissed her crotch. I left with an Astro-Boy keychain, Catwoman magnet, rubber squid, and Baby Spice doll.

And an open invitation for lunch any time I wanted it.

I was on a roll with druggies, because my next blonde was a platinum 24-year-old heroin addict with lovely eyes, rotten teeth, and plush breasts. She was shivering in 85 degrees heat sitting on a bench in Tompkins Square Park, and as I walked by she made a pitch for money in a surprisingly girlish voice.

"Dude, you gotta buck, I needa buck."

I looked at her sternly. "Do your parents know you're out here?"

She opened her eyes (or I think she did, hard to tell) and looked up at me.

"Shit, dude, my dad's a dog-fucker and my mom gave me my first taste!"

I sat down next to her.

"Gee, so you've had it hard, huh?"

"Fuck, yeah!" and she breathed in mucus. "Looka this," and she pulled up her T-shirt to show me scars on her stomach.

"Christ," I whistled, "what happened?"

"My dad used to beat me." She took my hand and placed it on the right side of her head. There was a valley in her skull. "He knocked me so hard one day I got dented," and she began to sniff.

"There there," I cooed to her, and she fell passively against my body. I stroked her hair and rocked her, breathing in her odour: essence of unwashed skin spiced with urine notes. I wanted to lick her right there.

"What's your name?"

"Dorothy."

"Where do you live, Dorothy?"

She shrugged. "Wherever, man," and I could see her eyes getting wet. I lifted her face.

"Tell you what, Dorothy, why don't I take you to dinner?"

Her eyes widened. "Yeah? You ain't shittin' me?"

"Nope. You deserve a night out."

She shook against me. "I'm kinda fucked-up."

I brushed my lips against hers and whispered in her ear. "We can take care of that, too."

"That'd be so cool, dude. I know where to get supremo shit."

"And you can, ahh, 'do your business' at my place, maybe take a shower."

She threw her arms around my neck in a very childish gesture. "Oh, dude!" she exclaimed, and kissed my cheek. "What's your name?"

I told her. She smiled at me.

"Know what?" she said with a Shirley Temple intonation.

"No, what?"

"You can fuck me if you want," she lisped. "I gotta very tight pussy. Everyone says so."

"Well, how nice of them."

"Yeah – and know what else?"

I already knew what I needed to know, but what the hey – In cases like this, more is more, you know?

"Nope, I don't."

"I really like my ass fucked," and she turned her baby eyes on me. "Would you like to fuck my ass?"

I smiled at her. "Maybe after dinner. I don't like to ass-fuck on an empty stomach."

She frowned. "Dude, you're not making funna me, are you?"

I kissed her full on the lips, taking in a mouthful of her bad breath, and said, "Let's get your shit." She shyly took my hand and led me out of the park to a street off Avenue B that must've been missed when the Lower East Side became the East Village. It was filthy. In the middle of the block, we stopped in front of a boarded-up tenement. She instructed me to wait out front, because "the dude'll freak if he sees you, dude!" I slipped her the necessary bills and she entered the building through a space in the boards. Some people passed me and glared. I smiled back. She suddenly reappeared.

"Done deal, dude!"

I put my arm around her waist and led her to 14th Street, where I hailed a cab. She sank back on the seat, her eyes glazing over. I hustled her into my apartment building in Chelsea, and felt her up in the elevator, running my hands over her breasts. She fell back against the wall and shut her eyes.

"You dig me, that's cool," she mumbled.

In the apartment she kicked off her ratty sneakers and pulled her shirt off, gleefully falling on my sofa and rummaging in her bag for her works. With an engineer's precision she assembled her needle and prepared the packet and spoon.

"Uh, would you like a candle?"

"Thanks, dude!" and spoon was set to flame. She looked

up at me, with serious eyes. "You wanna fuck me while I shoot?" She pulled the heroin into the syringe. "Really, I dig being fucked," and she wrapped a worn piece of surgical tubing around her arm, "while I do shit."

I knelt by her and kissed her, then filled my mouth with those nubile breasts, biting into her nipples while she squirmed. Her skin had an earthy, dirty flavour.

"Take my pants off, dude."

I tongued her breasts, then licked her navel, which was pierced with a small silver ring. I undid her pants and slid them off. The pungent odour of unwashed pussy wafted forth.

"Now you. I wanna see your cock."

Her eyes brightened as I threw off all my clothes.

"Dude, you're so clean!" and she grabbed my cock and licked it like a greedy child with a candy cane. she sucked it into her mouth. The sight of my cock going in and out of those young pillowy lips, while one of her hands held a needle and the other arm wore surgical tubing thrilled me to the balls. I twined her unwashed hair into my fingers and pumped her mouth. But before I could come she pulled my cock out.

"Fuck me," she said.

I prepared to roll a condom on, but she stopped me.

"Nyuh-uh, dude, you gotta do it raw."

"Dorothy –" I began to protest, but she cut me off.

"You ain't afraid of catchin' somethin', are ya?"

I paused.

"Cause if you think I'm dirty, I'm leaving, dude."

She arched and spread her legs, and revealed the raw sweet pinkness in her pubic hair (dyed blonde – very careful for a homeless junkie, I thought). I got on the couch and rubbed my dick along her crack.

"Wait, dude, I just gotta get ready," and she pulled the tubing tight with her mouth and positioned the needle. Then she smiled.

I pushed in and she shot up. The heroin took her and she

went slack and her arms drooped. "Baby's being fucked," she murmured in a sing-song girly voice. "Yummy yummy yummy, I got jism in my tummy, and I feel like nodding out." She stopped singing and giggled as I fucked her using long strokes, and she hadn't lied: she had a tight sweet twat.

Suddenly she kicked against me, forcing me out of her hole, my cock twanging stupidly in the air. "Jesus, Dorothy, what the hell!" but for an answer she twirled, got up on all fours, and presented her ass to me. There was a tattoo on her left cheek of a heart pierced by a bloody knife.

"Please dude, up my ass, fuck me up my ass!" and she pulled her cheeks apart. What the hell, in for a penny, etc. etc. I positioned myself while reaching one of my arms forwards to grasp her tits. I used my other hand to shove my cock into her rather unpleasantly brown small hole.

She screeched in delight, "Yeah, baby likes, oooh, yeah, hard, baby wants it hard!" and I began to pound her. Her face fell into a sofa pillow, and she drooled as she made little grunting noises. I never thought of myself as a fan of anal sex, but I dug the feel of her anal canal, and I dug the way my cock looked going in and out of that tight round ass of hers.

"You dig baby's ass?" she mumbled into the pillow.

"Yeah, I dig it!" I exuberantly replied, and fucked her harder. I could feel the come rising, pouring into my cock-head. I jerked, and came with a glorious spurt that curled my toes and made me moan. I even had some after-tremors, little oozing quakes after the main event. Sperm dribbled out her asshole, disgusting and exciting me. I pulled free, and saw brown flecks on my dick.

"Jesus," I whispered, and fell against her back.

We were soon sleeping side by side. I was in a deep post-coital sleep, but she – she was deep in junkie heaven, her mind in a black abyss, lost to the world and herself.

Afterwards, I scrubbed myself with scalding water and steel wool.

Oh, and I did take her to dinner.

Of course, there was a very brief interlude with a ditzy

single mom, black roots showing beneath a bad rinse job. I finger-fucked her in the furniture department at Macy's, while her kid jumped on chaise lounges.

But let me tell you about my prize: a plastic surgerized fifty-something with the proverbial penthouse on Park Avenue, courtesy of husband number three. Her face stretched behind her ears, her hair was like a mane of frizzled fools gold, and her pussy was shaved. She had one of those vulgar deep tans that showed off her age spots. Yet her breasts were real, small and charmingly flat against her chest. I met her in a bar off Union Square. She wore white Capri pants, red pumps, and a pale blue scarf twirled around her neck. Her shirt had one too many buttons undone, revealing a very expensive red satin bra. Depending on your zip code, her outfit was either retro-chic or suburban vulgar. She was finishing a Cosmopolitan, her loud red lipstick firmly imprinted on the glass. I stood next to her stool. Her perfume wafted against my nostrils. I ordered bourbon, water on the side. She glanced sideways, appraising me.

"You old enough for that drink, sonny?" she laughed, in a low voice, rich with alcohol.

"Old enough and then some." I tapped her empty glass. "Buy you a drink?"

She gave me another look, replied "Sure," quickly showing her tongue between her lips.

"Same thing?" and she nodded. I signalled the bartender, and she picked up the refilled glass with a very feminine gesture, showing off her carefully tapered fingers and lacquered nails. Two very expensive rings glittered in the light.

"To little boys." She smiled, and clinked my glass.

I tossed my bourbon back, swirled some water in my mouth, and savoured the burn.

"How's the drink?" I inquired.

"Nice," and she pushed the glass over to me. "Taste it."

You might think it imprudent to drink from a stranger's glass, but then my tongue's been up junkie twat and my cock's been in places brown, black, and blue, so I wasn't about to get sanitary now. I took her glass and sipped from the lipstick side, licking the imprint when I finished. She smiled.

"Ooooh, aren't we provocative?" and the way she said it told me I was in the pussy zone.

"Drink OK?" I asked. She studied the glass from different angles. "Yes, it's not bad, but it's missing something." Suddenly her hand was on my crotch. I moved closer, to hide what she was doing. She tugged at my zipper and skilfully snaked her cool bony hand into my underwear and around my cock. I leaned into the bar and let out a low gasp as she slowly began to jerk me.

"Yes," she repeated, in her low voice, "this drink needs something, something salty," and she squeezed harder on my cock, "Something only a sonny boy can provide – something with a head," and she began to seriously pump me. I tried hard not to gyrate my ass. I wondered if anyone around us knew what was going on, but I didn't care. I swallowed hard. I started to come. My companion quickly brought her glass to my squirting cock, the milky white swirling in the deep ruby of her drink. She gently pulled on my cock as she sipped her drink.

"Now that's a Cosmopolitan," and she plunged her tongue into the glass and coated it with the milky red drink. She pulled me by my cock until I was right next to her. It turned me on. Her eyes glittered as she let some of the drink dribble down the side of her mouth. And then she kissed me, one of those sloppy alcoholic kisses. She rolled her tongue into my mouth, and I could taste her saliva, my jism, and the bartender's idea of a Cosmopolitan all at once. It was gross. I was in heaven.

She pulled away, took a swig of the drink, and kissed me again, letting the liquid roll into my mouth. I let it roll back. We swirled it until we had no more left. There was a pause. We were both breathing deeply. Her hand was still on my cock.

"So," she whispered, "sonny boy wants his mama."

"Lady–" I began, but she slid her hand off my dick and brought it up to my face. Her fingers glistened, and she pushed them into my mouth.

"Be a good boy and lick them clean."

I licked. She slowly pulled away and dried the hand with a cocktail napkin. She laughed.

"Don't you think you better zip your dick up?" And she shook her head. "Mama's got to tell her sonny boy everything, doesn't she?"

She's really into this Oedipal shtick but I figured, as I tucked my organ as inconspicuously as I could into my fly, what the hell. I could go along with a gag, if it got me this perfect burnt blonde poon.

I looked up and could swear the bartender cocked an eyebrow at me. I took a deep breath. "By the way, it's not 'sonny boy'," and I told her my name.

She smirked. "Your name's sonny boy, all right. I knew the moment I saw you that you were my sonny boy." She rapped my ass with her knuckles, spiking me with her rings. It hurt. I jumped. "Besides, it's not polite to contradict your elders. Where's your manners?"

I opened my mouth, but she cut me off.

"If you want to play with the big girls, you have to have manners," and she slid drunkenly off her stool, falling against my chest. I caught her, and she looked up at me, her face flushed with liquor. She parted her lips, and I kissed her again, seizing her well-kept body and squeezing it to mine. I was in a frenzy to have her. Her eyes were laughing as we pulled apart.

"I've got to pee – escort me," and she drunkenly offered me her elbow. I walked her to the women's room, but as I turned to leave she laughed and said, "A gentleman helps a lady pee," and pulled me into the bathroom with her. It smelled of urine, vomit, and menses. She locked the door and grabbed my shirt.

"Let's see what we got," and she pushed me against the wall and jerked the shirt open. The buttons echoed against the tiled floor.

"Mmm, you're not bad for a little boy," and she ran her hands greedily over my chest. The contrast of her dark tanned hands against my never-been-in-the-sunlight skin excited me. Her fingers brushed my chest, and I closed my eyes. I felt her tongue on my neck, and she licked down to my nipples. She sucked them into her mouth, teasing them with her tongue, biting them gently, licking them some more, then biting them with an ever increasing insistence. When I could bear it no longer, I grabbed her face and kissed her, seizing her body close to mine. Her hands tugged at my belt.

"Take off the rest," she whispered.

I did, and she licked her lips as she watched. I tried to hang my clothes on a hook by the door, but she pulled them out of my hand and threw them on the ground.

"Fuck your clothes."

She stood back and shimmied her pants off, revealing red satin panties. There was a sweet odour that made me think she perfumed her pussy. She slowly slid her panties down her legs, and I saw her crotch was shaved. It made me hungry to see it, glistening like a pink mouth. She smiled and took her shirt off, walking over to the toilet to piss. When she finished urinating, she leaned back and pushed her pussy up.

"Lick Mommy, c'mon baby, come over here and lick Mommy clean."

I walked over, got on my knees, and without hesitation put my tongue on her urine-drenched pussy. I licked the wet skin, cleaning every crevice. Then I slowly pushed into her hole and tongue-fucked her slowly.

"Yes," she growled. "Oh, yes."

She gyrated against me, breathing in short gasps. Then she pushed me on to the floor, which caused a moment's panic as my skin hit the cold, filthy, unpleasant tiles. The moment passed when she slid off the toilet and on to my cock, her wet juicy cunt thrilling every nerve. She put her hands on my chest and leaned forwards undulating her hips slowly.

"Yes, yes, yes," she repeated, while I just breathed deeply, thrusting into her as best I could from my position. Suddenly, someone knocked on the bathroom door.

"Tell them it's occupied," she said in a low voice.

"Wh-What?" I gasped.

"Tell them it's occupied," she repeated.

"Me? But this is the women's bathroom."

She laughed and squeezed my dick with her pussy.

"Nothing gets by Mommy's little boy, does it?"

Another knock. She looked at me.

"It's occupied," I yelled out.

The knocking stopped.

"What if she complains to the bartender?"

She ignored me and began to fuck me harder, squeezing her muscles rhythmically. Her face began to flush as a much harder knock interrupted us.

"All right," a harsh male voice shouted, "you've had your fun. Now get out of there."

She was bucking wildly.

More knocks.

"Don't make me open this door."

This seemed to drive her crazy, and I thought she was going to bounce right off my dick. I was near coming, myself. She curled her fingers into my chest hair and let out a long low guttural moan. Her bouncing slowly stopped. I let myself go, coming with a quick spurt. She fell on top of me, kissing me sloppily.

"I'm losing patience," the voice on the other side yelled.

She looked up and yelled, "Can't a girl piss in peace around here?"

"Oh, uhhh," the voice sounded confused. "Sorry, ma'am, I thought a man might be in there."

"Do I sound like a fucking man?"

"No, no, you don't. Please excuse me. And take your time."

"Thanks, I will."

"Think he believes it's only you?" I whispered.

"Who cares?" and we kissed some more, until she finally lifted herself up. I watched her gather up her clothes.

"I could fuck you all night."

"That's because you're a loyal little boy, but you better get dressed."

We were ready to leave.

"You first," she said, and unlocked the door and pushed me out, where a small line of women glared.

"Sorry, girls," she said, laughing behind me, "but I needed help wiping myself."

We staggered out of the bar as the bartender eyeballed us all the way to the door.

Blondes. Burnt-out blondes.

Like a thirsty man needs water, like the condemned man needs a reprieve, I need dyed blonde pussy.

You see them on the streets, on the train, or in cabs.

And I crave them.

I crave them all.

Chameleon

Francisco Ibañez-Carrasco

[Wide angle: a motel bathed in the neon light of a huge number 6. As we pan into one of the windows, through the slight partition in between the curtains we hear the faint sound of Jimmy Scott's voice.]

He grabs her from the back and brutally glides into her. I moan. His hands keep a firm grasp on her hips and leave imprints, and then they creep up to her firm breasts, so white. The hardened nibs of my nipples kissing the cold tiles, my back curves in ecstasy, like a bow it readies to shoot an arrow, I moan. He thrusts in and out with the mechanical precision of a well-oiled machine, tongue and groove, he pulls and digs into my flesh. Then his hands slide again across the deep valley of her smooth and heaving stomach to land in her mound of pubic hair. I moan, and start to grow, I can't help it. He shrieks and recedes, pulls out of her in an instant, leaving me empty, his huge cock oozing angst, still throbbing. I turn around and his face in the twilight is a disgruntled mask of horror. He takes two steps back, lets out another shriek. You're a . . .! But . . . how? You, fucking sonnovabitch! His big hands are coming towards me; his cock now is limp, shipwrecked. Instead of scurrying, I wrestle and push him hard against the wall, laughing aloud, my fists land on his contorted grimace and swiftly I kick him out of the motel room, naked, beautiful, wealthy brat, college jock, broad shoulders, cropped blond hair, a mercenary of lust, not inebriated any more, so awake, so startled. Out! Out into the cold northwest starry night, in the middle of nowhere. While he, panic-stricken, kicks the door, then calls luke-warmly pleeease, then yells in rage. Poor fool, a Fred Flintstone, thinking fast but ineffectively about what to do, what to do and his poor butt getting colder. Inside, I look for his wallet, his gold watch, his BMW keys, his licence, and his credit cards. I'll ditch them later; it has to look like a robbery. Not that he would tell anyone. Who would? Tell what? Too embarrassing. I get dressed in his grey sweat pants, wrestling team T-shirt and runners, a bit too tight to envelop my flab, and slump out the back window.

[Cut to: Corporate building, a three-storey high erection soothed by a balmy breeze. Minimalist décor reception desk and stick chairs flank the entrance where a well poised receptionist with a thin wireless headphone greets us good morning in a clarinet voice. Jimmy Scott pauses in his tedious task to ponder. His two glassy eyes vacant like TV sets beaming dead air.]

Day after day in the mailroom I look at the agile young man of slender architecture walk on by in the company of other gorgeous young men or silvery hawk-like CEOs or women in little Gucci or Prada numbers. He is slick, Armani, Hugo Boss, not charming, arrogant, he barely looks at me with those strange grey eyes, black eyelashes, maybe Eurasian, he is twenty-five. When I deliver the mail, the faxes, small UPS packages, his hands do not receive, his index points, put it there, his nail impeccably manicured. When he is not around I have taken to checking his appointment book, later I fiddle with his Palm Pilot, it's never too hard to come up with a pass code – calculate his age, nine inches cut, and the number of fingers in his hands, add and subtract, and I got it – predictable, no one would think the moron-looking, middle-aged plump mail room guy could work that out (or any piece of technology for that matter). I say never trust an ugly face. I find out he is on his way up the corporate ladder, his dates with several women look more like business meetings, at least as they are officiously logged, older women; he's climbing, moving and shaking, only enough shaking, he reminds himself of the perfumes they like, memoes himself about the conversations that are successful, selected lines, the restaurants they like, the number of orgasms they fake, and small budgetary annotations, thrifty fellow he is, strategic to the max. I find out and memorize numbers, domicile, directions, and identifications. At times as I repeat the numbers like prayers I begin to sweat and I smell foully, "mendacity" someone once wrote in a play, mendacity. I have to pause; I turn the little gadget off and sneak out of the well-appointed office and hurry back to my fluorescent lair in the basement.

I pull my hair with desperation, it hurts, I pull harder until it has loosened about ten inches, I collapse in a decrepit sofa, cheap room and board, my hair is thinning, it hangs lovely, straight, later I will shampoo it with a temporary sensuous reddish tint that he will recognize because I know it is the hue he prefers, small amounts of money he will never notice have gone missing from one of the many company chequing accounts he manages. Later I will use hot wax, which exquisitely excoriates my skin leaving it smooth and sensitive to the slightest touch. I read *In Style* and *Vogue* and *Cosmopolitan* and about the lives of serial killers. I answer personality tests, examine culinary tips, aromatherapy, pheromones, aphrodisiacs, all the romantic stuff and I go about my tasks methodically. It's the long weekend. With my thick hands I grab my chest and pull on my skin until it caves under the pressure, to form a turgid bosom, and polish it into two alert round nubs that will barely insinuate themselves under a thin and light velvet moss green blouse casually thrown over a demure deep wine medium-length skirt *à la* Julia Roberts. I massage my neck, my hands, my buttocks, my legs and my feet for hours, refining them, until they have adopted the desired silhouette, the enticing curvaceous lines.

The day rolls on sluggishly and I am anointed by the purring of Billie Holiday, a day of frugal eating, only grapes and drops of water give my skin the complexion and the paleness I know he finds desirable, the anorexic heroine chic look he falls for, Uma Thurman, Winona Ryder, Gwyneth Paltrow, Jewel, girls he adores, petals. Finally, I am ready for the conclusive touch. The suffering is excruciating as I press hard, with all my might, on my cock with one hand, with the other on my Adam's apple, inwards into my skin, past the bones, until they amalgamate into my body, a process only soothed by my acidic tears. I am now complete and my voice is that of Kathleen Turner and Lauren Bacall, my eyes are not red any more, my luscious eyelashes, exquisite cheeks, my tears have evaporated into a subtle perfume of roses, old-fashioned yet not overwhelming in the least, a scent that will surely cast a subtle and elusive veil upon the senses of anyone who draws near.

[Close in on a renovated heritage house in a narrow street, quiet, under a roof of magnolia trees sweetly rocked by a slight breeze. A clicking of high heels approaches gently from the end of the street, a cab speeds away, a cat purrs on a nearby branch, two shapely legs walk up to the house, the living room light is on.]

It's late spring, evenings can be cool, deceiving, evenings can be dark but I soon take shelter in his front porch, quickly knock at his door, no one else in sight; slightly agitated, he opens, wearing evening pleated dark pants, dry-cleaned and pressed to perfection, no shirt on, a compact triangle of ribbed muscles gets lost down his leather belt that hangs undone. He is to meet with some middle-rank manager woman, I know, my timing is perfect, my eyes widen with a glimpse of fear, I utter a nondescript little sound, I deliver a heavenly mirage. I'm sorry, I say, he says, May I help you? I'm sorry, I barely pronounce. I begin to turn around to go back down the flight of stairs and exit from his life for evermore. He can see my petite waist, my slender calves, and the thin nap of my neck, damsel-in-distress, illuminated by the sepia light of the Chinese lanterns hanging in his porch. I slowly pause and turn to face him again, I didn't mean to bother you, I whisper like a rustle of leaves, I wonder if you could call the police for me, 911 that is, my well-rehearsed lines, Blanche Dubois' revenge. I will not be taken for granted. Is everything all right? He says and I know I am an intriguing creature under the pallid double moon of his eyes. Confidently, I explain to him who I am, where I work, about my co-worker, who lives down the street and invited me for drinks but wanted more, he said he thought that neighbour was gay, with undisguised smugness. I say that so did I, but he had tried anyhow, to force himself on me, my voice breaking like a small wave, I can't go on, choked, my car didn't start, I show him the BMW keys. In the meantime, he has run to the bedroom to put his pressed white shirt on and has poured a glass of ice water for me, I sit like I was taught, pressed against the soft brown suede sofa – I mean as if I had been trained in a finishing school – the wholesomeness of my legs barely showing.

A spring interlude, some Debussy, sensible meals, Jenni Craig, Martha Stewart, Oprah blessed be the many goddesses of good living, clean-cut love-making, missionary style, initially, hardly a sigh, a tremolo, the beginning of a lot of learning, unquestioned, unwrapping him layer by layer, imperceptible abrasions in the skin, with restrained drama, without extravagance because I wasn't just anyone, I was an adorable woman fascinated by his potency, his formidable chest, barren of all primeval hair, only glistening essential oils, his insistence in ingesting hormones for the body tone, the elimination of fatty tissue, lies, lies, tell me sweet little lies. The fact is that he was left spent every night, but greedy as males are he would come around for more, with eclipsed eyes, and found me like one finds a little orphan Columbine in a nest, vulnerable to any contact. I always came to him, told him how my ex-boyfriend had gone mad, stalking me, I showed him his notes asking me for the car he had given me back, in careful typing "I will not tell anyone about us". I cried, see how he denies my existence and what happened between the two of us, those cherished times, no, don't pick me up home, I'm sure he is around, stalking me, I'll see you this evening. He would hang up the phone with a smirk expression at first; happy to bail me out, to help so he can help himself to me that very same night. A minute later Jimmy sees the agile young man of slender Eurasian architecture shift the buttressing stud in his pants from the corner of his eyes as he meekly delivers crisp stationery.

I drained out every ounce of his anxiety, he was grateful, I tinged his dreams, contaminated like a metastasis; he was cautious at first but like the good rock climber in a sterile indoors he was, strong and adventurous, he yielded to the challenge, in the summer he would go back to windsurfing he said, so many dangers besiege the modern man, life is so fraught with dangerous desires. I smiled as he slowly let go of his hands, his selfish thick lips, his pristine teeth, his tongue, his words, his lukewarm saliva, the misty suburban memories of his life (that we all learn to describe as repressed childhood recall of abuse), nothing to shout about, and his juvenile ambitions (and his wallet, his apartment keys, his car keys). I taught him secrets, intimacy, to give in, to trust me, I should know well that shattered dreams, chard and turds can be satin, velvet or silk, it's all about lightning and location, location, location. I initiated him in the perverse secret of my flowers, the poisonous vibrations of the raging stems that can keep an erection solid for hours, the roses with thorns gently scratching his back until it bleeds, just barely, his bound wrists, his legs spread apart until the abductors are slightly strained, my lips around his shaft, careening his ravines, descending into every little crevice. One day my fingers fondled his sensitive ass, timidly, another rose that was, slowly blooming, a few seconds at first, later some more, longer, until finally bathed in that strange summer early morning light, the window wide open, the calm breeze blowing through it and through my lips like the fluttering wings of a hummingbird, his back tensed, his hands trapped in cuffs, his eyes blindfolded, his mouth gagged, his ears covered, deliciously moaning like the precious male animal that he was, that he is, and I couldn't hold my shape any more.

[Cut to: Inside the young businessman's gentle period house located in the shaded street.]

I say, you will kill for me, he says he doesn't understand her, that he will not drink what he drank last night (and the night before and the night before) on the rocks, that it gave him nightmares, a bad headache, that he felt strange. How strange that is? I ask. He admits that he rather not have her play with his ass like she did, it hurts, in fact, it is ablaze now. How good is it? I ask. He is befuddled. Good? He doesn't want to understand but for the time being we have more important things to occupy our minds, his life crisis, leaving that silly career job, getting more fat into his body, beer and fries, getting used to the sudden swings in my mood and the inflections in the sound of my voice, my late-night vanishings leaving him alone in the bed, wanting more, puzzled and in pain; we have to deal with the eviction notice slid under the front door, the concerned calls from cut-throat colleagues, ex-girlfriends, and faraway American relatives.

One day he says he doesn't know how it has all happened that everything seems to be tumbling down . . . but she is in his life and that is all that matters, that he knows that he loves her, that he wants to lose himself in her, kneel down in front of her, keel over, his eyes uncovered to see the things she does to him, how she tattooes bluish graffiti on his body. The atomic iron doors that barricaded this sanctuary have swung open, drums resounding in the sky of my soul, and the feelings imprisoned inside now overflow. He says he would do anything for her. I say, just wait until you come away from this neighbourhood into my house, no, you've never seen it, I seem to be here all the time, that's right, all the time, wait then, you say you would do anything for me, wait. In front of his eyes almost coming out of their sockets, I return to my original shape.

In my long life of foster homes, petty crimes, convenience store hold-ups, run-aways, screeching old tyres in the greasy pavement of road gas stations, I went scurrying from trailer park to trailer park like an itinerant circus freak show, eating road kill, for so long, couldn't let anyone see the real me, so whimsical, so damaging. Since I was a child I was looking for God, but there was no God for those like me and I understood I had to create my own. So I came, not looking for mister right, just looking for the right one for me, couldn't let the police get near me, the social services, the scientists, the counsellors. When it got too close for comfort I'd disappear and go and settle in the next squalor, amble around the fancy area of town, the towers, the wall-to-wall fantasy, do my little facts-finding, and proceed with extreme caution, handle with care, sheltered by the shadows. Shady identities I created, ghouls lifted right out of B-movies I watched late into the morning, being one of those who don't need to sleep much, did menial work, underpaid, until I found the next suitor, always hoping this would be the one, emotional mobility, transient, instability as noted in the psychiatric diaries. One by one I faced the many disappointments, a personal trainer in an uptown gym with expansive hands crowned in ten killer fingers, a roller coaster of bulging muscles, feet odour, I excused that, a small member, I excused that, it is not that I wanted children, voracious appetite for the kinky, there was my loophole, I thought I would hang on to that psychological handle, exploit that vein, but no one is as twisted as they would like to believe they are, that is why they watch movies, to compensate for what they don't dare to do, hesitant, envious, even in their fucking fantasies. Or the dutiful middle-class entrepreneurial father, *Fatal Attraction*'s victim, still so gullible after so many years of horror tabloid headliners, ready to fuck the baby sitter at the mere sight of her small cup bra. Don't these affluent businessmen read *The Enquirer*? Enchanting innocence is the innocence of these otherwise respectful citizens. Or the police chief in his early fifties who would eventually introduce me to his half sisters, half his age, whom he fucked avidly. Oh, sweet perversion, tailored and seamed into the staunchest uniforms! They became an acquiescent audience in one sultry evening viewing inside a 1950s motel room; two pairs of mesmerized owls they witnessed me, perched on top of him, something grotesque and alive, drying breasts, immersed in the delicious agony of metamorphosis that yielded no butterfly out of a cocoon but another worm, bigger and better, Aliens, the umpteen sequel, an improved "Me" in neon fucking lights pumping meat into this venerable patriarch, the keeper of the law and order, his generous sweat covering his heroic and medalled chest and his glistening ample forehead, imploring for his women's forgiveness, hard panting, as I completed my ferocious ramming up his ass with triumphant colors, the crying of the women, the Greek choir to his futile tragedy. With stories like these and so many other stories was cluttered my life before he came along, to all the men I loved before, big and strong, like songs, like clichés, like long and drawn puffs of smoke.

[Cut to: A decrepit and untidy trailer in a noisy suburban park. A radio blasts Meat Loaf.]

But men, they say, are like buses, they come every fifteen minutes, at least if you are in the city, they pick you up and you move on with them only to get off at your most convenient stop. Tired of the house in the shade of the magnolia trees, the number of distressed calls from friends and family, the number of people who have seen way too many reruns of

"The Silence of the Lambs" I needed to move on myself, so I called the jock, fine, I'll give you back your fucking BMW and I will stop the threats of sending an anonymous letter to the bride-to-be, lovely she is indeed, barren though . . . yeah, I saw the gynecologist's report . . . never mind how I saw that, fuck I've almost been inside her fucking cunt! Got pen and paper? You got something out of school after all, pretty boy. Did I mention you tasted positively good? A jawbreaker the crazy piece of yours is. No, I said *tasted* as in your oozing precome not *tested* as in HIV positive. Please, don't gag. Write this address down. Hey, you'll get to meet the real improved "Me" in neon fucking lights . . . click. How rude!

I dance for him the lewdness of a cheap 1980s punk song, endless love, each night the last, spirits rise, late into the morning light, every day a beginning, lap dance, and the dance is unrehearsed, a little stream of beer flows from the end of his lips, through his rough beard to his gut. The monumental energy of his early thirties help him lift me from the floor, shove his cock inside me, as if lifted by a huge crane and crashed against a brick wall, again and again until a gush of fermented liquid empties inside me, like the blood hurrying through the thick veins in his neck and the storm of his alcoholic breath as enraged as his temperament all deposited inside me. I had to teach you so much, my puppy love, now you love me for what I am, a bit of this and a bit of that.

As in the movies, the way I like it, the jock comes in as told, pushing with terror the door ajar and he finds us in the stinking room, he on top of me having his way, damsel in distress, and he goes to my help once more like that night I had been left behind in the highway near the motel where the he found me. He has found me again, he cannot see the resemblance, masqueraded I am by his own petty arrested adolescence desire, he sees a woman being devoured by a monster, a damsel properly saved is a sure shot damsel in the sack. Keep your eyes on the prize. Poor jock, so gullible, reaches fast for the fireplace tool and spears him good in the back. I fall back on to the suede sofa. Thank you. I cry inconsolably, monster blood, sweat and tears dripping down my lovely dress, with trembling hand I point out at the BMW keys, I sob that he was driving that when he picked me up in the nearby highway where I was stranded. I search for my cell phone, the monster hid it, I have to call my new job in the steel minimalist tower, I just started there, and they might be wondering what has happened to me. The jock finds it and hands it to me, frail and sitting on the floor in a corner of the revolting trailer. I dial 911. Police? Firefighters? No. Paramedics, from the closest station. Jimmy knows. Jimmy knows that Jag, 24, the one with the cinnamon skin, the turban and the dagger, has begun to work as a paramedic in the third shift a month before. Jimmy hopes to be moving on.

Butt Hutt

Matt Thorne

I first met Isobel in an Internet café. She was looking up hardcore pornography. Normally this wouldn't have caught my attention (especially if it was one of the places in the centre of Soho, where no one cares what their neighbours are accessing) but because it was the Internet Exchange in the Trocadero and she'd already attracted the interest of the muscular blue-shirted staff, I found myself taking the silver seat next to her and asking,

"What site is that?"

"The bald guy. It's a sex-tracker."

"Aren't you worried about getting in trouble?"

"Why?"

"You seem to be getting some dodgy looks."

She swivelled round on her seat and looked at the man coming towards her. "Oh, shit," she said, shutting the machine down, "it's all right, I'm going." I laughed. Picking up her stuff, she asked, "What's your name?"

"Terry."

"Have you got much to do, Terry?"

"Not really. Just checking my e-mails."

"Well, I'm going to McDonald's. Come join me for a drink when you've done."

I didn't say anything, instead tapping my password into the screen. Then I turned to check out her legs as she walked away.

Isobel was looking up porn at the Trocadero because her

home computer was broken. Too concerned about the secret stash on her hard-drive to take it to a repair shop (we joked about how computer repairmen should sue Gary Glitter for lost income), she was waiting for her friend to come round and fix it. In the meantime she was using Internet cafés around London, although this was the first time she'd tried the Trocadero, and had only really done so because she'd come into town to buy some CDs.

Delicately, I tried to raise the subject of why she was looking up porn, which so far she'd failed to explain. She told me that she supplemented her income from working at the Royal Bank of Scotland by putting together a weekly guide to Internet porn-sites for a small list of subscribers. She explained how most men and women (or at least those who subscribed to her magazine) tended to have one special peccadillo. Often these were quite subtle, and hard to find through uneducated surfing. The broader, grosser tastes could be easily satisfied (there were a cornucopia of coprophilia pics, and almost any single sexual word typed into a search engine would send you straight to donkey-fucking), but it was surprisingly hard to find say, softcore photos of redheads with unshaven vaginas, or even naked men alone without erections.

Not that she was only into soft stuff. If you had appetites you were ashamed of, chances were you'd find something satisfying in Isobel's cc'd catalogue. I didn't want to seem prudish, so I told her that the service she was offering seemed a useful one. Then I mentioned an article I'd read in the problem page of *Time Out New York* about a gay man who was irritated because his boyfriend made him wank him off while he looked at pictures of amputees.

"Stumps, yes, that's quite a common one." She looked me in the eye. "But what about you, Terry? What are you into?"

"It's stupid . . ."

"Everyone feels like that."

"No, I don't want to say, because it's not something that has anything to do with me sexually really, I just like it in pictures."

She smiled. "OK, Terry, I understand. How about I'll tell you mine and you tell me yours?"

"That seems fair."

"OK," said Isobel, "I'm into dressed genitalia."

"What?"

"You know, cunts with glasses placed on them so they look like Eric Morecambe. Cocks dressed up like Marilyn Monroe."

I frowned, unsure whether she was winding me up. Until now, Isobel had seemed a completely normal woman. She was very attractive, with the kind of distinctive features that meant she didn't have to worry too much about clothes or make-up, wearing today a pair of blue jeans and a smart blazer over a cream top. Her hair was brown, clean, and held back by a red Alice band. There was nothing about her appearance that suggested she'd be interested in Internet porn, still less that she got off looking at photographs of comedy cocks.

"Your turn."

"OK, I'm going to tell you, but sorry, I do have to ask. Your fetish . . . is that a serious thing?"

"Yes. And it's very popular. There's lots of sites dedicated to it. Although it sort of crosses over into insertions."

"Insertions?"

"Yes, you know, girls with bottles up their pussies or ice creams sticking out their backsides. A lot of the funny-face cunts actually cross over into insertions. Things like Winston Churchill, for example, because of the cigar."

"Of course."

"So . . ."

"Yes?"

"What are you into?"

"Socks."

She nodded. "Any particular colour?"

"Oh, only one colour. Pink. I like pink socks. On beautiful American girls."

"I see."

"I don't know why. I think it's a whole eighties thing. I don't really like magazine pornography that much, but when I moved into the flat I'm in now I found a whole stack of *Knaves* from the mid-eighties. I was in seventh heaven."

"So you go for all that eighties stuff? Madonna gloves, and legwarmers?"

"I used to, but not any more. Now it's just . . ."

"Socks."

"Yes."

We talked for the rest of the evening. I let slip that I was single early in the conversation, but Isobel retaliated by telling me how happy she was with her current boyfriend, Stephen. As it drew close to the time of my last tube, we swapped e-mail addresses and went home alone.

Three days later, I received an e-mail from Isobel. It told me I might like to check out a site called Butt Hutts. I typed the address into the server, and it took me to the usual page of disclaimers and a photograph of a small wooden shack. Butt Hutts was written in comic bubble-lettering, making the whole thing look like the video jacket of a Lemon Popsicle movie. With low expectations, I clicked on ENTER and waited to see what would come up.

The next graphic was a row of five huts. Each hut had a number above it but no description. Isobel's e-mail had instructed me to check hut three so I clicked that one first. The screen shivered and the next picture was of three fully dressed women. Next to each girl was their name and a small icon to click on. The girls pictured were called Amber, Candi and Helen, I clicked on Amber.

The next page was a full screen photograph of Amber. Dressed in a plain blue dress with the top two buttons undone, she had dyed red hair and a pair of sexy white boots. Beneath the photo was the following text:

Hi, my name's Amber, and I live in Butt Hutt #3 with my friends Candi and Helen. If you'd like to see me take something off, stroke now (the mouse, silly.)

Disappointed, I clicked on the photo and it was replaced by a second one which showed Amber without her boots. I'd come across these sites before, and they were always incredibly frustrating, usually consisting of a series of pictures which led up to a final one of the girl topless but still wearing knickers, and a message telling you that if you wanted to see anything more you'd have to input your credit card details, either because it was a pay site or because it operated an AVS. Still, I clicked through the pictures, wanting to see why Isobel recommended it. I expected it was probably because one of these three butt hutt babes was wearing pink socks in one of the pics. It clearly wasn't Amber, however, and after I'd got her down to her knickers I was about to move on, when, to my surprise, it seemed I could click again without resorting to a credit card.

The next picture was of Amber, fully naked. She had a nice shaved vagina and pretty tits, but the picture didn't really do it for me. I've always been pretty fussy about pornography. It only takes one detail (long, curled fingernails, ugly coloured varnish) and the picture is no longer exciting. But, and this is why I hate the tit-sites that shut off too soon, I find I am almost always aroused by a picture of a woman spreading her labium, no matter what the rest of her looks like. And when I clicked on Amber again I was amazed to find that was her next pose, lying back with her legs raised.

This was the last of Amber's pictures, so I clicked the icon that took me back to the main menu for Butt Hutt #3. I scrutinised the photos of Candi and Helen much more carefully, trying to guess which one might be wearing pink socks. But as both pictures were cropped at the calf line, it was hard to tell. Especially as it was a commonplace of almost all pornography that every woman pictured looked like she'd raided a dressing-up box, the desire to make sure every item of clothing was sexy overshadowing any concern about how the outfit looked as a whole. I decided to go with the woman I found most attractive, and clicked on Candi, a brunette with a mischievous smile and a plaid skirt. I found her sexier than Helen because she was sitting at a computer, nibbling at a pen and pulling at the shoulder of her white jumper.

I clicked on her first photograph and the next page showed her without that jumper, pleasantly plump breasts held back by a black bra. I clicked again and the bra was gone. Her hairstyle had also altered, spoiling the straightforward strip tease effect. Another mouse-tap and she'd brought her feet up onto the chair. No socks. I tapped through the other pictures anyway, aroused by the final shots of Candi sticking her green pen into her vagina and anus. Printing off copies of the last two pics, I went back to the initial menu and clicked on Helen.

She looked much more attractive in the second picture, partly because she'd rolled up her grey Butt Hutts T-shirt to reveal the bottom halves of her tanned breasts, but also because the focus was much clearer. There's nothing more disturbing than the strange visual effects that can occur when a picture has been inexpertly scanned on cheap equipment, especially the ovoid blotches that appear on the swells of arms and thighs, making the women look like they have liquid crystal skin.

Two more clicks and the T-shirt was off and she was kneeling on a bed with a metal frame, pushing her hand down the front of her panties. And there they were: the elusive socks. I unzipped my fly and took out my cock, too excited to print out the pages. I held my breath as I tapped again, hoping the photographer had realised the erotic potential of the socks and allowed her to keep them on as she divested the rest of her clothes. Another screen-shiver and there she was, entirely naked apart from the socks. But would she spread? I clicked again and there it was, the picture that did it. Helen, the socks, open legs, dildo pushed into her hole.

*   *   *

The following morning I e-mailed Isobel, thanking her for the tip. I didn't expect her to get back to me for a day or so, but her response came by mid-morning, asking for my phone number. I gave her the main switchboard, sensing it'd be a bad idea to mention my direct line. Twenty minutes later, she called and asked if I'd like to go on a date that evening. Surprised things were moving so swiftly, I asked after Stephen.

"Oh," she said, "don't worry about that. We've come to an arrangement."

"What does that mean?" I asked.

"Well, there's this girl he wants to fuck."

We agreed to meet at the Trocadero, then go for dinner and a movie, or a movie and then dinner, depending on programme times and whether we could find a film we both wanted to see. I hung up, and walked across the office to tell my friends about my good fortune.

We ate at McDonald's, skipped the movie, and headed to her house to fuck. I took her in the living room, from behind with her black dress hitched up. After it was over, I asked her if her friend had fixed her computer. She shook her head.

"Actually, that was something I wanted to ask you. Would you mind if I came round and used your computer while you're at work? I'll understand if you say no."

I looked at her. She smiled sweetly, Something told me she wouldn't understand if I said no, and I even began to worry that she'd fucked me just to gain access to my computer. But that was absurd. Unless this was some kind of complex sting, and I was about to be framed as the head of a paedophile ring.

"OK," I told her, handing over my spare key.

She said she'd come round in the morning. She'd invited me to stay over at her place, but I had to prepare my house for her arrival. I already had enough of an idea of what kind of person Isobel was to realise that to try to hide anything would be futile. No, if there was anything in my house I didn't want her to see, I either had to throw it away or take it to work with me.

The clearing operation took less time than I'd imagined, and I decided to log on to Butt Hutts again. Part of me wanted to explore the rest of the site, but once it had loaded, I was overwhelmed by the urge to visit Helen again. But when I checked Butt Hutt #3, she no longer seemed to be there. I knew I had the right number because I could see Candi and Amber, but in place of Helen was a black girl named Kelly. Trying to keep calm, I reminded myself that most web-masters are obsessive tinkerers and that he'd probably just shuffled the pictures. I checked huts one, two and four, and was about to do five when the computer crashed. Pissed off and tired, I abandoned my PC and went to bed.

I left for work before Isobel arrived, then sent her an e-mail mid-afternoon, asking her to find out what had happened to Helen. She didn't respond, and I left work early, fully expecting to come home and find my flat cleaned out. But she was still at my desk, a cup of coffee placed on my *Playboy* mouse-mat. I walked up behind her and squeezed her shoulders. She had accessed the Butt Hutt site, and was making notes in a small reporter's pad.

"Did you find her?" I asked.

"No," she said, "you're right, she's gone. It's very unusual behaviour for Adrian."

"Who's Adrian?"

"Adrian runs this site."

"You know him?"

"No, I just did a domain-search. I always do that with the sites I like. It's like trying to find out who directed your favourite film. You'd be amazed how many of these sites are designed by the same person."

"So, what do you know about him?"

"Well, lots, but that's involved some pretty complex hacking. The domain-search only gives you the most basic information about the designer, but with the right software you can use that to do much more complicated background digging."

"Tell me, then. Who is he?"

"He's a grad student at Princeton University."

She clicked back to the title page and keyed in a member-ship identification password.

"You belong to this site?"

She nodded.

"But aren't you worried about credit-card fraud?"

"Oh, I'm part of the problem, I'm afraid. I got the pass-word from one of those cheat-sites that break into other people's accounts."

She moved the cursor up to the WEBCAMS bubble and clicked again. The graphic of the five wooden huts reap-peared and she selected hut three. There was a short pause while various enables loaded, and then the screen was filled with a recording of a living room. I could see a tall lamp, a long sofa and a black girl (presumably Kelly) sitting watching TV. Her hand was under her skirt and she appeared to be masturbating.

"It's quite a weird one, this site."

"Weird in what way?"

"Well, usually, part of the appeal of these sites is that you can tell the girl what to do. You send your e-mail with your request, wave at me, flash your boobs, whatever, and she does it . . . but Adrian's gone to lots of trouble to make sure there's no way you can interact with his women."

She took a swig from her coffee cup and we both leaned in to look at the computer screen. We watched Kelly orgasm, and then I stroked my fingers down Isobel's back.

Isobel bought the tickets over the Internet. She used a real credit-card number. Mine. It was three months since I'd first met Isobel, and although we'd never officially become boy-friend and girlfriend, and Stephen was very much still in the picture, I'd fucked her almost every afternoon since she first started using my computer.

The trip was her idea, a combination of mutual dare and birthday treat. Although I'd started out reluctant, Isobel had persuaded me by pointing out that my challenge was much easier than hers. After all, I had a choice of fifteen girls, and one of them was bound to agree to a night alone with me. And I already knew what each of them looked like, right down to the most intimate details. For all she knew, her quarry could turn out to be a complete freak.

And from the information we had so far it seemed likely that this was the case. Over the last two months, Isobel and I had befriended two lonely Princeton postgrads through regular visits to an intercampus chat room. Neither of the postgrads was friends with Adrian, but both knew him, and said that he was a visible character around campus. Although Isobel and I were being very careful not to mention the Butt Hutt site in these sessions, we'd probed enough to discover that the straighter students thought Adrian was a drug dealer. The main reasons why they believed this was because he looked a bit like James Spader in *Less Than Zero* (albeit with a weird English accent) and was extremely popular with the more outgoing female undergraduates.

Isobel thought he sounded wonderful.

Isobel and I had decided we would be much more successful if we worked separately. Although my PC pal (Eric) was driving to Newark to collect me, Isobel's connection (Wendy) had told her to take the shuttle-bus. In order not to be spotted together, Isobel took the slow queue through Immigration.

I spotted Eric immediately. He was wearing a black vest, blue jeans and what looked suspiciously like slippers. In his hands was a cardboard sign with Terry written on it, the "e" turned into a smiley face.

"Eric?"

"Terry? Good to see ya." He clapped me on the back. "That all you brought?"

"Yeah," I told him, thinking he looked much older than twenty-eight, and wondering whether he'd lied to me about his age, "travelling light."

"No problem. I have some old shirts if you get stuck for clothes."

About a year before I had spent three weeks working in New York. That had been just long enough to get a general sense of Americans, although I had a suspicion that graduate students would turn out to be quite different to the people I'd been working with.

"This isn't that great a drive, Terry," he told me, "but it's best to do it quick. We can get something to eat once we get to Princeton."

"OK."

We walked to his car. It was a great car, a huge monster-mobile that had no doubt served someone's family well before Eric picked it up. I sat in the passenger seat, wondering why we'd never been allowed those weird self-fastening seat-belts in England. Eric looked at me.

"Did you bring the tapes?"

I nodded, unzipped my bag and handed him a yellow Tower Records carrier. He took out the tapes, looked through them, growled his approval and pushed *Generation Terrorists* into the car-stereo.

Eric was right. It wasn't much of a drive, and even the excitement of being in America didn't make the passing scenery any more interesting. Reaching Princeton was a real relief, and when Eric asked me if I was hungry, I nodded enthusiastically.

"Is there anything you'd especially like? We have pretty much everything here."

"I don't mind."

"OK," he said, "let's take a walk. Stop me if you see somewhere."

We ate in a place called "Tiger Noodles". I had Sesame Chicken, a meal that seems a staple of Chinese cuisine in America, but is rarely found in English Chinese restaurants. I'd developed a taste for this main course when I'd been working in New York, and eating it now took me back to that turbulent time.

"More rice, Terry?" Eric asked me as the waiter refilled our water jug.

"Mmm. Thanks."

"I gotta say, Terry, it's so good to have you here."

"Thanks, Eric. It's kind of you to put me up."

"Forget about it. I don't have that big a place, but it's a damn sight better than a butt hut."

I looked at him, amazed. "A what?"

"Butt hut. The Butler Apartments, if you want to get prissy about it. A bunch of prefabricated buildings on the edge of campus. I was stuck in one of those for my first two years here."

"Can you show me the huts?"

"Of course. Why?"

"No reason. I'm just interested in how they house students here."

"Well, Terry, if that's what gets you going. But, listen, a girl from my department is having a party tonight in her butt hut. Why don't we wait till then?"

"OK," I said, "that sounds great."

"Cool. I wasn't planning to go, but it'll be a good opportunity for you to meet some of the other students. And that guy you asked me about will probably be there."

"Adrian?"

"Yeah. He's at pretty much every party in Princeton."

"Great."

"You done there?"

"Yeah."

"Come on, then, let me show you my place."

Eric's room was revolting. I'm not an especially fastidious man, but this went far beyond any depths of students squalour I'd previously witnessed. The main reason why I found this mess so distasteful was that this was clearly the apartment of a relatively wealthy individual. All kinds of gizmos and gadgets were scattered around the apartment, including a complex laser system that sent cross-cutting red beams at just above ankle-level.

He spent the afternoon telling me about his studies. They seemed abnormally fascinating to him, which surprised me; as our chat-room exchanges had indicated that he devoted all his time to devouring popular culture. Discovering that he was much more interested in mediaeval music made me wonder when he found time to sleep.

I persuaded him to go out for food again before we went to the party, although it was obvious he would've clearly preferred to finish up the leftovers in his fridge. I knew from experience that while most Americans (especially those who want to be your friend) initially seem easier to push around, they also tend to turn on you more suddenly than English people, the switch from complete compliance to unwavering resistance often surprisingly violent. Usually I'd be more careful to avoid a future confrontation, but as I didn't intend to stick with Eric for long I was prepared to take advantage of his goodwill.

We ate in The Annexe, a pleasant bar-restaurant that served good veal. At the table next to ours was a group of Eric's fellow students. Although they didn't seem to like him that much, they were curious about his new English friend and invited us to join them for a drink in the D-Bar.

"You want to, Terry?" he asked.

"Sure," I replied, "it's still early, after all."

The D-Bar was like every other college bar I'd ever been in, no doubt the same the whole world over. A depressing day-after-the-party atmosphere, puddles of flat beer on every surface. An insufficient cash register, pool table with two broken pockets. A few stray souls surrounding a table with too many empty bottles. We stayed long enough to hear the last Wilco album and the first Liz Phair, leaving just as they were putting the Wilco back on again.

I hadn't thought about Isobel that much since arriving in

Princeton, but as we began walking down towards the butt
huts, I wondered whether she'd also found out about the
party. Given her formidable investigative skills, it seemed
fairly likely, but maybe her contact was too much of a social
outcast to have been told.

"Do we need to bring drinks?"

"You haven't told him then," one of the girls said, giggling.

Eric looked at her. I looked at Eric.

"What?"

"The woman who's organised this party always does a
huge bowl of this fatal blue cocktail. Everyone has to give five
bucks when they go in."

"She'll probably let you off," Eric told me, " 'cause you're
a guest."

The two women in our group were far too plain to be Butt
Hutt babes. They were also dressed in Princeton sportswear,
something absent from Adrian's Internet site. I tried to
image both the girls naked, just to be certain, but the thought
was too repellent to consider for long.

It was a pleasant evening, and everyone we passed seemed
to be walking down to the huts. The huts looked quite
different from the graphic representation on the title page
of the site, and made me think that the photograph was
probably a deliberate red herring. It seemed strange that
Adrian would use this phrase as the name of his site at all,
given that it was such a well-known euphemism on the
Princeton campus. Surely this was the sort of thing that
could get him kicked out of college if the authorities found
out.

There was loud industrial music coming from the party
hut, although I wasn't sufficiently schooled in the genre to
know if it was Ministry or Nine Inch Nails or some smaller
band. The woman I'd been seeing in New York had liked this
sort of music, and while I had no problem with it and it
certainly made for a lively party soundtrack, I found its
popularity hard to fathom.

By now, I was fairly certain that most of the other students thought Eric was a geek. If I was to have any success seducing a butt hut babe (assuming there were any at the party) I'd have to separate myself from him early on. From the attention I'd been drawing at the D-Bar, it seemed that being English was something of a secret weapon, and I'd already begun to exaggerate my accent.

A tall, skinny guy in a blue shirt was walking next to a bald man up ahead of us. The bald man had a Sesame Street voice and was getting extremely agitated. The skinny guy recognised Eric and raised his arm.

"He's another English guy," Eric explained, "do you want to ask him about Adrian?"

"No," I said, "that's OK."

Eric shrugged. "Suit yourself. Let's go say hello to the host."

He dragged me across to the doorway of the butt hut. The girl standing in the entrance had a large glass bowl into which she was depositing collected five-spots.

"Terry, I'd like you to meet . . ."

"Candi."

The girl looked at me, shocked.

"No, dude, this is Lisa."

It was Candi. After Helen's disappearance from the Butt Hutt site, I had spent many nights masturbating to my print-outs of Candi, and didn't need to see her poking a pen into her private places to know I had the right girl.

"I'm sorry," I said, "my mistake."

We went inside the hut and Eric scooped us both a glass of the blue stuff. Lisa kept looking at me, and I couldn't help worrying that I'd blown my cover too early. I was also anxious that I wasn't taking this whole thing seriously enough. After all, even if the very least these people had to worry about was being kicked out of college I'd spent enough time around Eric to know that was a pretty big deal. I tapped Eric on the shoulder.

"Is Lisa going to be collecting money all night?"

He grinned. "Unless some poor sap takes over for her."

"Eric?"

"Yes, Terry?"

"Would you be that poor sap for me?"

"Oh," he said, "you wanna talk to Lisa?" He looked around, then smiled and nudged me, "OK, but not for long."

"Sure," I said, "thanks."

Eric walked over to Lisa, took the bowl, and pointed in my direction. I smiled, and she walked across.

"What was your name again?"

"Terry. Look, I'm sorry about earlier. I didn't mean to embarrass you."

"Why would I be embarrassed about you getting my name wrong?"

"Right. I just wanted to say that I'm a friend of Adrian's and a big fan of your site."

Her mouth opened and she looked at me again. *Shit. Why had I said that? Another stupid mistake.*

"You?" she said slowly. "A friend of Adrian's? I don't think so."

"OK, I'm not really his friend, but I know some people he knew in England."

"Look, Terry, I don't know what you're doing here, but I don't think you realise what you're getting yourself into. And if you don't want to take my word for it, stick around and let Adrian warn you himself. Only don't expect him to be so nice about it."

Shooting me one last look, Lisa turned away and walked back across to Eric, angrily tugging the dollar-filled bowl away from him. He looked back at me, shrugged, and came over.

"Got shot down, did you? Don't worry, Terry, she's like that with everyone." He paused. "Except Adrian."

"Is she going out with him?"

"Oh no, I don't think so. She's probably fucked him once or twice, but then again so has almost every girl on campus. Let's go outside."

I followed Eric out of the already humid hut and joined the revellers on the grass outside. The English guy and his bald friend were still arguing about something, and after a few minutes of watching them I realised the source of the conflict was that the English guy didn't really want to be here. A few of the men outside smiled at Eric, but no one seemed interested in talking to him.

I was still checking the girls' faces for any other representatives from the Butt Hutt site. But most of the girls looked more likely to appear on some nihilistic bondage site. It seemed strange that the students of such an elite institution would go for an outdated fashion-phase like goth in such a big way, but maybe that was their form of rebellion. I also wondered why Adrian didn't have a goth hut on his site, as I'm sure he would have got plenty of volunteers, and that the girls would've thought it a totally punk thing to do.

I sat down next to one of the goth girls. Unlike most of the goths I'd seen in England, who seemed to take to that fashion as if it was the only way of making themselves sexy, most of these girls seemed gorgeous. The girl I'd sat next to could've passed for a film star if it wasn't for the purple hair.

"Hi, I'm Terry," I said, holding out my hand.

She laughed, and then said something to her friend. I couldn't work out what she said because she covered her mouth with her hand. The friend, who was slightly overweight and wearing a black lace dress leaned in to ask me, "Are you a friend of Eric's?"

I looked up at Eric, who looked embarrassed and on the verge of tears. "Am I your friend, Eric?"

He nodded, moving back and forth on the spot as if he needed to urinate.

"We met over the Internet," I explained. "I'm from England."

"Duh," said the girl next to me. Her friends laughed.

"Come on, Terry," Eric said, looking from side to side and pulling at my shoulder.

"What?" I asked.

"They don't like me."

"Who doesn't like you?" I asked. "These girls? That's not true, is it?"

I looked round their faces, enjoying the feeling of being back in control after Lisa had embarrassed me. Then I looked up at Eric.

"Sit down, Eric."

He shook his head. "I'll get some drinks. You want another drink, don't you?"

"Thanks, Eric, that would be lovely."

The girls handed over their empty cups, although I was fairly certain they were only doing it for the entertainment of watching Eric struggle back with so many drinks. I sensed the girls were beginning to relax in my company, so I asked, "Why don't you like Eric?"

The lace girl laughed. "We don't like anybody."

Isobel arrived at midnight. It was dark and I only noticed her because she was on Adrian's arm. Everyone at the party was in a hurry to greet him, rushing over to pat his shoulder. Eric had been completely wrong about Adrian's appearance. He looked nothing like James Spader. Instead, he looked like a cross between Malcolm MacLaren and John Lydon, albeit clad in a stained blue blazer. He had a shock of bright red hair, like a punk Tintin, and white, almost translucent skin.

I waited until the greetings had finished, then went over to say hello to Isobel. Adrian raised an eyebrow at her, and she introduced me.

"Adrian, this is my friend, Terry, the one I told you about."

"Ah, Terry," he said in a fruity English accent, "it's a pleasure to meet you."

After being seen with Adrian, my stock rose considerably. Lisa came back across to me and told me that her real name was Lisa, not Candi, although it was her in the pictures. I told her she was my favourite butt hutt babe, and then asked her what would be showing on the site tonight.

"Oh, it's Amber's night tonight," she said. "She's doing a home alone thing."

"Didn't she want to come to the party?"

"Yeah, but she needs the money. And Adrian's paying her double tonight."

We talked for a little while longer, and then Lisa invited me to a private party at Adrian's place. It wasn't due to start until two, but she promised me it'd be lots of fun.

"There'll be, y'know," she said, gently tapping the side of her nose, "and Adrian's got a hot tub."

The party had thinned out considerably by two, but Adrian was still careful to make sure we didn't pick up any uninvited guests. Eric had left at about midnight, after we'd had a brief argument. He told me that he needed seven hours sleep a night and couldn't stay any longer because he had breakfast commitments. I told him I understood, but still wanted to stay.

"Can't you leave a window open?"

"No way, Terry, I can't do that. Not with all my equipment."

"But Princeton seems a pretty safe place."

"I'm sorry," he said, shaking his head, "why don't you come back with me?"

"Because I've got something I need to take care of."

"Give it up, Terry. She already shot you down once."

"Things are different now I'm friends with Adrian."

"Let him put you up then. I'm sorry, buddy, I'll see you in the morning."

I wasn't too worried, knowing that Adrian's party was likely to last all night. But I did feel a little nervous now that I no longer had an escape route, especially as I knew I wasn't really in the same league as Adrian and Isobel, and worried that they might use this fact to humiliate me in some way.

"How are you doing?" Adrian asked as he sidled up alongside me. "Still up for another party?"

"Of course."

He patted my shoulder. "Glad to hear it."

"Which way is it?"

"Hang on a mo. Lisa's just rounding up the stragglers."

We turned and watched Lisa talking to two women and the skinny English guy. I was surprised that he'd been chosen for this select gathering, especially after his earlier protestations to his bald friend.

"Who's that guy?"

"Glenn? President of the Rocket Society. That's an unofficial position, of course. Why? Do you know him?"

"No, no, I'm just surprised he's coming. He seemed very reluctant about the party earlier."

"My party?" Adrian asked, frowning.

"No, the blue drinks do."

"Oh, that's just his way. And I expect he didn't want to upset Donald."

"Who's Donald? The bald guy?"

Adrian nodded. "The two of them are very close."

I hadn't realised how tired I was until we started walking to Adrian's. I suppose it wasn't that surprising, given that I'd now been up for almost twenty-four hours straight. I tend to always run on New York time, even when I'm in England. But the flight and excitement (and, oddly, the fresh air, not to mention the blue cocktails) had taken it out of me, and I could feel myself starting to flag. My eyes were closing when I felt someone take my hand.

"Tired?" Isobel asked.

"Exhausted. Aren't you?"

She nodded. "But I'm too excited to back out now. And I don't have anywhere to sleep."

"What happened to Wendy?"

"I've no idea. When I went to the address she gave me there was no sign of her. And no one I've spoken to seems to know who she is. Apparently, there's no one with her name at Princeton. The whole thing must've been a hoax."

"Probably some horny guy pretending to be a girl."

"I suppose so. It was stupid of me not to be more careful about checking her out."

"How did you find Adrian?"

"He found me," she giggled.

"Really?"

"Yes, it was ridiculous. I got off the bus and there he was. And, of course, he started trying it on straight away."

"What did you say?"

"That I'd be more than happy to be a butt hut babe. Apparently an opening's just about to come up."

She released my hand and skipped over to Adrian. We'd reached the road now, and began walking towards the main streets where Eric had taken me to eat earlier. I looked over at Lisa and she smiled back at me.

"Not far now," she said, "and I promise you it'll be worth it."

Adrian strode into his home, immediately heading for the dining room. The rest of us followed and stood in an awkward cluster at the far end of his large table. He rang a small bell and two maids appeared. They were both attractive women with long dark hair, dressed in a uniform that left their breasts and buttocks exposed. I chuckled to myself, thinking that Adrian had probably watched *Story of O* more often than was good for him.

"Champagne, everyone? I know I need something to wash away the taste of that horrible Harpic. Now does anyone want something more substantial to eat? Say now, because I predict in a short while you're all about to lose your appetite."

I looked up at him, feeling scared. Then I saw him bring out a small vial from his blazer and relaxed. I had no problem with drugs. Or sex, for that matter. But I've always shied away from violence, and hate it when S&M gets too serious.

We sat at the table, waiting while Adrian prepared the lines. I took this opportunity to check out the other two women that Lisa had brought back from the butt huts. They didn't look like they were the stars of his site, although it was true that I didn't remember the exact appearance of every girl.

The maids returned. On closer inspection I realised that one of the maids was blindfolded. She was the one with the bottle. The other girl arranged the glasses and guided the blindfolded girl's hand as she poured on the champagne. Adrian looked up from his chopping and smiled at this, before checking that everyone else was enjoying the performance.

"OK," he said, "who wants to go first? Terry?"

He passed the tile to me and I took out a ten-dollar bill from my pocket. Adrian noticed and shook his head.

"Oh no," he said, "there's a straw there. And you're the first to use it so there's nothing to worry about."

I picked up the thin straw and snorted the line. Aware that everyone was watching me, and wanting to make a good impression, I dabbed my fingers on the small crumb that was left and rubbed it on my gums.

"Jolly good," said Adrian. "Isobel?"

She snorted a line, and then passed it across to the skinny English guy. He grimaced.

"Problem, Glenn?" Adrian asked.

"No," he said, leaning down to snort the line.

The tile went round the table, and ended up with Adrian. He chopped out some more lines and it went round again. Two more times and I was feeling awake again, and oddly enthusiastic to see what happened next.

"OK, everyone," said Adrian, "how about a game?"

Lisa laughed. "Perfect."

"It's a very tame game, but seeing as we do have two new people with us tonight, I think it'll serve as a very good way of breaking the ice. It's a Swedish game, although for some reason it's called The Russian Post Office. Now, the rules are very simple, although we should probably move into the sitting room if we're going to have enough space to play."

Adrian stood up. Everyone else copied him, giggling and smiling at each other. He took Isobel's hand and pulled her behind him. The two maids retreated and I sensed that'd be the last we'd see of them for the evening. We walked through into the other room, which looked like Tony Scott's idea of an opium den, with billowy curtains with a fan behind them and cushions for everyone to lie out on.

"Music?" Adrian asked, as he walked across to the stereo. He placed three new CDs in a multidisc carousel and then brought the remote back with him as he sat down.

"Lisa," he said, "would you like to explain the game?"

She stood up, brushing a hand down over her top and looking at me. "What happens is, we each take turns to be the postman. The postman goes outside and knocks on the door. He then says he has a delivery. Adrian then asks him what sort of delivery he has. The delivery can be a kiss, which is just a kiss, a French kiss, a touch-up, which is a touch-up *under* the clothes, or a hamburger, which is where the post-man lies on top of the chosen person and makes out with them, but is not allowed to do anything under the clothes."

"You missed a bit," Adrian told her.

"Hang on, I was getting to that. When the person knocks, Adrian also has to ask who the delivery is for. He points at a person at random and says, 'is it for this person?' and then moves round the room until the postman says yes."

"OK," said Adrian, "Glenn, you've played this before. Why don't you start us off?"

Glenn smiled and got to his feet. He went outside the door and ended up giving a hamburger to Isobel. Although she was perfectly willing, the way they arranged themselves on the floor was awkward and he ended up kneeing her in the crotch.

"Christ," she said, pushing him off.

"I'm sorry," he told her, immediately standing up, "shit."

Adrian laughed. "OK, Lisa, your turn."

Lisa stood up and went behind the door. Adrian's head was lolling backwards. The maids had left two or three bottles of champagne and I refilled his glass. Lisa knocked.

"Yes?" Adrian called out.

"I have a delivery," she replied.

"What sort of delivery?"

"A touch-up."

"Ah," said Adrian, "but who's it for?" He pointed to Isobel. "Is it for this person?"

"No."

He pointed to one of the girls. "This person?"

"No."

He pointed at me. "This person?"

"Yes," she said, and opened the door.

We played The Russian Post Office for about an hour, by which time everyone had been comprehensively kissed and groped by everyone else. The only awkward moment came when I had to deliver a hamburger to Adrian, mainly because I didn't want him to know I wasn't really into it. After the last time round, Adrian said,

"OK, that's enough. Who wants to stay and fuck?"

Everyone did apart from one of the girls, who chose this moment to leave. This evened the numbers, but seemed surprising given that we could've easily coped with another woman. Unless she didn't like the look of the men on offer.

The six of us went through to Adrian's hot tub. He'd prepared some more lines and we did those before stripping and climbing into the water. Adrian looked at my erection and smiled at me as I slid into the tub. He had his arm around Isobel and was absent-mindedly stroking the tips of her nipples. There was something lazily proprietorial about this gesture that really irritated me, even though my claim on Isobel was slight. I knew I should be more excited about being coked up in a hot tub in America, seconds away from sex with an amateur porn star. But my libido was dulled by the fact that I'd also have to witness a woman who'd become one of my best friends being fucked by a gamy English pervert. There was also the worry of safety, as no one seemed about to put on a condom. I looked at Lisa as she moved through the bubbling water, trying to convince myself I was getting a fair trade. She had a better body than Isobel, muscular without being off-putting. But it was her smile that really got me excited; the look in her eyes that reminded me of the girls in my high school that I'd lusted after but never actually fucked.

Glenn's glasses were steaming up, but when his girl tried to take them off he barked at her to leave them alone. I could sense we were all waiting for a signal from Adrian that it was OK to start fucking, and it came when he pulled Isobel onto his lap.

I found it surprisingly easy to penetrate Lisa, even though I wasn't that used to underwater fucking. I sat back with my arms stretched across the tub while she moved up and down on my cock. Adrian and Isobel were facing each other, him underneath and her gripping his wet neck. I kept trying to look over Lisa's shoulder to see what Glenn and the other girl were up to, and was confused and distressed to see four feet sticking out of the water.

Adrian finished first, pushing Isobel off and standing up. Climbing out of the tub, he wrapped a towel around his skinny white frame and made straight for the cocaine. Lisa looked at him. Scared she was going to follow his lead and stop, I gripped her shoulder hard and sped up until I came.

"Who wants downers?" Adrian asked. "Everyone right, unless you're keen to see the sunrise."

He moved among our still dripping bodies, handing out pills from two different bottles.

"Is it safe to mix them?"

"Safe? I'd recommend it. It's taken me years to find a combo that cancels out each other's side-effects. But maybe we should all go upstairs first."

It seemed the arrangement was that we'd sleep in couples. Adrian and Isobel had the biggest bedroom, Glenn's and mine being of a similar size. Adrian gave Lisa a long kiss goodnight and then retired. I shook hands with Glenn, and then Lisa and I were alone.

We popped our pills.

"How long have we got?"

"Ten minutes max."

"Then I'll be brief. What happened to Helen?"

"Who?"

"The girl who was in your butt hut before Kelly replaced her."

"Oh, Amanda. Why, did you like her?"

I looked at her. "Yes, but that's not what this is about. I want to know what happened to her."

"OK," she said, "get into bed and I'll tell you."

The bed was only a queen size, and the two of us had to hold each other tight to be comfortable. Her fingers found my penis and she looked at me inquisitively.

"Oh no," I said, "I'm completely dead down there. And don't try to distract me. What happened to that girl?"

"Nothing happened to that girl. You know what people are like when they go to college. They experiment with sex, they experiment with drugs . . . and some people discover that they love that lifestyle, while others get scared and turn to something else."

"What d'you mean?"

"I mean Amanda found a boyfriend. She was never really that interested in appearing on the site in the first place. Adrian . . . preys on people at their weak moments, and makes it seem like everyone around him is having the most incredible fun. But he gets bored of people pretty quickly."

"OK," I said, "so explain this to me. What did Adrian mean when he told Isobel that there would be an opening on the site soon."

She looked at me. "Did Adrian say that?"

"Yes."

"And those were his exact words? There would be an opening?"

"Yes. What did he mean?"

She shook her head. "Nothing. Another one of the girls has probably dropped out is all."

I wanted to question her further but the sleepers had already kicked in and I drifted off into a dark, blank place.

The following morning I was awoken for breakfast by Isobel. She came into our bedroom and shook me awake, making me get out of bed and come outside onto the upstairs landing.

"I'm going to stay," she told me. "What about you?"

"I'm going home. Just as soon as I've found Eric and got my stuff back. And I think you should come with me."

She shook her head. "I knew you were going to say that. But listen, it's just an experiment, OK? This is something I've always wanted to do, and I'm desperate to experience it for myself."

"But, Isobel, I don't think you realise what's involved here. I'm convinced there's something sinister going on."

"Oh, come on, Terry, don't be stupid. It's just sex, OK? Just sex."

Eric was waiting for me. He opened the door on my first knock and gave me a hug. Surprised, I gripped him back. Then I realised he was crying.

"I'm so sorry, buddy."

"What for?" I asked, surprised.

"Last night. I shouldn't have left like that."

"It's OK. I got Adrian to put me up. Like you suggested."

"Still, I did a bad thing."

"Don't be stupid. But listen, Eric, I have to go back home."

"It's because of me, isn't it?"

"No, Eric, it's nothing to do with you. It's just that coming out here was a spur of the moment thing."

"And now you regret it?"

"No, of course not."

"Are we still friends?"

"Of course."

"And you'll carry on sending me e-mails."

"Definitely. Now, Eric, could you drive me to the airport."

"Sure thing, buddy. Just let me use the bathroom and we'll go."

The flight back was horrible. Although I hadn't suffered too much from my indulgence the night before, my body clock was out of whack and I couldn't tell whether I wanted to sleep or stay awake. So I tried to sleep, then got irritated and watched a bit of a bad movie, then played computer games for a while (unsuccessfully, due to my faulty handset) before trying to drink myself into a coma.

I don't know how to tell the last part of this story. Just writing this down, and ordering these events into a narrative makes me feel as if I am in some way culpable; as if I'm inviting my own punishment. I haven't said any of this to anyone, and sat in silence when Stephen came round to find out what had happened to his girlfriend.

I know that once I've written this I won't be able to stop myself feeling guilty, and maybe I'll even feel forced to report this to someone, although exactly who I don't know. Maybe I'll even have to conduct my own private investigation, fly back to Princeton and sort things out myself. But I can't help feeling that it's just a bad joke, and I've done nothing more serious than accidentally access a disturbing website.

I was feeling edgy from the moment I got off the plane. Certain I would be pulled over and strip-searched, I made little effort to disguise my dishevelment as I shuffled past the customs officers. But, for almost the first time ever, they let me through unmolested. Going down to the luggage carousel, I collected my bag and took a Piccadilly line tube home.

I fell into bed the moment I got through the door, telling myself I'd check on Isobel's progress as soon as I'd had some proper sleep. In spite of my intentions, it was two days before I returned to the butt hutts. Now I was no longer with Isobel,

I felt my past few weeks' indulgence all the more keenly, and felt eager to reconnect with my family and friends.

The only time I came near to telling anyone what'd happened was when two of my mates at work asked me about the girl I'd been seeing, the one I'd told them was "up for anything". But I knew if I described my time in America, they would think I was either boasting or lying, or, if they did take me seriously, this rumour would be something I'd have to live down if I ever introduced them to any of my subsequent girlfriends. And that would definitely be it for me with any of the women in the office.

I had known for ages that a time would come when I'd have to clean up my act, although I always thought it'd be a new girlfriend that'd prompt me to change. But now I'd begun to suspect that it didn't work like that. Most men didn't meet women like Isobel because they didn't spend their evenings in Internet exchanges, and even if they did, they didn't strike up conversations with odd-looking women accessing hardcore porn. If I altered my lifestyle, it would put me back in a world where I could meet normal women.

By the time I went back to the computer, I'd decided that I was glad Isobel had gone, and that rather than using this site to monitor her progress, I would just check it once and then forego Internet porn forever. It didn't really do that much for me, and if I went back to using my imagination for masturbation, it'd stop me feeling like I was hiding some terrible dark secret. So I clicked through the huts and there she was, the new girl in hut #5. And as I went through the pictures with a sense of finality, I felt pleased that she was wearing pink socks, thinking this a nice gesture and wondering whether they were the same pair that Helen had once worn.

I printed out paper copies of the pictures of Isobel, then did the same for the rest of the girls on the site. I tried to forget that I had fucked Isobel and Lisa, and found that at least for the moment this was surprisingly easy, and the fact that they were naked in the photos made me feel less emotional than I might have done if they were fully clothed. I shut down the computer and went to bed.

Putting the pages on top of a cupboard, I made myself think about an ex from a few years ago as I masturbated on to the sheet. But after I'd come I didn't feel satisfied, and, hating myself, returned to my PC. I looked through the pictures of the girls again, then accessed the webcam. What I saw there scared me as much as if I'd been directly connected to a disapproving god. Filling the screen was a huge close-up of Adrian's luminous face, staring straight into the camera. Within seconds he looked right at me, as if making sure I was there. I knew he couldn't really see me, but it felt as he was peering straight into my soul. Then he walked back from the camera, turned round so that his back was facing me, and pulled down his chinos. He wasn't wearing underwear, and he turned his backside towards me. Squatting, he began a bizarre sideways herky-jerky dance, fingers flipping as he crouched and shuffled.

He kept this up for about five minutes, before he stopped, stretched open his bum-cheeks and squeezed out a thick black turd. As he did this, the hut door opened and Lisa wheeled in a bed. Strapped to the bed was Isobel, naked apart from a pair of knickers. With the slow, halting nature of the webcam, it was hard to make out all of the action, but while I watched Lisa seemed to do something unpleasant and gynaecological to Isobel, the image on my screen changing without warning to a bloody close-up. Then the server disconnected. I kept trying to get back on, but every time I attempted access of the Butt Hutt site it flashed me a 404.

That was three months ago.

It's the only ending I have.

I'll let you know if anything changes.

Passenger

Sidney Durham

Yellow tank top, tight denim shorts, sandals, backpack. Tanned, blonde, twenties. No bra. Shoulder tattoo, a red rose. Her gum popped. "Well?" she said. "You gonna give me a ride or not?"

"I guess so," I said. She had approached me boldly, and at first I thought she was a hooker. No way, she said. She just needed to get to Gatlinburg. She said I looked safe.

I thought her incredibly naive to make such an assumption, but if I didn't take her, she might well get herself into trouble. Besides, I was going to Asheville; it would be on the way. Maybe she would be able to carry on an intelligent conversation.

Wondering what other travellers thought about her getting into my car, I pulled out of the rest area and punched the cruise control when I got the big Lincoln up to exactly five over the speed limit. I still had seven hundred miles to go, and now most of it would be with her in the car with me.

I could smell her. It was cloves, maybe her chewing gum, which seemed to pop incessantly. I cracked the window a little, but it made a whistling sound I knew would anger me quickly.

She slumped in the seat next to me, the impudent tattooed shoulder between us. She had kicked off her sandals and had her feet tucked up, toes moving slowly. Her shorts had inched up, revealing too much flesh. Her breasts sagged in the light fabric that covered them, and her nipples jutted. She needed a bra. She popped her gum again.

"Would you mind getting rid of the gum?" I asked.

She stared at me. I tried to keep my attention on the road, but her gaze drew me and I had to glance at her face. Her eyes were bottomless black, meaning her hair probably wasn't really blond. "What the fuck's wrong with it?" she asked. She was grinning, holding the gum between her front teeth.

"I can't stand cloves," I said.

She studied the armrest in the door, found the right button and punched it repeatedly, inching the window down in little bursts of motion. Each widening of the opening let in more baked August air. When she had the window all the way down she blew the gum out of her mouth and through the opening, where it disappeared. She punched the window back up again and looked at me. "You didn't like the popping, did you?"

"No. Thank you for getting rid of it."

"You a salesman?"

"Accountant."

"Bean counter. That's what Lyle calls them."

"Who?"

"Lyle. My dad. How old are you?"

"Forty-two."

"Man, I hope I don't live that long."

"Forty-two?"

"Sixty-eight. Lyle's sixty-eight. That sucks. Forty-two is bad enough."

"How old are you?"

"Twenty-six."

"Sure."

"Okay, twenty-three. My birthday's next month." She tipped her head back and closed her eyes. I could see fine golden hairs on her throat. "What's your name?" she asked.

"Albert. What's yours?"

"Albert? For real?"

"What's yours?"

"Indigo."

"Indigo? I don't think so. What's your real name?"

"It's Indigo. I'm gonna change it to Indigo."

"What is it?"

"Inez."

"What's wrong with Inez?"

She turned her head and looked at me. "It's stupid. You have to call me Indigo." She slipped her fingers down the top of her shirt and scratched the space between her breasts, making them move. "You married?"

"Divorced."

"Dumped ya, huh?"

"Something like that," I said. It seemed everybody assumed I was the one who got dumped.

"How long you been divorced?"

"It's not final yet."

She scratched again. "Does the radio work? Got a CD player?"

"They didn't put CD players in cars this old. You can look for something on the radio if you like." I hoped she wouldn't, but she began fiddling with the knobs, leaning forwards. Her breasts took a peek at me. She found something loud and harsh.

"How fast will this old heap go?" she asked.

"I don't know. I don't speed."

She leaned close and looked at the speedometer. I could smell cloves again. "You're doing seventy-five," she said. "That's speeding. And it says it'll do one-twenty. Try it."

"No way."

"Chicken. If you get it up to a hundred we'll get there sooner."

"Not good for the car. It would be dangerous and waste gasoline. I would get a ticket and have to pay a fine, and we would lose all the time we might gain."

"Bean counter." She threw herself back in her seat with a loud sigh. "Look. I'll show you my tits if you get it up to ninety."

"No. Forget it."

"C'mon, Al. Go for it." She turned in her seat so that she

was leaning against the door and yanked up her top. Her untanned breasts were like beacons, drawing my eyes. "Watch the road, Al," she said, pulling the top down again.

"Keep yourself covered," I said. "And stop calling me Al. And fasten your seatbelt."

"Ninety, Al, Al-bert. Ninety m.p.h. You can touch these babies when you get this heap up to ninety." She pulled the top up again.

"Cover up."

"Ninety, Al-bert." She pulled her top off over her head and rubbed her breasts with it. "They're real soft," she said, throwing the top to the floor in front of her.

"We'll get arrested. Put your shirt back on."

She got on her knees and leaned close. "C'mon, Al-bert. Push on the pedal."

"Sit down! People will see you!"

Indigo leaned and pressed her soft breasts against my arm. "Ninety, Al-bert. Do it now." She began rolling her shoulders, rubbing her breasts on me. Her head was very close to mine and I could feel her breath against my face.

I looked safe, she'd said. Right.

I did books. I didn't drink. I didn't even swear. I never watched racy movies, and I never went to nude bars. I wore bow ties and wingtip shoes. And a girl half my age was rubbing her naked breasts on me, offering to let me touch them.

All I had to do was push on the accelerator pedal. A simple muscular contraction, pulling my Achilles tendon, forcing my toe down, was all that was needed. Her breasts shifted amiably against my arm as she continued to urge me. My cock, so long dormant, was reacting, stirring, reminding me it was there.

It was cause and effect: I could press the pedal; I could touch her breast. But there were other effects. In my mind I built an inventory of things that could happen if I touched her breasts. The list scrolled in my head and I watched it, trying to examine the contents, looking for risk and danger. If only she would stop rubbing me with her breasts I would be able to concentrate! It would be irresponsible to "go with it", as she might say, without carefully considering the implications. I was not that kind of person.

I was a careful, deliberate person, starting a new life. And I was being asked to drive my car faster than I ever had by a young, firm-bodied, impudent girl named Indigo, who was rubbing her bare breasts on my arm. She would let me touch them.

Life is short.

I pressed the pedal to the floor. The engine roared and the nose of the car lifted as the automatic transmission shifted. Terrified, I let go of the wheel with one hand and grabbed one of her breasts. Her nipple was a hard button and she rolled her shoulders, rasping it on my palm.

"Attaboy, Al-bert," she said. "You've got soft hands, bean counter." She rubbed again and I felt her nipple stiffen even more.

The car seemed to vibrate dangerously and I wanted to step on the brakes, but I kept my foot pressed to the floor and my hand pressed against her softness. The engine began to scream.

"Go, Al-bert!" she shouted, her voice high. "Give it hell!"

I kneaded her breast as my eyes cycled from the road to the rearview mirror to the speedometer. The speed rose steadily as the heavy car gained momentum, and the sound of the tyres and the thick summer air we were plunging through became a roar. I began to wonder if I could get my mouth on one of her nipples without losing sight of the road.

Indigo took the decision from me, pulling away and moving back to the passenger seat. I took my foot off the pedal but our momentum had already brought us to a tractor-trailer and I swung out to pass. He blew his horn as we passed the cab, startling me. Indigo lowered her window and stuck out her arm to wave. "I think he liked me," she said, laughing and turning the radio up louder. "Pass another one."

I saw her hands move and glanced at her. She was tracing

her fingertips around her nipples, which had become quite distended. Her window was still down and her hair was floating around her head. I stepped on the gas and caught another truck. Another horn blew, and Indigo waved again. Then, as I began to slow the car, she opened the front of her shorts and slipped her hand inside. "Keep going," she said, looking at me. Her cheeks were flushed. "They're probably talkin' about me on the CB," she added, her hand squirming inside her shorts. "Find another fuckin' truck."

I looked back at the road. Another truck loomed in front of us. When I pulled out to pass, I saw there was actually a line of four trucks. As we drew abreast of the first cab I heard the horn, blasting loudly through the open window.

Indigo raised her hips and pushed her shorts off. I kept the speed up, glancing sidelong at her as often as I dared. Her pubic hair was wispy yellow, and I noticed for the first time the blue-violet color of her fingernails as she continued to stroke herself.

More trucks. More horns. I eventually realized the truckers were slowing to allow our travelling roadshow to catch them. The black asphalt seemed to be streaking under us as the car settled, almost floating over the road. The trucks appeared to be moving backwards towards us.

I began to grin like a crazy man and horns blared as Indigo moved her hand faster, harder, fingers fluttering in her crotch like a frantic bird. "Slow down," she grunted, reaching out the window with her free hand to wave the trucks forward. "Stay in the passing lane. And pinch my fuckin' nipple."

I slowed, turning off the cruise control. I reached, found her hard nipple and began rolling it between my thumb and forefinger. She was moaning, the sound muted by the wind rushing by her window. One by one the trucks caught and passed us, horns sounding.

Indigo came. It was a screaming, thrashing orgasm, and she raised her hips up, bucking like a boat tossed in heavy seas. She slumped in her seat as the last trucker blasted his way past, fist out the window, thumb in the air. "Holy fucking shit," she said, rolling up her window. I glanced at her and saw droplets of perspiration had collected on her upper lip and between her breasts.

In the closed cavern of the car I caught new scents: hot oil and metal, and woman. I glanced at her and she turned, grinning at me. "Now I blow you while you pass them again," she said, getting to her knees and reaching for my zipper.

I grinned and stepped on the gas. Indigo's bare ass was in the air, pointed at the window. I turned the radio up all the way as she freed my cock, and used the controls on my armrest to lower her window, knowing the horns would blow again. I got the car up to eighty-five and punched the cruise control as her sweaty upper lip grazed my cock. I reached down and grabbed a breast.

The trucks were still slow, waiting for us. Every driver gave me a thumbs-up as we roared past them, Indigo's head bobbing enthusiastically in my lap.

Just before I went off I decided to grow a pony tail.

The Survey

Mary Anne Mohanraj

So this guy walks up to me on the street at something like 8 p.m. on that deserted stretch over by the park, y'know? I'd be scared except he's just a kid, and he says, "Hey, you wanna do this survey?" And I say, "What's in it for me? I'm a busy woman." And he says, "Five bucks – and if you answer the long form, fifty."

Well, fifty bucks is not something to sniff at, y'know? There's a lot I could buy for fifty bucks. There's this long black velvet coat over at Goodwill, only twenty bucks, and a nice pair of rhinestone heels I've been eyeing, five bucks, and that leaves twenty-five for the kids – half for them, half for me. That's fair, right? And that sounds so good I can see the money's already spent, so I'd better answer his questions. So I tell him, "Shoot." And he says, "Do you masturbate?"

So I reach back my arm and I'm gonna belt him a good one right there, only he ducks and hollers out – "It's for the survey!" And I drop my arm and I say, "What the fuck kinda survey is that?" And he says, "It's a fucking survey, see? The university is doing a survey on fucking. I got stuck with asking women if they masturbate, which is not making me popular, believe me. My roommate, he gets to ask guys where the best places to get a blow job are, lucky bastard. You wouldn't believe how many women have tried to hit me already today, lady. Look, one of them got me." And he shows me this bump on his forehead, under where his greasy hair falls in his face. So I say, "What the hell kind of school do you go to that does a fucking survey? Never mind . . . I don't wanna know."

So he's standing there, waiting, and I'm standing there, thinking. "Do you gotta know my name?" I ask him. He says, "Well, we have to put down a name and an age, but you don't have to give me your real name. They won't know." And I think it over, and finally, I think, Sure. What the fuck. Give the kid a thrill. "Put me down as Esmerelda. Esmerelda Valentino, age twenty-eight." Ever since I watched *I Dream of Jeannie* as a kid, I've liked the name Esmerelda. "And the answer to your question is 'Yes.'" The kid scribbles something down on the clipboard he's holding, and then reaches into his pocket and hands me a five. And I say, "Where's my fifty?" And he says, "That's only for the long form, Miz Esmerelda. Nobody wants to answer the long form." And I say, "Show me."

So he hands over the clipboard, and there's this sheet of paper with big words at the top – *How Do You Masturbate?* – and a long list of questions below. Questions like "How many fingers do you use when you masturbate?" and "Do you prefer clitoral or vaginal stimulation?" and "Have you ever inserted foreign objects into your rectum?"

I hand back the board. "That's what they want to know? They got this list – that's supposed to tell them how we do it?" The kid nods his head, looking embarrassed. And I laugh. 'Cause it's just too damn funny, y'know? And I say, "Siddown, kid. Grab a patch of sidewalk. That little list of yours won't tell you nothin'. I'll tell you how I really do it." So we sit down on the sidewalk and I stretch out my aching feet, 'cause it's been a hard day at the diner, and I close my eyes and start talking.

"It all starts with Johnny, see. Not Johnny Stepanino, that lousy no-good bum that I've been seeing for the past six years, who keeps promising me a ring but do you see it on my finger? Not him – he's got stringy hair and doesn't remember to bathe half the time unless his mama tells him to; I wouldn't give him the time of day 'cept he's got a good business and could really take care of me and my kids. But he's never gonna get up the nerve, 'cause his mama don't like the idea of him marrying a girl who's only a little bit Italian, mostly mutt, and dropped out of high school when she got knocked up at sixteen. His mama don't like that idea at all.

"Anyway, the one I'm thinking of is Johnny Viaggi. Johnny Viaggi with the long black hair that falls into his face so cute – kinda like yours, kid. He smells clean all the time, clean as spring, with the smell of new bread hanging heavy over him – that's 'cause he works at Cantalini's bakery over on Fourth.

"That Nina Cantalini! How that little shit managed to snag Johnny Viaggi I'll never know – oh, she's all-right looking, I'll give you that, with that tight ass and those big tits. But them Cantalini women are all drinkers, which is why the men run the shop, and I swear that before she's thirty Nina will be drinking up the profits and lettin' her body go to hell. She's gonna swell up like a balloon and those big tits are gonna droop over the beer belly she's gonna have. And that tight ass is gonna loosen right up, and Johnny Viaggi is gonna be damned sorry he married such a worthless drunken lump of a woman when he could've had me.

"You're wondering why I'm telling you all this. See, when I'm getting off, I'm not alone. No, I close my eyes, and Johnny Viaggi is right there next to me. It's his big thick hands that lift me up and move me to my bed, his hands that unbutton my blouse and push it down my shoulders and off my arms. Slender arms, and a slender body, and if my tits aren't as big as that damn Nina's at least they'll still be standing up straight in ten years. I don't fucking care if I'm only a 32A – my nipples are sensitive as hell, and that's what counts. That's what Stepanino says, anyway, and for once the scumbag is right.

"I've got great little tits, and when I unhook the front of my cherry red bra and pull it off, that's Johnny's fingers doing it, and his big hands cupping my tits so that they disappear under his rough touch. Then my nipples stand up hard, so hard they poke out between his fingers, and he starts playing with them, rolling them between two fingers, squeezing and pulling a bit, all the while whispering words of love, '*Mi amore, cara mia*, darling Angie.' And I'm moaning under Johnny's touch 'cause it's so good, and my nipples are so sensitive, and his breath is soft against my ear, against my neck – I'm almost ready to come right there, but he likes to take it slow.

"Then his hands slide down my body, unzipping my skirt and pushing it down, so he can see the red silk garter belt and black stockings I wore just for him, just like he asked me to. No panties, and Johnny's fingers trail down and down, almost tickling but not quite, sliding over my shaved pussy until they're barely touching my clit. And he touches me then, and it is so sweet, so fucking sweet that I moan Johnny's name, oh yeah. I'm lying in my bed with his body warm beside me and his mouth on my nipple now and his fingers sliding into my pussy, warm and wet and slick and hard, pumping harder and harder until I'm almost about to come and it's then that he whispers, "Angie, will you marry me?" and that's when I scream "Yes, yes, yes!" and I'm coming hard and fast like you wouldn't believe.

"*That's* how I masturbate. You got all that down, kid?" He's staring at me with wide eyes, like he's never heard a woman come before.

Maybe he hasn't. And I'm standing up and shaking the dust from my ass, and he comes alive quick and reaches into his pocket, fumbling a little, and then counts out nine more fives into my hand. He's still not saying a word so I smile at him and turn away, walking down the empty street and not caring that my feet still hurt 'cause I've got fifty dollars in my pocket and a sopping-wet pussy.

Take *that*, Nina-fucking-Cantalini.

Muriel the Magnificent

Marilyn Jaye Lewis

When Muriel Bing was seven years old, in the course of a single Saturday afternoon, something happened that shifted the topography of her secret inner landscape forever. The day had started out harmless enough: an afternoon in late spring close to the end of her second grade school year. In high spirits, she and Tommy Decker, the little brown-haired boy whose family's backyard adjoined hers, played together on her brightly coloured swing set. Higher and higher they swung, until Tommy wagered with Muriel. "I'll bet you can't swing as high as me and jump when I yell 'jump.'"

"Yes, I can."

"No, you can't."

"I can, too!"

"OK," hollered Tommy, the bet underway. "The loser has to do whatever the winner says," he shouted.

Muriel's sturdy legs pumped determinedly as her swing kept pace with Tommy's. Her long auburn braids flying out behind her on the upswing, then smacking lightly against her shoulders as she swung down and back. Over and over, higher she climbed, until Muriel had reached an exhilarating height.

"Now!" Tommy Decker cried, "Jump!" as he flung himself free of the swing, soaring several feet out over the small backyard, landing in a tumble on the cool green grass, his empty swing chink-chinking to a sudden halt behind him.

Muriel, however, hadn't jumped. The sheer height she'd

reached had been too daunting. When it came time for her fingers to release their tight grip on the chains of her high-flying swing, when she'd heard Tommy's voice suddenly shout "jump" and her eyes had taken in the full scope of empty sky she'd be forced to sail out into and the hard expanse of ground beneath her, Muriel's bowels had clenched tight. She'd been too timid to jump.

Her feet dragged the swing to a stumbling stop. Tommy had already leapt to his feet and come running over, his eyes bright with triumph. "You lose, Muriel," he cried gleefully. "I won. Now you have to do whatever I say!"

Tommy Decker was only one Decker from a veritable sea of Decker boys. Unlike the Bing family, the Deckers were Catholics who'd had nothing but sons. In the Decker house, there were always boys as far as Tommy's blue eyes could see: in his bedroom at night there were boys, in the morning at the kitchen table, or in front of the television set when he came home from school – nothing but brothers. Tommy was drawn to Muriel Bing because she was an only child; a sweet, kind and smart little girl, but more because she was just that: a girl.

"Now you have to come behind the garage with me," Tommy announced.

Bravely, Muriel slid off her swing, knowing Tommy was fully capable of making her do something awful. Once, the summer before, he'd plucked a carrot from her father's vegetable patch, a carrot no bigger than Muriel's pinkie, and had forced her to eat it, then and there, dirt and all. Another time, he'd made her shuck unripe peas from their pods and eat them raw, giving her a churning stomach ache. Worse yet, Mr Bing didn't like Muriel and Tommy making a mess of his garden. He'd said as much, in no uncertain terms, on several occasions.

With a cursory glance back towards her house to see if anyone was watching her, Muriel followed Tommy behind the garage to her father's vegetable patch, her childish curiosity outweighing her reluctance, as usual.

When the pair were safely ensconced between the row of hedges that lined the edge of the Decker yard, and the garden at the back of the Bing's garage, Tommy told Muriel, "Pull down your pants."

She was stunned. "What?"

"I said, pull down your pants. You have to do it because you have to do anything I say."

Muriel stared at Tommy uneasily and did nothing.

"Come on," he persisted. "Do it. I just want to see."

In an unfamiliar mix of interest and fear, Muriel did what Tommy wanted. She unzipped her pants, tugging them down just a little bit.

"Those, too," he insisted, pointing at her cotton underpants.

Muriel hesitated. "No," she refused quietly.

"Come on, Muriel, just for one second. Just until I count 'one Mississippi' then you can pull them back up, OK?"

Muriel considered Tommy's offer, her cautious hesitation giving way to a growing intrigue. She liked the way it felt, Tommy staring at her underpants in earnest, she suddenly felt eager to show him what she knew the sisterless boy wanted to see. When she tugged her underpants down just enough to reveal her smooth mound and the pouting cleft at its base, the expression of wonder on Tommy's face made Muriel almost burst with pride.

He seemed so entranced by the sight of the strange nakedness that peeked out from between Muriel's legs, that Tommy forgot to count "one Mississippi". In fact, the two of them stood transfixed by the magnetic pull between them for several uninterrupted moments. When they finally were interrupted, though, it happened in the worst possible way: an unsuspecting Mr Bing rounded the corner of the garage.

"Muriel Bing, what do you think you're doing?" he sputtered, as Tommy Decker took off running for the relative safety of his own backyard.

Muriel's seven-year-old mind knew instinctively that she

had no satisfactory answer to her father's question. "I'm not doing anything," she replied weakly, hastily tugging her pants and underpants back up around her waist.

No sooner were her clothes in order, than Muriel's father grabbed her abruptly by her little arm, escorting her up the yard to the house, in through the kitchen door, down the hallway and into her room.

"You know better than that, Muriel!" he practically shouted. "What was going on out there?"

"Nothing," she replied timidly, realising in a panic that the most dreaded punishment was befalling her. The pants and underpants she'd pulled up to her waist only moments before, were coming down again, quickly, and her father was pulling her over his knee.

"Daddy, don't!" she cried feebly, as the spanking got underway. But there was no stopping Mr Bing. The smacks rained down on Muriel's bare bottom furiously, as he unleashed a litany of reasons why what Muriel had done was bad, bad, bad.

This degree of anger was uncommon in Muriel's father and she was unnerved by it. It wasn't so much the severity of the spanking that wounded her, she was pierced to the core by the sound of his words.

"I'm thoroughly ashamed of you, Muriel," he declared, as he unceremoniously yanked her from his lap when the spanking was over. "What made you do a dirty thing like that?"

He stood her helplessly in front of him while he continued to lecture her harshly about the wickedness of her immodesty. Throughout the entire scolding, poor Muriel's pants remained around her knees. The little mound whose unveiling had so recently filled her with pride was uncomfortably on display and now serving as the obtrusive source of her newfound shame.

At thirty-seven, Muriel Bing was as bony as a little bird; her modest breasts, her slender waist and narrow hips, always concealed beneath the finely tailored yet conservative dress suits she wore every day to the law office, where she specialised in real estate. She wore simple silk blouses, buttoned to her throat, and durable navy pumps on her small, sturdy feet.

Muriel lived alone in a well-appointed apartment in midtown Manhattan and almost never dated. She was no longer a virgin – she wasn't as pathetic as that – still she had become an expert at repressing any unseemly urges to satisfy her drives; not just the biological urges, but the appetites of her very senses. She ate plain, unseasoned foods cooked at home, almost never drank alcohol, not even wine, and her spotless apartment held no aromas of daily living except for the distinct odour of anti-bacterial cleanser.

The law firm where Muriel had been employed since she'd passed the New York Bar eleven years earlier, was a prestigious, well-equipped, state-of-the-art office on Fifty-seventh Street, just off Fifth Avenue. Each employee's desk had the latest model computer. They were on-line, networked, firewalled, intranetted, and secure on their dedicated server. No software program could be accessed without a valid password. Outside meetings took place in the form of on-line video conferencing. Office e-mail was monitored and noted in extensive personnel files.

At home, Muriel's fondness for technology lagged far behind the firm's. Until recently, she'd had a reasonably respectable computer, a modest printer, and the only software she'd deemed necessary was for word processing, which she did a great deal of late into the night. But gradually, the outside world had caught up with her. Only days before, Muriel had upgraded to a high-speed unit with all the frills, even free. Internet access – a needless temptation Muriel had previously withstood. The only e-mail correspondence she engaged in was work-related and so it stayed on the computer at the firm. Still, acquiescing to the advancement of technology into the privacy of her own home, Muriel logged on to the Internet and set up her first personal account.

Her free Internet access included the option of maintaining a small homepage. At first, she dismissed it out of hand, having no reason to display any part of her private life on something as public as a homepage. Yet, after some consideration, it occurred to Muriel that it could help advertise the law firm. She set about learning the software to upload a humble web page devoted to her occupation as real estate lawyer, listing her experience and the contact information of the office and nothing more.

It was quite late on a Friday evening when Muriel uploaded the newly created page to her allotted space on the server.

After she'd been alerted that the files had been sent successfully, she typed the URL of her homepage into the address locator and waited for her handiwork to load into her browser.

It seemed like she waited a long time. The simple page was loading very slowly, too slowly, as if it were laden with images or those space-consuming enhancements that frequently tried her patience on other websites.

Muriel walked away from her computer and went to the kitchen to peruse the contents of her refrigerator. While the browser continued to load her homepage, Muriel reached for an apple and a diet ginger ale.

In a particularly hot pink hue, the words "Muriel the Magnificent" blinked on and off incessantly on a pitch black background.

Muriel stared at her monitor, first in confusion, then in complete indignation, as jpeg after jpeg of a thoroughly naked woman, in all sorts of obscene poses, assaulted her vision. Clearly she had mistyped the URL. She checked the address in her browser against the address she'd been given by her service provider. It was the same.

Slightly panic-stricken, since Muriel had no ready faculties for processing lascivious feelings and the lewd images veritably bursting before her eyes in a riotous array of digitised colours aroused something primitive in her, Muriel hurriedly closed the page and prepared to resend her files to the server.

Carefully, she re-entered the ftp information, being especially observant about entering her user name and password. When the files had again been successfully sent, Muriel retyped her URL into the browser and loaded her homepage.

This time, in only a few seconds, the page had reloaded. "Muriel the Magnificent" flashed merrily on the screen.

A decidedly buxom, fleshy, full-figured woman in a myriad of wide-spread poses, of bending-over poses, or poses where her substantial boobs were squeezed together tightly – these assorted sordid images greeted Muriel again.

It must have something to do with our names being similar, Muriel decided. Perhaps there was a mix-up on the server because of that.

Yet there was something oddly familiar about this other Muriel, with the teased auburn hair, the heavily made-up eyes and glossy lips, wearing spiked heels and little else. Muriel scrolled down the page to the final photo: the voluptuous woman was bending over, lustily grabbing a sizable portion of her rear end in each of her well-manicured hands. Across the photo, just below a protuberance of shaved labial lips, the words "let's make contact" flashed annoyingly, while pointing to an e-mail link.

Muriel clicked on it, only to be more horrified when the preprogrammed e-mail address turned out to be her own.

Should I? she wondered. If I do, what will I say?

Muriel didn't want to make actual contact with this other Muriel, she only wanted to know where the e-mail would ultimately arrive.

She typed the words "testing 1,2,3" into the body of the e-mail and clicked "send", only to receive an e-mail several moments later notifying her that her e-mail was undeliverable as addressed.

"But how could I have received *this* e-mail if my e-mail address is incorrect?" Muriel demanded of her monitor in vain.

Anxiously, she dialled the number for twenty-four-hour

tech support. It was late enough on a Friday night that she wasn't on hold for more than ten minutes. After having explained her peculiar problem to the tech support person, he offered to go to her homepage himself.

"There's some information about a law firm," he said. "And some résumé or something for a real estate lawyer – is that what you're getting?"

"That's what I'd *like* to be getting," Muriel whined incredulously, "but what I'm getting is pornography!"

The tech support person was silent for a moment. "I don't know what to tell you, ma'am. There's nothing pornographic about what I'm seeing here."

As he read aloud, verbatim, the brief description of the law firm and work experiences Muriel had composed, Muriel was dumbfounded.

"Well, what am I supposed to do about all this pornography!" By now, Muriel was nearly hysterical. "I want to see my homepage. What if other people see these disgusting photos and assume it's me? That I'm *that* Muriel?"

Another uneasy silence came from the other end of the line. "I don't know, ma'am. I don't know what to tell you. Perhaps you should try to contact this other woman."

"But her e-mail address is the same as mine – and it doesn't work!"

"What do you mean, it doesn't work?"

"I tried sending an e-mail to her, but it came back as undeliverable."

"Well, maybe it's a dead website. It happens all the time."

"No, you don't understand. It's *my* e-mail address. It works just fine."

"I'm sorry, ma'am, I really don't know what else to tell you." The tone of the young man's voice was now edging into patronising impatience.

Muriel slammed down the phone. "You useless piece of . . ." Then she fumed silently for several minutes over her first personal encounter with on-line tech support.

*   *   *

Muriel stood rigidly in the hot shower, letting the water blast down on the back of her neck, hoping it would soothe her agitated brain. Her eyes closed in defeat and she sighed.

I must have sounded completely insane, she realised, as her conversation with tech support reverberated in her head. What the hell is going on with that computer?

In a burst of rage, Muriel had shut down the machine, overwhelmed by the extent of her unmitigated confusion. She'd elected to give it up for the time being and prepare for bed. Her anger had followed her from room to room, as she'd switched off the lights, secured the apartment, stripped off her clothes and gotten into the shower, but she was determined not to let the anxiety follow her into bed. Muriel was prone to bouts of insomnia, a state of mind she dreaded.

In a white cotton nightgown and a pair of equally white cotton panties, Muriel slid into bed. The sheets felt cool against her skin. Muriel felt noticeably calmer. With luck, she would sleep.

At 3 a.m., Muriel's eyes opened. She stared blankly into the darkness and the first thought that commanded her attention was this: why were so many grown women determined to look like parodies of little girls?

Muriel couldn't help thinking about that other Muriel; Muriel the Magnificent, with her womanly figure and shaved labia. It was absurd looking.

Muriel snuggled more comfortably into her pillow. Her hand absently playing at the stray strands of pubic hairs that poked through the leg bands of her cotton panties. As far back as she could remember, Muriel had had a generous thatch of dark brown pubic hair. She couldn't recall a time when she didn't have it.

Wait, she thought, remembering the Tommy Decker incident. But in an instant her mind skittered clear of the discomforting memory, and soon enough Muriel Bing was sound asleep.

*   *   *

On Saturday morning, Muriel slept in. It was uncharacteristic of her to even remotely surrender to the lure of sloth. However, her bed felt so comfortable, a cool breeze blowing in gently over the blankets, and a bird warbling merrily on a sill across the airshaft, that Muriel was lulled back to sleep before she knew it. When she finally roused herself, it was nearly noon.

She sat lazily on the edge of her bed, looking down at her loose-fitting nightgown, her skinny legs. The images of the other Muriel leapt to her consciousness.

How would it feel to be so fleshy? she wondered. What would it be like to always have one's boobs in one's peripheral vision?

She tugged open the top of her nightgown and stared down at her modest breasts. She tried squeezing them together in an unsuccessful attempt to create cleavage. She eyed her flat stomach, too. Then she noticed with interest how her cotton panties covered her slightly protruding mound so smoothly. She wondered what she looked like down there, under all that hair. And this time when her mind served her up the memory of Tommy Decker, she let it linger there.

"What's with me today?" she muttered, feeling her hormones beginning to stir. Then she realised she was thinking about her computer, about how easily salacious images could be summoned from it. Why not? she thought.

She didn't even put on the coffee pot. She went straight to her computer and booted it up. She got on-line and went directly to the images of Muriel the Magnificent. This time, she studied the images intently. She found herself especially intrigued by the photos of Muriel spread wide, where every labial fold was blatantly revealed. There was one shot in particular where Muriel held her spread knees up to her breasts. Her tummy bulged enticingly in this position and then the smooth-shaven vulva seemed somehow more garish, even the anus was visible.

"There's something really filthy looking about that," Muriel said quietly, realising that her pulse had quickened.

As she studied the rest of the images, she fondled her nipples through the material of her nightgown. Then she discovered that the crotch of her panties was soaking.

"Jesus," she sighed. "Enough!" She closed down the browser and got off-line.

Muriel was too distracted now to make coffee. She decided to go out for a cup instead. She got dressed and went down to the corner café. It was a beautiful sunny day, with a hint of spring in the air. Muriel surprised herself again, this time by ordering a double latte and, at the last minute, adding a cream-filled, chocolate-iced doughnut to her order! She couldn't remember the last time she'd tasted a doughnut and now, suddenly, she craved it.

Muriel sat down at a small table in front of the window and watched the people on the street walk briskly past. As her teeth sunk into the gooey pastry, her mouth filling with the rich flavour of fats and sugar, Muriel barely suppressed an audible moan. It was delicious, it was the best doughnut Muriel could remember tasting. She made a mental note to have breakfast out more often.

She shifted in the seat and caught the scent of herself. She was still wet between her legs. As she drank her double latte, her mind filled with pictures of the other Muriel's shaved pussy and spread legs. She watched the girls walking past the window and wondered which ones had shaved pussies concealed beneath their jeans or under their dresses.

This is crazy, she thought. Still, she loved the feeling of surrendering to the lusty pictures filling her head. She felt hypnotised. Before she knew it, her mind was made up. She tossed her empty cup into the trash can and headed home to her apartment, to her bathroom, where she was determined she would shave herself.

Muriel stripped naked and sat on the edge of her tub. By now, she was so aroused between her legs that even something as light as shaving foam felt incredibly exciting. The steel blade, repeatedly stroking her swollen mound, caressing it, revealing more and more of her increasing nakedness, drove Muriel to ecstasy. When she washed away the final residue and admired her handiwork in the mirror, she was thoroughly enchanted with the new vision of herself. She remained naked the rest of the afternoon, studying herself admiringly in the mirror, adopting many provocative poses, masturbating herself to orgasm seven times. When she had finally exhausted herself, she collapsed on her bed and stared up at the ceiling.

What good is it to look so inviting if there's no one around to appreciate it? she wondered, coming peculiarly close to admitting that she wanted a lover.

Suddenly, Muriel realised she was starving. She pulled on some clothes and headed outside for dinner. She chose a local Italian trattoria, an establishment that had been in her neighbourhood for years but which she had never once stepped inside.

It was early enough on a Saturday evening that the host was able to accommodate a single diner with no reservation without much difficulty. He showed Muriel to a small table in the corner. The restaurant was dimly lit, a single votive flickering seductively on every table, Frank Sinatra crooning out from the speakers.

"Something to drink before dinner?"

Muriel looked up at the waiter as if in a trance. The warm timbre of his masculine voice had melted into her ears. His dark eyes were beautiful, his shoulder-length black hair pulled into a neat ponytail behind his head. Suddenly Muriel wanted wine. Red wine. The best vintage. Maybe even a whole bottle if they wouldn't serve her the best vintage by the glass. She'd drink what she wanted, without concerning herself about being wasteful for a change.

When the waiter returned with the bottle of wine, Muriel noticed for the first time that he was probably much younger than she, but she didn't care. She remained entranced. As he poured her a glass to taste, he seemed to eye her seductively, making Muriel wonder if he could smell her from where he was standing. She found herself hoping he could. Soon a busboy hovered around her with a basket of bread, then another came near to pour her some water. A different waiter came by for her food order, and, later, the host was back to see how she was enjoying her meal.

She felt flushed. Never had Muriel been surrounded by so many attentive and attractive men. She returned to her apartment reeling from the thought of so much seemingly available masculinity in the world.

She couldn't resist booting up the computer one more time.

The page was back to loading slowly, but within a few moments, "Muriel the Magnificent" was flashing on her monitor once again. Only this time, the selection of jpegs had changed. Muriel felt slightly alarmed: this was an active web page after all. Who was this other Muriel whom she was so voyeuristically enjoying?

She studied the new photos with acute interest, for now Muriel the Magnificent was no longer solo, she had a male companion – one who was remarkably endowed. In one photo, the companion stood behind her, clutching two good-sized handfuls of Muriel's boobs, while his stiff erection poked up between Muriel's spread legs. The images became more provocative as the page continued to load. In fact, in one photo after another, a purely pornographic tryst between two rambunctious lovers was thoroughly exposed.

Oh, God, this is what I *want*, thought Muriel deliriously, as picture after picture assailed her eyes and her fingers worked tirelessly down under her skirt.

The male companion looked satisfyingly familiar – much like the waiter at the trattoria who had poured Muriel her wine, who had kept her glass enticingly filled throughout the course of her incredible meal. The same waiter who had eyed her knowingly, as if he were ready to scoop up a bit of her smell with his fingers; as if he were aching to taste her.

In one photo, the lovers were passionately entwined, their

copulating genitals readily captured by the camera's lens. Another pose illustrated why Muriel was so magnificent: her lover's substantial shaft filled her mouth to capacity. There were still more shots of the lovers performing intercourse in every position. The final parting shot, of course, was a daunting close-up of Muriel's snug anus stretching to accommodate every thick inch of her companion's probing tool.

When the final image loaded in front of Muriel's eager eyes, she succumbed to another orgasm. Her eighth for the day – by far, a personal record. Muriel forced herself to shut down the computer and find her way to a hot shower. But what a glorious day it had been.

Later that night, Muriel couldn't sleep. She felt too keyed-up. Finally she gave up any pretence of drifting off to slumber. She got out of bed and went in to the dark living room. Clad in her white cotton nightgown and white cotton panties, she sat on her open window sill in the cool night air and watched an occasional taxi zip across the nearly deserted street below. From where she sat, she could see the trattoria closing. It was nearing 3 a.m. The neon sign blinked off suddenly and then Muriel watched several of the employees exit the restaurant together. Most of them walked away from her building, but one walked in her direction. Muriel's heart fluttered when she realised it was her favourite waiter.

"Hey," she called out quietly, surprising even herself. "Hey, you – hi!"

The young man looked around curiously.

"Up here."

"Hello," he called back to her, seeming to recognise her immediately, even though it was dark. "What are you doing up? It's so late."

"I couldn't sleep."

He crossed the street and was now standing on the sidewalk three storeys below her window. "I was just thinking about you," he said, reaching into his bag and retrieving a half-empty re-corked bottle of red wine. "I swiped this from your table," he called up to her, showing her the bottle. "I didn't want it to go to waste, but it's too good to drink alone, no?"

Muriel's heart raced. She couldn't believe it was happening. Her mouth opened and words came out of their own volition. "Why don't you come up? I'll buzz you in," she offered.

"OK," he replied, seemingly unfazed by her ready acquiescence.

He must do this a lot, she thought, as she buzzed open the front door of her building and listened to his feet hurrying up the steps in the quiet stairwell. He sounded eager, perhaps taking the stairs two at a time. When he reached her floor, she stood in her open doorway waiting for him.

He eyed her thin cotton nightgown, her skinny legs and bare feet. He smiled, a little out of breath. "What's your name?" he asked. "I'm Antonio – from Canarsie."

"I'm Muriel," she replied.

"Well, Muriel," he said, lifting the bottle once again from his satchel, "do you have any glasses or do you drink from the bottle?"

Antonio and Muriel sat together on the couch in her dark living room, a faint light shining in from the kitchen doorway. They were only on their first glass of the leftover wine when Antonio set his glass down on the coffee table and reached for Muriel's, setting hers aside, too. He slid closer to her on the couch.

"You know, you look really inviting in that little nightie," he began quietly. "Do you ask a lot of guys up here in the middle of the night?"

"No," Muriel replied nervously. "I haven't even been on a date in I don't know how long."

"Well, that would explain it."

"Explain what?"

"You have this air about you, you know? Like you're really

ready for it. Am I right?'' he asked, his hand sliding up her thigh, under her nightgown, his fingertips brushing along the leg band of her panties.

Muriel caught her breath and didn't reply.

"What's the matter, Muriel?'' Antonio taunted her, his warm hand slipping down between her loosely parted legs, then fleetingly across the crotch of her panties.

"Nothing,'' she managed to answer.

"Are you sure?'' he persisted, his other hand reaching for the back of her head now.

"I'm sure,'' she said, her mouth finding his in the darkness and locking on.

He tasted like wine, cigarettes, coffee. He smelled of all the robust flavours of every Italian meal he'd been in the vicinity of at the trattoria. It was a heady mixture, an unfamiliar but not unpleasant scent for Muriel, because above all, he smelled like a man, and her entire body responded.

Antonio was all over her, his hands everywhere: under her nightie to fondle her nipples, then running through her hair as they continued to kiss, then down along her thighs, then grabbing her arse. Finally he tugged her panties down and discovered the smoothness of her shaved mound with his fingers.

"One of those naughty little girls, huh?'' he whispered. "For some reason that doesn't surprise me.''

In a mere moment, he had her panties completely off, her thighs spread and his face buried between her legs. It wasn't the first time Muriel had felt a man's mouth on her down there, but it was the first time she let herself enjoy it. It was exhilarating. Antonio's tongue explored the swelling folds of her inner lips, then found her clitoris and lingered there while his fingers pushed into the sopping wetness of her hole.

She followed his lead effortlessly, her eager body assuming whatever position Antonio favoured with only the slightest word of encouragement from him; positions she'd shied away from in the past because she'd feared the lewd postures too immodest, perhaps even degrading. But now, as Antonio mounted her from behind, her knees pulled up under herself while she gripped the arm of the couch and felt the plunging fulness of his erection filling her, she found herself suddenly grateful for the happy, inexplicable accident of Muriel the Magnificent and her lurid web page.

Remembering some of the images that had filled her head earlier, Muriel found herself taking the initiative now. She straddled Antonio, impaled herself upon his substantial shaft. She explored the length of him with her mouth, sucked his erection ardently. Then squatted over his face and let his tongue go at her again.

Finally she invited him into her bed, where it was easier for him to pound into her relentlessly from behind, his thumb sliding into her anus while his thick cock tormented her Muriel couldn't remember ever having felt so filled up, so completely appreciated, so thoroughly aroused. She took the force of his pounding as if she were born to be the receptacle of his fucking, his endless fucking, she never wanted to stop fucking . . .

Muriel and Antonio lay entwined on Muriel's bed, the Sunday morning dawn inching imperceptibly closer outside her bedroom window.

"You're too skinny, you know," Antonio teased her quietly. "We're going to have to fatten you up. Put some meat on your bones."

It sounded to Muriel as if he had intentions of sticking around, that he didn't consider them a one-night stand. She wondered how she felt about that.

"You should come by the restaurant more often. I can slip you some food on the house," he assured her, seeming to think she was thin because she couldn't afford to eat. "What do you do, anyway, Muriel? Where do you work?"

"I'm a lawyer," she replied.

"A lawyer? Then forget about it – you're taking *me* to dinner."

Antonio drifted to sleep while holding Muriel in his arms.

★   ★   ★

As soon as the sun poked through her curtains, Muriel's eyes opened. Antonio was sound asleep. She was relieved that he hadn't left her. Still it concerned her that she was plunging herself headlong into such unfamiliar territory. Muriel had never done anything so rash in her life. And it had all started with that web page. Her whole life had changed simply because she'd gotten on-line.

Then her curiosity got the best of her. It was uncanny how Muriel the Magnificent's experiences were only one step ahead of her own. She studied Antonio while he slept, then decided to slip out of bed and consult her computer: what erotic pleasures did Sunday have in store? Would they include him? Was the other Muriel still cavorting wantonly with the other Antonio?

The computer booted up and Muriel got on-line. The web page loaded slowly, an indication that the jpegs had probably changed. Muriel's pulse quickened; what was she likely to see?

"Muriel the Magnificent" flashed again, as usual. The first image loaded. It was Muriel with the other Antonio, they were getting down to business. They were both facing the camera. Muriel was astride Antonio with her legs spread, making it plain that Antonio's cock was deeply imbedded up her shaved hole. But just outside of the picture stood another man, his erect penis was clearly discernible in Muriel's right hand.

"Oh, my God," she murmured breathlessly, as picture after picture revealed the other Muriel getting lewdly penetrated in every orifice by two good-looking men at once.

"Caught you!" Antonio blurted, startling Muriel, making her jump.

She whirled around in her chair to find him standing naked behind her. She blushed. "I didn't know you were up."

"Hey, it's OK," he laughed. "Don't be embarrassed. Everybody likes to look at dirty pictures. This is a nice computer," he went on. "It looks brand new. So you're on-line?"

"Yes," Muriel answered sheepishly.

"Me, too. I spend a lot of time on-line. It's the wave of the future, right? Soon enough everyone will be on-line."

Muriel looked away from Antonio and stared at her monitor distractedly. "Yes," she agreed quietly. "Soon enough, everyone will be on-line."

Wasabi Punani

Christine Pountney

When I was just sixteen years old, I went to San Francisco on a school trip. To the boys in my class I was sexless. I was too tall, too gangly. My breasts were too firm, too high, and my hips were too much like their own. For all their bravado and sexual boasting, they were unsophisticated and lacked imagination. They required the cumbersome trappings of obvious sexual characteristics to arouse their desire and preferred the Greek girls, with their hairy forearms suggesting advanced pubic growth, and the physical handicap of fully developed, oversized breasts.

Sexless as I may have seemed to my peers, I had already attracted the attention of various older men, and I knew with the instinct of a vixen when the scent was up and a man was snared. I liked the attention I received from older men, and I assumed the coy and sullen persona that my teenage years allowed. But above all, I assumed a passive yet provocative sexual role. I wore my school kilt as short as I could get away with, without actually getting expelled, and let my tie hang as loose and indolent as my morals.

It was a glaringly bright day, and we were taking a walking tour of San Francisco's vast and labyrinthine China Town. I was dawdling at a stall with an exotic array of sea creatures, fish eyes and large phallic molluscs. Entranced by the purple tentacles of a squid, I stood there fingering its tiny little suction cups. When I finally looked up, I realised that my class had moved on and that I was alone.

I didn't mind; in fact, I felt exhilarated and relinquished myself to the muscular movement of the sidewalk throng. I let the crowd nudge me forward, brush past me, stroke me anonymously and urge me down a side street; the smell of jasmine and rice filling my nostrils; the shrill cry of hawkers and the cawing of seagulls overhead colluding to heighten my sense of disorientation. I looked up past the sharp edges of the buildings at the liquid blue sky and let the sun fizzle on my retina.

Temporarily blinded, my eyes watering, I collided with a woman running down the street. She knocked me sideways into a bunch of garbage cans at the edge of an alleyway. I scrambled to my feet and, groping my way along the walls, I retreated from the din of the market. When my vision cleared, I saw that I was at a dead end and that in front of me was a door, slightly ajar. A blue light seemed to beckon me inside. I entered a hallway and the door closed quietly behind me.

At the end of the corridor was a curtain of blue glass beads, from behind which quavered the stretched elastic tones of oriental music. I brushed the beads aside and stepped into a smoky, windowless room. It was in fact a *sushi* restaurant and was filled with Japanese businessmen in immaculate dark suits, with white starched shirts and silver ties that shimmered as if they were made of fish scales. They were seated in clusters, huddled around a wide *kaiten* that snaked its way slowly around the room. There was very little conversation, just the clicking of chopsticks like cockroaches scuttling across chrome.

Slowly the men turned to look at me standing there, my hair tousled, my lips slightly parted, my breath quickening at finding myself suddenly the centre of attention. The air was cooler than outside and I could feel goose bumps rising on the sensitive skin behind my knees and spreading up the length of my thighs, sending little shock waves of pleasure across my hips and buttocks.

When all the men had stopped eating and were looking at

me, I heard a harsh whisper like a command and a beautiful young man came over, gave me a quick bow and then, placing his hand gingerly on the small of my back, ushered me forward. There was more whispering and suddenly the room exploded like a stock market as the men began to argue between themselves. It was as if they were heckling over a slave. I looked at the man who was standing beside me and he seemed defiant. He was stomping his feet and yelling something in Japanese. Eventually the chef, an old man wearing a white *kapogi*, came out from behind a counter and raised his hands. The businessmen obediently surrendered to his seniority and the room fell silent again.

The old man bowed to me, then said, in clipped English for my benefit, "She too young. No touch. Only look."

There was some dissent among the men, which the old man quelled with another command barked in the staccato rhythm of his dialect. The young man with the delicate features then turned to me and holding up his hands in a gesture suggesting he wouldn't lay a hand on me, deftly removed my school tie and then my shirt without once touching my skin. There was a murmur of approval among the men. He handed my tie and shirt to another man who folded them neatly and placed them to one side.

All eyes were upon me and I felt an overpowering sexual fire light up inside my body. My groin began to ache as the blood rushed to my vulva. The old man clapped his hands and the nice young man sat down and another man came forward. He was shorter than the last one and plump. He was breathing rapidly and little beads of sweat stood out on his upper lip. He looked at me and I thought he was going to grab me. I wanted him to! Instead, he gave me a short, sharp bow, walked around behind me and unzipped my kilt. He didn't let it fall to the floor, but drew it down slowly and carefully. I could feel his breath on my legs as he held it in place while I lifted my feet and stepped out. He took my skirt back to his table and also folded it neatly. He never once touched me.

Another man came forward and, kneeling in front of me so close I could feel the static coming off the hairs on his head, he removed my shoes and socks. He too bowed quickly then sat down. I stood there exposed, with only the air to caress my naked skin. I squared my shoulders and stood there in my white cotton panties and white lace bra, a hundred eyes burning on my adolescent body, driving me crazy with desire. I wanted to be touched. I felt craven, as if there was a growing hollow in my body and I wanted it filled, but the men were quiet, admiring their captive; and like a deer caught in the headlights of a car, I couldn't move.

It was the old man who came forward again, this time with a large knife. The blade glistened and flashed blue in the light from the paper lanterns. He stood in front of me and, with several deft flicks of his knife, he denuded me. My underwear and bra fell to the floor in little pieces like cherry blossom. It took all the strength I had not to reach out and place the old man's hands on my breasts, but I didn't dare displease him. He clapped his hands again and barked an order and a large man came over and got down on all fours. He pointed to the conveyor belt. He wanted me to use the man's back as a step and get onto the *kaiten*, along with the *sushi*.

There was *sushi* all around me, *tekkamaki* rolls on ebony *saras*, and wooden *getas* with two or three pieces of *sashimi*; lying side by side like praying Muslims. I pushed the dishes aside but couldn't avoid squishing a few pieces underneath my body. When I had reclined on the conveyor belt and was slowly gliding like Cleopatra on her burnished throne around the room, the old man shouted, "He who overcome desire grow strong! Now eat!" and all the businessmen obediently resumed the clicking of chopsticks. With dizzying efficiency, they selected dish after dish from the moving conveyor belt and began lifting succulent bits of grey mullet dipped in soya sauce into their hungry mouths. The men seemed intent on ignoring me and the air was charged with disciplined restraint, with a desperate stifling of desire.

I rolled over onto my stomach and tried to catch their gaze.

I rolled onto my back. I lay on my side and smothered my breasts with the palms of my hands. Some of the men looked askance, some fidgeted, one began to choke on his *miso* soup. I saw the beautiful young man shoot a glance at the chef as if to challenge him, but most of them simply refused to look at me and stared at their plates. I was approaching the counter where the old man was preparing his perfectly wrought edible works of art and, as I passed him, I picked up a handful of *sushi* rolls wrapped in seaweed and placed them on my belly. I lay back and felt around me and picked up a cool slice of red snapper. I placed it on my nipple. I didn't dare move. I lay there, slowly drifting around the room and waited until, finally, with the speed of a frog's tongue, a pair of chopsticks darted out and the slippery fish was plucked, with a little pinch, from my nipple.

I gasped with pleasure and placed another piece of fish where the last one had been. It was immediately removed. I began frantically covering my body with more *sashimi*. I placed them on my breasts, my belly and my pubic mound. I rolled over and got on all fours and placed a piece of *sushi* snug between my buttocks. I felt the little flick of a pair of chopsticks before it was plucked out.

I rolled onto my back and lifted my legs until my knees were level with my chest and placed a piece of *tamango* in the silk cup of my vagina. I pulled my knees apart and it sank deeper into my cunt and I felt a faint suction when it was removed. I tucked a piece of *temaki* firmly between the swollen folds of my labia and suddenly all hell broke loose. Men started jumping up, knocking their chairs over. The beautiful young man scrambled onto the conveyor belt to my delight while the old man tried desperately to impose some order and control by yelling over and over again, "She too young. No touch! No touch!"

The young man got on all fours between my legs. I could feel his hot breath on my skin. His tie slipped out of his jacket and caressed my thighs. I panted breathlessly, "Touch me! Touch me!" and pulled my legs even further apart with my hands. A kind of suspended hush fell over the other men as they waited to see what would happen. I could hear the old man repeating his mantra in a whisper, "She too young. No touch. No touch." The young man bent ever so slowly forward and took the wet glistening morsel of *temaki* between his teeth and slowly sucked it out of my cunt. My hand immediately shot out and found another piece of *sushi*. In fact, the men were providing them now and there was no end to the raw fish that appeared at my fingertips.

Then another man jumped onto the conveyor belt. He too got on all fours and sucked a piece of *sushi* up, along and off the tip of my clitoris. "Touch me," I kept whimpering in unison with the old man's "No touch, no touch." The businessmen were hopping on and off the conveyor belt, tousling and wrestling each other to the floor. And amidst all of this commotion I lay there unviolable, untouched except for the sucking and popping out of bits of fish, until finally the men fell into a rhythm, lining up like schoolboys to feed off me. Kneeling before me as if before the Buddha to bend, kiss, bite and suck until I began to convulse with pleasure. So hot was my orgasm that when it had passed I lay shivering with exhaustion, while the men lay sprawled around the room, glutted and satiated by our mutual feast.

And then, as swiftly as I was swept up in their Epicurian ritual, I was lifted down, presented with my clothes and ushered back through the curtain of blue glass beads into a bright San Francisco alley.

Below the Beltway

Simon Sheppard

"Senator, Mr Sherwood of the Family First Foundation to see you."

"Thank you, Larry. That'll be all. Please close the door as you go."

"Thanks for meeting with me, Senator."

"No problem, no problem at all, Mr Sherwood. As you well know, the cause you represent is near and dear to my heart."

"Please, Senator, call me Rick."

"Well, then, Rick, I want to thank you folks for the generous support you've given my campaign. And I want to assure you that anything I can do for the cause, I will do. I surely will."

"Senator, in trying times like these, it's inspiring to know that men like yourself are not afraid to stand up and be counted."

"Rick, the values that you and I hold dear are the values that have made America great. You know, some of the people on the other side, heck, *all* of the people on the other side think of me as a hick, a born-again fuddy-duddy. Make no mistake – we are under attack. Our entire Christian way of life is in peril. That's why it's so encouraging to see men like you, young, vital, vigorous men, joining the cause. Are you married, Rick?"

"Pardon?"

"Married, Rick."

"Engaged, sir."

"Well, she's a lucky girl. Yes, indeed. You know, my boy, there's nothing like marriage, nothing in the world. My wife and I, though . . ."

"What, sir?"

"Oh, nothing, nothing. And please stop calling me 'sir'. I feel like *I* should be calling *you* 'sir'."

"I'm sorry, I don't understand."

"Well, now, a big, strapping, handsome fella like you . . . Look at the shoulders on you. You go to the gym, Rick?"

"A few times a week, sir, I mean, Senator."

"Excuse me while I take this call . . . Who's calling, Larry? Well, tell him not to get his Oval Office panties in a twist . . . No, no, just tell him I'll get back to him as soon as I can. And hold all my calls . . . I'm sorry, Rick. Where were we?"

"Talking about the gym."

"Big, strapping man like you. Look at you. Look at those feet. What size shoes you wear, Rick?"

"Thirteen, Senator."

"Thirteen, huh? I bet you'd like to have somebody at your feet, those great big feet of yours, wouldn't you? You ever think about it? That little gal of yours, for instance?"

"What?"

"At your feet, man. Kissing those feet. Looking up at you, worshipping you. Ever want that, Rick?"

"My feet, sir? No, can't say that I . . ."

"Feet are a funny thing, y'know. Most people don't think about them much. But there they are, working away for us. And if you treat 'em right, they can give you so much pleasure."

"Senator, about the legislation I came here to discuss . . ."

"Take your shoes off, Rick."

"Sorry, Senator?"

"I said take the shoes off those big feet of yours."

"I don't think . . ."

"Don't you worry about your legislation. Who the hell's gonna be on your side if not me? You want to get your way with Congress? Then take off your shoes."

"Listen, Senator . . ."

"Take your damn shoes off. Please. Please take your shoes off. Please, sir."

"You just want me to take off my shoes?"

"And put them on my desk. That's right. Put that one right up here. And now the other one. Hmm, nice shoes, soft leather. Feel nice. Smell nice, too. Don't smell too much, but I can tell you been in 'em."

"Senator, I think that's enough. If you don't mind . . ."

"Rick, do you know how powerful I am? You are not talking to some perverted peckerwood here. You are talking to a senator of the United States of America. A damned important senator. Now stretch out your feet, let me see 'em . . . Damn, they *are* big. Nice socks, too. Some guys go for those thin black socks, you can see the toes through 'em. Not me, always seemed kinda fruity to me. Right? Kinda fruity . . . Now, why don't you lean on back and relax? Just prop your feet on my desk. There now, doesn't that feel good, getting your feet massaged like this? Your fiancée doesn't do this for you?"

"No, she doesn't. But y'know, it does feel kind of . . . kind of pleasant."

"See, what did I tell you? Now then, those socks are nice and thick and masculine, but they do get in the way. Why don't I just peel them off? There we go. Hey, your feet are kind of sweaty. Nervous?"

"I was, but this feels okay. And I . . . guess there's no harm in it. As long as it doesn't go any further."

"No, my boy, no harm in it at all. Just my fingers kneading your big, manly foot, the arch, the instep. Going to work on your toes. Here, you comfortable like that? Why don't you just put your feet back on down? . . . That's it. Now I'll just get right down here and . . ."

"Hey, not your mouth. Your fingers are okay, but your mouth . . . that's faggotty stuff."

"So what does that make me?

"I . . . I don't know."

"It makes me a faggot, doesn't it? Say it. Say 'You faggot'."

"I can't."

"SAY IT, BOY."

"You, er, faggot."

"Louder."

"Faggot."

"Like you mean it. You want that bill to pass, doncha?"

"YOU FAGGOT! . . . That's . . ."

"Go on, Rick, go on . . ."

". . . that's right, you . . . suck on my toes. You're, er, gonna make me feel real good. Oh, yeah . . . real, real good. Oh, Christ! That's it, you just open wide and get them all in there."

"Mmmmf . . . Oh, Rick, sir, it tastes so fucking good, sir. Please, would you stand up so I can just kneel here at your feet and look up at you? Oh, God, thank you, sir. Here, sir, let me run my tongue between your beautiful toes . . . Sir?"

"What is it, er, footslave?"

"Sir, if I keep my face buried between your feet, may I run a hand up your powerful legs?"

"Yeah. Fuck, yeah, that's it."

"May I touch your big straight-man's cock, sir?"

"Yeah, you can touch it through my trousers, but . . . That's enough. Back off."

"Oh, thank you, sir. It's so big and hard."

"Enough."

"I'm sorry. I'm sorry, sir. Rick, sir . . ."

"Yeah?"

"Would you step on my face? Please?"

"Uh . . . Listen, Senator, I'm not sure . . ."

"I TOLD YOU TO STEP ON MY FACE, RICK."

"Like this?"

"Harder. Harder. Oh, yeah . . ."

"Stop playing with yourself, Senator."

"What?"

"Hand away from your dick."

"Sorry, sir. Y'know, Rick, I think you're getting the hang of this."

"Who cares what the fuck you think?"

"Oh, God, yes, yes . . ."

"Now then. Take your fucking clothes off. Now. And fold 'em up neatly . . . NEATLY, I said."

"Now what, sir?"

"Back on the floor. On all fours. No, no, lie on your back. You want my foot? Well, you got it. There. There's my big foot. On your face, down over your chest, your belly, that pathetic excuse for a hard-on."

"Oh yes, yes, grind it in."

"Did I tell you you could talk?"

"Sorry, sir."

"Now shut the fuck up. You only speak when spoken to, you sick fuck. Now, tell me about Larry."

"Larry? What do you want to know about him? He's my aide, college junior . . ."

"I mean, does he know what a fucking faggot you are? Does he know about your little games?"

"No, of course not."

"Okay, call him in here."

"What?"

"Are you fucking deaf? I said get up, get on the intercom, and tell him to get his ass in here. And do it NOW!"

"Larry, would you please come in here for a moment?"

"There now, that wasn't so hard, was it?"

"What do you want, Sena . . . Dang, what's going *on* here?"

"Your boss would like to worship your feet, Larry."

"Really?"

"You tell him, Senator Slaveboy."

"Please, Larry, please let me lick your feet."

"Jeez, REAALLLY??"

"Just do it, would ya? Take off your shoes and socks and let him do your feet. Actually, it'll feel pretty goddamn good.

Hey pigboy, you gonna do as good a job on him as you did on me?"

"Yes, SIR."

"You'd fucking better. Okay, Larry. Stand there while he gets on his back – lie back down, Senator Pigboy – and stick your toes in his mouth while I stand here between the senator's legs and grind my heel into his crotch like THIS."

"Oh, God, oh, God, oh, Jesus."

"Shut up and get your mouth back on Larry's toes."

"Mr Sherwood, are you sure this is okay? I mean . . ."

"He's your boss, isn't he? And he wants your feet, doesn't he? So give 'em to him. If you want to hold onto your job."

"But jeez, Mr. Sherwood, I'll bet that hurts."

"How about it, Senator Faggot? You had enough pain? Maybe I'll lighten up if you make me feel real, real good. I'll just drop my pants and squat over you – back off, Larry – squat over you like *this*, and now I wanna feel that born-again, right-wing tongue shoot straight up my ass. Oh, yeah, that's it, you just go ahead and clean me out real good. Hey, Larry, this feels really good. Look good to you? You want to take a turn? Oh, yeah, I can see by that big bulge in your pants that you do. Strip down and you can have a crack at him. No pun intended . . . Hey, Larry, nice legs."

"I'm on the track team, Mr Sherwood."

"And look at that dick. Meaty head, big old piss-slit. Pretty, huh, Senator?"

"Sure is."

"Sure is, SIR!"

"Sure is, sir."

"Yeah, that thing is drooling . . . And what a fuckin' nice hairy ass. Larry, you just go ahead and sit on his face."

"Like . . . like this?"

"Yeah, like THAT, college boy."

"Uh, Mr Sherwood, do you think you'd mind if I jerked off some?"

"Yeah, I think it would be all right if you played with that big, stiff pole of yours. Just don't shoot. Not yet. I bet your big, important dickhead of a boss would like that hot spunk for himself. Ain't that right, Senator?"

"Mmmmff."

"Hey, take your butt out of his mouth for a second, Larry. I can't understand a fucking word he's saying. Now then, you fucking piece of senatorial shit, repeat after me: 'I'm going to eat this boy like he was Jesus Himself'."

"Blasphemy, that's blasphemy . . . Ow!"

"Say it!"

"OWWW!"

"Say it, motherfucker, or you'll *really* hurt."

"I'm gonna eat him like he was . . ."

"You fucking pussy, say it."

". . . eat him like he was Jesus Himself."

"Okay, Larry boy, why don't you go ahead and fuck his face? You ever fuck a man's mouth before?"

"Never."

"Hear that, fuckpig? You make sure you do an extra-good job on this boy's virgin pecker. Larry, you got any complaints, you let me know and I'll give him a good kick in the ribs, like THIS."

"Unhh."

"Shut up and get sucking. That's it, you right-wing fuck-boy, tongue that piss-slit real good. Meanwhile, I got me a big ol' hard-on of my own, and it needs some attention. Hey, college boy, you ever touched somebody's dick before? Besides your own, I mean."

"Not since I was a kid. It's against my religion."

"Shit, it's against EVERYBODY'S religion."

"Yeah, but . . ."

"That boss of yours making your dick feel good? Yeah, he is. I can tell by that shit-eating grin of yours. Okay, now *you're* going to make *my* dick feel good. Spit in your hand and jack me off. I'm sure you know how to jack off."

"Uh, okay."

"That's it, Larry, grab it real good. Up toward the head.

Faster. Oh, yeah. You must've practised on yourself a lot. Right? Just you and yourself on those long, cold nights . . ."

"Mr Sherwood?"

"Yeah?"

"I wanna shoot. I really wanna shoot."

"Hang on a minute. Take your hand off my dick. Play with my balls."

"Like this?"

"Yeah, like that. And keep skullfucking him. Pump that big, hard thing of yours right down his throat. I'm gonna finish myself off, I'm gonna sperm off right . . . in . . . his . . . goddamn . . . fucking . . . face . . . ohh, YEAHHH!"

"Oh, dang, you came right on his mouth, right on my crotch. Oh jeez, I'm gonna come, I'M GONNA COME . . . ohhh . . . jeez."

"Fuck . . . oh, yeah . . . fuck, yeah. Looks like you had big fun, Larry. You still got a fucking boner. You liked fucking your boss's face on the goddamn floor of his goddamn office, huh?"

"Oh, jeez. Oh, jeez. What've I done?"

"Shot a load of come down the throat of a United States senator, near as I can tell. Hey, is there a towel around here, Senator? Senator?"

"You can . . . you can use my shirt."

"That'll do. As long as you wear it afterwards."

"Mr Sherwood?"

"Yeah, college boy?"

"Mr Sherwood, shouldn't the Senator be allowed to get his rocks off? I mean . . ."

"Nice how you look out for your boss's interests, Larry. Yeah, okay, I guess so. Senator, you got my permission. You may jack off that pathetic excuse for a penis. Just be quick about it."

"Unh. Unh. Unh. Unh. AAAAHH! Oh . . ."

"Dang, what a load!"

". . . God, oh, God, oh, God . . ."

"So how about it, you boys have fun? Larry?"

"I surely did."

". . . oh, God."

"Enough piety, Senator. You got what you wanted?"

"Yep."

"Y'know, I'll bet you usually do get what you want."

"Got that right, You surely did get that right. Hey, Larry, go get the man his money. How much was it?"

"Usually charge two-fifty for an outcall. But this required some extra acting. So make it an even four hundred."

"Well, now, that seems like a lot."

"But you've gotta admit I'm worth it. And you wouldn't want any undue publicity, now, would you?"

"I surely do hope that's a joke and not a threat. Because I am a very powerful man with very powerful friends, and shitheads who cross me wind up regretting their folly, more often than not."

"Split the difference. Three-seventy-five."

"Pay the man, Larry."

"Thank you kindly."

"You're not going to count it?"

"I believe I can trust you. If you can't trust the government, who can you trust, eh? So I'll just bid you gentlemen a good afternoon."

"Show the man out, Larry."

"Well, Senator, I must say that I enjoyed myself. That hustler fella sure seemed to know his business. You going to use him again?"

"Mebbe so, though things did get a bit edgy toward the end. Still, he did do a good job pretending to be you, Sherwood. He's not a half-bad actor. Comes to that, you did a good job playing my aide. I don't think he caught on."

"Enjoyed it, Senator, enjoyed it a lot. Though it was a tad strange, you calling him by my name. Say, is there really a Larry?"

"Um, he's a boy who worked for me a couple of years back."

"And did he . . ."

"Let's move on to more pressing matters, shall we?"

"Sure thing, Senator."

"Good, good. And?"

"You can rest assured, sir, that when I get back to Family First, I'll talk the board into shooting you another nice, fat campaign contribution."

"And it goes without saying, Sherwood . . ."

"Please, call me Rick."

". . . Rick, that the legislation you and your fellow patriots so ardently support will make its way swiftly through the legislative process."

"Veto?"

"He wouldn't dare. Wouldn't dare."

"Well, thanks again, Senator."

"My boy, next time you're in town, let's do it again."

"Mighty, uh, generous of you."

"Not at all, not at all. It is, after all, the least I can do to preserve the values that made this country what it is today."

Subculture

Sarah Veitch

The story so far:
Lisa has travelled to Malta to live and work at Vitality, a prestigious health clinic – but when she arrives there she finds that the owner, Dr Michael Landers, physically disciplines his staff. Now she's made a work-related error and is trying to talk her way out of being soundly spanked . . .

Michael blinked twice, then he smiled lazily down at her: "It's no secret that I enjoy roasting a womanly bottom. All of the staff at Vitality have been recruited because of their sexual submissiveness." He waved a hand in the direction of the window which led to the gardens and the stables. "I've got a veritable sub-culture here."

"But I'm not like that." Lisa made herself look at him square on, pushed her shoulders back in what she hoped was a dominant gesture.

"Oh, but you are. I knew that you had a subservient side the moment I met you," Dr Landers said. He clapped his right hand softly down on his left palm three times with hellish slow precision. "I bet you used to fantasize about being spanked."

Damn him again – was the bastard psychic, or did he use this line with every new member of staff? Lisa made a mental note to talk to Carmen, Marie-Rose and Jamilla about the doctor's conversational gambits.

"I might have done," she said cagily, trying to ignore the

tingle which spread through her groin following his actions and words.

"Don't tell me – and then you forced your desires back because you found out they weren't politically correct," Michael Landers continued. He was right again. Lisa fingered the legs of her olive green shorts. She wished that she was wearing more dignified clothes, that she could find the words and expressions to satisfactorily end this talk.

"I'm a businesswoman now. I believe in men and women being equal," she said.

Michael Landers smiled. "So do I – equal but different." He raised his eyes upwards, obviously searching for the right phrases and emphasis. "When a woman agrees to being punished by me, she momentarily hands me her power. She has to be powerful in the first place or she'd have nothing to give."

"But Jamilla's a servant, so . . ."

"A servant who knows what she wants and how to get it," the doctor answered simply. He paused. "I assume you watched her being caned through a window or doorway. After the caning, did you stay?"

"I . . . yes." Lisa felt caught out, at a loss again.

"Then you'll know she cried out louder and longer in orgasm than she did when she submitted to her thrashing," the English doctor said.

Lisa took a deep breath: "But that doesn't . . . I mean, she still wriggled and begged for mercy when the rod fell over her bare bottom."

The doctor nodded: "Of course she did. It hurt like hell, and she felt ashamed. I would, too, if I was bent over a desk and soundly beaten. Deep down, though, she's submissive, so she got off on it none the less."

He paused, then leaned forwards again. "Did it excite you to watch?"

"No, I thought it was an assault," Lisa lied, remembering the traitorous rush of pleasure to her pubis.

"You'd react by calling the police if it really was an

assault," Dr Landers said. He smiled over at her. "You're a woman of honour and of courage. You wouldn't have stood by if you really believed that domestic violence was taking place."

"So I'm honourable yet you still want to spank me?" Lisa muttered.

"Very hard indeed."

Worse and worse. The twenty-eight-year-old cleared her suddenly tight, clogged throat: "And if I don't agree?"

"Don't agree to live by your employer's rules whilst you have a live-in job?" The suited surgeon shook his head. "In that case I'll put you on the next plane back to England and we'll both forget that this sad little interlude ever took place."

Lisa looked round the clean, wholesome and hope-bringing medical room. Then she walked over to the window and stared down at the Cactus Garden with its yellow rock backdrop.

"I don't want to leave Malta," she wailed. She stiffened as she heard the man approach, felt his strong arms on her shoulders.

"Then come over to the couch now and accept your first ever spanking," he said.

How much could a palm-slap hurt? She'd just force her mind to think of other things. Feeling strangely nerveless and ashamed and just a tiny bit curious, Lisa allowed her employer to guide her towards the couch.

"Usually I stretch a naughty girl out so that her head hangs down on one side of my knees and her legs are stretched out on the other side," he said conversationally. "Point is, when the legs are stretched out the thrashing hurts more." He looked thoughtfully up at her as he settled himself on the couch, his feet firmly on the carpet, legs parted. "But as you're new to being spanked I'll let you put your belly across my lap and rest your weight along the couch." She sensed him smile. "Now, isn't that kind of me? And I'll stop and start to let you get used to the heat."

It was to be a long chastisement, then. Lisa stood where he'd guided her. Nibbled her lip as he patted his lap.

"I'll add on an extra punishment if you don't bend over my knee of your own volition," he warned, smoothing his cream suit trousers.

The twenty-eight-year-old considered his words.

"Make me if you can," she said. She braced her sandals firmly against the carpet. Put her hands behind her back. Dipped her head down like a see-nothing-so-fear-nothing ostrich. Squealed with surprise as he grabbed her around the waist and positioned her over his lap and across the examination couch in a virtually seamless move. But surprise wasn't all that she felt – the sudden rush of blood to her clitoris unnerved her, and she pushed her slim thighs together and moaned.

"Oh, angel, is that pussy you're so intent on keeping hidden feeling horny already?" Michael Landers murmured. "Will that clit that's been wearing all these 'Keep Off' signs want to come?"

"Only with Reece. You said you wouldn't touch me sexually unless I begged you to," Lisa countered, raising her head from the surgical couch and twisting it back.

"And I'll stand by my word," Michael Landers said. His prick seemed to be standing to attention, none the less: she could feel the head of it pushing into her shorts-clad belly. Still, he couldn't help his sexual cravings just as she couldn't control hers. What they could control, Lisa reminded herself, was whether or not they gave in to them – and she couldn't give in as she was engaged to Reece.

Waiting for the first spank was hellish. It seemed to take an age. Lisa closed her eyes and waited for the palm to fall. Waited. Waited. Waited.

"Why haven't you started yet, you bastard?" she muttered eventually.

"Are you so keen to feel my palm?" The voice was low, amused. "You're not going anywhere for a long time so I'm just contemplating your naughty bottom. Just examining the shape of an error-making arse."

"Thought you'd have seen hundreds by now," Lisa spat out into the medical couch, feeling a little of her spirit reassert itself.

"But each girl and her cheeks is substantially different," her employer replied. He patted and palpated her shorts-hugged orbs. "Some backsides know that they've done wrong from the start. They jerk and writhe and . . . well, sometimes the owner tries to wriggle away before I raise the hardwood paddle. Whereas a bum like yours is a touch arrogant, almost relaxed."

Lisa certainly didn't feel relaxed. Her heartbeat was pounding its tattoo through her chest. Her braless breasts were rising and falling within the loose confines of her lemon polo-shirt and new lines of electricity were snaking their way towards her crotch.

Then Michael Landers raised his palm – and she forgot all about the crotch-based electricity. Felt her attention shift to her bum and analyze the new sensations that were happening there. Mm, that spank had been surprisingly light, surprisingly enjoyable. Maybe this chastisement wasn't going to be so bad after all. Her new boss spanked on and on and on. His palm flattened first one small cheek then the other, bringing new stimulus to the hidden curves beneath the garments. He said nothing as he punished, his entire focus obviously on her clothed backside.

After an indefinite duration the heat began to build substantially in Lisa's rear. "Ouch," she muttered, and "That was a hard one!" and "Oh! Aaah!"

"Just another twenty, I think," the doctor said. "Then we'll let you stop and regain your composure."

"What makes you think I've lost it?" Lisa muttered darkly, then yelped as he doled out six much harder spanks. He'd been holding back so far, then – she hated to envisage the force of a no-holds-barred spanking. She shut her eyes tightly and concentrated on keeping quiet as he pained her with the other fourteen smacks.

"Right, that's the warm-up taken care of," he said, sounding pleased with himself. She felt his palm tracing the full swell of her hips, "It renders the flesh more supple, prepares it for its proper punishment."

"You mean there's more?" Lisa managed, shocked to hear her own voice reduced to a breathless squeak. She searched for her businesslike tone, but found it sadly lacking. There was no hiding behind a power suit or a briefcase here.

"Of course there's more. You can't endanger life and not expect a serious reprimand," her employer retorted. "A bum that's put others at risk of fever deserves to experience a similar prolonged temperature itself."

"But it already feels quite sore, sir." Lisa forced out the hateful words to get herself off the hook. Her clitoris twitched slightly.

"Don't forget that it's your first spanking, so you've no yardstick to compare it with," Dr Landers said.

He continued to lightly stroke her curves. Lisa felt the heaviness increase in her labial region. Forced the whimpers of pleasure back, damned if she'd give him the satisfaction of knowing he was turning her on.

"Right, I think you've recovered," the thirty-something said a few moments later. "You're ready to go on to Phase Two."

"Phase Two?" Lisa repeated. It sounded like the title of a bad science fiction film.

"Mmm, Phase Two is where I pull down your shorts and spank you over your pants. You are wearing panties, I take it?"

"I am, but . . ." Stunned, Lisa tried to remember which pair of briefs she'd put on.

She put her palms back to her cheeks to hold the olive cotton in place. "You can't take down my shorts, you bastard."

"Believe me, my dear, I can."

"But isn't that getting . . . rather sexual?"

"As I said before, I won't fuck you unless you plead for it," Michael Landers said.

"You'll wait for the rest of your life, then, mate," Lisa replied, enraged at his conceit and arrogance. She mentally examined her plight some more. If she let him strip off her clothes he'd presumably get even more aroused and frustrated – and she'd let him stay that way.

"Go on, then," she said, taking her hands away. "You can always wank in the toilets afterwards," she added crudely.

"Oh, I think I can find someone to take care of me," Michael Landers said.

He probably could. Lisa felt a new unexpected pull of disappointment in her chest. Somehow she hated the thought of him being pleasured by another woman. Sensed that if she chose to she could make him spasm into rapture and groan with more ecstasy than he'd previously felt.

But she was the one to groan softly with shame as he removed her olive green shorts. The awareness of him contemplating her bum in the cheek-hugging peach pants was just too degrading.

"Like what you see, do you?" she taunted.

"Well, I'll certainly enjoy spanking it," Michael Landers said.

Lisa buried her face in the surgical couch as best she could. She wished she could put a blanket over her head and just go to sleep till this humbling ordeal was over. Unfortunately her hot flesh was very much awake.

"I can feel the heat of your arse through your pants," her new employer said conversationally.

"Congratulations. Means your faculties are in working order," Lisa snapped.

"For a girl who's bent over my knee," the doctor continued, "you're mighty uppity."

"That's medical speak, is it?" the twenty-eight-year-old taunted, determined that she wouldn't be bested by this supercilious man.

"No, that's straight talking, which is what a naughty bum deserves," the former surgeon said.

Lisa flushed and held her breath as he fondled that self-same bum. The peach panties covered her cheeks from thigh to waist, would hopefully afford her poor bottom some protection. If nothing else it meant he couldn't stare down at the folds of her labia or her dark dividing crack. He could doubtless see their shape, though, for the knickers were very close-fitting. And she could tell that the crotch was already damp.

The young woman trembled as he flexed his fingers. "Well, I can't sit around chatting all day," he continued. "There's a girl here that needs a damned good thrashing. And my palm is itching to oblige." He roasted his right hand against her waiting left cheek. Then he spanked the neighbouring orb. Found a slow assured rhythm. Chastened the lower and upper globes. He saved his hardest spanks for the centre of her cheeks where the flesh was as its fullest. Soon her small spheres started to glow. I can take it, Lisa told herself, pushing her belly forwards in a vain effort to avoid the worst of each slap, then arching her body up again before the next stinging encounter. I won't give him the satisfaction of knowing that I feel anything, she thought stubbornly.

Spank followed spank followed spank. "How many more?" she muttered at last.

"How many more do you deserve for endangering the public?" Michael asked softly.

If she said too few he'd accuse her of being self-lenient. The herbalist searched for a suitable figure. Finally she muttered: "Ten?"

"Ten it is." Lisa relaxed across his knees, relieved that her chastisement was almost over. "Ten on the bare, my dear," Michael said.

"But you're a man and . . ." Lisa tried to scramble from his lap but his firm hands held her easily in situ.

"I could call in one of my female employees to correct you, if you'd prefer that?" he enquired.

"Christ, no, I . . ." She thought of how much more humiliating it would be for the likes of Carmen to chastise her. "All right, you bastard – just do it," she said resignedly.

"And another six spanks for calling your employer a bastard," Michael Landers said. He squeezed her flesh through the warmed cotton. "Trust me, my dear, you're getting off lightly. I'd have used my belt on Marie-Rose or the others if they came out with insults like that."

His belt was a matt black leather affair – Lisa's eyes had been drawn to it earlier. She shivered and swallowed hard: "How do they bear . . .?"

"They can bear it because I've built them up gradually over many months." There was an absolute certainty in his tone, "When they've been bad girls I slowly take them to their limits." She heard the slight smile enter his voice. "Then I take them just a little bit beyond."

"I think I've reached my limit," Lisa muttered, trying to stave off the moment when he pulled down her panties.

"Don't ever cry wolf, dear – it just earns you extra chastisement," her tormentor said.

She felt his fingers on the waistband of her briefs. "Right, let's see how this wicked bottom is getting on underneath the cotton." She winced as her knickers were dragged down and left just below her naked thighs. Winced with shame as he laid both palms over her flesh as if taking her temperature. "Lift your head, Lisa," Michael Landers said, "and look at the mirror on the ceiling. Enjoy the glow of your recalcitrant rump."

He had to be joking. He couldn't have . . . Lisa looked up and saw her own face and her back and her scarlet bottom reflected back at her from the ceiling-based looking-glass. "Pervert," she muttered, glancing quickly away.

"The word would be *voyeur* – and isn't everyone, these days?" He shrugged both his shoulders, keeping both hands on her back. "I actually installed this mirror for practical reasons. It reassures my patients by letting them see exactly what I'm doing to them during an intimate exam."

"And the band played believe it if you like," Lisa murmured. On one level she felt quite pleased with herself – she was still showing him that she wasn't at all submissive. She wasn't saying the shameful things which poor Jamilla had said. There again, Jamilla's bum had trembled beneath the swishing force of the merciless cane, whereas she, Lisa, was just getting a hand spanking. Though some of those spanks had almost made her yelp.

"Such bold little globes," Michael murmured. "I'll have to double the number of spanks they receive because you're so insolent. I'm usually more lenient with a new girl but still have to teach her manners and respect."

"If this is you being lenient, I'd hate to see you on a bad day," Lisa countered, wriggling shamefacedly over his lap.

As if in answer, Michael renewed the spanking with greater zeal. God, how she wished she had her panties back on to protect her! Lisa winced as the man toasted her unclothed flesh. Being spanked on the bare was a whole new experience – the cotton had obviously diffused the earlier slapping. Now his palm made stinging contact with a small section of helpless nude flesh. Dr Landers spanked her centre swell, he spanked to the sides, he spanked below so that his fingers strayed near her quivering thigh tops. His hand rose and fell till every centimetre of her hemispheres was writhingly aflame.

"Aaah!" At last Lisa put her hands back, fingers spread over the scalding contours. She twisted her head back, "I can't take much more, honest, sir."

"Then let's stop for a little rest and a chat," Michael said. Lisa kept her hands protectively over her curves, but she put her face down upon the couch again. "Do you agree that you were neglectful?" Michael asked.

"Yes, sir." She didn't want to fight with him any more, just needed to go to her room and touch her clit.

"And you agree that this thrashing has made you wet?"

"It hasn't. I . . .." She fought to find the words which would save her dignity. "You promised no sexual contact, so you're not allowed to check," she added, biting her lip.

"And I'll stand by my word," the doctor said steadily,

"But if you're not telling the truth you'll have to be chastened further on the bare."

"I'm truthful," Lisa lied, feeling another fervent rush of delight to her Mount of Venus.

"Then stand up with your legs apart and show me that you're dry as a desert," the doctor said.

"And if I don't, you'll . . .?" She daren't even think about his reaction.

"I'll continue spanking you till you do. That's only fair." He stroked her bare bum. "You have to obey my house rules, Miss Steen. After all, I'm obeying yours by not touching you sexually."

"Right, let's get this over with," Lisa said. She put her palms flat on the couch and slowly hoisted herself back on to her knees. She refused to look at him. Spent a moment reorientating herself before swinging her feet around and onto the ground. Her pubis felt heavy with stimulus, yet surely her desire wasn't visible to the casual eye?

"Wider, sweetheart," Michael said with a smile. Lisa moved her thighs further apart, further, further. Felt the wetness start to slick from her body and looked down to see the long gelatinous threads. "The proof of the pudding is in the eating," the doctor continued. His words made her think of his tongue trailing wild sparks across her clit and through the lush folds of her labia. He'd lick gently down each petal then back up again until . . . "Come on, angel, over my lap for a final twenty," the surgeon said softly. "Accept a sound thrashing for telling a lie."

Lisa toed the ground: "And after that my punishment will really be over?"

"Providing you don't commit further acts of negligence, then yes."

Going over his knee again took almost all the courage she possessed. He knew she was sexually on fire, damn it. He might try to touch her clit – and if he did she'd be lost. Suddenly Lisa wanted him to caress that peaking bud, to give it the release it so obviously needed. She'd come so quickly.

"Was I right or was I right?" Michael Landers murmured, starting to stroke her sore cheeks as she lay over his knee. Lisa quivered at the indignity. Suddenly she hated him all over again.

"Right about what?" she countered coolly.

"I was correct in assuming that though your arse hates being reddened your pussy gets off on it," her employer said.

"That's what you think. I was fantasizing about Reece before . . . before you laid a finger on me," Lisa lied.

"Before I laid a palm on your bare arse, you mean?"

He seemed determined to humiliate her. The twenty-eight-year-old writhed with sexual shame. Her clitoral hood rubbed against his thigh and sensation almost overwhelmed her. Jesus, she was so near . . . "Twenty spanks on an already sore rump for not being honest," Michael Landers said as if pronouncing a legal sentence. His right arm came down across her shadowy buttock crease.

The slap seemed to ricochet through her helpless globes to her equally immobile clitoris. Lisa moaned with increasing lust. She pushed down hard against his thighs again and felt her body start to move towards the ultimate pleasure. Bucked forwards against his trouser leg as he dished out each echoing whack. Then she flattened her body out for a second, only to push forwards strongly again.

". . . five, six, seven," Michael said out loud as he added each hard bum-spank. "That's it, sweetheart, you just rub against my leg like a little animal, like a dog frigging a lamp post when it's in heat." Lisa winced at his words but their taunting level took her strangely closer to Eden. He spanked, she writhed, she pushed against his suited leg and groaned.

Somewhere between spank fifteen and sixteen she felt the beloved signal go off in her groin, signalling climax. Shoved the entire lower half of her body against him, jerking her hips forwards with tiny hard movements to keep the stimulus sending the pleasure through. Never before had she felt such a strong, focused orgasm. Never before with her own fingers or with her ex-husband or with Reece. "Uh," she kept muttering, her clenched teeth unable to hold back the grunts of increasing rapture, "Uh, Uh, Uuuuuh, Uuuuuuh, Uuuuuuuuuh!"

For long moments after the last frissons had died away, she lay semi-naked over Michael's lap. She wished that he'd stroke her hair or kiss her neck or tell her she was wonderful. She looked up at him when he did none of those expected things. He was smiling enigmatically down at her, his fingers still circling her slender waist . . .

Threesome

Daniel James Cabrillo

1 Two Obsessions

1

You walk across the golf course in your short denim sundress, carrying your sandals in your hand. The kids run ahead, I lag far behind, taking pictures of you and them and the palm trees swaying in the warm, late-afternoon breeze, the surf banging against the rocky shore in the background, everything tinted gold by the sun low in the sky.

A man on a golf cart drives towards you. Because you're looking at the kids, he studies you more frankly than he could if you were aware of him. He likes the way you move, the tilt of your head, your barefooted stride on the moist green grass. He likes your voice when he hears you call the kids. He likes your body. Your sundress is his co-conspirator and teaser, revealing, concealing, hinting: the bib stretches across your breasts, hugs them together, exposes their round white tops and your bare shoulders; the denim stretches across your flat stomach and squeezes your buttocks, defining each as you walk; the hem sits high on your thighs, shows the good shape of your athletic legs; he'd like to see what happens where your thighs meet.

He'd like to fuck you.

As he guides his cart close to you, you turn and see him and smile. He smiles back. To you the smile is pleasant and polite, the greeting of strangers in a good mood at a Hawaiian resort, nothing more. To him it is much more; it is contact, and contact changes thought into feeling. Looking at you had been a critical function, an evaluation. When you made contact the centre of his appreciation dropped from his brain to his scrotum.

He wants to fuck you.

He passes, looks back over his shoulder for a last glance, turns around to look where he's driving – and sees me. Our eyes meet: he knows immediately that he is caught.

I know what he's thinking, what he's feeling.

He wants to fuck my wife; I know it; he knows I know it.

I nod at him, he nods back, guests at a resort. I let him off the hook.

But in the split second after eye-contact and before the smiles I believe I perceive – what? Embarrassment? Yes, of course. You get caught coveting somebody's wife, you're going to be embarrassed. Yet I think I see more. What? Devastation? Desperation? No, those are too strong. Disappointment? Definitely. Embarrassment and disappointment.

He moves on.

The sun sets. We go to dinner. Halfway through our meal the man comes into the restaurant with his wife and kid and another couple. His impulse to look at you is irresistible – he even chooses his seat to have a clear line of vision – but my presence disorients: he can't look at you without checking to see if I'm watching him watch you. I inhibit his freedom to openly covet, and it upsets him. At one point I catch him looking not our way but down into his plate, mouth set, almost angry.

It begins to come clear to me. There's more to this than casual lust for a sexy woman.

The two women at his table get up to go to the buffet. The other man glances at our table, does a little double-take when he sees me, says something concise and cryptic to his friend. I'd bet anything that what he said was something like: Oops.

So the man was that interested in you. Interested enough to tell his friend, or interested enough so that his friend noticed he was interested. They'd talked about it, about you . . . that single mom over there, the little number with the hot little body. I flash back to an incident – not even an incident, a passing perception – that occurred last night.

You and the kids had picked me up at the airport in the evening. Back at the hotel, the kids went to their *hale*, we to ours and we made love. Afterwards I went into the dark sitting room to get my bag, which I hadn't unpacked. I glanced outside for a look at the tropical night under the waxing, nearly full moon and saw a figure standing in the dark, looking towards our *hale*. I'd thought nothing of it: for all I knew he could have been meditating, or sneaking a smoke.

Now I wonder if the man who wants to fuck you had been the figure in the night shadows, looking for you, perhaps hoping you'd step out for a breath of air or an evening walk.

Now I know why my appearance has upset him.

He had big plans.

You never see these things. You should: you'd like them.

He's been looking at you since you or he first arrived earlier in the week. He saw a woman alone with three kids at a Hawaiian resort, assumed – not unreasonably these days – that you were a single mother. You weren't cruising for men – this isn't a place for that – but that only made you more attractive. And after all these days alone with our kids, you were probably getting horny . . .

Probably he started thinking about ways to meet you, get to know you, get away from his wife, seduce you. As the days went by, what started as admiration evolved, became desire, then fantasy.

I'd like to fuck her became I *want* to fuck her.

I want to fuck her became I *need* to fuck her.

I need to fuck her became I *am going* to fuck her.

Then I showed up.

Poor guy. He has only one place to go from here:

I *must* fuck her.

Obsession.

2

You used to want to be invisible. You were quiet and meek and you dressed not to be noticed. You cultivated nondescript. You also were a great piece of ass. In bed you were extremely descript: distinctive, creative, aggressive, daring, full of fire. It took me a while to learn that your sexual self was closer to your real self than your shy public self.

In other words, the real you was the distinctive, fiery you I loved to fuck. As I gradually began to understand this, I gradually fell in love with you.

Through the years you've let the sexuality come forwards. You're not meek, you're not invisible, you dress great, you know you're sexy. You know it, but do you feel it? I'm not sure you do. I tell you often enough, but I'm your husband.

The fact is that I'm as obsessed by you as the man in the golf cart, but it doesn't count. Somebody who loves you can't convince you that you're as sensual as he thinks you are. What does he know? He loves you.

I want you to feel it, though.

You deserve to feel it.

I want you to believe it.

3

At night, after the kids go to sleep, we go down to the beach, find a nice, secluded spot so we can take some pictures. I bring the Hasselblad, so you know I mean business. I put the Polaroid back on the camera to take proofs first.

I ask you to take your sundress off and I chronicle every button unbuttoned, the naked revelation of all your parts: one breast, the other, the sweet, rounded belly, your buttocks, the hairy mound in the centre of your body. One picture in particular moves me. You unbutton all the buttons down to the last, at crotch-level. One breast is fully exposed, half the other, and your belly. You hitch the dress to lift it up and off; I snap the picture just as the dress is high enough to expose the underside of your buttocks and the bottom of your pubic thatch. There's a nice expression on your face, not seductive but provocative: you're looking forward to getting the dress off. You're looking forward to what we'll do when it's off.

I, too, am looking forward to what we'll do when the dress is off.

Horny and hurried, I take fewer pictures than I'd planned. You redress; I gather up my camera gear and proofs, and we walk back to our *hale* to take your dress off yet again.

On the way we pass the ground-level *hale* of the man and his wife and kid, and I drop the proofs. I glimpse the man inside, watching as we bend down to pick them up. I miss one of the proofs. It's the dress-hitching picture I just described. It stays on the ground as we continue on.

I know he will find it.

4

I give you the news: he wants to fuck you.

We're enjoying a beach near the hotel; the man and his wife and kid and friends are just arriving.

Who? you ask. I point him out.

I have a feeling he was very choosy about which beach to come to this morning, I say. I bet they drove from one beach to the next, and he found fault with each until they came here. What he found here was you.

You laugh.

I'm not kidding, I say; I saw it on the golf course and in the restaurant. I know the look.

You study him and his entourage.

His wife is cute, you say.

What's that got to do with it? I ask. *My* wife is cute; that doesn't mean I would like to fuck his.

You lean up, shade your eyes, study him. Now that I've pointed out his interest, you can't help but notice how often he looks your way.

He's not my type, you say.

That's true: he's good-looking in an Izod shirt way, tall, slim, with a tennis player's body. But, your type or not, he's attractive, and you're flattered.

I leave you and go snorkelling, knowing that my absence will make him bolder. He'll look at you more, and now you'll be more aware of it. He may even try to make contact. From the reefs I see him playing frisbee with his kid. You're lying prone, the top of your swimsuit untied and your breasts mashed against the beachtowel. I call every play: his moving closer to you; his one or two near misses; his jackpot – the runaway frisbee skips across the sand and comes to a stop a foot away from you. He crosses to it, kneels to retrieve it, apologizes. I can see you telling him it's no problem; he remains kneeling, chats a little with you. As you roll over and sit up, you almost expose your breasts, but cover them with the swimsuit top in the nick of time.

Perfect!

Our kids close in, wanting you to settle a dispute, ending the man's stolen moment with you. That's okay, too.

When I return I lie beside you, read my book, occasionally and conspicuously whisper in your ear, telling you what the man would like to do to you now . . . and now . . . and now. You giggle a lot.

For his benefit, of course.

A lot of this is for his benefit. Maybe all.

5

It's warmer tonight and the moon is one night short of full. You and I return to the secluded beach where I took pictures last night – this time without the camera. We lie down in the soft sand, smooch a little, take some clothing off, feel around each other to make sure everything we love is still intact.

Before long you get to your knees and recreate one of our beach interludes of thirteen years ago.

Back then, you were the best cocksucker I'd ever known or dreamed existed. Now you're ten times better. Impossible, but true.

After a while, I want a turn, so I scamper away, get my face between your legs, and feast. We're very romantic tonight, I notice – passionate but slow, gentle, delicate. Is it the moon? The warm breezes? The tropical setting? Or is it the knowledge that our lovemaking, which is so much a part of us and comes so easily to us, is something denied to yet desperately desired by someone else?

All of the above.

I eat until you begin your climb; you reach for my arms, draw me up, take hold of my cock and guide it to the niche. We fuck a slow, clingy fuck, but your climb has started and won't stop. I try to change pace, to slow down, but you won't let me, you don't want this one to last, you want to come and you want me to come while you're still coming, and so you clasp me to you, and the clingy walls of your inner cunt grab at my shaft like a thousand little suction cups, and, as you wish, I come. With my first shot your orgasm begins and keeps coming like currents in a choppy sea.

We hold each other, calm down, cool down, relax. It is very warm and very quiet.

I am aware of another presence. I open my eyes and look up toward a cluster of rocks and foliage not far away. He stands very still. Can he tell that I am looking at him? He probably can't, but even if he could he would not flee.

What he has seen is what he has been dreaming about. You make love the way he knew you would, with your whole body, with all your will, with your entire consciousness.

He would do anything, give anything, to be with you as I have just been.

We close our eyes and cling together. I hear him walking away.

6

Christmas Eve Day. I spoke to him. His obsession made him vulnerable, and I exploited his vulnerability. Relentlessly.

I believe that at one point it crossed his mind that I was a homosexual, using you as my beard. And the remarkable thing about that was, if I had been a homosexual, I'm sure that this straight, handsome, intelligent man – this Flyover – would have done whatever I asked – even a homosexual act – if it meant getting to you.

Someday I'll tell you how I made it happen. Some aspects were amusing. But now it doesn't matter how I made it happen.

I made it happen because I want it to happen for you. I want you to feel in yourself what you project to others. I want you to know what power you have, to feel that power, to appreciate it and love having it, and love yourself as I love you.

7

Christmas night. A bath. I help you bathe, spreading suds all over, rinsing you with my hands and warm water. I help you from the tub, pat-dry you with a towel, lead you to the sitting room, lay you down onto a comforter on the floor, give you a slow, gentle massage.

Afterwards I help you into the negligee I bought you in the hotel shop – not as trashy as I'd like but as provocative as they had, and in any case you look sexy in it. You model it for me, sit in the chair, take the glass of champagne I pour for you.

I leave you alone while I go into the bedroom and get into my robe. On my way back there's a soft knock at the door. I cross to the door, open it.

The man steps inside with his wife.

Her expression is cold, set, but her eyes are slightly swollen, her cheeks a little streaked. Not long before, we can tell, she was crying. Now there's hardness in her face.

She is going to do what he wants her to do. (I wonder why. Because he begged? Because he bullied her? Or was there something he had to get even with her for – an affair, perhaps – and this was his chance? No way of knowing.)

I look at you. Your expression is not a lot more revealing than hers, except that yours projects no hostility. You like the way he looks at you, the way he crosses to you so slowly, never taking his eyes off you. He looks like a knight who's just found the holy grail. I'd thought he'd be more desperate-looking than this, maybe a little pitiful in his desperation, but, to his credit, his bearing, while nearly worshipful, is dignified, confident. He stands above you, looking down, extends his hands. You take them and stand up, look at me.

I lead the wife to the sofa. She won't let me take her arm but goes where I show her. I offer her champagne. She refuses. I put the glass on the table next to the sofa.

You won't have to do anything, I tell her. Just watch.

What? she asks, surprised.

It was just my way, I explain, of making sure he wants her enough. My wife for his.

Oh, he wants her enough, she says.

I know, I say. But . . . this is for her, not me. For them. You and I will just watch.

The wife nods, sits, still livid, but she reaches for, takes the glass of champagne. In spite of her anger, what I have just told her makes her feel better.

After we sit, you return your attention to the man. You offer him your glass of champagne. He drinks what's left, puts the glass down, takes you in his arms, kisses you. It is strange for you at first, I can tell: it has been a long time since you've been kissed so deeply and romantically by another man, and it catches you off guard, unsure. But there is so much passion in the kiss, so much depth of feeling, that you can't help but respond. Your arms slide around him, your hand on the back of his neck, and you kiss him with as much fervour as he kisses you.

When the kiss ends he steps back, takes your hands in his.

You glance at the bathroom door, and he gets the message. He lets go of your hands, crosses to the bathroom. While he's inside you refill your glass of champagne, refill the wife's, smile at her. She does not smile back, but she doesn't glare at you, either. She lowers her eyes.

Her husband is in the bathroom for a minute, then he comes back into the sitting room, wearing a hotel robe. He crosses to you, takes another taste of your champagne. Then he unties the tie at the neck of your peignoir, takes it off, leaving you in a small nightie. He caresses your arms with his fingertips, your shoulders, your neck. He kisses you again. He lowers a shoulder strap, puts his hand inside, takes hold of a breast. He holds it, feels its heft and shape, then releases it, removes his hand to slide the strap down your arm, turn back the fabric, expose your breast. He looks at it, touches the nipple with his fingertip, then – quickly but not hurriedly – he slips off the other strap, lets the nightie drop to the floor a puddle at your feet. He steps back, looks at you naked.

You untie his robe; it, too, drops to the floor.

He takes you in his arms and kisses you, feels your naked body against his. His hands caress your back and buttocks, yours caress his, and kiss follows kiss as the two of you drop down to your knees, then to the floor. He kisses your mouth and neck, your tits, one, then the other; when his tongue finds your nipple his hand settles on your pussy. His fingers play with the lips until they give way, and as his fingers slide between them your hand wraps around his hard cock and slides gently up and down.

Foreplay is brief: he is hard, you are wet. He climbs over you, kisses your mouth and breasts. His torso raised on his hands and stiffened arms, he lowers his middle – you lift your hips and turn your cunt upwards to meet him – and rests his shaft lengthwise along your pussy-lips. He moves slowly, remaining outside, the underside of his shaft sliding in your channel. You caress his buttocks with little grabby pinches, match his movements with hiprolls. Any second now: you will open and he will enter.

And here, I admit, I begin to have a problem. Yes, I want this man to fuck you. Yes, I all but planned it. Yes, I want you to experience this display of your own sexual power. Yes, I want to watch it all. But what I am watching is not happening exactly as I had expected it would. I had expected to see an obsessed man achieving his longed-for goal with a virtual seizure of your body, followed by an eruption of sexual energy and an ecstatic explosion. That's certainly how I would have reacted.

The man who is about to fuck you, however, does not react as I would. Confronted with imminent realization of the holy grail, he becomes patient, deliberate. A serenity comes over him. He is determined to savour the experience. He wants you to feel it as intensely as he feels it.

And, for a moment or two, this does bother me. I watch the two of you playing each other's bodies like virtuosi playing their instruments, and something deep inside me tells me to intervene, to stop it now, to take you away. It's strange: I am willing – no, eager – to have this man fuck my wife – really fuck her, give it to her, fuck her to kingdom come – but the prospect of his making love to her in a practised, deliberate, loving way makes me feel uncomfortable.

The man's wife, too, seated beside me, is changed by the imminence of the event. Her change, however, is the opposite of mine: while I have grown jealous, she has become more sanguine. The anger and most of the sorrow leave her face, and she can't take her eyes from her husband and you. She is intrigued by what she is watching and surprised by her measured, curious response to it.

But if I feel an impulse to stop the event, the example set by the man's wife forces me to think more clearly. I did not, after all, set terms for this encounter; I did not say, Here, fuck my wife but don't be good at it. That his performance is more expressive than I expected, I have to tell myself, is a positive element. Once I accept this, I return my attention to the two of you on the floor, glad that he will be a worthy lover.

He raises his hips back; his cock dangles, points downwards; he lowers himself and finds your outer cunt-lips with the dome of his cock. He pushes; resistance is negligible; your lips give way; the head of his cock enters and blazes the trail for the slow entry of his whole long shaft.

We watch it, his wife and I. We see that dangling moment, and the positioning, and the entry. While his cock sinks in, the man's wife catches her breath, holds it until the whole pink shaft disappears inside you and out of sight. Then she exhales.

When he is fully impaled you cry out, a half-sob, and slide your hands up from his ass, across his back, down to his ass again. Your cry is like a prod to him; he pulls his prick out, shoves it back in, each thrust faster and faster, until soon he is a pile driver pile driving into your juicy cunt, making your whole supple body quiver all around it.

His wife is saying, *Do it to her. Do it to her, Do it to her!* very softly but in rhythm with his thrusts.

I wish she would say: *Fuck her!*

You thrash beneath him, slide your hands wherever they'll reach, clutch him to you. You plant your heels in the carpet and push, raising your ass up off the floor and pressing your pelvis against his so you can savour every thrust, feel the full length of every plunge. You and the man interlock limbs, meld all flesh, share every spasm and tick, rotate your hips together, lift and sink together, and as you begin your climb you cry out again.

This time the sound of your cry has the opposite effect on him. He continues pumping into you but more slowly, each thrust slower than the one before. You get right into the slower rhythm, substituting intensity for speed, lifting your hips higher, pressing against him harder, intensifying every aspect of the act. It's a beautiful sight to see, a magnificent fuck, and yet there's something gloriously off-kilter about it. It's clear you're climbing towards your peaks; the closer to it you get, the slower you fuck. And when you finally climax, you're jammed together almost immobile, his shaft fully buried in the wet, clingy inner walls of your cunt. He freezes for a moment, then shoots his cream into you; you take it with spasms that I can barely perceive – but I know from having been there what's happening inside your cunt. You both collapse, still interlocked, embracing, very still.

His wife gets up, stands above you, looking down at his body sprawled on yours, locked against yours. If he feels her watching, he doesn't respond. You do, though, and look up and her and smile. She turns away, not knowing how to react, looks at me. I shake my head, as if to say no, no, leave them alone. I know you're not through.

She sits down next to me, very tense. She doesn't know what to do with her hands, folds, unfolds, refolds them in her lap. I reach for them, but when I touch one she pulls her hands back as if burned. I try to smile comfortingly at her, and it works. She extends her hands to me. I take them both in mine, hold them.

The room is very still, the only sounds the sounds of your breathing, his, mine, hers . . .

8

Eventually – it might have been minutes later, an hour later – the man rolls off you, gets to his feet to fetch the champagne. While he is gone you scamper to your knees, creep across to his wife and me, take her hands from mine, and undress her quickly. She does not resist; she does not cooperate. You open my robe, exposing my erection.

The husband returns, refills the glasses. He sits on the floor, you lie down with your head on his thigh; both of you watch his wife and me. You reach back for his flaccid cock, toy with it; she reaches for my hard cock, takes it in her fist, strokes it. You turn your head and kiss the tip of his cock. She drops her head into my lap and engulfs my cock with her mouth. She lacks your finesse, but I'm not complaining. She sucks me off and plays with her cunt at the same time; I like the way that looks. She's not far away from a quick climax, I can tell, and so I make her stop, lift her face away. She's confused but a moment later doesn't care as I get her down to the floor on her back, climb between her legs, find, plunge, fuck.

She's like a bucking bronco, just released, not yet broken, tossing and turning and thrashing. I try to stay with her.

Do it to me! she cries. *Do it to me, Do it to me, Do it to me!* I do it to her. I wish she'd say *Fuck.*

Do you turn the light out, or does he?

Your tits flatten on my back; I don't need light to know what's happening. You're on your knees beside me, doubled over me, your arms on the far side of me, your ass in the air. The man is on his knees behind you, his cock under your buttocks, sliding in and out of your cunt.

He fucks you while I fuck her; your body is the conduit, the link that unites his fucking to mine, yours to hers.

Rolling now . . . me off her, he off you . . . and we weave limbs and hands and fingers, just flesh now, eight arms, eight legs, four asses, two cocks, two pussies, four mouths, four tongues, eight lips, four tits, slipsliding, fucking, sucking, whose is it? who cares? and she never says fuck.

I am buried inside her when she comes; she comes loudly, almost violently, clutching the skin of my back with her fingers, jerking her ass upwards with each spasm, and with the last spasms straightening her legs flat on the floor, closing her legs within mine, her cunt squeezing my cock and making me come with a series of explosive jerks. She is still trembling when I have given her all I have, her clamped thighs and tightened cunt holding my cock inside even as I subside and shrink until, finally, I've scarcely anything left for her cunt to hold on to, and I slip out.

Then she is negligible.

She was always negligible: she is neither obsessed nor the subject of obsession.

Exhausted, we drain together, all of us, just short of sleep, flesh against flesh, hands lazily stroking, not quite dozing, dozing . . .

9

Later – no way to tell how much later – I feel your cool ass against my hip, rolling gently, and I surmise that his hand is stroking your pussy. I turn to my side and press my front against your back, my cock nestling lengthwise in the crevice between your buttocks. I put my arms around you, reach for your breasts; one of my hands encounters his face as he suckles. He lifts his face away, takes my hand and places it on your tit. Then flattens himself against your front as I press against your back.

I'm not sure how I know, but I know that his wife is gone; and that's fine, we are just us three, as it should be.

For only he and I are obsessed, and you are our obsession.

So we, the obsessed, close in on you, our grail, touch, feel, kiss, embrace, adore you, in perfect rhyme, he in front, I in back, head to toe, then turn you around and reverse the ritual, I facing your front, he your back, up, up . . . When I reach your face I kiss you as deeply and lovingly as I ever have, and know that he wants to kiss you, too, so I turn you yet again.

The communication between us two men is wordless and perfect and wholly committed to you. Our hands meet at your juncture, share your juices, then depart, leaving our cocks to find their niches, and they do, and enter you in concert, his cock in your cunt, mine in your ass, both sliding slowly, surely inward until we are fully impaled, the domes of our cocks separated only by a thin membrane, and then we move in harmony, stroking within you, adoring you with our cocks, our length and hardness and endurance testament to the depth of our passionate obsession.

We stroke, we love, we fill you up together through the night, and when you come so do we, together, until we're drained, and sleep.

When dawn breaks you and I are alone.

2 Pique & Melissa . . . & Doc

Doc's Tale

Pique and Melissa met at the Mommy & Me playgroup; for a time they were inseparable. They were about the same height, just over five feet tall, and under a hundred pounds, and they both looked like teenagers, but everything else about them was different. Pique was dark, Melissa fair. Pique was quiet, tending to shy, and Melissa was the classic coquette, more than a bit of a tease. Pique was a mystery: you never knew what she was thinking until she told you, if she told you; Melissa never kept a secret thought in her life. Each was sexy on her own, but together they were sexier than the sum of their parts. You almost couldn't look at them without thinking of the delights they promised together.

They were hands-on friends. They walked with their arms around each other's waists, like young Italian women. They fussed with each other's hair. They applied suntan lotion to each other, a treat to behold. But, physical though they were, they were never overtly sexual: their touching always had to have an innocent-seeming basis.

We were better off financially than Melissa and her husband, and Pique had a larger wardrobe, which Melissa would hit whenever she had someplace dressup to go. Then, or sometimes just for the fun of it, she would come over and she and Pique would try on Pique's dresses. During those sessions Melissa would take every opportunity to handle Pique, holding Pique's breasts as she admired them, running a hand down her own belly and then down Pique's for a comparison test of flatness; touching, stroking anywhere, everywhere, as they discussed muscle tone and clarity of skin and roundness of tush. Though Melissa was the more aggressive, Pique was not totally passive, and they were not at all furtive about all this touching, which came across as quite natural.

I was attracted to Melissa and made no secret of it; the vision of a threesome with her, Pique, and me was so exquisite it gave me headaches. And, I was sure, it was eminently achievable. Melissa's husband was a musician and their marriage off as often as on, with the off-periods providing opportunities. Pique never denied that it could happen. "If it can happen," I'd say, "let's make it happen." And Pique would say, "Maybe," or, "We'll see," or other nice things to string me along. Melissa knew I wanted it, too. So together they teased me; maybe "tortured" is a better word. For my birthday they gave me a videotape of the two of them modelling trashy lingerie. I loved that tape.

One night we took Melissa and her husband to a benefit dinner-dance.

While Melissa and I were dancing a slow dance, she could feel me getting a hard-on. This is a good way to characterize the difference between Pique and Melissa. If Pique were dancing with her friend's husband and he got a hard-on, she probably would step back and pretend not to notice. It's not that she wouldn't like it; she was just more discreet than Melissa. But when Melissa felt my hard-on, she looked me straight in the eye, smiled, and pressed herself against it. "Oh, how wicked," she said. "Your wife's best friend, tsk tsk." But as she said it she slipped her hand between our bodies and touched the bulge in my pants.

"Why shouldn't I want to fuck my wife's best friend," I asked, "when my wife's best friend wants to fuck my wife?" Melissa gave my cock a little squeeze and withdrew her hand.

"Do it," I said.

"Do what?" she asked.

"Fuck her," I said. "If you want to fuck her, fuck her. You do want to. And I want you to."

Melissa didn't say anything then, but a few days later – either coincidentally or because my encouragement emboldened her – she did take her relationship with Pique into a new realm.

We were renting a beach house at Malibu that summer, and it had a sauna. Melissa had come over late in the afternoon, and that night I asked Pique what they'd been up to. I should mention at this point that whenever I knew that Pique and Melissa had been together, I always asked Pique what they had done, and Pique would make up a sexy story just to get me hard and horny. This time was no exception.

Pique told me that they had taken a bottle of wine and some nice camomile oil into the sauna, that they had shared the wine and oiled themselves and each other, that Melissa had stretched out on the top step and Pique on the next step down to enjoy the heat, and that, when she was half-dozing, Pique had felt a pressure gently pushing her legs apart and opened her eyes to find Melissa kneeling between her up-raised knees, a hand on each knee, pushing them outwards. Melissa smiled guiltily but said nothing – neither did Pique – and ran her hands down the oily insides of Pique's thighs. Her fingers met at Pique's mound and combed through the hair there; her thumbs stroked softly. Pique laid back and closed her eyes; Melissa bent down and kissed Pique's pussy. When Pique did not protest, Melissa licked the soft bud, sipping and supping until Pique began to tremble; then Melissa slid up Pique's body and pressed herself against Pique, breasts mashing against breasts, pussies meshed together, Melissa's tongue probing deep into Pique's mouth as Pique's orgasms coursed through her.

Pique let it all happen. She didn't reciprocate, but she did nothing to stop Melissa, either.

When it was over, Melissa sat up and said sheepishly, "I couldn't resist, you looked so beautiful, all oily and sexy . . ." And Pique just giggled about it, took it matter-of-factly as an extension of their play – although in truth it was a little one-sided.

As I said, Pique had told me similar stories before. But this one was the best, the most realistic. It aroused me so much that we started fucking while she was still telling it to me.

And as we fucked and I listened I realized the story was true. Don't ask me how I knew; I just did; I could tell it had really happened – and that got me hotter still. We must have fucked for two straight hours.

There were a couple of other incidents, in which Melissa was the aggressor and Pique the willing recipient. I was sure that with the right kind of encouragement Melissa would be glad to join me and Pique in bed. Pique agreed. "Then why haven't we done it?" I asked. "Do you think she'll try to take me away from you, is that it?"

"No," said Pique. "I think she'll try to take me away from you."

One night after midnight Melissa called to say she was at the end of her rope with her husband and could she come over?

She could and she did. I heard the soft din of their voices as they sat in the living room, drinking wine and commiserating quietly long into the night.

Presently I slipped into my robe to get a bottle of water from the kitchen. En route I stopped at the living room entrance and looked in. Melissa, all cried out, was lying on the sofa, her head propped against an arm cushion, her legs extended across the seat and crossed at the ankles. She was wearing a fuzzy, low-cut sweater – Pique's, I think – and a pair of slacks, and she looked cuddly, sad, and sexy, all at once. Pique was wearing a silk robe and nothing underneath; she kneeled on the floor beside Melissa, absently stroking Melissa's hair. It was an intimate scene, one friend comforting another, but there was a palpable sexuality to it; either way I felt like an intruder and turned to go.

But just then Melissa noticed me, and so did Pique, and they smiled and said hi.

"Is everything okay?" I asked.

"Sure, come on in," said Pique. I hesitated. "Really, it's all right, isn't it, Mel?" And Melissa said, "We need you, just to prove that there are good men left," and she pulled her stockinged feet back to make room for me on the sofa. I sat beside her, and she extended her legs straight out again, and put her foot in my lap. As the two women sketched in Melissa's unfortunate marital crisis, my cock stirred and stiffened under Melissa's feet. There was no way she could not feel it.

I took Melissa's feet in my hands and gently massaged them. I don't remember much of what was said. I do remember realizing that while I may have intruded upon their intimacy, I had not shattered it, and with that realization I felt more at ease. At one point Melissa shifted a little, turning more towards Pique. I released her foot, and she immediately pressed her heel against the hardening lump that was my cock, and at the same time slipped her hand inside Pique's robe and took hold of her breast.

Both Pique and I were surprised: we simultaneously stiffened at the gestures and sucked in air. Melissa smiled; so did we; then we relaxed. I moved my hands up Melissa's legs under the full-cut pants she was wearing, but my eyes were fixed on where Melissa's hand disappeared into Pique's robe. How I longed to see what it was doing.

Melissa read my mind, which probably wasn't difficult, and pushed the fabric aside, exposing Pique's beautiful white breast in Melissa's softly caressing hand, Pique's hard dark nipple pinched between the tips of Melissa's index finger and thumb. Pique and I both responded, I moving my hands further up Melissa's legs, Pique leaning forwards to undo the catch of Melissa's slacks and slipping her hand inside.

When I took hold of the cuffs of her slacks, Melissa raised her ass so I could pull them down her legs and off. Pique's hand was under the pink panty satin, her fingers combing through the hair, her middle finger stroking.

Without taking my eyes off the event, I stood up and moved the coffee table away. When I'd done that, Pique looked up at me then down at Melissa's panties, into which Pique's hand disappeared. It was a signal to me; I pulled Melissa's panties down just enough to expose her pussy and the lovely sight of Pique's two fingers gently stroking Melissa's clit, then slowly disappearing into Melissa's cunt.

Just as slowly, and watching my face, Pique withdrew her fingers, turned to me, untied the sash of my robe, and pushed the robe off. It puddled at my feet, leaving me standing dumbly naked before them, my hard cock bobbing in front of me. Pique took it into her mouth for a moment or two, and then she backed off, sat up on her knees and took her own robe off. Pique and I were both naked now, and we turned to Melissa.

While I rolled Melissa's panties the rest of the way down her legs and pulled them off, Pique took hold of the bottom of Melissa's cashmere sweater and lifted it over her head. Melissa wore no bra, so now she, like us, was naked.

When Melissa sat up, Pique put one hand on my ass and pressed me forwards, and the other hand behind Melissa's head and pushed it forwards. Melissa's lips met my cockhead and opened, and she took my hard prick into her mouth. She sucked softly and enthusiastically, but only briefly, for Pique separated us, drew Melissa down to the floor on her back, got behind her, and cushioned the back of Melissa's head between her breasts.

I, too, was on my knees, kneeling between Melissa's outstretched legs. Pique took hold of Melissa's breasts, one in each hand, and offered them to me. I bent forwards and sucked on each nipple in turn; at the same time my fingers probed her pussy-lips, entered between them, pussy-played. Melissa reached for my cock; I had to scamper closer so she could reach it; she stroked it in her fist and kneaded the balls. Our hands played in each other's genitals in perfect concert.

Melissa smiled up at me, opening her mouth a little, wanting a kiss.

"Don't you want to kiss Melissa?" Pique asked. "I think she wants a kiss."

Of course I obliged, lowering my face to hers and kissing Melissa's mouth softly but deeply as our hands continued to caress each other. After a few minutes of smooching and handplay, Pique smiled lovingly at me and nodded, and I moved forwards, knees closer to Melissa's body.

Melissa lifted her hips and placed the head of my cock at her opening. I left it there, head against those plump, waiting lips. Then Pique took Melissa's head in her hands and gently laid it flat on the floor and straddled it; she reached under and spread her pussy-lips and lowered herself over Melissa's mouth. Melissa's tongue shot up and flicked at Pique's clit. I bent forwards and sucked Pique's beautiful tits. Melissa took Pique by the hips and pulled her down against her open mouth, shot her tongue out to lick Pique's pussy, then shoved it in to slurp and explore.

Pique lifted my face away from her tits. She wanted to watch this: she put her hands on my buttocks, urged me forwards. There was a brief tug as my cock-head pushed against Melissa's pussy lips; then they parted and I entered, my hard cock sliding smoothly into the soft, wet warmth. I felt my whole body slacken with pleasure as I watched my prick pump into Melissa.

I looked up along Melissa's body, watched her stomach contract and relax as she fucked back; I saw her unattended tits trembling; then I saw Pique's middle moving against Melissa's mouth and tongue in sympathetic rhythm. I looked up along Pique's body, saw Melissa's hands on Pique's hips, guiding her movements, and Pique's hands squeezing her own tits. And finally I saw Pique's face, looking at my face and smiling as she and I matched movements into and against the pleasure-giving supine figure beneath us.

"I love you," I said without sound, just mouthing the words, and Pique said the same, the same way.

Melissa and her husband split up for good shortly thereafter, and for a time we were a classic *ménage à trois*. Well, almost classic. We couldn't really live together because of the kids. The month or two that followed were truly among the most exciting of my life. We really had the knack. It was seldom about configurations with us; we soon tired of those. Most of the time we would two-on-one; that is, two of us would make love to the third. At other times we would be two with the third looking on.

Much as I loved being the male lover with two women, the thing about it that excited me most was watching Pique and Melissa fuck. And fuck they did, even though they both remained women. They used no dildos; neither assumed the male or female role; but they embraced, entangled, mashed and thrashed as any fuckers would, and they were beautiful.

The very first weekend of our three-cornered relationship we had another of those black-tie benefits, and we asked Melissa to join us. (We offered to get her a date but she said, "Why do I need a date?" I loved that.)

Anyway they were both so pretty that night, Pique in an elegant black gown, Melissa in a stunning red one, both looking sexy and scrumptious and youthful. I felt great. I don't know what was closer to bursting that night: my head, my chest, or my cock; they were all swollen.

I was talking to a friend during the evening and turned around and there they were, Melissa and Pique, talking to "a vertically challenged actor" (who isn't that much taller than they). And flirting. And turning him on. And I knew exactly what he was thinking. And what he wanted, I had.

Before long, though, it became obvious that Pique's reservation about a threesome with Melissa had been correct. Melissa wanted Pique much more than she wanted me. Indeed, after a while it was easy to see that Melissa fucked me because that was the only way she could get to fuck Pique. I didn't care; I'd take it any way I could get it.

Then Melissa insisted on having time with Pique alone, which was okay with me, although Pique didn't like where Melissa was headed. Finally Melissa started working on Pique to leave me so they could go off together. Pique wasn't interested, so Melissa, rejected, tried to get me to leave Pique for her. Not a chance.

Now twice rejected, Melissa became totally destructive, and not only did the *ménage à trois* fall apart, but so did the friendship.

The outcome is sad, I think. They were such good friends. And though I don't think she'll admit it, Pique still misses Melissa.

I know I do.

Pique's Postscript

Soon after our threesome began, Melissa started getting seductive when Doc wasn't around. She wanted us to make love without Doc. I felt uneasy about it but when I told her about my doubts, she made it clear to me that that was part of the package.

Melissa was smart. She knew how much Doc was enjoying our threesome, and she knew it wouldn't be easy for me to take it away from him. So I was in a quandary. I'd fuck the Oakland Raiders if I could, but only if Doc suited up with them. I don't cheat on him, period.

So I explained my dilemma to Doc. Or, rather, I started to – as soon as he realized what I was getting at, he let me know that it was okay with him. If my making love with Melissa was the price of keeping our threesome with Melissa going, he wanted me to pay it. It wasn't as if it was a sacrifice or anything. He saw how much I enjoyed doing sex with Melissa; "You like it, do it!" was Doc's attitude.

And we did have fun. Melissa was no newcomer to women. Even before we started our threesome, Melissa used to tell me stories. When she and Rudy first got married they shared a house in Toronto with the other two married guys in Rudy's band and their wives. The band was on the road a lot and whenever they were, the three wives played. (I think she used to tell me these stories as a way of coming on with me, getting me aroused. I guess it did – at least, it made me curious, which is step one.) Sometimes the women prowled – they once picked up a kid who was hitch-hiking and brought him back to the house and kept him there for three days – but mostly they did each other. I'm not sure if, or how often, she had seen the women since that time, or if she'd seen other women, but the point is, she'd had experience.

Not that I needed teaching. I'd had my share of touchy-feely experiences as a teenager, and there was nothing in the idea of making love with a woman that repulsed me – especially when the woman was Melissa, who was so cute and cuddly and affectionate and feminine. Besides – let's face it – a woman doesn't need to be taught what to do to make another woman feel good.

God, it was great. Doc's blessing gave me the freedom to let myself go. And how Melissa exploited it: she was at me constantly. I was willing, eager, even greedy sometimes. When we were apart I craved the look and feel and smell of her; my mouth watered for her lips and the silly way she'd run her tongue along my lips and teeth, and for the feel of her nipples puckering in my mouth, and for the taste of her sweet salty pussy.

But mostly I craved the things she did to me, which was everything, anywhere, all the time. We always seemed to be doing something. She ate me in the ladies room of Jimmy's restaurant, with ladies coming in and out. I came. We fingered each other when we went to see *Back to the Future* together one afternoon. We both came. I buzzed her with a little vibrator the whole time she was on a conference call with her lawyer and her soon to be ex-husband – and made her come then, too, without missing an issue. It seems to me that we were always coming. I never knew it was possible to come that much.

But the worries I had about this affair before it started weren't wrong. Melissa had an agenda and it was me. And it was dangerous. You know how it is when you're in the throes of a new sexual relationship – it's new, it's intense, and you want it every minute. Alongside it an older relationship can't possibly stay as exciting. Melissa knew that; she knew how exciting this was to me, and she knew all the sex we were doing would begin to drain away some of the heat from sex with Doc. I knew it, too, so I made sure that I – and I and Melissa – kept Doc happy. But it required acting sometimes, forced effort; for the first time ever sex with Doc became almost dutiful.

And then Melissa began to cut the underpinnings of my marriage. She was my best friend, she knew everything about Doc and me, and she would create situations that highlighted the weaknesses of my marriage – and the strengths of my relationship with her. At first it was very subtle. For example, I'm a jock, a much better athlete than Doc. I always beat him at tennis, and I'm a far better skier. He always went skiing with me, though, until he had surgery a couple of years ago and gave it up. Anyway, Melissa had the great idea that we should go skiing. Doc fell right into Melissa's trap by saying that he couldn't go, but Melissa and I should. And we did – and had a fabulous time. It was one way of Melissa's showing me that we can have more fun without Doc than with.

And from there on, Melissa escalated, obliquely putting Doc down, creating circumstances that made him the third element of the threesome. Until finally I said, "Melissa, what do you want? Do you want me to leave Doc for you?"

She said, "Would that be such a terrible idea?"

"Yes," I said, "it would. And if you think it could ever happen put the idea out of your mind right now because it never will." And she took it pretty well, and we went on.

About a week after that conversation we were having lunch at the Polo Lounge, and our waiter was young, cute, and flirtatious. Melissa encouraged him, of course, flirting back, asking him what time he got off, using double entendres.

"He likes us," she said.

"I know," I said.

"I'm going to do him," she said.

"Melissa!" I said. "He's a baby."

"Doesn't bother me," she said. "Besides, the only guy I'm fucking is Doc. I've got to find a prick of my own."

She was serious, though at the time I didn't realize how serious.

After lunch we went back to Melissa's house and took a long, lazy bath together. We were seated face to face with a glass of wine, our toes toying with each other's pussies, enjoying a lazy foreplay, when I noticed Melissa looking past me, smiling. I looked to see.

There in the doorway stood the cute young waiter. It seems that in the restaurant, while I went to the ladies' room, Melissa had slipped a note into the check folder. The note contained her address and the suggestion that he come straight over after work and let himself in; she'd leave the door unlocked.

I turned back to Melissa. "Oh, no," I said.

But she interrupted. "No, no, no, no," she said. "He's just for me. I just thought we'd give him a little show first . . . Then you can watch."

I didn't like it, and if I hadn't been so light-headed from the wine and aroused from the foreplay I would have dressed and left. But, to tell you the truth, I liked the idea of performing for the kid, of turning him on and then watching as Melissa fucked him.

There's a robe behind the door, Melissa told the boy, and as we continued our bath, sudsing each other up, cleaning and scrubbing, the boy undressed slowly and slipped into the robe. Poor thing – he couldn't resist the urge to stroke himself as he watched. "Better be careful," Melissa said to him. You don't want to . . ." But it was too late, he was too worked up; he came in several big spurts.

"Tsk, tsk," said Melissa as she and I climbed out of the tub. "But of course at your age . . . it won't take long, will it?"

She kissed him, then kissed me, and said, "We'll just have to put on a show for him, won't we – to help him along." And so we dried each other in big, fluffy bathtowels and put a little powder on each other, doing everything very slowly and sweetly, showing off for the waiter, and then we went into the bedroom and sat the boy down in the easy chair where he could watch, and we dropped our towels and climbed into Melissa's bed and Melissa went to work on me.

She was truly inspired. She laid me on my back and used her hands and mouth on my face, my breasts, my belly, the insides of my thighs; in fact she used her whole body, now rubbing and sliding her flesh against mine, now lifting away and tracing my contours with her nipples until I was squirming and writhing with joy and desire. And then she scooted down and put her mouth around my pussy and pushed her tongue between my pussy-lips and found my clit. She licked, she sucked, she nipped, and she was wonderful. I raised my ass up off the bed and pushed my centre against her, the better to feel her tongue pressing my clitoris back into the pelvic bone. Oh, the noises I made!

When she saw that I was close to coming she slowed down, eased up to prolong the fun. She turned me over onto my stomach, massaged my back and the insides of my thighs, kissed my buttocks and licked between them, and darted her tongue under, dabbing at my cunt again, prodding me up, up again, towards my peak, and then she laid down flat on top of me, pressed her tits into my back and pushed her pubic hair into the flesh of my ass and kissed me on my neck and licked my ears.

As I started to tremble Melissa reached under me and took hold of my tits, put her legs inside mine and hooked my ankles with her feet and suddenly, quickly, turned us both over.

Now we were both face up, with me on top, Melissa's hands on my tits holding me against her, her ankles inside mine pushing my legs apart. And then I got it, I understood: she had gotten me into position and locked me there, spread-eagled and exposed, open and ready.

And sure enough, as soon I realized it, the waiter was there, climbing onto the bed, kneeling between my legs, looming. Inside my head I was saying, "No! no! Stop this, I've got to stop this, no . . ." But when I saw him move at me with his prick in his hand, ready to go, I knew I couldn't get away and didn't want to get away: I wanted to feel that prick more than I wanted him to stop.

The waiter placed his cock-head at my niche; Melissa squeezed my tits and raised our legs to cross over his calves. I was fully committed now: not only did I not resist; I thrust my hips upwards to capture the waiter's invading prick.

The second his fat cock-head pushed through my lips and entered my channel, I came. I kept on coming, coming in great spastic clenchings, and so the entire fuck was contained within my orgasms. The waiter drove into me like a piston, his cock rockhard and strong and unstoppable, each down-plunge filling me up and keeping me coming. Sharp pangs of pleasure – stripes of ecstasy – streaked from my womb and coursed through my innards, galvanizing my flesh, sparking my nerve endings, singeing the very tips of my nipples and fingers and toes. It was all peak and no valley and it made me crazy: I thrashed, I bucked, I grabbed, grabbed any way I could, with my fingers, with my cunt-walls, fucking him back as hard as he fucked me.

The orgasm never faded, just kept rolling, but there was only so much bucking and clenching my body could do before I started to cramp, and eventually the pain overtook the pleasure and I had to stop. I tried to push him away or squirm free but I was trapped between him and Melissa, and all I could do was reach my hand down and pull the waiter's cock out of me. I wanted to bend it downwards and back and put it in Melissa, but the waiter, panicked to find himself close to coming but bobbing unsheathed, momentarily eased up and I scampered out from between them, and he placed his cock himself and plunged into Melissa.

I lay on my side beside them, took his balls in my hand and held them gently as he fucked her, and I looked at her face and she looked at mine and we kept our eyes locked like that, even as the waiter started coming, and as he shot inside her, she smiled at me.

I was first to move. I got up off the bed and went to the bathroom. I won't say that I was disgusted with myself, although I'm sure that on some deep level I was, but I was defensive; my thoughts ran to, "Okay, great, now I've done it, I fucked another man, big deal, it was great, the greatest fuck of my life, and I'm going to fuck again because I loved it and I want more and what difference does it make?" When thoughts of Doc flashed in my head I told myself he'd pushed me into this, which wasn't all there was to it, but it was true to the extent that he wanted me to keep it going with Melissa no matter what. This was a what.

When I got back to the bed Melissa was on her hands and knees sucking the waiter's diminished but not hopeless cock, and she looked at me and kept sucking him, taking him full inside her mouth, fucking him with her lips and bathing him with her tongue, but watching me, all the while looking straight at me, until at last he came, shooting into Melissa's mouth.

From there on it was a debauch. I called home and said I was spending the night at Melissa's – which was fine with Doc, of course. Melissa and I fucked each other while the waiter slept, and took turns fucking him when he woke up. I kept drinking wine and passed out.

At around midnight I woke up being fucked. Great, let's get going, and I was into it. But as I fucked I became aware that the bed was shaking more than it should have been and the moaning and groaning and giggling contained too many voices. I opened my eyes and there beside were Melissa and the waiter fucking.

Who was fucking me, for God's sake?

I looked up and saw someone I'd never seen before. "Oh, God I'm lost," I thought as I thrashed and writhed beneath the stranger. Lost, as I lifted my ass up to meet his plunging prick. This was a first, even for me. The first time I lay eyes on somebody is while he's laying me. Lost lost lost, as I fucked and fucked and fucked the night away.

Seems that while I slept the waiter had called a friend to come over, to even out the numbers. Melissa's suggestion, no doubt.

Since we'd used Melissa's car the day before, she had to drive me home in the morning.

During the ride I told her I thought we had to stop. I loved her, she was my friend, but I felt I was becoming somebody I didn't want to be.

And it was true. I'm the first to admit that sexually there's not much I won't do. I love sex; to me it's the greatest of all amusement park rides. But Doc is my honey and I love him and I won't betray him. And I just had.

"And loved it," Melissa said.

"Yes," I said, "I loved fucking the waiter, loved the way it felt physically, loved fucking his friend, loved fucking you, but talk about amusement park rides, that's all that night was – thrilling, but only thrilling, and when it was over, empty."

"Like us?" she asked.

"You know better than that," I said.

She was quiet for a while, then she took an audio cassette from her handbag and slipped it into the player.

It was a recording of Melissa and Doc, in bed, fucking, sucking, laughing, having a fine and dirty old time.

I didn't say anything or shut it off. I let it play. It was still playing when we got to my house and I got out.

And that was that.

The funny thing is, I think our friendship could have survived but for one thing: that tape. Doesn't that sound odd? She fucked my husband behind my back; okay, that's Melissa, I could've lived with that. She did all in her power to make me betray my husband, and she succeeded, but somehow I think that wasn't malicious: it was her way of showing me I was no better than she was.

But making that audio tape – she did that for one reason only: to hurt me. And it did.

Melissa tried me first, then Doc. When we both rejected her, she punished us by proving to us, separately, that we were both as capable of betrayal as she was.

Of course we were. Of course we are. Big deal. Betrayal's our exception, not our rule. We're together. She's alone.

Eventually I told Doc about the waiter. Eventually he told me about his fucking Melissa alone. And – no question about it – the admissions caused pain and strain for a while. But we got past it – not by blaming Melissa, but by realizing what we knew down deep all along: that indulging our lust for her was going to cost us something.

I still miss the friend she was, though. I really loved her. And when I think about what happened, I don't regret anything, because early along, our threesome gave me some of the sexiest, hottest, most loving moments of my life.

A few times after we all three became lovers, we would go down to Doc's and my bedroom, and instead of getting into bed with Doc and Melissa I'd plop myself down in the chair and say, "Okay you two, never mind me, go to it!" And I'd watch them. I would watch them undress each other. I would watch him go down on her. I would watch her blow him. I would watch them fuck. Now and then they'd look my way and I'd say, "No, I'm not here, forget me." And they would. And you know what? They were the hottest, most stimulating sight I'd ever seen. I loved watching them. I loved the sight of her lips on his cock and his tongue on her clit and his cock pumping merrily in and out of her pussy. And lord, how I loved watching them come, Doc shooting his cream into her in great spastic jerkings, Melissa tossing her legs straight up in the air when she started to peak, heaving her hips upward, slamming her pelvis against Doc's to make sure her cunt captured every available cock inch. Eventually I would join them, and love it, but it's the watching I remember best, the watching that got me hot, the watching that put images in my memory that get me hot even now.

My husband and my best friend, fucking each other. Nothing ever made me hotter. Or happier.

3 One Night

Sarah wakes up in a champagne fog with questions:
  Where is she?
  Is it night or day?
  Is she drunk or hung over?
  Is she dreaming or is this real?
  Whose mouth is eating her pussy?

The pleasures generated by that mouth make it hard to concentrate on anything else but, in addition to pleasure, Sarah feels something a little like panic because in fact she doesn't know where she is, or if it's night or day, or if she's drunk or hung over, or whether or not she's dreaming . . .

And then it begins to come back to her: how she and her husband – already tipsy – took another cold bottle of champagne and walked along the beach until they found a nice little niche in the dunes; how they'd cuddled and smooched like teenagers; how when she was sucking his cock they'd heard a titter, looked up, and found they had an audience: a young couple, beautiful, maybe twenty, as tipsy as she and her husband.

Don't let us stop you, the boy had said, and Sarah had giggled and said, with a mouthful of cock, I won't, but after another suck or two she'd stopped, self-conscious.

The kids had joined them in the dune, and they'd all chatted and shared the champagne, which was soon gone. Her husband went back to the house for more, and in his absence the boy and girl kept talking with Sarah but couldn't keep their hands off each other. At one point the girl's halter top fell away and her tits tumbled free, plump and white, and at the same time her hand disappeared into the boy's fly and reappeared with a stiff white cock. A minute later the girl went up onto her knees and framed the cock with her down-pointing tits, then engulfed the cock with her mouth . . .

It is coming back to her, but recollections are mixed with sensations of the present as Sarah draws her knees up and turns them outward and lifts her hips to better access her cunt to the mouth making love to it – a mouth she knows is not her husband's: it's different, doing different things . . .

She is in her own bedroom, she knows that now, and it is still night. Does she remember returning to the house?

And this is no dream.

She'd watched the girl suck the boy's cock, and at one point the girl had stopped sucking and offered the cock to Sarah. Sarah had simply sat in place, her eyes on the cock, but hadn't moved, and the girl had resumed sucking. A few minutes later, with the cock bobbing and trembling and swollen to its grandest, the girl had offered it again, and this time Sarah had felt a hand behind her head, urging her to do it – her husband's. And she had: she'd gotten to her knees and lowered her mouth and taken the boy's cock in her mouth and tasted it all around, and then returned it to the girl . . .

She feels fingertips caressing her hips as the tongue caresses her clit, and then the fingers slide round to her ass and fingernails score her buttocks – long fingernails – and Sarah is sure now of what she has been suspecting: that her present lover is the girl.

She remembers drinking more champagne. She remembers watching the young couple escalate from sucking to fucking. She remembers admiring the boy's lean body lying on the girl, his tight round ass clenching as he pumped his fine young prick into her pussy. She remembers liking the way the girl flattened her heels beside his knees and used them for leverage, raising her hips to match his downward plunges, and then, when the boy was about to come, wrapping her legs around his thighs and clamping him to her as he shot. She remembers watching the boy thrash and twitch and drain into the girl, then roll off onto his back, exhausted, and she remembers the girl, spreadeagled on the sand, still unsatisfied, masturbating . . .

And Sarah remembers the look in her husband's eye as he watched the girl.

Sarah tosses her head from side to side as the girl lavishes her pussy with her tongue, knowing, as only a woman can know, where and how. Sarah tightens her fingers and realizes – or has she known all along? – that she has a hard cock in each hand, and she strokes them . . .

"You want to fuck her, don't you?" Sarah remembers saying to her husband as they watched the girl on the beach separate her cunt-lips with the fingers of one hand and expose her clit to the ministrations of her other hand. She remembers her husband nodding, and she remembers saying, "Then fuck her . . ." and she remembers taking the girl's hands from her crotch and urging her husband to his knees between the girl's legs, and she remembers saying, "Go on, fuck her," and he did . . .

Sarah trembles as soft waves of pleasure ripple outwards from her womb; but just as they start her lover abandons her clit and cunt and slides up along her body, kissing her stomach, her tits, her neck, her mouth . . .

She remembers the four of them swimming naked in the surf, and then all their hands on her, all over her, caressing her. Her turn. Everyone had come but Sarah. But that's all she remembers.

They must have brought her here. Home.

The girl flattens her plump tits against Sarah's tits, presses her pussy against Sarah's pussy, explores Sarah's inner mouth with her cunt-flavoured tongue, and Sarah kisses her back, lifting her middle upwards the better to match the labial mesh of flesh and hairs, trying to continue the climb started when the girl was eating her.

Then, as if reading Sarah's mind, the men slide their cocks from her fists and rearrange the girl, turn her around so that the girl's face returns, blessedly, to Sarah's cunt, and the girl's pussy lowers to Sarah's face. Sarah takes the girl's buttocks in her hands and pulls her down so Sarah can eat the girl as the girl eats her. Once again waves of pleasure begin rippling from deep inside Sarah's cunt, the waves take her to the shore, to the edge, she's going to come . . .

And on the very edge, virtually as she tightens in advance of her first orgasmic spasm, the girl lifts her face from Sarah's pussy and lifts her pussy from Sarah's mouth and departs, but there is no abandonment here, no frustration – the interruption is only temporary, only momentary – for when the girl crawls aside, she is instantly replaced by the boy, who lowers himself between Sarah's legs and with one smooth stroke slides his rock-hard cock into her wet, hot cunt.

As soon as he enters her Sarah comes at last – oh, how she comes! – and thus the whole, glorious fuck is contained within an orgasm. The boy fucks Sarah – oh, how he fucks her! – with long, even, pistonlike plunges of his big, hard, youthful prick, each thrust of the shaft stretching and filling her cunt until the bulbous crown taps her womb and stirs the hot, lavalike liquids there; then it vacates, then fills her up again, each in and out an ecstatic journey, each penetration a prod activating her every muscle, awakening her every nerve-ending. The pit of her stomach clenches and contracts with an exquisite cramp that shoots tremors outwards and up-wards, inside and out, up into her stomach and tits and head, down through her cunt-walls and clit and all over her skin. This is no mere orgasm, it is the climax of the climax, and it keeps coming, coming, turning her into a thrashing, grip-ping, chattering organism.

"Comecomecomecome on," she cries out. "Oh, fuck me, fuck me, ride me, keep coming, fuckfuckoh, God, fuck me . . ." and she wraps her arms around his back and clamps him down against her and wraps her legs around his and kicks the heels of her feet into the back of his legs and against his ass as he fucks her and fucks her and fucks her until at last she asks him to stop, begs him to stop, not because she's done – she could come forever – but because it hurts, she needs to rest, just for a minute, a moment, Oh, please, stop but wait, wait, wait . . .

And he stops.

She clamps him to her, keeping his cock inside and, with his cock still fully implanted, the boy gently takes hold of Sarah's buttocks and turns himself and Sarah over until they have reversed positions and he lies flat on his back and she lies on top of him, his cock undisturbed.

For a while they are still, and during this rest Sarah notices that the bed is bouncing with the same rocking rhythm that it rocked with when they were fucking; then she hears a feminine grunting behind her, which matches the squashing sound of a cock-in-cunt, the slapping of flesh against softer flesh. Sarah knows without looking that the girl is on her hands and knees on the bed, and that her husband is on his knees behind the girl, fucking the girl – but she looks anyway, smiles at the girl, then looks down at the boy beneath her. A moment later she feels the girl's breath under her; the girl is licking Sarah between cunt and ass, and licking the boy's balls, and Sarah – almost involuntarily – begins ever-so-slowly to rotate her middle around the boy's imbedded prick. The girl's tongue and Sarah's twisting, turning cunt realert, reactivate the boy and he begins lifting his hips upwards to meet Sarah's downward, prick-engulfing movements. At the same time the girl points her tongue and touches Sarah's asshole, licks and slurps and drenches it with saliva.

Within seconds Sarah is where she was minutes ago, back at her peak, almost out of control, bouncing, heaving, rotating, clenching, squeezing, as if desperate to feel more of the boy's cock, or feel it differently, or feel it someplace else.

She cries out – a wordless cry – part scream, part squeal, part laugh.

The room resonates with all their noises now: grunts and groans and fuckwords and the squishy-wet, Jello sounds of pricks in cunts.

The bed bounces with the unrelated rhythms of four fucking bodies; and Sarah is only vaguely aware when behind her, the girl scampers from the bed and urges Sarah's husband up behind Sarah until his cock-head nestles at her asshole. The boy spasms and shoots his first shot; at that instant her husband's cock-head pushes past the tight opening and leads the way for his shaft to move onwards, inwards into Sarah's ass, completing the filling of Sarah.

There is nothing left in any of them to exploit this new configuration; its beginning is also the end. The boy's cock and her husband's cock meet, separated only by the membrane inside her; both cocks twitch, swell, and come, shooting together, exploding together as Sarah, out of control, thrashes and jerks and clutches and clenches and grabs and gives and receives until she has taken all the men have to give her and she collapses, drained and done.